SARAH MORGAN

New York, Actually

ONE PLACE. MANY STORIES

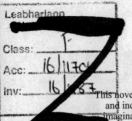

HQ
An imprint of HarperCollins*Publishers* Ltd.
1 London Bridge Street
London SE1 9GF

This paperback edition 2017

1
First published in Great Britain by
HQ, an imprint of HarperCollins*Publishers* Ltd. 2017

A catalogue record for this book is available from the British Library

ISBN: 978-1-84845-674-7

Printed and bound by
CPI Group (UK) Ltd, Croydon, CR0 4YY

Dear Reader,

As a child I was a voracious reader and one of my favourite books was Dodie Smith's *The Hundred and One Dalmatians*. As well as the warmth and originality of the storyline, I loved the fact that each dog had a distinct personality.

I've often included dogs in my books (the first was Maple, from *Sleigh Bells in the Snow*), but the dogs have always played a small background role until one day last winter when I came across a photo of a Dalmatian with a heart shaped nose. I knew I had to give him a central role in a book, and I knew he had to be called Valentine.

Some people find dogs easier to love than humans, and that is the case for Molly the heroine of this story. When it comes to giving advice on other people's relationships she's an expert, but she's not so good when it comes to her own. She can't imagine loving anyone more than she loves her dog Valentine, but then she meets sexy lawyer Daniel. Daniel knows more about depositions than dogs, but he'll do whatever it takes to get Molly's attention, even if that means borrowing a dog.

At first Molly and Daniel appear to have everything in common, but as the truth gradually reveals itself both are forced to re-examine everything they believe about themselves.

This is a story about letting go of the past, but it's also a story of friendship and love (both human and canine!), family and community, and it takes place against the glamorous backdrop of New York City. From the leafy paths of Central Park to the glittering skyscrapers, there's something for everyone in New York and, as Molly discovers, sometimes the city that never sleeps can be the perfect place to find love.

I hope you enjoy the book, and thank you for reading!

Love Sarah

xxx

To the Washington Romance Writers,
a fun, fabulous group of people.
Thank you for inviting me to your retreat. xxx

"Some of my best leading men have been dogs and horses."

Elizabeth Taylor

One

Dear Aggie, I bought my girlfriend an expensive coffee machine for her birthday. First she cried, then she sold it on eBay. I don't understand women.
Yours, Decaffeinated.

Dear Decaffeinated, the important question to ask yourself in any relationship is what does your partner want? What makes them happy? Without knowing all the details it's impossible to know exactly why your girlfriend cried and sold the coffee machine, but the first question that comes to mind is—does your girlfriend drink coffee?

Molly stopped typing and glanced at the bed. "Are you awake? You have to listen to this one. It's obvious he is a coffee drinker and the gift was really for him. Why do men do that? I'm so lucky to have you. Of course, if you ever sold my coffee machine on eBay, I'd have to kill you, but that won't be the advice I'm posting online."

The body on the bed didn't stir, but that wasn't surprising given the amount of exercise they'd both had the day before. The hours they'd spent in each other's company had left her sweaty and exhausted. Her body ached, a reminder that although her fitness levels had increased since she met him, his stamina still surpassed hers. His relentless energy was one of the many things she admired about him. Whenever she was tempted to skip an exercise session, all it took was one look from him to have her reaching for her running shoes. He was the reason she'd lost weight since arriving in New York City three years earlier. Some days she looked in the mirror and barely recognized herself.

She looked slimmer and more toned.

Best of all she looked happy.

If someone from her old life walked in now, they probably wouldn't recognize her.

Not that anyone from her old life was likely to show up on her doorstep.

Three years had passed. Three years, and she had finally rebuilt her shredded reputation. Professionally, she was back on track. Personally? She glanced at the bed again, feeling something soften inside her. She hadn't imagined ever getting close to anyone again, certainly not close enough to let them into her life or her home, and definitely not her heart.

And yet here she was, in love.

She allowed her gaze to linger on the perfect lines of his athletic body, before returning her attention to her email. She was lucky so many men struggled to understand women. If they didn't, she'd be out of a job.

Her blog, *Ask a Girl*, attracted a large volume of traffic

and that, in turn, had attracted the attention of a publisher. Her first book, *Mate for Life, Tools for Meeting Your Perfect Life Partner* had hit the bestseller lists in both the US and the UK. That, in turn, had led to a second book deal, all under her pseudonym Aggie, which meant that she had both anonymity and financial security. She'd turned misfortune into a fortune. Well, maybe not a *fortune* exactly, but enough to enable her to live comfortably in New York City and not to have to limp back to London. She'd left one life and moved on to a new one, like a snake shedding its skin.

Finally, her past was exactly where it should be. Behind her. And she made a point of never looking in her rearview mirror.

Happy, she settled herself more comfortably in her favorite chair and shifted her focus to her laptop.

"Okay, Decaffeinated, let me show you where you've been going wrong."

She started typing again.

A woman wants a man who understands her, and a gift should demonstrate that understanding. It isn't about the value, it's about the sentiment. Choose something that shows you know her, and that you listen to her. Choose something—

"And here's the important part, Decaffeinated, so pay attention," she muttered under her breath.

—something that no other person would think to buy her, because no one knows her like you do. Do that, and I guarantee your girlfriend will remember that birthday forever. And she'll remember you.

Satisfied that if the man listened to her advice he might have a half-decent chance of pleasing the woman he loved, Molly reached for her glass of filtered water and checked the time on her laptop. Time for her morning run. And she didn't intend to go alone. No matter how busy her working day, this was time they always spent together.

Shutting down her computer, she stood up and stretched, feeling the whisper of silk brush against her skin. She'd been typing for an hour while barely moving and her neck ached. She still had a stack of individual consultations waiting for her attention, but she'd deal with those later.

She glanced through the window, watching as darkness slowly melted away to be replaced by a wash of sunshine. For a moment the view was filled with streaks of burnt gold and the dazzle of glass. It was a city of sharp edges and towering possibilities, its darker side masked by the shimmer of sunshine.

Every other city would be waking up at this time, but this was New York. You couldn't wake up, when you'd never been to sleep.

She dressed quickly, swapping pajamas for a soft T-shirt, Lycra leggings and her favorite dark purple running shoes. At the last moment she grabbed a sweatshirt because an early spring morning in New York City could still bite through a layer of clothing.

Scooping her hair into a careless ponytail, she reached for a water bottle.

There was still no movement from the bed. He lay in a tangle of bedding, eyes closed, not stirring.

"Hey, handsome." Amused, she nudged him. "Did I finally wear you out yesterday? That's a first." He was in his prime. Fit and shockingly attractive. When they ran together in the park, heads turned in envy and it made her glow with pride because they could look, but she was the one who got to go home with him.

In this world where it was almost impossible to find the right person, she'd found someone who was protective, loyal and affectionate, and he was all hers. She knew, deep in her heart, that she could depend on him. She knew, even without marriage vows, that he was going to love her in sickness and in health, for richer for poorer, for better or for worse.

She was lucky, lucky, lucky.

What they shared was free of all the stress and challenges that so often marred a relationship. What they shared was perfect.

She watched, her heart filled with love, as he finally yawned and stretched slowly.

Dark eyes locked on hers.

"You," she said, "are *insanely* handsome and everything I've ever wanted in a man. Have I told you that lately?"

He sprang from the bed, tail wagging, ready for action, and Molly dropped to her knees to hug him.

"Good morning, Valentine. How's the greatest dog in the whole wide world feeling today?"

The Dalmatian gave a single bark, licked her face and Molly grinned.

Another day was dawning in New York City, and she was ready to roll.

* * *

"Let me get this straight. You want to borrow a dog so that you can use it to meet a dog-loving girl? Have you no shame?"

"None." Ignoring his sister's disapproval, Daniel carefully removed a dog hair from his suit. "But I don't see how that fact is connected to my request."

He thought about the girl in the park, with her endless legs and that sleek dark ponytail swinging like a pendulum across her back as she ran. Since the first day he'd seen her, pounding her way along one of the many leafy trails that cobwebbed through Central Park, with her dog bounding ahead of her, he'd been smitten. It wasn't just her hair that caught his attention, or those incredible legs. It was the air of confidence. Daniel was drawn to confidence, and this woman looked as if she had life by the throat and was strangling the hell out of it.

He'd always enjoyed his early morning run. Lately it had taken on a new dimension. He'd started timing his run to coincide with hers even though it meant arriving in the office a little later. Despite those sacrifices on his part, so far she hadn't even noticed him. Did that surprise him? Yes. When it came to women, he'd never had to try too hard. Women tended to notice him. However, the girl in the park seemed unusually preoccupied by her running and her dog, a situation that had led him to the decision that it was time to raise his game and tap into his creative side.

But first he had to talk his way past one of his sisters and so far that wasn't looking good. He'd been hoping for Harriet, but instead he'd gotten Fliss, who was much tougher to get around.

Eyes narrowed, she planted herself in front of him and folded her arms. "Seriously? You're going to pretend you own a dog in order to hit on a woman? You don't think that's contrived? Dishonest?"

"It's not dishonest. I'm not claiming ownership. I'm simply walking a dog."

"An action that suggests a love of animals."

"I don't have a problem with animals. Can I remind you I was the one who rescued that animal from Harlem last month? In fact he would do fine. I'll borrow him." The door opened and Daniel flinched as an energetic Labrador sprinted into the room. He didn't have a problem with animals unless they were about to get up close and personal with his favorite suit. "He's not going to jump up, is he?"

"Because you're *such* a dog lover." Fliss caught the dog firmly by its collar. "This is Poppy. Harriet is fostering her. Note the 'her' in that sentence. She's a girl, Dan."

"That explains why she finds me irresistible." Hiding his laughter, he lowered his hand and played with the dog's ears. "Hello, beautiful. How would you like a romantic walk in the park? We can watch the sunrise."

"She doesn't want a walk in the park, or anything else. You're not her type. She's had a rough time and she's nervous around people, especially men."

"I'm good with nervous women. But if I'm not her type, then tell her not to drop hairs on my suit. Especially blond ones. I'm due in court in a couple of hours. I have a closing." Daniel felt his phone buzz, pulled it out of his pocket and checked the message. "Duty calls. I need to go."

"I thought you were staying for breakfast. We haven't seen you in ages."

"I've been busy. Half of Manhattan has decided to divorce, or so it seems. So you'll have a dog here ready for me at 6:00 a.m. tomorrow?"

"Just because a woman goes running on her own, doesn't mean she's single. Maybe she's married."

"She's single."

"So?" Fliss scowled. "Even if she *is* single, that doesn't mean she wants a relationship. It bugs the crap out of me when men assume a single woman is only single because she's waiting for a man. Get over yourselves."

Daniel studied his sister. "Which side of bed did you climb out of this morning?"

"I can climb out of any side I like. I'm single."

"Lend me a dog, Fliss. And don't give me anything small. It needs to be a reasonable size."

"And there was me thinking that you're secure in your own masculinity. Such a big, macho guy. You're afraid to be seen with a small dog, is that it?"

"No." Busy typing a reply to the message, Daniel didn't look up. "The woman I'm interested in has a big dog so I need one that can keep up. I don't want to have to carry the animal while I run. Even you have to admit that would look ridiculous, not to mention being uncomfortable for the dog."

"Oh for— Stop looking at your phone! Here's a clue, Dan. If you're going to ask me a favor, at least pay me a small amount of attention while you do it. It would be a sign of love and affection."

"You're my sister. I handle all your legal affairs and I never bill you. That's my way of showing love and affection." He answered another email. "Stop overreacting. All I want is one cute dog. The sort that's going to stop a woman in her tracks and make her go gooey-eyed. I'll do the rest."

"You don't even *like* dogs."

Daniel frowned. Did he like dogs? It wasn't something he'd ever asked himself. A dog was a complication and he kept his life free of complication. "Just because I don't own a dog doesn't mean I don't like them. I don't have time in my life for a dog, that's all."

"That's an excuse. Plenty of working people own dogs. If they didn't, Harriet and I would be out of business. The Bark Rangers is turning over—"

"I know your turnover. I can recite every number in your company's balance sheet. That's my job."

"You're a divorce attorney."

"But I stay on top of my sisters' business. Do you know why? Because it's a token of my love and affection. Do you know how? Because I work a hundred hours a week. It's barely a life for a human. It's certainly not a life for a dog. And might I point out that your dramatically increased turnover came as a result of your new relationship with that up-and-coming concierge company, Urban Genie, a partnership I arranged through my friend Matt. You're welcome."

"Sometimes you are so smug I could punch you."

Daniel smiled, but still didn't look up. "So are you going to help or not? If not, I'll ask Harry. You know she'll say yes."

"I *am* Harry."

Finally Daniel looked up. He studied her closely, wondering if he'd made a mistake. Then he shook his head. "No, you're Fliss." It was a game the twins had played on him hundreds of time growing up.

Which Twin?

His score was 100 percent. They'd never fooled him yet.

Her shoulders slumped. "How do you do it?"

"Tell the two of you apart? Apart from the fact that you're as abrasive as an armadillo, I'm your big brother. I've had plenty of practice. I've been doing it for twenty-eight years. The pair of you have never fooled me yet."

"One day we're going to."

"Not going to happen. If you really want to pretend to be Harriet you need to tone down the attitude. Try being a little softer. Even in your crib you were always the one yelling."

"Softer?" Her tone had a dangerous edge. "You're telling

me to be soft? What sort of sexist comment is that, especially as we both know that 'soft' gets you nowhere?"

"It's not sexist, and I'm not telling you to be soft. I'm giving advice on how you might be able to convince some poor fool you're Harriet. And that's not me, by the way, so don't waste your time." He looked up as the door opened.

"Breakfast is ready. I made your favorite. Pancakes with a side of crispy bacon." Harriet walked into the room carrying a tray. She had the same hair as her sister—a smooth, buttermilk blond—but she wore hers pinned haphazardly at the back of her head, as if her objective was simply to move it out of the way so it didn't interfere with her day. Physically, they were identical. They had the same delicate features, the same blue eyes, the same heart-shaped face. Temperamentally, they couldn't have been more different. Harriet was thoughtful and calm. Fliss was impulsive and fierce. Harriet loved yoga and Pilates. Fliss favored kickboxing and karate.

Sensing an atmosphere, Harriet stopped and glanced between them, her expression changing. "Have you two had a fight already?"

How, Daniel wondered, could three siblings from the same family be so different? And how could twins, who on the surface were indistinguishable to most people, bear no resemblance on the inside?

"Us? Fight? Never." Fliss's voice was heavy with sarcasm. "You know how much I adore our big brother."

"I hate it when you fight." The anxious look in Harriet's eyes made him feel guilty and he exchanged glances with Fliss. It was a glance they'd shared a million times over the years. A tacit agreement to suspend hostilities until Harriet wasn't in the room.

They'd all developed their own way of coping with conflict. Harriet's was to hide from it. As a child, she'd hidden under the table to avoid the screaming fights that had been part of their early family life. On one occasion Daniel had tried dragging her out to remove her from the fallout. Her eyes had been squeezed shut and her hands over her ears, as if not being able to see it or hear it might mean it wasn't happening.

Remembering how impatient he'd felt at the time, Daniel felt a needle of guilt. They had all been so self-absorbed, his parents included, that none of them had understood what was going on with Harriet. It had become apparent in the most public way possible and even now, twenty years later, he couldn't think about that evening at the school without breaking into a sweat.

On the surface Harriet didn't appear to be particularly tough, but he and Fliss had learned that there were different kinds of tough. Despite appearances, Harriet was made of solid steel.

He watched as she set the tray down and carefully unloaded plates of food and napkins.

Napkins. Who bothered with napkins for a casual breakfast with family?

Harriet bothered. She was the architect of all domestic comfort in the apartment she shared with her twin.

There were times when he wondered if the three of them would still be a family if it weren't for Harriet.

As a child she'd had an obsession with her dolls and her dollhouse. With the insensitivity of an eight-year-old, he'd dismissed it as a typical girl activity but now, looking back, he could see that she'd been constructing something she didn't have, clinging to her image of home and family when their own had fallen short. She'd found some semblance of stability in her own private world, whereas he and Fliss had found other ways to dodge the cracks and the shifting emotional landscape of their parents' marriage.

When Harriet and Fliss had moved into the apartment, Harriet had been the one to make it a home. She'd painted the walls a sunlit yellow and had chosen a rug in muted shades of green to soften the wooden floor. Hers was the hand that arranged the flowers on the table, plumped the cushions on the sofas and tended the plants that clustered together in a junglelike profusion of green.

Fliss would never choose to own a plant. Like him, she wouldn't want the responsibility for something that required care and attention. It was the reason neither of them had any interest in a long-term relationship. The only difference between them was that Fliss had tried. Only once, but still it was enough for Fliss to feel she had proved her point. Been there. Done that.

None of them talked about it. The Knight siblings had learned that the only way to make it through a bad day, a bad month or a bad year was to keep moving forward.

"We weren't fighting." Daniel kept his tone slow and easy. "I was giving her brotherly advice, that's all."

Fliss narrowed her eyes. "When the day comes that I need your advice, I'll ask. And, by the way, hell will have frozen over at least eight times before *that* day comes."

Daniel stole a piece of bacon from the plate and Harriet slapped his hand gently.

"Wait until I've set the table. And before I forget, Fliss, we had two more jobs sent through from Urban Genie. We have a busy day ahead."

"So does Daniel." Fliss stole a piece of bacon, too. "And he's not staying for breakfast."

"You're not?" Harriet handed him a napkin. "But I thought that was why you were visiting."

Daniel frowned at the implication that he only saw them whenever he wanted to be fed. Was that true? No. He visited because despite, or perhaps because of, his combative relationship with Fliss, he liked seeing his sisters. And he liked to keep an eye on Harriet. But it was true that his visits almost always coincided with food. As long as that food was prepared by Harriet, he was happy. Fliss could burn water.

"I had a message from the office, so this is a flying visit. But it's good to see you." On impulse he stood up and hugged his sister and heard Fliss mutter something under her breath.

"Yeah, right, use affection. Harry will fall for that."

"I'm allowed to hug my sister."

Fliss gave him the eye. "I'm your sister, and you don't hug me."

"I don't have time to spend the rest of my day removing thorns from my flesh."

"Fall for what?" Harriet hugged him back, and Daniel felt a rush of protectiveness. He knew she had found her perfect niche in life, but still he worried about her. If Fliss had a problem, the whole of Manhattan would know within minutes. Harriet kept things to herself.

"How are you doing?"

Fliss snorted. "Charm alert. He wants something, Harry." She forked a generous portion of bacon onto her plate. "Cut to the chase, Dan, preferably before I throw up my breakfast."

Daniel ignored her and smiled at Harriet. "I need a dog."

"Of *course* you do." She smiled back, delighted. "Your life is so focused on work, so emotionally empty, I've been telling you for *years* that what you need is a dog. It will give you permanence, something you can really love and connect with."

"He doesn't want a dog for any of those worthy reasons." Fliss waved her fork, her mouth full of bacon. "He wants a dog to help him score."

Harriet looked puzzled. "How does a dog help with that?"

Fliss swallowed. "Great question, but this is our big brother we're talking about so there's the biggest clue right there. He wants a prop. A canine prop. He yells 'fetch,' and the dog brings him the girl." She stabbed another piece of bacon. "Even if you managed to meet this woman with your dog plan, you'd never keep her. What happens when you invite her back to your place and she discovers the dog doesn't live there? Have you thought about that?"

"I never invite women back to my place so that isn't going to be a problem. My apartment is a dog-free, woman-free, stress-free chill zone."

"Even so, sooner or later she'll find out you're not a dog person, and then she'll leave."

"By then I'm sure we'll both have had enough of each other, so that sounds perfect to me. It will be a mutual parting of ways."

"Mr. Heartbreaker. Don't you ever feel guilty that you're leaving a trail of sobbing women around Manhattan?"

Daniel released Harriet. "I don't break hearts. The women I date are exactly like me."

"Insensitive and obtuse?"

"He isn't insensitive." Harriet tried to keep the peace. "He's a little afraid of commitment, that's all. And so are we. Daniel is hardly alone in that."

"I'm not afraid of commitment," Fliss said blithely. "I'm committed to myself, my happiness, my personal growth."

"I'm not afraid either." Daniel felt sweat prick the back of his neck. "Am I cautious? Yes, because that's the job I'm in. I'm the type of guy who—"

"—makes a woman decide to stay single?" Fliss helped herself to another pancake.

"I don't want to be single," Harriet said. "I want to love someone and be loved by them. But I'm not sure how to make that happen."

Daniel caught Fliss's eye. Neither of them was in a position to offer advice on that subject.

"Given that I spend all of my extremely long working week unraveling the lives of those who didn't choose to stay single," he said, "I'd say the female race should be thanking me for remaining commitment-free. If you don't get married, you can't get divorced."

"Well, that's a positive outlook." Fliss tipped maple syrup over her pancake. "One of these days, some very smart woman is going to teach you a few lessons about women. These are delicious, Harry. You should open a restaurant. I'd help out."

Harriet flushed. "I'd muddle up all the orders and, as much as I love you, I wouldn't let you near a kitchen. It wouldn't be fair to the New York Fire Department."

"I don't need lessons about women." Daniel stole a piece of bacon from Fliss's plate. "I already know everything there is to know."

"You only *think* you know everything there is to know about women, which makes you a thousand times more dangerous than the man who admits to being clueless."

"I'm not clueless. Growing up with you two was an intensive training course in how women think and feel. For example, I know that if I don't get the hell out of here right now you're going to explode. So I'm making my exit while we're still friends."

"We're not friends."

"You love me. And when you're not scowling, I love you back. And Fliss is right—" he smiled at Harry "—you're an incredible cook."

"If you loved me," Fliss said between her teeth, "you'd be staying for breakfast. You *use* me, in the same way you use all women."

Daniel reached for his jacket. "Here's a tip from inside the mind of a guy. Stop being cranky or you'll never get a date." He watched his sister's face turn puce.

"I'm single through choice," she spluttered, and then sighed and glared at him. "You're winding me up. Why can't I see when you're winding me up? You drive me bat-shit crazy and then I can't think straight. It's one of your tactics and I know that, but I still fall for it every time. Are you this annoying in court?"

"I'm worse."

"No wonder you always win. Opposing counsel probably wants to get as far away from you as quickly as possible."

"That's part of the reason. And for the record, I don't use women. I let them use me, preferably after dark." He bent to kiss her cheek, thinking that teasing his sister was his second favorite game after poker. "So what time can I pick up this dog?"

Two

Dear Aggie, if men are from Mars, when are they going back?
Yours, Earthbound and Exasperated

She noticed his dog first. A German shepherd who was as strong and athletic as his owner. She'd seen the two of them every day for the past week, just after sunrise. She'd allowed herself a glance or two, because…well, she was human, wasn't she? She had as much appreciation for the male form as the next woman, especially when that male form was as well presented as it was in this guy. And besides, studying people was her job.

Like so many other people in the park at this time, he wore running gear, but something about the way he moved told her that when he wasn't pounding the paths, he dressed in a suit and was commander in chief of whichever empire he presided over. His hair was dark and cropped short. Doctor? Banker? Accountant? Judging from the air of confidence he exuded he was very good at whatever it was he did. If she'd had to make more guesses about him, she would have said he was focused to the point of driven, spent too long working, and found it hard to empathize with weakness. He'd have his own weaknesses of course, everybody did. Being smart, he probably even knew what they were, but he would hide them because weakness wasn't something he'd share with others. He was the type of guy who, if he knew what she did for a living, would laugh and then express surprise that anyone needed advice on something as straightforward as relationships. A man like him would have no idea how it felt to lack confidence, to not be able to find the courage to approach a woman you found interesting and attractive.

A man exactly like Rupert.

She frowned. Where had *that* thought come from? She was careful to never think about Rupert. She had enough self-insight to know her experience with him had colored her view of the world. In particular, it had colored her view of relationships. In all probability this man was nothing like Rupert.

The only piece of information that jarred with her impression of him was that he had a dog. She wouldn't have expected a man like him to want responsibility for a dog. Maybe the dog belonged to a friend who was sick, or maybe it had belonged to a deceased family member, but if that was the case then she would have expected a man like him to use a dog-walking service, like the one she occasionally used for Valentine. The Bark Rangers.

The dog was the one misshapen piece of the jigsaw that stopped her picture of him fitting together perfectly.

Determined not to be caught staring, she ran on, her feet pounding the ground in the comfortable rhythm she now found instinctively. Running was a way of testing herself. Of pushing herself outside her comfort levels. And pushing made her aware of the power and strength of her own body. Running reminded her that when she thought she had nothing more to give, she could still find more.

Even though it was early and the park wasn't yet open to traffic, it was busy. Joggers mingled with cyclists riding hill repeats and dawn laps of Central Park. In a few hours they'd give way to parents with strollers, and tourists keen to explore the eight-hundred-and-forty-three acres of parkland that ran from 59th Street to 110th and east to west from Fifth Avenue to Central Park West.

She could never decide which season in New York was her favorite, but right now she would have voted for spring. The trees were thick with blossoms and it flavored the air with a heavy sweetness. Crab apple, cherry and magnolia bathed the park in a creamy, pink glow and exotic birds from Central and South America gathered ready for the spring migration.

She was pondering its near-bridal magnificence when Valentine shot in front of her and almost tripped her up.

He bounded after the German shepherd, who was thoroughly overexcited and refusing to come back when called.

"Brutus!" The man's voice thundered across the park.

Molly slowed her pace. Seriously? He'd called his dog Brutus?

The dog ignored him. He didn't even turn his head in the direction of his owner. There was no acknowledgment that they even knew each other.

Molly decided that either Brutus was the sort of dog who loved to challenge authority, or else he didn't often find him-

self in the company of other dogs and wasn't about to prioritize obedience over a good time.

Clearly there was one thing that power couldn't command, and that was a misbehaving dog. Was there any better leveler?

She whistled to Valentine, who was having fun with his
new friend.

His head came up and their eyes met across the expanse
of grass. After a split second of thought he came bounding
toward her, all long lines and lean muscle, and as graceful
as a ballet dancer. She heard the muted thud of his paws on
the soft grass, the rhythmic panting, and then he skidded to
a halt in front of her, the rear end of his body moving with
each swing of his tail, that canine barometer of happiness.

There was surely no more uplifting greeting than a wagging tail. It conveyed so much. Love, warmth and unques-
tioning acceptance.

He was followed by his new friend, the German shepherd,
who skidded untidily to a halt at her feet, more bruiser than
ballet dancer. He gave her a hopeful look, seeking approval.

Molly decided that for all his bad-boy tendencies, he was
cute. But like all bad boys, he needed a firm hand and strong
boundaries.

His owner was probably the same.

"Well, aren't you adorable." She dropped to her haunches
to make a fuss over him, stroking his head and rubbing his
neck. She felt the warmth of his breath on her skin and the
smack of his tail against the leg as he circled in excitement.
He tried to put his paws on her shoulders, almost knocking
her on her butt in the dirt. "No. Sit."

The dog gave her a reproachful look and sat, clearly questioning her sense of fun.

"You're cute, but that doesn't mean I want your muddy paws on my T-shirt."

The man stopped beside her. "He sat for you." His smile was easy, his gaze warm. "He never does that for me. What's your secret?"

"I asked nicely." She stood up, conscious of the sweaty tendrils of hair sticking to her neck and annoyed with herself for caring.

"Looks like you have the magic touch. Or maybe it's the British accent that does it for him. Brutus—" The man gave the dog a stern look. "Brutus."

Brutus didn't even turn his head. It was as if the dog didn't know he was talking to him.

Molly was puzzled. "Does he often ignore you?"

"All the time. He has a behavioral problem."

"Behavioral problems usually say more about the owner than they do about the dog."

"Ouch. Well, that puts me in my place." His laugh was a rich, sexy sound and heat ripped through her body and pooled low in her abdomen.

She'd expected him to be defensive. Instead, she was the one who was defensive. She'd built walls and barriers that no one could pass, but she was sure that this man with the dangerous blue eyes and the sexy voice was used to finding his way around barriers. She felt breathless and swimmy-headed, and she wasn't used to feeling that way.

"He needs training, that's all. He's not very good at doing what he's told." She focused on the dog, rather than the man. That way she didn't have to deal with the laughing eyes of his insanely attractive owner.

"I've never been too good at doing as I'm told either, so I'm not going to hold that against him."

"It can be dangerous for a dog to challenge authority."

"I'm not afraid to be challenged."

That didn't surprise her. One glance told her this guy knew his own mind and walked his own path. She also sensed that the smooth layers of charm and charisma concealed a core of steel. He was a man only a fool would underestimate. And she was no fool.

"You don't expect obedience?"

"Are we still talking about dogs here? Because this is the twenty-first century, and I like to think of myself as progressive."

Whenever a situation or person unsettled her, she tried to detach herself and imagine what advice she'd give as Aggie.

Feeling breathless and tongue-tied around a man can be uncomfortable, but remember that however attractive he is, underneath he has his own insecurities even if he doesn't choose to show them.

That didn't make her feel better. She was starting to think this man didn't have a single insecurity.

It doesn't matter how you feel on the inside, as long as you don't show it on the outside. Smile and act cool and he is never going to know that he turns your insides to the consistency of pulp.

Smile and act cool.

That seemed like the best approach.

"You should try taking him to obedience classes."

He raised an eyebrow. "That's a thing?"

"Yes. And it might help. He's a beautiful dog. Did you buy him from a breeder?"

"He's a rescue. The casualty of a vicious divorce case up in Harlem. The husband knew that Brutus was the one thing the wife loved more than anything in the world, so he fought for him in the divorce. His lawyer was better than hers, so he won and found himself with a dog he didn't want."

Molly was appalled enough to forget about the strange melting feeling going on inside her. "Who was his lawyer?"

"I was."

Lawyer. She'd missed that one on her list of possible professions, but now she wondered why because it was a perfect fit. It was easy enough to imagine him intimidating the opposition. He was a man used to winning every battle he fought, she was sure of that.

"Why didn't he give Brutus back to the wife?"

"Firstly because she'd moved back to Minnesota to live with her mother, secondly because the last thing he would ever do was something that would make his ex-wife happy and thirdly because, much as his wife loved the dog, she hated him more. She wanted to make his life as difficult as possible so she made him keep the dog."

"That's a horrible story." Molly, who heard plenty of horrible stories in her working day, was shocked.

"That's relationships."

"That's one divorce. That's not all relationships. So you rescued him?" That revelation exploded all her preconceived ideas about him. She'd assumed he was the sort who put himself front and center of his life, rarely inconveniencing himself for anyone, but he'd saved this beautiful, vulnerable dog who had lost the only person who had ever loved him. He might be handsome and a sharp talker, but he was obviously a good person. "I think it's great that you've done this." She rubbed Brutus's head, sad that this animal had paid the price for people's failure to work out their differences. When relationships fell apart the fallout was far and wide. She knew that better than anyone. "Poor guy." The dog nudged her pockets hopefully and she smiled. "Are you looking for treats? Is he allowed?"

"He's allowed. If you have a spare."

"I always carry them for Valentine." Hearing his name, Valentine was by her side in a flash, possessive and protective.

"Valentine?" The man watched as she fed both dogs. "Is he a man substitute?"

"No. Last time I checked he was definitely a dog."

He flashed her a smile of appreciation. "I thought maybe you'd given up on men and settled for the love of a good dog."

That was closer to the truth than he could have imagined, but she had no intention of admitting it to anyone, least of all someone who seemed to have the world at his feet. What would he know about how it felt to have your weaknesses publicly exposed? Nothing.

And she had no intention of enlightening him.

Her past was hers and hers alone. More private than a bank account, hidden securely behind a firewall that allowed no one access. If there was a password, it would be Screw Up. Or possibly Major Screw Up.

"Valentine isn't a substitute for anything or anyone. He's my number one dog. My best friend."

Her gaze collided with his and she felt the connection like a physical jolt.

She had the jitters, and she couldn't remember when that had last happened to her. It was his eyes. She was willing to bet those devilish eyes had encouraged more than a few women to throw caution to the wind. There was probably a label on him somewhere saying Handle with Care.

She tried to ignore the way she was feeling, but her heart had other ideas.

Oh no, Molly. No, no, no. Her inbox was filled with questions from women wanting to know how to handle men exactly like him, and while she might be excellent at giving advice, her expertise ended there.

Somehow sensing he was the topic of conversation, Valentine wagged his tail hard.

She'd found him abandoned when he was still a puppy.

She still remembered the look on his face. A little startled and a lot hurt, as if he couldn't quite believe someone had actually chosen to dump him in the gutter rather than keep him. As if that action had caused him to question everything he had ever believed about himself.

She knew the feeling.

They'd found each other, two lost souls, and bonded instantly.

"I called him Valentine because he has a heart-shaped nose." That was the only detail she was prepared to share. Time to leave. Before she said something, or did something, that might lead her on a path she had no intention of walking. "Enjoy your run."

"Wait—" He put out a hand to stop her. "This isn't the first time I've seen you. You live near here?"

The knowledge that he'd been watching her while she'd been watching him gave her pulse rate another workout.

"Near enough."

"Then I'll be seeing you again. I'm Daniel." He held out his hand and she took it, her body ignoring the warnings of her brain. She felt his fingers close around hers, the pressure firm. She imagined he knew what to do with those hands and imagining it gave her that breathless feeling that made it difficult to think properly.

She was having trouble focusing, and in the meantime he was looking at her expectantly, waiting.

"Let's try this again," he murmured. "I'm Daniel, and you're—"

Her name. He was waiting for her to tell him her name. And judging from the amusement in his eyes he knew exactly why she was tongue-tied.

"Molly." There were still days when it felt unnatural using that name, which was illogical because Molly *was* her name. Or one of them. The fact that she'd only started using that name since she'd moved to New York shouldn't matter.

She gave him no more than that but still she saw him file it away and knew it would be remembered. She sensed he wasn't a man who forgot much. He was smart. But even if he found out her last name and looked her up, he still wouldn't find anything. She'd checked.

"Join me for a coffee, Molly." He released her hand. "I know a great little place near here that makes the best coffee on the Upper East Side."

It was somewhere between an invitation and a command. Smart and smooth. An effortless overture from a man who didn't know the meaning of the word *rejection*.

But he was about to learn, because there was no way she would be joining him for coffee or anything else.

"Thanks, but I have to get to work. Enjoy your run, you and Brutus."

She didn't give him a chance to argue, or herself a chance to doubt her decision. Instead she ran. She ran through the dappled sunshine and the scent of blossoms, Valentine by her side and temptation nipping at her heels. She didn't turn her head even though not doing so made her neck ache and was a bigger test on her willpower than anything she could remember for a long time. Was he watching her? Was he annoyed that she'd turned him down?

Only when she'd covered what she considered to be a safe distance did she slow her pace. They were close to one of the many ankle-level dog drinking fountains, and she stopped to catch her breath and let a thirsty Valentine drink his fill.

Join me for a coffee...

And then what?

And then nothing.

When it came to relationships she was great with the theory but bad in practice. How bad was a matter of public record. First came love. Then came pain.

You're a relationship expert, but you're hopeless at relationships. Do you even know how crazy that is?

Oh yes, she knew. And so did a few million strangers. Which was why these days she was sticking with the theory.

And as for smooth lawyer Daniel, she guessed it would take him around five minutes to forget everything about her.

* * *

He couldn't get her out of his mind.

Annoyed and a little intrigued by the novelty of that experience, Daniel pressed the buzzer and Harriet opened the door.

He smelled fresh coffee and something delicious baking in the oven.

"How was your run?" She had a tiny Chihuahua under her arm and Daniel clamped his hand on Brutus's collar, intercepting the enthusiastic surge of energy that was about to propel the dog through the door.

"Are you seriously going to leave these two together? Brutus would eat him in one mouthful."

Harriet looked confused. "Who is Brutus?"

"This is Brutus." Daniel removed the lead and the German shepherd bounded into the apartment, his tail smacking into one of Harriet's plants and scattering soil and blooms across the floor.

Harriet put the tiny dog down and picked up the shattered remains of her pot without complaint. "That dog is called Ruffles. And he's too big for this apartment."

"I refuse to stand in the middle of Central Park and call for 'Ruffles,' so I renamed him. Do I smell coffee?"

"You can't rename a dog."

"You can if someone was stupid enough to name him Ruffles in the first place." Daniel strolled into the bright, sunlit kitchen and helped himself to coffee. "What sort of name is that for a big macho dog? It will give him an identity crisis."

"It's the name he was given," Harriet said patiently. "It's the name he knows and responds to."

"It's a name that embarrasses him. I've done him a favor." Daniel took a mouthful of coffee and checked his watch. There were always demands on his time, and lately there was never enough time, a factor due in part to the extended length of his morning run.

"You're later than usual. Did something happen? Did she finally talk to you?" Harriet threw the shards of pottery away and carefully scooped up what was left of her plant.

Daniel knew that the moment he left she'd be repotting it carefully and giving it whatever attention it needed to make a full recovery.

"Yeah, we talked." If the few words they'd exchanged could be counted as talking. He'd asked a few questions.

She'd responded. But her responses had been brief and de-signed to offer him no encouragement whatsoever. She'd made it clear she was more interested in his dog than in him, which might have crushed the spirit of a man with less knowledge about relationships.

Although there had been no verbal indication that she was interested, there had been nonverbal cues.

In the fleeting second before the barriers had gone up, he'd seen interest.

He wondered who was responsible for those barriers. A man, presumably. A relationship gone bad. He saw plenty of examples in his working day. People who had affairs, grew apart or simply fell out of love. Love was a chocolate box of heartbreak and disaster. Pick your flavor.

"She talked to you?" Harry's face brightened. "What did she say?"

Very little.

"We're taking it slowly."

"In other words she's not interested." Fliss walked into the kitchen. She was wearing yoga pants, a sweatshirt and a pair of black running shoes with a neon purple flash. She grabbed her keys from the countertop. "Obviously a woman of sense. Either that or you're losing your touch. So does this mean you won't be walking Ruffles tomorrow?"

"I'm not losing my touch and yes, I'll be walking *Brutus*. And, by the way, he has a few behavioral issues, the most significant of which is not coming when he is called."

"That must be a whole new experience for you."

"Very funny. Any tips?"

"I don't have any advice to offer on relationships except maybe don't do it."

"I was talking about the dog."

Three

Dear Aggie, if there are plenty of fish in the sea, why is my net always empty?

Molly let herself into her apartment, dropped her keys into the bowl by the door and headed straight to the shower.

Ten minutes later she was back at her computer. Valentine curled up in a basket underneath her desk and put his head on his paws.

Sunlight flowed in through the windows, bouncing off the polished oak floor and illuminating the handwoven rug she'd picked up from a textile design studio she'd discovered on a trip to Union Square. In one corner of the room was a large wooden giraffe that her father had shipped to her from a trip to Africa. No one glancing at her overflowing bookshelves would have been able to discern much about her character. Biographies and classics nestled against crime fiction and romance. Also on the shelf were a few remaining author copies of her first book, *Mate for Life, Tools for Meeting Your Perfect Life Partner.*

Do as I say, don't do as I do, she thought. She'd dedicated it to her father, but probably should have dedicated it to Rupert. *For Rupert, without whom this book would never have been written.*

But to do that would have meant risking exposure, and she had no intention of letting anyone discover the real person behind "Dr. Aggie."

No. Her father was the safest option. That way she could ensure that everything she'd built stayed standing and she could push the whole Rupert episode, as her father called it, into a mental box labeled Life Experience.

When she'd first moved to New York, she'd shared a room in a dingy walk-up in the outer reaches of Brooklyn with three women who had an addiction to beer pong and all-night parties. After six months of panting up one hundred and ninety-two stairs (she'd counted every one) and taking the subway into Manhattan, Molly had blown the last of her savings on a small one-bedroom on the second floor of a building several blocks away from Central Park. She'd fallen in love with the apartment on sight, and with the building, with its cheerful green door and iron railings.

She'd fallen in love with her neighbors, too. On the ground floor was a young couple with a baby and one floor above them was Mrs. Winchester, a widow who had lived in the same apartment for sixty years. She had a habit of losing her keys, so now Molly kept a spare set. Directly above Molly were Gabe and Mark. Gabe worked in advertising and Mark was a children's book illustrator.

She'd met them on her first night in her apartment when she was trying to fix a misbehaving lock on her door. Gabe had fixed it, and Mark had made her dinner. They'd been friends ever since and new friends, she'd discovered, were sometimes more reliable than old ones.

The friends she'd had from childhood had abandoned her in droves when her life had fallen apart, reluctant to be sucked down into the deadly quicksand of her humiliation. At first there had been a few supportive phone calls, but as the situation had worsened, the support and friendship had trickled to nothing. They'd behaved as if her shame was infectious. As if by standing side by side with her, they might catch whatever she had.

And in a way she didn't blame them. She understood the hell of having reporters camped outside the house and of having your reputation shredded online. Who needed that?

Plenty of people wanted fame and fortune but no one, it seemed, ever wanted to trend on Twitter.

It had made her decision to leave London even easier. She'd started a new life, complete with a new name. Here in New York, she'd met new people. People who didn't know. The people in her apartment block were wonderful, and so was the Upper East Side. Amidst the vast grid of tree-canopied streets and avenues, she'd discovered a neighborhood flooded with New York history and tradition. She loved it all, from the ornate prewar co-op buildings and brownstone row houses to the classic mansions along Fifth Avenue. It felt like home and she had her favorite haunts. When she couldn't be bothered to cook she'd nip out and pick up a panini or homemade pastry from Via Quadronno between Madison and Fifth, and when she felt like celebrating she'd head to Ladurée and indulge herself in a selection of macarons.

She'd explored Manhattan and discovered hidden salsa clubs, arts clubs, jazz clubs. She roamed the galleries, the

Sarah Morgan

Met, the Frick and the Guggenheim. But her favorite place was the sprawling expanse of Central Park, a brisk ten-minute walk from her small apartment. She and Valentine spent hours exploring hidden corners together.

She flicked on her laptop and reached for her water while she waited for the machine to boot. Her desk was cluttered. Papers stacked high, scribbles and notes, two coffee mugs abandoned and forgotten. When she worked, she focused and that included blocking out the mess.

When her phone rang she checked the caller ID and answered immediately. "Dad! How are you doing?" She listened as her father told her about his latest adventure. He'd moved from London a few months before her embarrassing fall from grace, something for which she would forever be thankful. Having retired from his job in an electronics company, he'd bought himself an RV and proceeded on an epic road trip of the continental US, exploring his homeland state by state. In a dusty, sunbaked town in Arizona he'd met Carly and they'd been together ever since.

Molly had met her once and liked her, but what she liked most of all was that her father was so happy. She remembered watching him, stumbling his way through those first few years after her mother had left, his confidence drowned in the wake of monumental rejection.

She couldn't remember exactly when she'd started encouraging him to date. It had started in school, during her teenage years, when she'd realized that she was more interested in observing other people's relationships than in having one herself. And observing had uncovered an ability to match people up. She could see it so clearly. Who would be good together and who wouldn't. Whose relationship would last, and whose would crash on the rocks at the first sign of rough seas. Word had spread that she had a gift. And she loved using that gift. Why not? It was hard to find the right person in this crowded, crazy world. Sometimes people needed a little help.

They'd called her The Matchmaker. Which was a lot better than the name she'd earned herself a few years later.

At school, most of her lunchtimes and a large chunk of her evenings were taken up giving relationship advice. Having seen her father exhaust himself trying to please her mother and failing, she'd always encouraged people to be themselves. If you weren't loved for who you were, a relationship had no future. She knew that. If you weren't enough for someone, you'd never be enough.

No matter how hard he'd tried, her father hadn't been enough for her mother.

Molly hadn't been enough for her mother either.

Her father's voice boomed down the phone, dragging her back to the present. "How's my girl?"

"I'm good." She deleted a few spam emails with a stab of her finger. "Busy. Working on proofs of my next book."

"Always helping other people with their relationships. How about your own? And I'm not talking about Valentine."

"I have plenty of men in my life, Dad. I have a packed schedule. Tuesday and Friday is salsa dancing, Thursday is spin class, Wednesday is cooking class, Monday is theater group—there are men at all those places."

"But you're single."

"That's right. It's *because* I'm single I can do all those things."

"Relationships are important, honey. You're the one who always told me that."

"I have relationships. I had supper with Gabe and Mark a

few nights ago. Mark is taking an Italian cookery class. His tortellini is incredible, you should taste it."

"Gabe and Mark are gay."

"So? They're my closest friends." Although she'd never truly tested that friendship, of course. She'd discovered to her cost that the test of true friendship was whether you were willing to stand by someone being named and shamed. She seriously hoped she never had to test that out again. "And friendship is a relationship. They're great listeners and very happy together. It's good to be around them."

"You know you're a hypocrite? All those years you tried to pair me up with someone and told me to take the risk, but you won't take the risk yourself."

"That's different. I didn't like seeing you on your own. You have wonderful qualities that were crying out to be shared with someone special."

"You have wonderful qualities, too, Molly." He made a little sound. "Still feels weird calling you that."

"It's my name, Dad."

"But not one we ever used until you moved to New York. Do you feel like Molly?"

"I definitely feel like Molly. I like being Molly. And I share Molly's qualities with a bunch of people who appreciate them."

A sigh reverberated down the phone. "I worry about you. I worry this is all my fault. I feel responsible."

"You're not responsible." It was a conversation they'd had numerous times over the years, despite the fact that in the weeks and months after her mother had left, Molly had only ever cried in the bathroom where her father couldn't witness her distress. The rest of the time she pretended she was coping well because she hadn't wanted to make it worse for him. It was hideously unjust, she thought, that he felt guilty about something over which he'd had no control.

"Carly read your book. She thinks you have abandonment issues."

"She's right. I do. But I came to terms with that a long time ago." Molly picked up her pen and started doodling on the pad next to her desk. Maybe she should get a coloring book. They were the latest non-medicinal stress reliever. She glanced at Valentine. "Maybe I could use a black marker pen and join your dots."

"What?" Her father sounded confused. "Why are you using marker pen?"

"I'm not. It was a joke. Dad, you need to stop worrying about me. I'm the psychologist in this relationship."

"I know, and I know people talk to you about everything. But who do you talk to, honey? Do something for me. Go on a date. Do it for me."

"Do you have anyone in mind? Or should I just grab the first person I meet on the street?" She thought about the man in the park with the wicked blue eyes and the sexy smile. Just thinking about him was enough to get her heart pumping a little harder.

"If that's what it takes. Just get out there. Get your confidence back. In all those things you go to, you're telling me you haven't met a single man who has gained your attention?"

"Not one." Molly glanced at Valentine, pleased that he couldn't talk. If he could, right now he'd be calling her a liar. "So where are you and Carly going next?"

"Traveling north to Oregon. We're going to hike part of the Pacific Crest Trail."

"Have fun and send me photos."

"Carly has started a blog, *You're Never Too Old to Be Bold.*"

"I'll take a look. And now I need to go, I have a ton of work to do. Go and be bold. Only try not to do it in public. And give Carly my love." With a smile, she ended the call and returned to her computer.

She was happy being single. And if that seemed like a strange admission for someone who specialized in relationships, she didn't care. These days she separated her work life from her real life.

Her mind wandered back to the guy in the park. For a few forbidden seconds she wondered what it would be like to be with a man like him and then she snapped herself back to the present.

She knew what it would be like to be with a man like him. Trauma and trouble.

She wasn't going to wonder if she was a coward for not accepting his offer of coffee.

It wasn't cowardice, it was common sense.

It meant that she'd learned from experience, and experience told her that an invitation to coffee didn't stop there. It was a beginning, not an end, and she wasn't in the mood to begin anything. Especially not with a man like Daniel. Daniel…? She realized she didn't know his last name.

She opened an email and read the question.

Dear Aggie, my mother picked out sexy underwear for my girlfriend but she's refusing to wear it. Why?

With a groan of despair, Molly sat back in her chair and reached for her water.

Was the guy serious?

Because nothing says "I care" like underwear picked out by your mother.

Some men didn't have a clue.

She sighed and started to type.

Not only was she making a good living by doing what she did, she was performing a public service.

* * *

The next day there was no sign of him.

Valentine ran in circles, sniffing the ground and the air, looking hopeful. When it was obvious that he was going to be playing alone he sent her a long reproachful look.

"Not my fault." Molly paused to draw breath. "Or maybe it is my fault. I gave him the brush-off, but trust me, it was the right thing to do. Let's go."

Valentine sat, refusing to budge.

"There is no point in us hanging around because I can tell you now he's not going to show. And that's good. I'm glad he's not here." She felt an unfamiliar tug in her gut. "You have a lot to learn about relationships. They're complicated. Even friendships. My advice is to lower your expectations. People let you down and disappoint you. I'm guessing dogs might be the same. Looking out for Brutus is a very bad thing."

Valentine ignored her and sniffed the ground, passing up the company of a sleek-looking Labrador and an overenthusiastic bulldog in his search for his preferred companion.

Breathless from her run, Molly stretched and then sat down on a bench.

That feeling inside her couldn't possibly be disappointment, could it? She'd spoken to him once. Once, that was all.

But they'd been exchanging glances for a week, and those glances had shifted from a look to a smile, and then the smile had shifted from polite to personal. The result was that she felt as if she'd known him for a while.

Annoyed with herself, she stood up and was about to continue with her run when Valentine gave an ecstatic bark and all but pulled the lead from her hand.

She turned her head and there was Daniel, strolling toward her, Brutus's lead in his right hand and a tray filled with four cups in his left.

Even from this distance he was striking. A female jogger slowed her pace as she passed him, turning her head to check whether the rear view was as good as the front, but Daniel didn't spare her a glance. Molly wondered if attracting female attention was so much a part of his life that he no longer noticed it.

Or maybe the reason he didn't notice was that his gaze was fixed on her.

As he drew closer, her heart bumped hard against her ribs. Her dormant sexuality woke from its long sleep and awareness spread across her skin and settled somewhere deep in her belly. The knowledge that she wanted him came with a tremor of shock.

It brought back memories of the first time she'd met Rupert. It had been like touching an electric fence. Five thousand volts of pure sexual energy had shot through her, frying her brain and fusing her entire early warning system. Deprived of its protection, she'd stumbled blindly into that relationship, forgetting her personal limitations in that area. She'd recognized later, while analyzing it with the benefit of hindsight, that she'd been dazzled.

She'd never allowed herself to be dazzled again. No more broken hearts.

Dear Aggie, there's this guy I really like, but I sense that getting involved with him would be a bad idea. On the other hand he makes me feel the way no other man ever has. What should I do?

You should listen to the voice telling you it's a bad idea and run, Molly thought. *Sprint, don't jog. Sprint fast in the opposite direction.*

The past three years had all been about rebuilding her career and her confidence. She wasn't about to do anything that might threaten that.

There were areas of the park where dogs were allowed off the lead at certain times of the day, and this was one of them, so she let Valentine off the lead and he bounded toward Brutus, greeting him with tail-wagging ecstasy.

She removed the cap from her water and took a few hasty swallows.

Had he seen her sitting? Did he think she'd been waiting, hoping to see him?

She wished now that she'd carried on running.

Her father was right. She was a hypocrite. If she'd been offering advice she would have warned women to stay away from him, or at least be wary, and here she was as eager to see him as Valentine was to see Brutus.

"Sorry I'm late." His smile would have lit a dark night and she felt something flutter behind her ribs.

It was a good job she was excellent at resisting men, otherwise she'd be in trouble.

"What are you late for?" She managed to sound normal. Relaxed. But it was all for nothing because his smile told her he knew she'd been waiting. And hoping.

She was sure that a man like him was used to women waiting and hoping.

How many hearts had he broken? How many dreams had he shattered?

"I would have been here ten minutes ago but the line was longer than usual."

"The line?"

"At the coffee shop. Since you refused to come with me for a coffee, I brought the drinks to you."

She'd come to the conclusion long ago that there were two types of people in life. There was the type who saw an obstacle and gave up, and then there was the type like him—people who ignored the obstacle and simply found a different way to reach their goal.

"I don't drink cappuccino."

"Which is why I bought tea. You're British, so you have to drink tea." Still holding Brutus, he sat. "English Breakfast or Earl Grey? That I couldn't figure out."

"So which did you bring?"

"Both. I'm a man who likes to cover all bases."

"Are you always this persistent?"

He smiled, untangling Brutus from the lead with his free hand. "Fortune does not favor those who give up at the first hurdle."

"Old Chinese proverb?"

"All American. One of mine. Sit. I said *sit*."

Molly raised her eyebrows. "Me or the dog?"

His eyes gleamed. "Both of you, but I'm guessing neither of you are going to listen. That's how my day rolls."

She didn't sit, but she did smile. "What if I tell you I only drink peppermint?"

"Then I'm screwed." He fed the lead under Brutus's leg in an attempt to untangle it. "But you don't seem to me to be a 'peppermint' type of woman. Maybe you don't drink coffee, but you need your caffeine."

"I do drink coffee. But not cappuccino. And I happen to love Earl Grey tea."

"I'll try not to be smug." He handed her one of the cups. "Earl Grey. With a slice of lemon."

"You're kidding me."

"I never joke about beverages, especially after the week I've had. Caffeine is my drug of choice, during the daytime at least."

She watched as Brutus and Valentine played together. "We can let the dogs off the lead here."

"Brutus isn't good at coming back when he's called."

"He'll come back if Valentine is here."

He evaluated the risk and then unclipped the lead. "You'd better be right about this or I have a feeling that the next time I see him I'm going to be picking him up from New Jersey."

"He'll come. Watch. Valentine!"

Valentine skidded to a halt and turned to look at her. Then he shot toward her and Brutus followed.

"Good boy." She made a fuss and sent him off again.

"Do you have that effect on all guys?"

"Always." She peeled the top off her cup to cool the tea. "I can't believe we're sitting on a bench in Central Park and I'm drinking Earl Grey tea with lemon." She sat next to him on the bench, leaving enough space between them to be sure her leg wouldn't accidentally brush against his. If talking to him had this effect on her, she didn't want to risk touching. "Do you ever take no for an answer?"

"Only when no is the answer I want. And in this case it wasn't."

Laughter drifted across to them and she glanced up and saw a woman in a long white bridal dress embracing a man in a suit while a photographer snapped away. The couple staged a few intimate embraces and Molly wished they'd picked a different place for their photos. The scene made her feel awkward. It didn't feel as if it was something she should be witnessing, especially not with a stranger.

"Never understood the point of that." Daniel stretched out his legs, as relaxed as she was tense. "Staged photos. As if they need to make a public statement about how happy they are."

"Maybe they are happy."

"Maybe." He turned his head to look at her. "You believe in Happy Ever After?"

There was something about the intensity of that gaze that made it hard to remember what she believed about anything.

"Of course." She believed in it for other people, just not for herself. Happy Ever After Together was her goal for other people. Her own goal was Happy By Herself. And she was doing well with that. "I guess it's a good time of year for wedding photos. The blossom is pretty."

"Let's hope they don't look back on those photos in five years' time and think, 'what the hell were we thinking?'"

It was exactly the sort of remark she might have made herself, except in her case she would have also been wondering how they met and what they had in common. *Would it last?*

"I gather you're not married." She took a sip of her tea, thinking that a man like him, who probably had the pick of women, was unlikely to tie himself to just one.

"I'm not married. How about you? Have you left some guy sated and exhausted in the bedroom?"

"Ten guys. There's a chance they may never recover. If they're still there when I get home, I'm calling an ambulance."

He laughed. "The moment I laid eyes on you, I knew that

about you. If you're ever looking for one guy to replace the ten, you know where I am."

"You have the stamina of ten?"

"Want to test it out?"

"Not right now." This was the type of exchange she was comfortable with. The type that went nowhere and was all superficial. And he was good at it. Good at that breathless, heady flirtation that was as light as a butterfly and just as unlikely to linger in one spot. "How about you? Do you have ten women waiting at home?"

"I hope not. I'm pretty sure I locked the door."

He was so outrageous it was impossible not to laugh, too.

"You don't believe in marriage?" The moment the question left her mouth, she regretted it. She wished she had picked an impersonal topic, like the unpredictable weather, or the sudden rush of tourists crowding the New York streets. Anything other than the intimate topic of relationships. Now he'd think she was invested in the answer, and then he'd wonder if, for her, this was more than a cup of tea on a park bench on a sunny spring morning.

"I've taken a lot of risks in my life—parachute jumping, BASE jumping—never marriage." His tone suggested that wasn't likely to change anytime soon.

"You see marriage as a risk?"

"Of course it's a risk. If you find the right person, I'm sure marriage is great. But finding the right person—" he shrugged "—that's the hard part. Easier to get it wrong than get it right. How about you?"

The dogs chased each other back to the bench and Daniel leaned forward to make a fuss over Brutus. She saw his shirt pull tight over his shoulders, molding to powerful muscle.

"Never." She watched as he picked up one of the other cups and took a sip. "Who is the fourth cup for?"

"Me."

"You bought yourself two drinks? You have a problem with decision making?"

"No. I have a problem with staying awake when I work until two in the morning. As I said, it's my drug of choice. I need two coffees in the morning. These are my two coffees. So what do you do, Molly? No—let me guess. Your dog is well trained and you're clearly a strict disciplinarian so you could be a teacher, but I sense that you're not. I think whatever it is you do, you're your own boss. You're clearly smart, so I figure you have your own business. You work from home, maybe? Somewhere close to here. Writer? Journalist? Am I right?"

"To a point." She felt herself instinctively retreat. She reminded herself that she worked under a pseudonym. It was like sliding on a disguise. "I do some writing as part of my job, but I'm not a journalist."

"What do you write? Or are you going to make me guess? Is it dirty? If so, I definitely want to read it."

She knew enough about human nature to know that not telling him would simply make the subject more interesting. "I'm a psychologist."

"So you're analyzing my behavior." He lowered his cup. "I don't mind admitting that's a little unsettling. And now I'm going back over our conversation trying to remember what I said. On the other hand you're still sitting here so it couldn't have been anything too bad."

She *was* still sitting here, and no one was more surprised about that than she was.

"Maybe I'm still sitting here because I think you're a lost cause who needs help."

He nodded. "I'm definitely that." He watched as Brutus and Valentine played a rough game that involved rolling on the grass. "So are you going to take me on?"

"Excuse me?"

"You said I need help. It's only fair to give me that help. If you want me to come and lie on your couch, that works for me."

"You wouldn't fit on my couch. How tall are you? Six-two?"

"Six-three."

"Like I said. Too big." In fact he was too everything. Too handsome. Too charming. Too much of a threat to her equilibrium.

As if to confirm that, he smiled at her. Might as well have turned a blowtorch on to ice, she thought, feeling herself melt. "It won't make a difference if you smile at me. You still won't fit on my couch."

"You don't need to worry." He leaned in and lowered his voice. "I promise to be gentle with you."

"Oh *please*—did you really say that?" Because her hand shook, she sloshed tea over her leggings. "Ow!" She sprang to her feet and his smile turned to concern.

"Take them off."

"You're not funny."

"I'm not trying to be funny. I'm serious. Basic first aid for burns. The fabric will carry on burning your leg."

"I am not removing my pants in the park." But she tugged the Lycra away from her skin and sure enough the burning eased.

"I'm sorry." He sounded genuinely contrite.

"Why are you sorry?" She grabbed a handful of napkins and pressed them against her thigh. "I was the one who spilled my tea."

"But only because I made you nervous." His voice was soft, his gaze intimate, as if they'd shared something personal.

"You didn't make me nervous," she lied. "I'm not used to sexual innuendo this early in the morning. Or men like you. You're—"

"Cute? Irresistible? Interesting?"

"I was thinking more of annoying, predictable and inappropriate."

His smile promised fun and sin and a thousand things she didn't dare think about while she had hot tea in her hand.

"I made you nervous. And flustered. And if I were to analyze you, I'd say you're a woman who hates to feel either of those things."

Flustered? Oh yes, she was flustered. Being close to him made her feel light-headed and dizzy. She was agonizingly aware of every single detail, from the dark masculinity of his unshaven jaw, to the wicked glint in his eyes. But beneath the humor was a sharp eye for detail, and that worried her more than anything.

She had a feeling he saw far more than people usually did.

It was like hiding in a cupboard and knowing that someone was right outside the door waiting for you to reveal yourself.

And that was closer than she ever let anyone step.

"Thanks for the tea." She threw the cup away and reached for Valentine's lead.

"Wait." He reached out and caught her hand. "Don't go."

"I have to work." It was true, although that wasn't why

she was leaving. She knew it. He knew it. Conversation, a light flirtation—that was all fine. She didn't want more. "Goodbye, Daniel. Have a great day." She whistled to Valentine, put him back on his lead and took off through the park without looking back.

Tomorrow she was going to take a different route.

There was no way she was going to risk bumping into him again.

No way.

Four

He didn't have a great day. He had a frustrating, long and tiring day during which Molly kept popping up in his thoughts. He wondered where she went after she'd run in the park. He wondered who her friends were and what sort of life she led. He had a million questions about her, and very few answers.

Most of all he wondered what he'd said to make her run off.

He'd enjoyed the snap and spark of the conversation, the flirtation. It was the verbal equivalent of waterskiing—speeding and bouncing over the surface, but never delving into the deeper, murky waters below. It suited him fine, because he had no interest in going deeper.

He guessed she was the same.

He knew from the look on her face that she had issues. He'd seen that same look across his desk more times than he could count and he recognized the shadows of hurt. It didn't worry him. He'd never met a human being over the age of twenty who didn't have some issues. That was what being alive did for you. If you engaged in life, eventually you'd have scars to show for it.

He wondered who was responsible for Molly's scars.

It was that urge to know more that drew him back to the park the next morning, with Brutus tugging at his lead. It didn't occur to him that she might not show up. For a start she had to walk Valentine, and something told him she wasn't going to change her habits in order to avoid him, so he took the usual path, Brutus by his side.

Without Valentine to keep him in line there was a strong chance the dog wasn't going to come back, so he kept him on the lead. He'd even yelled "Ruffles" once to see if that made a difference but all that had done was confirm what Daniel already suspected, that the dog didn't have a problem recognizing his name. He had a problem recognizing authority.

As someone who had grown up challenging and questioning, Daniel empathized.

He was hauling the dog's nose out of a muddy puddle when Valentine appeared.

There was no sign of Molly.

"Where is she?" Daniel stooped to pat the Dalmatian. He was no expert, but even he could see that Valentine was a beautiful dog. And that heart-shaped nose was pretty cute. "Maybe that's where I'm going wrong. I need a heart-shaped nose to win her over."

He was wondering whether he should hold on to the dog or let him go, when Molly appeared, out of breath and annoyed.

"Valentine!" She reached them and frowned at the dog. "What did you think you were doing?"

Valentine wagged his tail hard.

It seemed to Daniel that whatever the dog had thought he was doing, he'd done it.

He guessed Molly hadn't intended to walk this way today, but what the hell. She was here. That was all that mattered.

Today she was wearing a pair of running leggings that clung to her body in a swirl of purple and black. Her sleek dark ponytail curved like a question mark over her back.

Daniel unclipped Brutus's lead and he sprinted off with Valentine. "Whenever I let him off the lead, I worry that might be the last I see of him. I only let him off when Valentine is here."

"Valentine never usually runs off." She frowned after the dog. "I don't understand it."

"I guess he wanted to play with his best friend. Look how happy they are." He gambled on the fact that seeing her dog so content would stop her leaving and judging from her smile, he was right. She'd decided to forgive the dog for his transgression. "So how do you persuade a dog to come back when you call?"

"Training."

"And if that doesn't work?"

"Then you're in trouble."

He loved the way her eyes lit up. He loved the tiny dimple that flickered at the corner of her mouth. He loved the way her hair whipped across her back when she ran. He loved the way she ran like she owned the park. He loved the way she loved her dog—

He was definitely in trouble.

"Are you in the mood for an Earl Grey tea? Say the word." He couldn't believe he was suggesting tea when what he really wanted was champagne, moonlight and her naked.

"What's the word? *Please?*"

"Fetch."

The smile turned into a laugh. "You 'fetched' last time. It's my turn."

He liked the way that sounded, as if this was something regular that was going to happen again. "But then I'd have to watch the dogs, and you're the responsible adult."

"You're not responsible?"

He looked at her mouth. "I've been known to be irresponsible once in a while."

* * *

Molly sat on the bench, watching the dogs play. Irresponsible? Irresponsible was her sitting here waiting for him to come back instead of finishing her run and going home.

She'd started the day being responsible. She'd taken a different route on her run, but Valentine had protested. He'd sprinted away and for the first time ever had refused to come back when she'd called him. And now she was here again, on their bench, waiting for Daniel.

It was still superficial, she reminded herself. It was everything light and fun.

A heart couldn't break if it wasn't engaged.

"Tell me about him," she said to Brutus, but he was too busy trying to bite Valentine's ear to pay any attention.

Daniel returned as Brutus was tangling himself with Valentine. "I don't suppose you specialize in dog psychology? My dog needs help."

She took the tea from him, careful not to touch his fingers. "I'm better at understanding human behavior."

"Behavioral psychology? That's what you do?"

"Yes." She saw no reason not to be honest about that.

"And do you prefer good behavior or bad behavior?" His smoky voice slid under her skin. She sensed this man could deliver a hefty dose of bad when it suited him, probably another thing that made him a magnet for women.

"Most people are a mixture of both. I observe. I don't judge."

"Everyone judges." He took another mouthful of coffee. "So what does a behavioral psychologist do? Do you ever advise on relationships?"

"Yes."

He lowered the cup. "So if you're a psychologist, and you've studied this stuff, all your relationships must be perfect."

She almost laughed, but knowing it would be a hysterical sound she held it back.

It was surprising how many people assumed her relationships would be perfect. It was like expecting a doctor never to get sick.

"You're right. My relationships are all totally perfect."

"You're lying. No one's relationship is perfect." He glanced from her to Valentine. "And you're here in the park every morning with your dog, which tells me he's your most meaningful relationship."

The conversation had somehow edged into the personal and she instinctively backed away. "I agree that no one's relationships are perfect. The best you can do is make them perfect for you."

He stretched out his legs, relaxed and comfortable. "Perfect, for me, would be short. I don't like to get involved past a certain point. Judging by the way you react, I'm guessing you're the same."

He guessed correctly. And she couldn't help being curious.

"You're afraid of intimacy?" Why was she even having

this conversation? What was wrong with her? She should be drinking her tea and leaving.

"I'm not afraid of intimacy. It's more that I don't have time for the demands that come with intimacy. My job is pretty all-consuming and in the time I have to myself, I don't want complications."

"That's common among people with avoidance issues."

"You think I have avoidance issues?"

"Love avoidance." She noticed Valentine nosing something in the grass and stood up to pull him away from it. "People who avoid intimacy often do so because they're afraid of being hurt. It's a self-protection mechanism. Typically those in avoidance relationships don't introduce their partner to friends and relatives because they don't think the relationship will last long enough. They use a variety of distancing techniques. And it isn't really about the current relationship, but about what has happened in the past. Often the roots of the problem are established in childhood. They are often people who didn't establish a proper parent-child dynamic and healthy bonding."

"My childhood wasn't what you might call nurturing, but I put that behind me a long time ago. If you're wondering about the origin of my views on relationships, I can assure you it has nothing to do with my parents. I'm not the sort of person who believes in carrying the past into the future."

"Everyone carries at least a little of their past."

"So what are you carrying?"

She'd walked right into that. "We were talking about you."

"But now I'd like to talk about you. Or do you always deflect conversation when it becomes personal?"

"I don't deflect." She sighed. "All right, maybe I do. Sometimes. You asked me if my dog is my most meaning-

ful relationship. The answer is yes, right now he is. I'm enjoying the simplicity of my life."

"So are you avoiding intimacy?" He mimicked her question and she gave a reluctant laugh.

"Definitely. And I've never been happier."

"So if we carry on seeing each other, are you going to be
analyzing my every move?"

"We're not going to carry on seeing each other. We're
having a conversation in the park, that's all."

"You already know me better than the last three women
I dated, and you're telling me that's it?" He was smiling,
and it was the smile that proved her downfall. That and a
late night updating *Ask a Girl*, which had left her tired and
lowered her defenses.

Sleep deprivation had a lot to answer for.

She sipped her tea, almost spilling the last of it as Brutus nudged her leg.

"Sit." Daniel gave the dog a severe look. "This animal is
out of control."

"He needs to know who is boss."

"He thinks *he's* the boss. It's a problem we're addressing."

"Brutus!" Molly said his name firmly but the dog didn't
even turn his head. "Maybe it's not a behavioral problem.
Is there something wrong with his hearing?"

"Not to my knowledge. Why?"

"Because he doesn't seem to know his own name. It's
unusual for a dog to ignore his name, even if he ignores
the command that goes with it. Hey—Brutus." She pulled
a dog treat out of her pocket and the dog's head turned like
a whip. "You know your name when there's food involved.
Why doesn't that surprise me? How long have you had him?"

"Not long. How long have you had Valentine?"

"Three years."

"Is that when you moved to New York?"

Molly reminded herself that thousands of people moved to New York every day. He wasn't likely to take her picture and do an image search. "Yes."

"What brought you to the US?"

Romantic disasters.

Professional and personal humiliation.

She could have given him a list.

"Career advancement. And I have family here. My dad is American. Born in Connecticut."

"Career? For a moment I wondered if it was heartbreak." He studied her face. "So do you think you'll go back at some point?"

"No." She kept her smile in place and her tone light. "I love New York City. I love my job, my apartment and my dog. Going back doesn't interest me."

"How about dinner?" Daniel reached down and stroked Valentine's head. "Does that interest you?"

Molly watched, transfixed, as those long, strong fingers caressed her dog. Her pulse sped forward. Her insides tumbled and turned. And still she stared at those hands, watching as he seduced her dog with easy, comfortable strokes.

He'd asked her something. What was it? Why was it so hard to concentrate around him?

Dinner. That was it. Dinner. "You're asking me to dinner?"

"Why not? You're good company. I'd like to buy you something other than Earl Grey tea."

There had been a time when she would have been tempted. She certainly would have been flattered. What woman wouldn't? But that time had passed.

"I'm pretty busy right now." She sprang to her feet, clumsy in her haste, and stepped on Valentine's foot. He gave an outraged yelp and leaped away. "Sorry." Racked by guilt, she stooped and kissed his head. "Sorry, baby. Did I hurt you?" Valentine wagged his tail, endlessly forgiving. "I should go." She was aware that Daniel was watching her, his blue gaze speculative and a touch amused.

"I'm assuming you don't have a fatal allergy to food, so I'm going to take that personally."

"I don't date guys I meet in the park."

"How is it different from dating a guy you meet in a bar?"

"I don't date them either."

He finished his drink and rose, too. He was more than a head taller than her, his shoulders wide and powerful. His hair gleamed in the early morning sunshine. "What are you afraid of?"

"I turn you down and you assume I'm afraid? Isn't that a little arrogant? Maybe I simply don't want to have dinner with you."

"Maybe. But then there's the alternative possibility. That you *do* want to have dinner with me, and that is freaking you out." Brutus nudged his leg, hopeful of another game, but Daniel kept his gaze fixed on Molly.

Awareness seeped through her skin and sank deep. "I'm not freaked out."

"Good. Do you know the little French bistro two blocks from here? I'll meet you there at eight. It's a public place, so that should satisfy your 'is he a stalker or a serial killer' worries."

"Even if I wanted to, I can't. Today is Tuesday. Tuesday is salsa dancing."

"Salsa dancing?"

"I go Tuesday and Friday nights whenever I'm free."

"Who do you dance with?"

"Anyone. Everyone. It's pretty casual." And hot, sweaty, sexy and fun. Harmless fun. Nothing deep. Nothing serious. Nothing that made her feel the way she felt when she was with Daniel.

"So you're happy to dance with strangers, but you won't have dinner with one. How about tomorrow?"

"Tomorrow is Wednesday."

"And Wednesday is...? Tango?"

"Wednesday is Italian cooking class."

"You're learning Italian cooking?"

"I started recently. I want to make tortellini as well as my neighbor. If you'd tasted his tortellini, you'd understand."

"Thursday?"

"Thursday is spin class."

"I never understood the point of cycling hard to get nowhere. Saturday? Don't tell me—Saturday is quilting." The paths around them teemed with joggers, walkers and people pushing strollers, but they were focused on each other.

"Saturday I keep free. I usually meet up with friends."

"Great. Eight o'clock Saturday it is. If you don't want to meet me in a restaurant, you can cook. I'll bring the champagne." He was comfortable and relaxed, whereas she felt as if she was floundering in the deep end of a large swimming pool.

"If you want to eat dinner with me you can join me at Italian cooking class."

He shook his head regretfully. "Italian cooking is Wednesday, and Wednesday is poker night."

"You play poker? Of course you do."

"Why 'of course'?"

"Ruthless killer instinct combined with the ability to mask your emotions. I bet you're good."

"I'm good." There was a devil in his eyes. "Want to find out how good?"

Her mouth dried. If he was flirting, she was going to ignore it. "I don't play poker."

His smile widened but he let it go. "It's mostly an excuse to catch up with friends and drink alcoholic substances. I'm not that competitive."

"I don't believe that for a moment."

He laughed. "I should take you along. You could read their minds and send me clues."

"I'm a psychologist, not a clairvoyant."

"So with this packed schedule of yours, when do you date?"

"I don't." Damn, she shouldn't have said that. Not only did she sound like a loser, but a man like him would take it as a challenge. "I mean right now, I don't date. I'm focusing on my work. I love my life exactly the way it is."

"Now I understand why you do so much exercise."

"Because I like keeping fit."

"No, it's because you're not getting hot sex. So you have to find another way of relieving pent-up frustration and releasing endorphins."

Molly gasped. "I am not frustrated! We don't all walk around thinking about sex the whole time." Until she'd met him. Since meeting him that was pretty much what she did.

"Not the whole time, but a lot of the time. And you must know that. You're a psychologist. We cloak ourselves in the trappings of civility because that's what society expects, but underneath we're all driven by the same primal urges. Want to know what those are?" He leaned closer and she saw the devil gleam in his eyes. "To procreate and win bigger than the other guy."

"This is why we are *never* having dinner."

"We're not having dinner because you're too busy. And you're too busy because you've substituted spin class and salsa for sex."

"I would rather take a spin class than have sex with you."

"Shouldn't you have sex with me before you make that decision?" His smile widened and his gaze dropped to her mouth. "Maybe you're turning down the night of your life, Molly-with-no-second-name."

"I have a last name. I just don't choose to share it with you."

"One meal." His voice was wicked temptation. "And if you're bored, I'll never bother you again."

Bored? No woman would ever be bored with him. But they'd be a lot of other things. Most of all they'd be vulnerable. There was no male weapon more lethal than dangerous charm. And this guy had it in spades. "No thanks."

He gave her a long, searching look. "So who made you scared, Molly? Who made you choose spin class and salsa over sex?"

She was so used to hiding herself, it shook her that he'd seen through her veneer.

"I need to go. Thanks for the tea." She tossed the cup in the waste bin, grabbed Valentine and ran back through the park, taking a shortcut that led to her apartment.

He was right of course.

She was scared.

If you fell, next time you were more careful where you stepped. And she'd fallen hard.

Five

"Daniel! Thank goodness you're back. I need to talk to you about the summer party and you need to sign these." Marsha, his assistant, met him at the door with a file full of papers and a list in her hand. "And Elisa Sutton is in your office."

"Elisa? Happy birthday, by the way."

"Happy would be a day at a spa. Instead, I'm here." She pushed the file into his hands. "I hope you appreciate my loyalty."

"I do, which is why a ridiculously extravagant bouquet of flowers is currently on its way to you. Now tell me about Elisa."

"She turned up half an hour ago, desperate to talk to you." Marsha lowered her voice. "I've sent out for more tissues. Last time she used a box and a half."

"You'd probably cry a box and a half if you were married to her husband."

"He's a box and a half kind of guy. You're the only man

I know who is good with crying women. Why are you so patient?"

He'd had plenty of experience.

A vision of his mother flashed into his mind and he pushed it away.

He wasn't a man to wallow in the past. He dealt with it and moved on. So why the hell had that image sneaked into his mind now?

The answer was Molly.

Molly, with her searching questions about his childhood.

She'd dug around in a wound and now it ached.

That, he thought grimly, was what happened when you went deeper than the superficial. There was a lot to be said for not getting to know a person better.

Annoyed with himself for allowing the situation to intrude on his day, he focused on work. "Divorce is always emotional. Handling it is my job."

"It's Max Carter's job, too, but he just abandoned a client who was crying a river in his office. He said he was giving her time to 'compose' herself. If I didn't know for a fact that the guy is a brilliant lawyer, I probably wouldn't believe it. Are you mad that I let Mrs. Sutton into your office without an appointment? You can fire me if you like."

"The day you leave is the day I leave. We'll walk out of here together, clutching our dead houseplants."

"Hey, I water those houseplants."

"Then you need to stop watering them. They're dying."

"Maybe the clients have been crying into them. Or maybe they're depressed. If I had to listen to all the sad stories you're told, I'd be depressed, too." Marsha had started working for him when her youngest daughter had left for college.

The same day her divorce had become final. The divorce he'd handled.

Her maturity, humor and air of quiet calm made her invaluable.

"Do you know why Elisa is here?"

"No." Marsha glanced toward the closed door and lowered her voice. "Last week she was in here crying over that lazy, cheating, no-good husband of hers, but today she's smiling. Do you think she's killed him and hidden the body? Should I refer her to one of our colleagues in criminal law?"

Daniel gave a flicker of a smile. "Let's hold the decision on that."

"Maybe she's here to tell you she's taken a lover. That might be the best revenge."

"Maybe, but it would make the custody battle more complicated so I hope you're wrong." Whatever the reason for the sudden visit, Daniel was sure it wasn't going to be good. "Why do you want to talk about the summer party?"

"Because I'm in charge of it and last year was a fiasco. We used Star Events and I had to deal with an awful woman with a power complex. I can't remember her name, but I do remember wanting to punch her. Cynthia. Yes, that's it. Can I use someone different?"

"Use anyone you like. As long as the alcohol flows, I don't care."

"There's this fresh, young company called Urban Genie…"

"Owned by three very smart young women who were previously employed by Star Events. Paige, Frankie and Eva. Good idea. Use them."

Marsha gaped at him. "Do you know everyone in New York City?"

"Matt Walker designed my roof terrace. He's Paige's older brother. And Urban Genie has done a lot to support my sisters' dog-walking business. Not only that, they're good. And they were fired by that 'awful woman,' which makes this karma."

"You don't believe in karma."

"But you do. Call them."

"I will." She crossed it off her list. "Just a couple of things before you talk to Elisa—you've been invited by Phoenix Publishing to cocktails at the Met in a couple of weeks. Do I make your excuses?"

"Definitely."

She crossed that off her list, too. "The interview you gave is published today. Do you want to read it?"

"Will I like what I read?"

"No. They call you a heartbreaker and New York's most eligible bachelor. They should have interviewed me. I would have told them that no sane woman would date you."

"Thank you."

"You're welcome. So do you want to read the interview?"

"No. Next?"

"Next is Elisa. Oh, and congratulations."

"On what?"

"The Tanner case. You won."

"In a contested divorce, there are no winners. Everyone is a loser."

Marsha studied him. "Is everything all right? Now I think about it you're later than usual, and you look different."

"I'm good." Braced for marital drama, he walked into his office. There were plenty of days when he wondered why he did this job. Today was one of them.

But Elisa Sutton wasn't crying. Instead she looked animated.

Even Daniel, experienced as he was in handling the emotional roller coaster that accompanied divorce, was surprised.

And suspicious. Was Marsha right? Had she taken a lover?

"Elisa?" Anticipating a confession of a sexual nature, he pushed the door shut. If his client was about to fill his office with her dirty laundry, he intended to contain it. "Has something happened?"

"Yes. We're back together!"

"Excuse me?" Daniel put his laptop down on his desk, playing catch-up. "Who? I didn't know you were seeing anyone. We talked about the risks of you getting involved with someone else at this point—"

"It's not someone else. It's Henry. We're back together. Can you believe that?"

No, he couldn't believe it.

Elisa had cried so many tears over the past few months he'd considered issuing a flood warning for midtown Manhattan.

"Elisa—"

"You're using your serious lawyer tone. If you're going to warn me this isn't a good idea, don't waste your breath. I've made up my mind. At first when he said he was going to change, I didn't believe him, but after a while I realized he was sincere. We're making a go of it. He is still my husband, after all." Tears welled in her eyes and she pressed her hand to her mouth. "I never thought this would happen. I didn't see it coming. I thought it was over."

Daniel stilled. He hadn't seen it coming either. From what he'd observed so far, Elisa and Henry's marriage was so bad that if they'd been able to bottle the vitriol there would have been enough toxins to poison the whole of New Jersey. And although he'd learned that the blame was usually shared, if not always equally, in this case the lion's share belonged to Henry, who was the coldest, most selfish man Daniel had ever met.

He'd employed a lawyer who was known to be as savage as a Doberman, and he'd set him on his wife, the woman he had supposedly once loved and with whom he shared two previously happy, but now traumatized children.

Fortunately Daniel had no problem being a Rottweiler when the need arose.

He frowned. Since when did he use dog analogies?

Walking Brutus was clearly getting to him.

"Last week you were in here crying," he said carefully. "You told me you didn't care what it took, but you never wanted to see him again." He kept his tone free from emotion. Clients invariably brought so much emotion into his office he'd learned not to contribute anything extra.

"That was last week when I thought there was no hope for us. He *hurt* me."

"And you want this guy back?"

"I really believe he is committed to changing."

Daniel felt a ripple of exasperation. "Elisa, once they reach a certain age people rarely change, and they certainly don't do it overnight." Did he really have to say this stuff? Didn't people know this? "There's a phrase about leopards and spots. You've probably heard it." He waited for her to acknowledge this, but she ignored him.

"I've already seen the change. On Saturday he turned up at the house with gifts. Thoughtful gifts." Her eyes were bright. "Do you know Henry has never bought me a proper gift in all the years we've been married? He's a practical guy. I've had kitchen equipment and once he bought me a vacuum cleaner, but he has never bought me anything personal or romantic."

"What did he buy you?"

"He bought me a pair of ballet shoes and tickets to the Bolshoi. They're touring."

Ballet shoes? What was she supposed to do with ballet shoes? In his opinion it was Henry who needed to wear the ballet shoes to help him tiptoe over the thin ice he was standing on.

He kept his expression neutral. "And you were pleased with that gift?"

Elisa flushed. "He bought them because I loved the ballet when I was a little girl. When we first met I was still hoping to make it a career, but I grew too tall. I don't know how he came up with the idea. It was so *thoughtful.* And he bought me roses. One for every year of our marriage. He took one off for the year we were separated."

Daniel waited for her to comment on the irony of that, but she said nothing.

"That's what it took to persuade you to forget the fights and the misery and start again? A pair of ballet shoes you can't wear and a bunch of roses? Those roses will be dead in a week." And their marriage in even less time than that.

"He also bought me a ring."

"A ring? Elisa, two months ago I had to stop you from throwing your current ring into the Hudson River."

"I know and it was good advice. I had it valued and— well, never mind. That's history now. Henry told me he'd been doing a lot of thinking and that whatever we had when we first met must still be there. He wants to work at rediscovering it and he gave me another ring as a token of his commitment."

"Commitment? This from a man who consistently undermined your confidence and then walked out, leaving you with no support?"

"He needed space, that's all. Our children are at an age when they're very demanding."

"Did he tell you that? Because from what you've told me he left that part pretty much entirely up to you."

"And because I was so wrapped up in the children, I didn't give him the attention he deserved."

Daniel sat down behind his desk and breathed deeply, banking down the anger. Something was happening to him and he didn't like it. "They're children, Elisa, and he is supposed to be the adult. Parenting should be a shared thing. I know you're scared and I understand that staying together can seem like the easy option, at least in the short term. Unraveling a marriage, particularly when there are children involved, is daunting to say the least. But—"

"Oh, we're not doing this because it's the easy option, we're doing it because of the children."

"It was because of them you originally wanted a divorce."

"But children are always better off with two parents, don't you agree?"

He thought of Harriet, hiding under the table with her eyes squeezed shut and her hands over her ears. "I don't agree." He kept his face expressionless. "My personal opinion is that children are better off being raised in a calm, positive environment with one parent than an explosive environment with two." Damn. Never before had he expressed his personal feelings in front of a client.

"But then you're a divorce lawyer." Fortunately Elisa

didn't seem to notice that anything was wrong. "I wouldn't exactly expect you to be a supporter of reconciliation. You need to justify your billing hours and the more we string this out, the higher your bill."

Daniel felt a flash of annoyance. "I'm no saint, Elisa, but I can assure you that my advice comes from a desire to do the best for you and the children, not from a need to add hours to my billings. And my advice in this case is don't do it. You first came to me because your daughter had started wetting the bed and was displaying behavioral problems, and your son's asthma was getting progressively worse. You were convinced that the atmosphere in the house was responsible."

"And I was partly to blame for that. I was very upset about the affairs and I didn't do a good job of hiding my feelings."

"He was the one who had the affairs." Daniel reminded himself that his job was to offer legal advice, not marital advice. Normally he had no problem with that, but today—

"Is something wrong? Are you sick?" Elisa was peering at him closely. "You don't seem like yourself."

"I'm not sick." With an effort, he hauled his emotions back inside. "Don't rush into anything. For the time being continue to live separately and give yourself breathing room."

"He wants us to renew our vows and I want to do that as soon as possible in case he changes his mind. This time we both really want this to work. And it's funny that we paid a ton of money on couples' therapy, and in the end the best advice we got was free."

Daniel was suddenly alert. "Somebody else has been giving you advice?"

"Yes. I never thought I'd thank another woman for giving me my husband back, but if I ever meet Aggie, I'll hug her."

"Aggie? Are you saying Henry has been having another affair since you separated?"

"No! I'm talking about *the* Aggie. The one who's everywhere. She has a great blog, *Ask a Girl*. Anyway, Henry was so confused about what was happening he wrote to her, and she pointed out that as we had children it was worth trying extra hard. Surely you've heard of her. She knows everything about relationships. How to fix your marriage, or choose the perfect gift, or whatever. She has millions of followers on social media."

"You're saying Henry is taking advice from a blogger? Some sort of advice columnist?" Daniel tried and failed to hide his incredulity. "That's what this is about? What did you say her name was?"

"Aggie."

"Aggie what? Aggie Interference. Aggie-doesn't-know-what-the-hell-she's-talking-about?" He saw the first flicker of doubt and misery in Elisa's eyes and felt a stab of guilt. "I'm sorry, Elisa. But I don't want you to make a mistake. If you're going to do this, I want to be sure it's what you want and a stranger who has never met you cannot help with that decision, no matter how many followers she has on social media."

"But sometimes an impartial observer can see things more clearly."

"We have a team of qualified people here who can—"

"No. And Aggie *does* know what she's talking about. I don't think she has a last name. But she's a doctor."

"Everyone has a last name. If they don't reveal it there's usually a reason." And he doubted Aggie was a "doctor" of anything, except maybe deception. "All I'm suggesting is that you should think twice about taking advice from someone who isn't qualified to handle the issues you're dealing with."

"Aggie is good. You are so suspicious."

"That's my job. I'm paid to be suspicious. I'm asking the questions you should be asking." Daniel scribbled the name on his pad. In his experience people who didn't give their last names were hiding something. Right now "Aggie" had better be hiding herself because he was going to track her down and tell her what he thought of her advice. And it wasn't going to be a polite conversation.

The thought of Elisa and Henry back together under the same roof made his whole body chill. Elisa would shrink to half the person she was, and as for the children…

He kept thinking of Harriet, and that awful night at the school when their father had unexpectedly shown up in the audience. Even now he couldn't think about it without shuddering.

Elisa stood up. "Daniel, you're the best divorce lawyer in Manhattan and you've been great, but I don't need a divorce lawyer anymore because I'm not getting divorced. What Aggie said struck a chord with us. She told us to think of the life we've created together. Our home. Our friends. Our children."

"Didn't he refer to them as baggage?"

She flushed. "He'd had a few drinks. We've both realized we should be putting the children first."

She left the room and Daniel stayed at his desk, staring through the floor-to-ceiling windows that wrapped his office on two sides. From his desk he could see the Empire State Building, and farther in the distance the gleam of glass and steel of One World Trade Center.

Normally the view soothed him, but not today.

Who was this Aggie, that she'd tell a dysfunctional family to stay together? How could she make such an important judgment based only on a letter? And whatever letter or email Henry had written, Daniel was sure he wouldn't have passed on the deep trauma suffered by his children as a result of their marriage.

He still couldn't believe Elisa was willing to overlook everything that had happened.

And he couldn't understand why everything today was affecting him so deeply.

Cursing, he pushed back from his desk and stood up.

His office was sleek and uncluttered, like the rest of his life.

It was the way he preferred it. He preferred to sail through life with neither anchor nor baggage. That way if he crashed his ship on the rocks, he wouldn't take those around him down with him.

How would he have turned out if his childhood had been different? Would he have chosen to be a lawyer? Or would he have taken a different, gentler path?

The door to his office opened and Marsha walked in with some files and a mug of coffee.

"I thought you might need this. Looking at your face, I'm guessing I was right."

"I feel as if I spend my entire day fighting. Why wasn't I a boxer or an MMA fighter? It might have been cleaner."

"You love fighting. You get that look about you. Clenched jaw. Dangerous 'don't mess with me' glint in your eyes. I assume Elisa didn't say anything you were pleased to hear."

"My eyes glint? Why have you never told me this before?"

"Because when they glint I'm mostly too scared to open my mouth in your company, and when they stop glinting I forget to mention it. The flowers arrived and they're beautiful, thank you. Now tell me why you're stressed."

"I'm never stressed. Only calm, and slightly less calm." Giving up the pretense, he rubbed the back of his neck to relieve the tension. "The ability of the human being to screw up its own life never ceases to amaze me."

"I hate to be the one to point this out, but that's the reason this is a busy and thriving law firm. If we all got it right, you'd be out of a job." She set the files down on his desk. "These are for you. And in case you've forgotten, it's Audrey's birthday today, too. They're in the kitchen eating cake. If you have a minute, I know it would mean a lot if you could join them. I don't want to contemplate what our working day would be like without Audrey, and Max is driving her insane. A few words from you would be compensation."

Audrey was one of the paralegals. She'd been with the firm for two years and had proved herself indispensable after five minutes.

"Thanks for the reminder. And I'll speak to Max." Pushing aside thoughts of Elisa and what a reconciliation would mean for the children, Daniel checked the documents and signed. "Have you ever heard of someone called Aggie?"

"The relationship expert?"

"How is it that everyone knows this woman except me?"

"Are you in the habit of asking for advice on relationships?"

"Why would I ask for advice on relationships? I've seen every permutation of relationship known to man. And woman."

"And yet you're single."

"Which is *why* I'm single. So tell me what you know about Aggie."

Marsha smiled. "She's wonderful. I bought her book."

"She's written a *book*?"

"*Mate for Life*. You didn't see it? It was at the top of all the bestseller lists and in every bookstore."

"I shop online, a consequence of never leaving my office during store opening hours."

"It was online, too. Excellent book. She's wise and sensible."

"Really? Because she told Elisa and Henry they should get back together for the sake of the children. I don't see anything wise or sensible about that."

Marsha pursed her lips thoughtfully. "Perhaps it would be better for the children."

"Are you kidding? Elisa and Henry loathe each other. Their children will be permanently scarred. Why people think that is the best outcome completely escapes me." Intercepting the curious look in Marsha's face, Daniel inhaled slowly and gestured to his laptop. "Find me something she has written. I need to know more about her."

"That should be easy." Marsha walked around his desk. "You could start by reading the letter Max wrote to her."

"He wrote to her?" Daniel shook his head in disbelief. "As a joke, I assume?"

"Why would you assume that? We both know Max needs serious help in the relationship department. Remember the coffee machine he bought his girlfriend as a gift?"

"Call me insensitive, but my interest in my team's personal life only extends to serious life events, not gift choices."

"This was serious." Marsha clicked on a link. "He bought her a coffee machine. She sold it on eBay. They broke up."

Daniel frowned. "Why did she sell it? Wrong brand?"

"She doesn't drink coffee."

Daniel started to laugh. "And he had to write to ask what he'd done wrong?"

"This is Max we're talking about, so yes. He said that a coffee machine made him happy, and that she should be happy that he was happy. She didn't see it that way. How he ever passed the bar I will never know."

"As you say, he's a brilliant lawyer and ferociously bright."

"Not when it comes to women. Here." She scrolled down. "Read. Not that you need any help with relationships."

Ask a Girl.

The words were picked out in a bold blue.

Daniel frowned. "'Ask a Girl' what? What sort of things do people ask?"

"Anything. Everything. Her advice is honest and direct. She has a huge following."

"So she really knows how to milk it."

"She's a businesswoman. She has a gift, and knowledge, and she uses it. It's not like you to deride a woman for being smart."

"I'm not deriding her for being smart. I'm deriding her for taking advantage of the vulnerable and giving dangerous advice."

"That's your opinion, Daniel. And although plenty of folks pay squillions of dollars an hour to hear your opinion, it doesn't mean you're always right on everything."

"I'm right on this."

"Her column is good. Interesting. I read it every week. We all do."

"All?"

"All of the women here, and even some of the men. The blog is only part of it. She answers questions, and I think she offers one-to-one relationship counseling over the phone."

Daniel scrolled through the pages of her website. "There's no photo. What does she look like?"

"She never uses a photo. Just the heart logo."

"So she doesn't have a last name, and she won't show her face. Anyone who won't show their face must have a reason. Maybe she's not a person. Maybe she's a bunch of computer tech guys laughing their heads off."

"No way would the advice she gives ever have been written by a guy."

"That's sexist."

"It's true," she said drily. "Read for yourself."

He read.

Dear Aggie, there's a woman at work who is a goddess. I'm an ordinary guy, nothing special. How can a man like me ever attract the attention of someone like her? Am I wasting my time? Yours, Underconfident.

Daniel glanced up in disbelief. "This is a joke, yes?"

"It's real."

"And does she give an answer? Mine would be, yes, you're wasting your time. Grow a spine."

"Which is why you're not the one answering the question. Not that I expect you to understand, but some men have trouble approaching women. They don't all have your success rate."

Daniel thought about the woman in the park. His success rate had taken a serious tumble. "Does she reply?"

"Scroll down. Her reply is underneath. And people are allowed to post their advice, too. It's a community."

"A community of people who don't know what they're talking about. Kill me now. *Dear Underconfident—*" his gaze flicked briefly to Marsha "—can you believe someone actually called himself that?"

"I think it's adorably honest."

"It's prophetic. You are what you think you are." He read on. "*Dear Underconfident, everyone is special in their own way*—seriously? Can you get me a bucket? I'm feeling ill."

"Just because you're not the sentimental type, doesn't mean it's rubbish. Not everyone is afraid of emotion."

"Just because I have full control over my emotions, doesn't mean I'm afraid. But I do have a healthy respect for the damage emotion can cause. In relationships, emotion drives bad decisions." His voice shook and Marsha stared at him as if he'd grown horns and wings.

"Are you sure you're feeling okay?" She spoke cautiously. "Is there something personal going on here I should know about?"

"No."

"We've worked together for five years and I'm old enough to be your mother. Despite your claim to being heartless, we both know you're not. You helped me when I was at my lowest point and I hope you know you can always talk to me in confidence."

"There's nothing I need to talk about. And you are nothing like my mother." Realizing he'd said too much, Daniel dragged his hand over the back of his neck and hauled his feelings back inside. He didn't want to think about his mother. He'd long since come to terms with what had happened. He'd been a kid, for goodness' sake. He'd done what he could. And he'd helped numerous women since then. More than he could count. "Emotion is what brings people streaming into my office. If more people engaged their brains instead of their hormones, the divorce rate would be lower."

"And you wouldn't be earning millions."

"I know you don't believe me, but the money has always been secondary." Trying to distract himself, he scanned a few more questions on the site, fascinated and appalled. "Real-life people actually write in asking her this stuff? They can't figure it out for themselves?" He tried to imagine what sort of person would be comfortable exposing such intimate, private secrets in such a public forum.

Marsha looked amused. "Have you ever asked advice about women?"

"I already know everything I need to know about women, including the fact that *this* woman is exploiting people who are emotionally vulnerable." Daniel flipped the screen shut and caught a glimpse of Marsha's expression. "What?"

"Please tell me you see the irony of that. You're the divorce attorney everyone hopes their spouse won't hire."

"Meaning?"

"It could be argued that you also charge people when they're at their most vulnerable. You can't blame her for trying to fix something instead of breaking it."

"I've never broken anything that could be fixed. And trying to fix Henry and Elisa is like trying to glue together a shattered vase with nothing but spit and hope." The muscles of his shoulders ached with tension. He wished he were back in Central Park watching the sun spill through the blossoms and Molly and Valentine pounding their way along the paths.

"Maybe her advice is sound," Marsha said. "Maybe it's something to celebrate. They have two young children, Daniel."

"I can never understand why people seem to think that growing up with unhappy parents is better than growing up with a happy single parent."

"I don't expect you to understand. You don't have children."

But he had two younger sisters. He knew a lot more on that topic than Marsha probably imagined.

"If they get back together they'll be divorced in a year."

"I hope you're wrong. But if you're not, then at least they will have made that decision themselves and they won't be blaming their lawyers."

"No, instead they'll be blaming this agony aunt." Daniel dismissed the topic and made for the door. "Do you own a dog?"

"Two. Why?"

"Do they come when you call them?"

"Usually. Unless they spot something better in the distance." She looked baffled. "Why are you asking me about dogs?"

Daniel was about to tell her about Brutus and then decided against it. Walking the dog was only a temporary thing. He didn't need to become an expert.

"I had no idea so many people owned dogs in New York. What happens to them during the day when you're here?"

"I use a dog-walking company. Is this your way of telling me you're about to become a dog owner?"

"Why the horrified look?"

"I— No reason. I guess I didn't see you as a dog person."

"And what does a 'dog person' look like?" He thought about Molly's long legs and the way she smiled at Valentine. If that was how a dog person looked, then it just might be his new favorite thing.

"For a start they don't generally wear custom-made suits and work eighteen-hour days. And dog people usually have a soft side."

"I have a soft side, which is why I'm about to walk away from that mountain of work on my desk and go and wish Audrey happy birthday. Team bonding. Oh, and Marsha—" he paused in the doorway "—let's find out who 'Aggie' is. Get Max onto it."

"You need advice on dating?"

"No. I need to tell her to stay the hell away from my clients."

Six

Dear Aggie, why do women say they're "fine" when they're obviously not fine? What exactly does "fine" mean? I suspect it's a code word and I need it deciphered. Yours, Confused.

"How can human beings treat animals so badly?" Harriet shifted position so that the puppy on her lap was more comfortable. "He's six weeks old. How can anyone want to harm something so vulnerable?"

"I don't know but he's safe now because he has you, and you're the best place for lost and abandoned things." Fliss pulled on her running shoes and pulled her hair into a ponytail. "I need to go. I have a packed day."

"Already? You haven't eaten breakfast." She sniffed the air. "What's that terrible smell? Are we on fire?"

"My toast was on fire but don't worry. I can't cook, but I can douse flames."

"You can't leave without eating something."

"Energy bar." Fliss dug her hand in her pocket and produced the evidence.

Harriet shuddered. "That's not breakfast. That's a nutritional insult."

"I don't have time for anything else. I'm seeing a new client, taking Paris the poodle to the vet for Annie because she's going to be out of town overnight and then I have twelve private walks. At least it keeps me slim. Which is good because I intend to stop in at Magnolia Bakery on my way home and buy something that someone else has cooked. Can I tempt you with anything?"

Harriet shook her head. "I'm going to have a baking session later, though, so you could save your bakery trip for another day."

"Your famous chocolate chip cookies? Yum. This is why I love you." Fliss swept up her keys on her way to the door and paused. "By the way, Molly has booked Valentine in for three walks next week. She has to proofread her book and she has a meeting with her publisher."

"No problem. I adore Valentine. He's the cutest dog on the planet."

"You say that about every dog."

"True." Harriet stroked the puppy's soft fur with the tip of her finger. "Have a good day. You don't want to wait to see Daniel? You were in the shower when he picked Brutus up." She flushed as she saw Fliss raise her eyebrows. "What? I actually think the name suits him better than Ruffles. Ruffles should be a cute poodle, or maybe a schnauzer. A griffon. Not a sturdy German shepherd with muscles in all the right places. Daniel is right."

"Don't tell him that. He'll be insufferable."

"I like seeing him with the dog."

"Why? Because you think it's good to see him caring about something other than himself?"

"He's always cared for us," Harriet said stubbornly and Fliss sighed.

"Yeah, I know. Don't make me feel guilty. And you and I both know he's going to dump the dog as soon as he gets the girl. And then he'll dump the girl soon after that. It's standard Daniel operating procedure. No exceptions. So don't start spinning happy endings."

"At least he dates. It's more than we do."

"You want to date?"

"Yes." Harriet was honest. "I do. I'd like to meet someone. I want a home and a family." She caught the puppy before it could wriggle off her lap. "Don't you?"

"I'm too busy having the time of my life to let a man mess it up. See you later." Fliss strode to the door with a long, loping stride, and as the door slammed behind her the puppy in Harriet's lap gave a startled jump.

"She only knows one way to close a door," Harriet soothed. "You'll get used to her." And then she realized he wouldn't be getting used to her because he wouldn't be staying. He was a puppy, and a cute one at that. It wouldn't take long for them to find him a family. "We need to find you a perfect match. People you'll be happy with."

And maybe she should do the same for herself.

It was no good saying she wanted to date and then doing nothing about it.

She transferred the puppy from her lap to the sofa. "Maybe I should put myself up for adoption."

* * *

Molly sprawled on the sofa and watched while Mark slowly added hot stock to the risotto. "So I've seen him in the park every day for the past two weeks walking his dog, and we've chatted a bit. Well, a lot in fact. And then he asked me to dinner. Dinner isn't an accident. Dinner isn't a casual meet-up. It's a decision. It's a step. And I said no. Do you think I'm a coward?" She decided there was nothing more relaxing than watching Mark cook. His movements were smooth and unhurried, nothing like the panic that occurred when she was in the kitchen. Mark was as much an artist with food as he was with a pencil and paper. "When you know you're bad at something, should you simply give up? Or should you practice? If you fall off a horse because you're a truly terrible rider surely it's better to decide that horseback riding isn't for you and take up swimming instead?"

"It doesn't matter what I think." He added another ladle of bubbling stock. "It's what you think that matters."

"There's only room for one psychologist in this friendship and I've already nabbed that position."

"So you don't need me to explain your behavior. But for what it's worth, I don't think you're a coward. There's nothing wrong with protecting yourself, Molly."

"I know but—" She bit her lip. "My dad said I was a hypocrite. I made him get back out there after Mum left and he says I'm refusing to do the same after Rupert."

"From what you've told me, Rupert was a dick."

Molly felt her face heat. She'd only told him a small portion of what had happened. "He was, but it was complicated." *You have no idea how to be in a relationship.* She swallowed. "I have a few issues."

"Everyone has issues, Molly."

"Mine impair my ability to engage in healthy relationships."

"Listen to yourself, Dr. Parker. If you can diagnose it, why can't you fix it?"

"I'm not sure I want to fix it. Love is a risk. I'm wary for a reason."

"Big risk comes with big reward."

"I'm not sure I see it is a reward." She took a deep breath. "It isn't only about protecting my heart, it's about professional security. I've rebuilt my life and I'm happy. I don't want to mess with that. It's important to play to your strengths in life. Relationships aren't my strength."

"That's not true. You're a great friend."

She thought about all the people she'd lost touch with. People who had cut her out when her life had fallen apart. "Friendship is different."

"What's a partnership if you don't have friendship?" He tilted the pan slightly and stirred again to stop the rice sticking. "I think being happy and fulfilled is the goal. Maybe you don't need another person. It's not as if you don't have plenty of friends. Good friends." He stopped stirring and sent her a look. "Friends who are going to be there for you through thick and thin."

She'd told him that part. How when her life had fallen apart in a very public way, her friends had distanced themselves.

"You'd trend on Twitter for me?"

He smiled. "For you, honey, anything."

Her insides warmed. "That's good, but I've had as much thick and thin as I can handle in one lifetime. And I agree with everything you say. So why does part of me wish I'd said yes to him?"

Mark lowered the heat under the pan. "Blame it on hormones."

"I hate hormones. And I hate the way society puts pressure on us to behave in certain ways and conform to certain stereotypes. If you're single, people always pat you on the head sympathetically and say that they're sure you'll meet someone soon. Then you get married, and they ask when you're going to have a baby. There's an order to things. It's assumed that not being part of a pair makes you someone to be pitied. As if single is an abnormal state that needs to be rectified."

Mark added the last of the stock to the risotto. "If you want to explore the pressure society puts on an individual to conform, try being gay. Try being the one weird kid in high school."

"I *was* the one weird kid in high school until they discovered I was great at matching people up. Then I had a purpose. And I love it. I think it's my vocation. Helping other people find the right person. Why does it matter that I can't do it for myself? Orthopedic surgeons don't have to break a leg to know how to fix a fracture."

"That's all true, but don't you find it exhausting leading this whole double life?"

"It's not really a double life."

"You have a pseudonym and a whole persona you don't tell people about."

"That's not exhausting, it's fun. I happen to love that part. It's my invisibility cloak. My disguise."

Mark put the ladle down. "I know all about wearing a disguise. For years I walked around with this huge secret inside me. It was like wearing a fancy dress costume. No one knew who I was underneath."

"And didn't that make you feel safe?"

Mark paused. "Honestly? No. It made me feel alone and

isolated. That's the downside of keeping secrets." He turned back to the stove. "I hope Gabe is back soon or this will ruin."

There was nothing better, Molly thought, than having neighbors who turned into great friends.

Their apartment was on the floor above hers, and it was filled with charm. Sunshine flowed through the big bay window, flooding the room with light. Books filled every inch of available space, crowding two deep on shelves and stacked high on the floors. Mark's art covered the walls, large canvases covered in bold strokes of color. On hot summer nights they opened the doors and sat on the fire escape sipping mojitos and pretending they were on a beach somewhere instead of trapped in an airless city, sweltering in the New York heat.

"I'm not having dinner with a stranger." Molly returned to the subject. She slid off her shoes and curled her legs underneath her while Valentine settled himself on the rug by the sofa. "At the end of the day Daniel is a random guy I met in the park. That's crazy, right?"

"Depends on how hot he is." Gabe walked into the apartment carrying a crate of champagne.

Molly raised her eyebrows. "Wow. When you said 'drop in for a drink' soon, I didn't realize you were taking it so seriously."

Gabe flashed her a smile.

He was classically handsome, with sculptured cheekbones and blue eyes. Mark had told Molly once that on Gabe's first day at the advertising agency where he worked as creative director, he'd spread the word that he was gay. Apparently that approach had saved him a whole lot of embarrassment and awkward moments in previous jobs, but it didn't seem to have stopped the women he worked with from falling in love with him.

"Mark texted that you want to talk about a guy. Tell me all." Gabe shrugged off his jacket. "Is he hot?"

"He's hot. I mean, if you think looks are important."

"Charming? Charismatic?"

Molly thought of the conversations they'd had. "I guess. He's comfortable with himself. That's always attractive." Oh, who was she kidding? He was more than attractive. And that was what scared her.

"Then what are you waiting for?"

"I don't want a relationship."

"How about fun?" Gabe cut a thin slice off a slab of Parmesan cheese and ate it. "Don't you want some of that?"

"I don't find relationships fun when they're mine."

"You know more about relationships than anyone I've met. You have a sixth sense when it comes to people. I don't understand why you can't apply that common sense and experience to your own relationships."

"I don't understand it either." Except that she did. Molly stroked Valentine's head. It was one thing holding back when you were talking to a stranger in the park, quite another to keep secrets from dear friends who kept none from you. "Okay, I'm lying. I do understand it. But understanding something doesn't mean you can fix it. Which is annoying, because as a psychologist I should know how to put my baggage in long-term storage."

"Baggage is baggage, sweetheart. You can try dumping it in the lost and found for a while, but somehow it always finds its way back." Gabe removed a bottle of champagne from the box and put it in the fridge.

Mark raised his eyebrows. "Are we celebrating something I should know about?"

"We're pitching for a champagne account. It's going to be wall-to-wall bubbles for the next month."

"Pitching means drinking the product?"

"Of course. I can't pitch for something that isn't wholly and completely familiar to me."

Molly grinned. "We should all be grateful he's not pitching for cough syrup."

"I pick my accounts carefully." Gabe started unbuttoning his shirt. "I need a quick shower. Talk amongst yourselves."

He walked back into the room ten minutes later, as Mark was serving the risotto and Molly was laying the table. Valentine lay with his nose on his paws, watching her protectively.

"I've said it before and I'll say it again, that dog would make a wonderful nanny when you have kids." Gabe was wearing a clean shirt and jeans. His feet were bare. "So why are you hanging out with us and not this hot, charming guy you met in the park?"

Molly carried plates through from the kitchen. "I like hanging out with you."

"Because we're comfortable and safe."

"Because you're friends." These days she chose her friends very, very carefully. Life had made her cautious.

Mark sat down at the table. "What does Mr. Hot Guy in the Park do? Choice of career tells you a lot about a person."

Gabe frowned. "I disagree."

"People choose to become doctors because they're caring."

"Not always. There's also the money and the status. And

the doctor in the book I'm reading right now is a serial killer. He went into medicine because he likes dead bodies."

Molly pulled a face. "You need to change your reading."

"I can't. I'm addicted to Lucas Blade. Whatever he writes, I read."

"Well, Man in the Park isn't a doctor. He's a lawyer."

"So he's smart and good with words. I'm liking him already. And how many times have you met?"

"Once or twice." Molly felt her cheeks heat. "Maybe more."

"How many times more?"

"He's been there every morning for the past couple of weeks."

"Whoa." Gabe's eyes widened. "This is a serious, long-term relationship."

"We sat on a park bench. We were in public the whole time. Our dogs are friends."

"So you're chatting with him so Valentine can have some guy time?"

"That's part of it. It's like a doggy playdate."

"Honey, you're not fooling anyone. You're interested in this guy, I can tell. So why didn't you say yes to dinner?"

Molly squirmed. "Because he's too—" She bit her lip and Gabe raised an eyebrow.

"Too?"

"I don't know. He's too—everything. Too good-looking, too charming."

"No man can be 'too' anything for you." Gabe sat back in his chair. "You, Molly Parker, deserve the very best of everything. Including champagne. Speaking of which…" He stood up, retrieved the bottle from the fridge and eased the cork out with a satisfying pop.

"You're biased." Molly watched as he poured the sparkling liquid into three glasses.

"Why would you think you're worth less than the best? Because some jerk with a big ego made you feel the size of a grain of rice a thousand years ago?"

"Three years ago. That's not so far away." She'd told them part of the story. Not all of it of course. No one knew all of it. But a large part of it had tumbled out one night when they'd shared Mark's spaghetti Bolognese and a bottle of wine. That same night Gabe had told her that his father hadn't spoken to him since he'd come out in his last year of high school and Mark confessed he had a closet full of pink shirts because his mother thought that was what gay men wore.

Families, she thought. The most complex relationship of them all.

"Honestly? I'm not great with his type."

"Hot, sexy and charming? Yeah, that's a killer combination. I can see why you'd struggle."

"Very confident men make me wary."

"Because they're more likely to trample all over those defenses you've built? Honey, confidence is sexy."

"Confidence can be intimidating. And then there's the fact that he's a divorce attorney. I'm a supporter of relationships."

"Even though you don't have one." Mark dissected the risotto with his fork, examining the texture, apparently satisfied. "Does your hot guy in the park know about your secret identity?"

Molly felt a rush of alarm. "No! Of course not. I'm Molly."

"So he doesn't know about Aggie?"

"No one knows I'm Aggie apart from you, my dad and my publisher. And it's staying that way."

"You should be proud of your success."

"I am. But these days I separate my work life from my personal life." Molly glanced at Valentine and Gabe followed her gaze.

"He's cute. Shame humans can't marry dogs. He's a keeper."

Molly nodded. "Even Mrs. Winchester loves him and she isn't easy to please."

Gabe topped up their glasses. "Speaking of Mrs. Winchester, I saw her a moment ago. Her hearing aid has been fixed, so no dirty talking in the stairwell."

"She shouts when her hearing aid isn't working." Mark drained his glass. "Hopefully now she might stop yelling, 'you're that nice gay man who lives upstairs,' every time I meet her."

"I get 'at your age I was married,'" Molly said. "That's one of my favorites." She took a mouthful of champagne, enjoying the fizz and the warmth that spread slowly through her veins. "There is nothing better than drinking champagne with friends. It makes every day a celebration."

Gabe stared at her. "That's it!"

"That's what?"

"Champagne—makes every day a celebration." He leaned back, his chair rocking precariously as he grabbed a pen from the side and a piece of paper, which happened to be an advertisement for pizza delivery. "I need to write that down before I forget it. Shit, Molly, you're a total genius."

Mark rolled his eyes. "Language. Mrs. Winchester can tolerate dog hair and the fact that we're gay, but if she hears you swearing you're out of here."

Molly frowned. "Shouldn't champagne be saved for special occasions?"

"If people save it for special occasions, the company

doesn't sell as much and won't increase their profits. This way, people drink it all the time and I get a big, fat bonus." Dropping his pen, Gabe raised his glass. "To friends. And to Mrs. Winchester's hearing aid, which will hopefully last longer than the previous one."

Seven

The day started with a dark threatening sky, but Daniel didn't alter his plans. The day before, he and Molly had spent half an hour discussing their favorite places in New York, while Brutus and Valentine had romped in the grass together. True, she still hadn't said yes to his invitation to dinner, but he sensed that pretty soon she would. Of course, finding a time was a challenge. The woman might not be dating much, but she certainly wasn't sitting around.

Harriet handed over Brutus. "Do *not* be late today. Someone is coming to meet him. Don't take him through any puddles. I need him to look his best."

"You're running a dog-dating agency?"

"He's a rescue, Daniel. I've been fostering him because the shelter was overloaded, but ultimately our goal is always to find every abandoned dog a new home. Poppy went last week."

"Who is Poppy?"

"The golden Lab you met last month."

It hadn't occurred to him that Brutus wouldn't be with his sisters permanently.

Daniel glanced down at the dog who had been his daily companion for the past few weeks. Brutus wagged his tail and nudged Daniel's thigh with his nose, eager to start their walk. "I assumed he'd stay here with you."

"With all the animals I foster there isn't room for another permanent inhabitant."

Daniel wondered if the dog knew he was about to go and live with a bunch of strangers. "He's a very intelligent dog. You can't let him go to just anyone."

"We won't. The shelter carries out extensive background checks on anyone who wants to adopt. They take it very seriously."

"How can they when they haven't spent time with him? It isn't only about the suitability of the environment—it's about the person. It needs to be someone who understands that he's a real dog. He's not going to be happy with someone who ties pink bows around his neck and calls him Ruffles."

Harriet glanced down at Brutus. "What do you think? Do you see yourself in a pink bow, Ruffles?"

The dog wagged his tail.

Daniel glowered at her. "It's the tone you're using. He thinks you're offering him a juicy bone."

"He likes hearing his name."

"I can tell you that animal is a lot happier now than he was when his name was Ruffles. I rescued him from a major identity crisis."

Harriet looked at him cautiously. "Why do you care so much? It isn't like you to become attached to anything."

"I'm not attached to him." Or was he? "The dog has already had one bad experience. He shouldn't have to go through that again."

"No one wants a rescue dog to have another bad experience. They run extensive checks which take time, so don't worry. You'll be able to use him for your 'dog dating' for a little longer. I presume that's why you're worried?"

"That's probably it." He dragged his gaze from Brutus's trusting eyes. "What sort of checks do they do? How do they know a person isn't putting on an act to get a dog and then they're nasty once the dog is theirs?"

"The team members are experienced. They're good at spotting fakes. Often the people they select have already been dog owners in the past." Harriet studied him. "You've grown fond of him, haven't you?"

"What?" The thought brought on a ripple of panic. "No. He's a dog!"

"Dogs are easy to love."

"I don't love him, but I admit he's been pretty useful. And he's a real character. I wouldn't want him to go to someone who didn't understand him."

The gleam in his sister's eyes made him wonder if he'd said something funny. "He certainly knows you. He barks when he hears you at the door. And look, he's wagging his tail."

"I could be anyone." Not in a million years would Daniel admit that he was starting to enjoy his morning walks with the dog. Brutus nudged him and Daniel lowered his hand and stroked the dog's head. "Are you ready, boy? Shall we go and see what the park has to offer us this morning?"

"Is the woman still showing up every morning? You should ask her out, Daniel. Before Brutus gets rehomed and you don't have an excuse to walk there anymore."

"I'll take a different dog." He saw Brutus turn his head. "Stop looking at me like that. You're making me feel guilty. You're supposed to be my wingman."

"Wingdog." Harriet giggled. "You can't show up with a different dog. That would be weird. Unless you've told her the dog doesn't in fact belong to you?"

"No." And he knew he should. It was starting to bother him that he hadn't. The more time he spent with her, the more he liked Molly. Not that he'd ever told her Brutus was his. Not in so many words, but he knew she'd probably made that assumption. He made a point of never allowing his life to become complicated, but suddenly it was complicated. It was time to tell her the truth. "I thought I'd get talking to her the first time I walked Brutus. I figured she'd say yes to a date on the second walk. I didn't think I'd still be doing this. Maybe Fliss is right and she isn't interested."

"She's interested. There are no shortage of places to walk a dog in New York City, Daniel. If she wanted to avoid you, she could do it easily."

"Then why hasn't she accepted my offer of dinner?"

"Because saying yes to dating a guy you met in the park is a big step. You could be a creepy stalker."

Fliss walked past, a slice of burned toast in one hand and a coffee in the other. "He borrowed a dog to chat up a girl. He *is* a creepy stalker."

Harriet ignored her. "A walk is easy. You don't have to make a decision. You simply do it. Dinner is—" She paused, thinking. "Dinner is a commitment."

"Dinner is not a commitment when the invitation comes from me. I'm inviting her to eat with me, that's all. Share a meal, not a life."

"It's still a step."

"A step?"

"Yes. Your woman is probably nervous." The wistful note in Harriet's voice made him think it was a step she'd love to take herself.

"She's not my woman."

"Well, you'd better get her to that point soon, before you no longer have Brutus to walk."

* * *

He and Brutus arrived at the park at the same time as Molly. Valentine immediately bounded toward Brutus, ecstatic to see his friend.

Molly felt like doing the same. Seeing Daniel again gave her a tiny jolt of shock. The image of him was burned into her brain, and yet in person he seemed bigger, sexier, more of a threat to her emotional equilibrium. A strange lethargy spread through her limbs and she sat down on what she'd come to think of as their bench. Would he ask her to dinner again? Would she accept?

She had no idea. Her mind was a mess.

"Did you know there are around 9,000 benches in Central Park?" She was babbling, but talking was the only way she could break the sudden seam of tension. "I love the dedication plaques. Every bench tells its own story. Look—" She twisted in her seat so that she could read. "*To the love of my life, on our wedding day.* That's optimistic, don't you think? Putting that on a bench is permanent. People are going to carry on reading it forever, so you have to mean what you say. Do you ever wonder about the people behind the inscription?"

"Not until now." Daniel sat down next to her and handed her a cup of Earl Grey. "If we had a plaque, it would say my dog loves your dog."

She could feel his leg brushing against hers. The pressure was light, and yet she could feel the hard length of his thigh.

Unsettled by the sudden thrill of sensation, she leaned over and made a fuss over Brutus. "I used to be a bit wary around German shepherds, and he is such a big, macho dog, but he has such a kind nature. I love him."

"Have you ever considered getting another dog?"

"Why? Are you selling Brutus?" She was joking, but something in his eyes made her think she might have wandered onto sensitive ground. "I was kidding. I can see the attachment between you."

"You can?"

"Of course. You always look so happy when you're with him. I feel the same way about Valentine. No matter how bad your day is, it's pretty hard to be miserable when you have a dog. They cheer you up."

"That's true." He looked surprised, as if it was something that hadn't occurred to him before.

"And then there's the fact that you play these weird games that no one else has ever heard of, like Don't Chase the Stick."

"That's weird?"

"Yes, because most people *want* their dogs to chase the stick. That's the game."

"I'm teaching him self-control. And he seems to like it."

"He likes the praise. It's cute. When I first saw you, I couldn't believe you were a dog person. You didn't seem the type."

He hesitated. "I like dogs."

"Obviously, or you wouldn't have Brutus." And there was something achingly sexy about the way this strong, powerful man handled his dog with such patient, gentle humor. "What happens to him when you're working?"

"My sisters look after him." There was a pause. "Molly, listen—"

She felt a flash of breathless panic.

"You've never told me much about what you do. All I know is that you're a divorce attorney." She spoke before he had a chance to ask her to dinner again, not because she was afraid to refuse him, but because she was afraid that this time she might accept. And accepting would lead to hurt and a possible threat to the life she'd built for herself.

He glanced at her. "Judging from your expression, you don't love divorce attorneys. How did my kind wrong you?"

"I've never had any involvement with divorce attorneys, but it's true that generally I think divorce is a horrible thing."

"I would agree with you." He took a sip of coffee, taking his time. "Which is why a good lawyer can make all the difference. And if there's one thing more horrible than divorce, it's being trapped in a horrible marriage. The horrible part generally starts long before I'm involved. I try not to escalate the situation."

Whatever her thoughts on the subject, she was sure he was a very, *very* good lawyer. "You don't find it depressing? Working with people at the end of their relationship the whole time?"

"Sometimes. And sometimes it's satisfying, helping someone extract themselves from a situation they find intolerable. Either way, I try and maintain an emotional distance."

Could someone be that close to another person's distress and not absorb at least some of it?

"Divorce is so final. Don't you think it would be better

if people tried to mend things before they went seriously wrong? It's like ignoring a hole in a sweater."

"What if the sweater didn't fit properly in the first place?" He leaned forward, resting his forearms on his thighs. "Sometimes people can fix what's wrong, and sometimes they can't. If they can't, then maybe they can part amicably, but sometimes that isn't possible and they need to lawyer up. That's my professional opinion."

"You don't feel bad about it?"

"About being good at my job? No. The truth is that sometimes marriage is nothing more than a big mistake and you have to cut your losses and get out." His words slid deep into a sensitive part of her she usually kept protected.

Was that what her mother had done?

Had she seen her husband and her only daughter as a big mistake?

She swallowed. "How do you know you're not breaking something that could possibly be fixed?"

"By the time people walk in through my door, what they have is already broken. I show them how to move forward with the least damage."

"What if there are children involved?"

The change in his expression was so brief she would have missed it if she hadn't been staring right at him.

"You're one of those people who think parents should stay together no matter what? You think that's a good thing?" To someone less obsessed with studying people, he would have seemed relaxed. But she noticed the small signs of tension. And that tension told her that his attitude was colored by something more than professional interest.

"I'm one of those people who think if two people loved each other enough to get married, they should at least try and rediscover some of those feelings they had at the beginning. I think sometimes people give up too easily."

"Is that a professional observation or a personal one?"

"Professional." She paused. "And maybe a little personal."

"A little? Did your parents divorce?"

"My mother left when I was eight. I've put it behind me, but I suppose I'm still a little sensitive about that particular topic." She had no idea why she'd told him something so private. It wasn't something she usually talked about, certainly not with someone she barely knew. She felt embarrassed, as if she'd removed her clothing in front of him, but he didn't seem at all uncomfortable or disconcerted.

Instead he reacted as if exchanging confidences was something they did regularly. "How's your relationship with her now? Is it awkward when you see her?"

"I don't have a relationship with her, so no, it's not awkward."

"You don't see her?"

"She thought a clean break was easier for everyone."

"And was it?"

Molly lowered her cup. She'd told him this much, there didn't seem much point in stopping now. "At the time, no. It was hard. It isn't easy to cope with the knowledge that your own mother doesn't want you in her life in any shape or form. But as I grew older I realized that it probably was easier this way."

"Because having her come in and out of your life would have been like having a wound reopened time and time again."

"Something like that." She felt the warmth of the cup through her hands. "Mostly because I don't think my dad would have been able to deal with it."

"He took it badly?"

"Very badly." She didn't elaborate. She didn't tell him there had been days when she'd been afraid to go to school and leave her father alone, and other days when she'd dreaded coming home, afraid of what she might find. "We had a rough year, and then one day I came home and smelled burning and that was when I knew things were going to be okay."

"Burning the house down was a good sign?"

She laughed. "No, but the fact that he was cooking was a good sign. After that, things gradually improved, although it was a while before my dad found the courage to date anyone again. That was the hardest part. He couldn't see his own worth. He hadn't been enough for her, and he took it to mean he'd never be enough for anyone."

Daniel watched as two squirrels chased each other across the grass. "That explains why you're wary of relationships."

"It's part of it, but not all of it. The real reason is simpler. I'm not good at them." She thought about how her relationships always ended. Not cleanly, but messily. Pain. Anguish. "How about you? You spend your day seeing relationships that are all screwed up and wrong. Must make it hard to believe one could ever be right."

"It certainly makes me careful."

She blew on her tea, wondering why talking to him felt so comfortable and natural. "So why did you choose to become a divorce lawyer? Why not criminal law or corporate law?"

He leaned down, his fingers closing over a stick. "I became a divorce lawyer because I grew up with parents who should not have stayed together. I would have given a lot for someone to help them untangle their marriage. Instead I learned firsthand what it's like to grow up with parents

who don't like each other." He threw the stick in a graceful arc and made Brutus wait before finally giving him the
command to fetch it.

His frankness surprised her. She'd expected him to be
emotionally guarded.

"That explains why you don't think it's always a good
idea for a couple to stay together simply because they have
children."

"Case-by-case basis." He watched as Brutus retrieved
the stick. "Maybe for some people that would be the right
thing to do."

"Did they divorce eventually?"

"Yes. But not until my sisters had left home." He turned
to look at her. Trapped by that intense gaze, it was hard to
find a single professional thought.

"Why did they stay together so long?"

"Because my mother was afraid to leave. And because
my father told her that if she left, she'd lose her kids." He
finished his coffee and threw the cup in the trash, his aim
perfect.

Molly sat still, shocked. "He was abusive?"

"Not physically, verbally. But that can be as bad. He di-
minished her and stripped her of her confidence until she
was convinced that without him she wouldn't be able to sur-
vive. You want to know why I became a divorce lawyer?
That was why. She told me one day that if she left he'd get a
fancy lawyer who would make sure she never saw us again.
She'd lose us, and her home. She wasn't willing to take that
risk. I told her that when I grew up I was going to be a fan-
cier lawyer than any of the ones he would have hired. I told
her I'd make sure she had us, and her home." He leaned forward to remove a twig that had become tangled in Brutus's

fur. "And that is way too much information to give to someone I just met in the park."

"I was thinking the same thing about what I just told you." Molly watched, transfixed, as his fingers moved gently and patiently over the dog's neck until he'd extracted the offending twig.

He gave Brutus a rub behind his ears and sat back. "Is your mother the reason you don't date?"

All she could think about were his fingers caressing the dog. She wondered if he was that gentle in everything he did. "I— Date? Oh. Not really. I'm having fun being single."

He leaned closer. "Have dinner with me and I'll prove there are some things more fun than being single."

Disorientated by his voice, it took her a moment to answer. "That's not going to happen."

"Why not?"

Because she had more sense. Because this man was already making her behave in a way that was completely out of character. Since when did she spill all her secrets to a stranger she met in the park? "Maybe I don't like you enough."

"That's not it." He gave her a slow, sure smile and she decided that smile could probably get him through a locked door without a key.

"Are you always so confident about everything?"

"Not everything, but I'm confident about this. Admit it, we've had a connection since the first day our dogs met in the park. It's the reason you keep coming back and the reason I keep coming back. Our dog-walking relationship has already lasted longer than some marriages." His gaze was direct and searching and she stared into his eyes trying to formulate thoughts and words.

It was true that they had a connection. It was the reason she was sitting here now. She hadn't felt this way about anyone in a long time. And last time had ended in heartbreak.

"The reason you're interested is because I keep saying no."

"Not true. You have a great sense of humor and I like talking to you. And then there's the fact that now you know all my deep, innermost secrets so I have to neutralize you in some way before you do me damage."

He made her laugh.

"Admit it, you're competitive."

"Maybe. A little. But I also find you interesting. And sexy. You have great legs and your butt looks good in running pants. And your dog is cute."

"You find my dog attractive?"

"I find the way you love your dog attractive. So how about it? Instead of sitting out here and watching the sunrise every morning, how about we share a good bottle of wine and watch the sun set for a change?"

She could imagine him in court, a formidable opponent with an answer to everything. He'd use a lethal cocktail of charm and verbal acuity to get the response he wanted. He'd find the weakness and use it. "I love sunrise."

He watched the sun bounce across the tops of the trees and spotlight the skyscrapers that framed the park. "I love it, too, but it would be nice to spend time with you without the whole of Manhattan jogging past."

"I bet you're the type who hates losing."

"I don't know. I've never lost. But if I ever do, I'll let you know how it feels." The conversation was light, but she was conscious that underneath the banter was an undercurrent of delicious tension.

She was trying to work out how to respond when it started to rain, a light patter that chilled her skin.

Daniel cursed softly and rose to his feet. "If we move fast we can shelter under those trees."

"Shelter? It's only a few spots. Don't be a wimp."

There was a dangerous gleam in his eyes. "Are you calling me a wimp?"

"Yes, but don't worry. It's good to know you have a weakness." The rain grew heavier and huge drops thundered down, soaking everything they touched.

"You're right. We should shelter." She called Valentine and ran, her feet splashing through newly formed puddles, the rain soaking through the thin fabric of her shirt and flattening her hair to her head.

Valentine barked, excited and fired up by the new urgency and Brutus followed, the two dogs side by side as they made for the shelter of the trees.

She dived through the long, pendulous branches of a weeping willow, feeling the leaves brush her face and her arms. She knew Daniel was behind her. She could hear the heavier thud of his running shoes on the ground and awareness chased across her skin, the feeling so intense it was like pressure. He could catch her easily, and when he did—

She stopped under the tree, unsettled by the explicit nature of her own thoughts.

It had been a while since she'd been interested enough to risk getting involved with someone. The last three years had been spent focusing on rebuilding her life, and sex hadn't been part of that.

She turned and met his gaze.

She told herself it was sprinting that made her chest tight and her breathing rapid, but she knew she was lying to herself. It was him. This man with the wicked eyes and the slow, dangerous smile. This man who made her feel a million things she never wanted to feel, all of which terrified her.

Did he know? If so he was a sadist because he gave her no breathing room, no space in which to gather herself.

Instead he stopped right in front of her, so close she was forced to take a step back or touch him.

She felt the rough bark of the tree press against her back and knew there were no more steps back to take. From here it was stand still or move forward.

"What are you doing?"

"I'm keeping you dry. Protecting you from the rain." He gave a slow, sexy smile. "Showing you my weakness."

But this close she saw nothing but strength. There was strength in the arms that caged her, in the dip and swell of muscle, in the width of the powerful shoulders that blocked her view of the world. There was strength in the lines of his cheekbones, and in his jaw, shaded by stubble.

Her gaze was trapped by his and his eyes made her think of long summer days filled with blue skies and endless possibilities.

"I don't mind the rain."

His mouth hovered close to hers. "I forgot you were British. We probably have a different relationship with rain."

"Rain and I are intimately acquainted."

"I never thought I'd envy the weather." He lifted his hand and stroked her damp hair back from her face. She felt the tips of his fingers brush across her skin, lingering, and knew this wasn't about clearing her vision of damp hair and rainwater. It was about exploration. Possession.

It had been so long since she'd been touched like this

and she was supersensitive, her imagination and her senses keenly aware of every touch.

Dear Aggie, there's this guy I find impossibly sexy, and when I'm with him I forget everything. I know that anything we share will be short-term. I'm worried a relationship will end in pain. What should I do? Yours, Light-headed.

The rain was coming down harder now, but only the occasional drip managed to squeeze its way through the cascading branches of the weeping willow. They were sheltered in their own private glade, protected by the tangled labyrinth of green and gold.

She'd thought there would be plenty of people seeking shelter, but it seemed everyone else had chosen to leave the park. They were alone, or at least it felt that way, trapped by the weather and cocooned by nature. It was as if someone had drawn the curtains around them, concealing them from the world. She was aware of the muted thud of raindrops as they pounded the canopy of the trees, of the rustle of leaves and the whisper of the breeze through the branches. And she was aware of the beat of her heart and the uneven note of his breathing.

She raised her hand and brushed a raindrop from his jaw, feeling the roughness of stubble under her fingers.

Dear Light-headed, not all relationships end in pain. Once in a while it's worth trusting your instincts and taking a risk.

As he lowered his head, she rose on tiptoe and lifted her mouth to his, meeting him halfway. Or that was what she told herself. The truth was that from the moment his mouth met hers there was no doubt who was in control. He cupped her face in his hands, kissing her with slow, leisurely purpose. There was something aggressive about the way he held her prisoner, but something infinitely gentle about the coaxing pressure of his mouth on hers. With each brush of his lips and each stroke of his tongue, he stoked the heat until she was shaking and dizzy with desire. The pleasure was disorientating, a low drag in her belly, a shimmer of electricity across her sensitized skin. Her fingers speared the soft silk of his hair as she tried to pull him closer.

Reason and logic were drowned by the rising tide of arousal. She was unable to even pose a question, which was a good thing because she wouldn't have been able to answer. All she could do was feel. She didn't believe in magic, but for a moment she saw stars. The world around them vanished until there was only the erotic touch of his mouth and the soft patter of rain on the leaves.

She melted under the dizzying strokes of his tongue, swaying against him, and felt his hand stroke down her back and linger on the base of her spine, pressing her close. That touch confirmed everything she already knew about his body. That it was hard and strong, conditioned and athletic. The unyielding pressure of his muscles suggested he did more to keep himself fit than chase a dog around the park.

She didn't know how she got there but somehow she was trapped between the sturdy tree and the power of his frame.

And still he kissed her. He left her nowhere to hide, exploring, demanding, discovering until she was a trembling mass of nerve endings. He showed no signs of stopping and her brain wasn't functioning well enough to come up with a single reason why she should be the one to stop doing something that felt so good.

His hand moved to her breast, his thumb stroking over the tip. The delicious friction made her shudder and she moaned and pressed closer. She felt his fingers at the hem of her T-shirt and then the warmth of his hand settling on bare skin.

It was like being on fire, the excitement burning over her skin and settling low in her belly.

She had no idea how far they would have gone, but at that moment Valentine barked.

Daniel eased back with obvious reluctance. "Maybe we should take this indoors."

Indoors?

The word seeped through the clouds of desire fogging her brain and finally settled into her consciousness.

She wrenched herself out of his arms, and winced as she grazed her arm on the bark of the tree.

"Hey, slow down." Daniel's voice was rough and sexy. "Good thing you picked a weeping willow, otherwise we would have put on a public display."

Hearing those words was like being plunged headfirst into a bucket of cold water.

Panic swarmed up her skin. What had she been thinking? She was careful never, ever, to put herself in a position where her professional credibility could be questioned, and yet here she was kissing in the park like a teenager, in view of anyone who happened to be passing.

All it took was a single photograph. A post online. Before you knew it your life was trending, every single private thing about yourself uncovered and laid out for the malicious delectation of an audience thirsty for another public shaming.

She took several deep breaths, reminding herself that even if someone had seen them, no one would have connected her with "Aggie." She'd created that persona for exactly this reason. For protection. An extra layer of defense, to add to the other layers.

And that was the scariest thing of all. Since she'd arrived in New York, no one had breached a single layer of her defenses. No one.

Until Daniel.

"Come home with me." He framed her face in his hands and spoke the words against her mouth. "We'll get out of these wet things and take a shower together. You know it's going to be good."

Yes, she knew. Which was why she was backing away. Fire like that inevitably ended up with someone being burned.

How had this gone from fun flirtation in the park to something so real? But she knew the answer to that. The moment he'd started kissing her, she'd forgotten everything. Even now, she was tempted to ignore the sensible voice in her head and go with him.

"No." She pulled away from him so suddenly he had to plant his hand against the tree to steady himself.

She empathized. From the moment he'd kissed her she'd lost faith in the ability of her knees to support her. If Valentine had been a few inches taller she would have climbed on his back and ridden him home.

She bent and grabbed his collar, clipping on the lead quickly.

"Molly, wait." Daniel's voice was thickened; he sounded almost drugged, as if he'd indulged in a serious binge on an illegal substance.

She knew the feeling. Only in her case he was the illegal substance.

She really liked him, and with that extra connection came the risk of heartbreak. She wasn't going near that again.

Eight

Daniel glanced across the office to check his door was closed, then opened his laptop and typed in *Ask a Girl*.

Maybe Aggie would have some advice on how to handle a woman who sprinted away from something good. The kiss had blown his mind and he was pretty sure it had blown Molly's, too. She was sexy, smart and unattached. He'd told her things he hardly ever discussed with anyone, and certainly not someone he barely knew. He still didn't understand why he'd done that, except that there was something about his connection with Molly that had accelerated the pace of their relationship. And he was sure she felt the same way, which was why he couldn't think of a single logical reason why she wouldn't want to take it to the next level.

He scrolled through the site, reading some of the questions. Not that he would ever have admitted it, but her site had a strangely addictive quality.

Daniel only ever saw relationships at the point where they'd broken down. He'd never given much thought to the rocky path that brought people to his office. Was this how it started, he wondered, with a simple question? A simple misunderstanding? One crack that, if left unattended, widened into canyons too big to breach.

He'd never imagined so many men would be prepared to write to a woman asking for advice. That, he supposed, was the power of the internet. You were anonymous. Or at least you thought you were. And Aggie had an opinion on all of it. What to say. What to think. What to feel.

Dear Aggie, my girlfriend leads such a full life I sometimes wonder if she even needs me. How can I persuade her to prioritize me over her book group or her quilting group? Yours, Insignificant.

Daniel raised his eyebrows. If a guy struggled to be more interesting than a book or a square of fabric, he was in trouble, surely?

Then he thought of Molly with her salsa dancing, spin class and cooking class, and felt a flicker of sympathy.

Maybe it wasn't as easy as he thought.

Intrigued, he read Aggie's answer.

Dear Insignificant, instead of asking your girlfriend to choose you over her favorite activities, why not join her? Sharing a hobby can be an intimate and emotionally bonding experience. While it's always healthy to maintain separate interests, it's also good to share things. It can deepen the understanding between you and lead to a more fulfilling relationship.

She expected the guy to take up quilting? The woman was deluded.

Daniel stared at the screen, thinking of Molly's interests. He didn't really want to take a cooking class and he'd never seen the point of a spin class, so all that was left was salsa dancing. But the only type of salsa he knew anything about was the sort that was served with nachos, and there was no way he was shimmying around on a dance floor in Lycra and sequins, however attractive he found Molly. He'd rather walk a poodle in the park.

Why couldn't she love baseball or poker? Or even jazz? He'd be happy enough to join her for any of those activities. Art? Theater? He'd be there like a shot. But spin class? Paying money to ride a bike going nowhere seemed like a crazy idea to him.

There had to be a better way.

How low had he sunk that he was considering writing to an advice columnist who probably knew less about relationships than he did?

He'd show up at the park tomorrow, at the usual time, and hope she was there. If she still wouldn't agree to dinner he'd take it down a notch and persuade her to join him for something less likely to crush his spirit in the first five minutes.

There was a tap on the door and he minimized the screen a few seconds before Marsha walked into the room.

"Your two o'clock has canceled so I moved up Alan Bright."

"No problem. Do you dance?"

"Excuse me?" Marsha stared at him.

"Dance. You know—tango, salsa, that kind of thing."

She smiled. "Daniel, if I did the tango, I'd spend the rest of the week with a chiropractor. Why do you ask?"

"No reason."

"You mean no reason you want to talk about. I'm intrigued." She folded her arms. "Are you going to tell me why you asked?"

"No."

Marsha rolled her eyes and made for the door. "That's what I thought. But if you're not going to share, stop teasing."

The moment the door closed behind her, Daniel typed New York Salsa Dance Club into the search engine.

After two minutes he was able to understand Marsha's response.

Why not join her at an activity she loves?

How about because he didn't have a clue how to dance? He'd fall over his feet or, worse, he'd fall over her. That would hardly advance his cause, although it would be a novel way to find himself on top of her.

Dating was complicated. It was no wonder Aggie was busy. He was still in the process of trying to find out her identity, but right now it wouldn't have surprised him if Aggie had turned out to be a team of forty people. Judging from the volume of advice that was given out, each of them was probably working full-time on researching answers.

And he didn't need to write a letter to know what to do next.

It was time to tell Molly the truth. He'd tried to do that earlier, but she hadn't given him a chance.

Thinking about giving people chances made him think about Brutus. He wondered whether the people who had come to look at him had liked him. Should he have mentioned to Harriet that the dog liked to drink from puddles?

He sat back in his chair, wondering how Molly was going to react when she discovered the dog wasn't his.

Hopefully she'd be flattered that he'd gone to so much trouble to get her attention.

She had a keen sense of humor, so he was pretty sure she'd find it amusing.

He'd tell her the truth, she'd laugh and then they'd go out to dinner.

* * *

She'd overreacted. It was a kiss, for goodness' sake. One kiss.

What she *should* have done was give him a smile, thank him and walk away with her dignity intact. Instead she'd run like Cinderella hearing the first chime of midnight.

Thinking about it made her cringe, and she'd cringed her way through a mostly sleepless night and woken early with a head full of cotton wool.

She'd taken Valentine for a quick walk in the park, going earlier than usual and taking a different route so that there was less chance of bumping into Daniel.

Valentine had been unimpressed by the change in routine and the lack of canine company.

She'd let him off the lead for a short time and sat on a strange bench, trying to think about the meeting she had with her publisher later, but only managing to think about Daniel.

Would he show up in the park later?

Would he wonder where she was?

No, he probably thought she was crazy now.

Having cleared the clouds from her head, she called Valentine and returned to her apartment.

"You're going to spend the day with Harriet. I'm going to meet my publisher." She talked to him as she got ready, taking extra care with her appearance.

They wanted her to tour, which she'd refused, just as she had refused to have an author photo on the jacket of her book. Touring would mean showing her face, risking exposure. She didn't want Aggie to have a face. On her website she used a logo—a heart with a question mark inside it. She used the same image on her social media. What was the point of using a pseudonym if you put your face up there for everyone to see?

She stared into the mirror as she finished applying her makeup.

When she was answering questions online, or writing her book, she became Aggie, the persona she'd invented. Aggie was fearless in the advice she gave. She was strong, confident and wise.

Right now Molly felt like writing to Aggie to ask her how to unravel her complicated life. She frowned. She'd never felt that way before. She'd always been comfortable compartmentalizing her work and her private life.

It was that conversation about divorce that had rattled her. Or maybe it was the kiss. What advice would she give herself?

Be yourself.

Or maybe that wasn't what she'd say. Who, in reality, revealed all of themselves? Most people had a side they showed the world, and a side they kept private.

She was no different, except that she'd given a name to her public persona.

"You're good at what you do," she told her reflection sternly. "You know more about relationships than anyone you've met, you have hundreds of grateful emails to prove it."

So if she was such an expert on relationships, why had she run from Daniel?

One kiss wasn't a declaration of eternal love. No feelings had been involved.

There had been no reason to overreact, except that she knew kisses like that inevitably led to other things and before you knew it someone got hurt.

On the other hand Daniel wasn't the type to get involved past a certain point, so maybe they could have the passion without the pain.

Was that even possible?

Remembering the kiss brought flutters of excitement low in her belly.

Where he was now? In the park?

Maybe, or maybe not.

Maybe he had assessed her running-away routine and dismissed her as too complicated. Who wanted to get involved with a woman who behaved as if zombies were chasing her when a guy kissed her?

Valentine watched her reproachfully as she stepped into a pencil skirt and teamed it with a shirt with tiny shell buttons.

"Don't look at me like that. I can't go and see my publisher wearing yoga pants. I need to look professional and competent. And I can't take you with me. You'll have fun with Harriet." She slid her feet into a pair of flats and put heels in her bag. "This is what pays the bills. And in New York City I can tell you those bills are big, so be a good boy and I'll take you to the park this evening."

He whined and lay across the door, looking pitiful.

"Don't guilt-trip me! You know you love Harriet." She dropped her phone into her purse, and glanced around to see what else she'd forgotten. "Do you miss Brutus?"

Valentine sprang to his feet and barked.

"You recognize his name? It's more than he does." She

stroked Valentine's head. "We'll go to the park tomorrow and, if Daniel is there, I'll apologize for behaving like a crazy person and say yes to dinner." Dinner, she promised herself. Nothing more. He was attractive, and he was a dog person. That gave him extra points in her book.

She grabbed Valentine's lead and a few dog treats, and made for the door.

It was a ten-minute walk to Fliss and Harriet's.

Fliss opened the door, looking flustered. "Molly. You're early."

"I'm sorry. Do you mind? I'll pay you extra of course, but I need to buy a gift for my editor on my way to the office." She smiled as Valentine shot past her into the apartment. "He's so at home here. He loves it."

Fliss's response was drowned out by a cacophony of excited barking.

Molly peered over Fliss's shoulder toward the noise. "Is Harriet fostering again? What—" She broke off as Valentine came bounding back to her, a large German shepherd by his side.

Even if his markings hadn't been unmistakable, Molly would have known who it was from Valentine's ecstatic greeting. "Brutus? What are you doing here? That's a coincidence." Smiling, she bent to rub Brutus's head. "I know this dog. He belongs to a guy I see in the park most mornings. He's adorable. The dog, I mean, not the guy. Although if I'm honest the guy is pretty adorable, too." She flushed as she realized she was babbling like a teenager. "He never told me he used dog walkers." She glanced up and saw the frozen expression on the Fliss's face. "What's wrong?"

"Say that again. That thing you said." Fliss spoke between

her teeth. "You meet a guy in the park—you mean you see him and run past him?"

"To begin with, but then we got to talking. Now we meet up most mornings. It's no big deal. This is definitely his dog. I'd know him anywhere. Brutus."

Brutus wagged his tail crazily and Fliss swallowed. "Crap. Molly—" She opened the door, her face a few shades paler than it had been a few moments earlier. "You'd better come in."

"Why? I have a ton of things to do, and—"

"Come in. Harriet!" Fliss bellowed her sister's name. "Come in here now, I need you. We have a situation, and I'm not good with situations."

"What situation?" Confused, Molly followed Fliss into the apartment while Valentine and Brutus played a lively game that involved barking and rolling on the rug in the center of the room. "The two dogs are great together. It will be like a boys' day out, so you don't need to worry about walking them together."

"What's wrong?" Harriet appeared, a toothbrush in her hand. "Hi, Molly. I'm a bit behind because I had to go and pick up some abandoned kittens in the night. We're so looking forward to having Valentine today, though. He's the best dog ever."

"Hold that thought. She may not be leaving him with us," Fliss muttered and Harriet looked puzzled.

"Why not? What's happened?"

"I have no idea." Uneasy now, Molly glanced from one twin to another. "What's going on?"

Fliss clenched her jaw. "Molly has been walking Valentine in the park every morning, and she's been meeting up with Brutus. He and Valentine know each other well."

Harriet's face brightened. "That's great. It makes it so much easier that they're already friends, because now the two of them can—" She stopped in midsentence and her eyes widened. Delight changed to consternation. "Oh!"

"Yes, oh." Fliss jabbed her fingers into her hair. "Molly, there is no easy way to say this, so I'm going to come right out with it and then you can blacken my eye. Go for it. Don't hold back. That man in the park... Brutus doesn't belong to him."

Molly smiled. "Yes, he does. I've seen them together every day. They love each other."

"I *knew* we should have said 'no.'" Temper boiling, Fliss paced across the floor. "He came to us last month and said he wanted to borrow a dog so that he could meet a hot girl. How the hell was I to know it was you?"

"Excuse me?"

"Daniel. Came to us."

"Wait. How do you know his name?"

"I've known his name my whole life. Daniel is our brother."

It took Molly a moment to comprehend what Fliss was saying. "Your *brother*?"

"Yes." Fliss let out a breath. "It didn't occur to us that you were the hot girl. You're going to kill me. And then you'll probably kill him. And neither of us would blame you for that. In fact there have been plenty of times when we've been tempted to do the same thing ourselves."

Molly stared at Brutus. Daniel's dog. Except that he wasn't his dog.

He'd borrowed the dog so he could meet her. And she'd fallen for it.

Fliss looked unhappy. "Say something. Are you flattered

or are you about to go batshit crazy? My money is on crazy. Go ahead. Yell or shriek. Throw something, only not a ball or the dogs will try and fetch it."

Harriet looked stricken. "We're so sorry, Molly. We never should have let him borrow Brutus, but our business is exploding right now and that dog is a handful, so to be honest we were glad to have someone walk him."

"And then there's your romantic side." Fliss turned her accusing gaze on her sister, who flushed.

"I know this is partly my fault. Fliss thought it was a bad idea, but you have to understand, Daniel has never really shown attachment to anyone or anything. I really thought having responsibility for the dog every day might be good for him. If I'd thought he was going to be unkind—"

Molly thought about the way Daniel had gently removed the stick that had become embedded in Brutus's fur. "He wasn't unkind. Not to Brutus." She couldn't get her head around it.

He'd borrowed a dog. Brutus wasn't his.

Anger started to simmer.

"But he didn't actually *lie*," Harriet said, her expression hopeful.

"He lied by omission. He knew I thought the dog was his." Molly's legs stopped functioning and she sat down on their sofa, sinking into throw cushions. Something sharp dug into her thigh and she realized she'd sat on a book. She hadn't even noticed it. She tugged it out from under her leg and saw the title.

Mate for Life.

"That's mine." Harriet snatched it from her and tucked it under a stack of other books. "I was hoping for some tips. Although this is too advanced for me. I need the beginner version. Mate for Five Minutes. That would be a start, but unfortunately Aggie hasn't written that one yet. Have you read it? It's good."

Molly made a noncommittal sound. What an irony, she thought. Harriet was reading her book and she had no idea Molly was the author. And it hadn't crossed Molly's mind that Daniel was the twins' brother.

"I thought if Daniel spent time with the dog, he might form an attachment," Harriet confessed. "I admit I wasn't thinking about the woman he was chasing. I apologize."

"Don't. It wasn't you, it was him." She told herself it was normal to feel angry, but the truth was she felt so much more than that. She felt sick.

All her first instincts had been right. The only thing that had confused her had been the dog, and it turned out Brutus wasn't even his. None of that was real. To think she'd actually been excited about seeing him again and finally accepting his invitation to dinner.

"I shouldn't have interfered," Harriet muttered. "It's not as if Fliss and I make attachments either, so we're not so different to him."

"We make attachments," Fliss protested. "I'm attached to you, and to my clients, and to the dogs I walk. I just happen to not have a man in my life right now."

Harriet looked at her sister, challenging. "Ever."

"Being attached to a man comes with strong feelings and when it all goes wrong you have to find something to do with those feelings that doesn't involve breaking the law. And there's the fact that I love being single."

"Daniel did a bad thing, but that doesn't make him a bad person." Harriet's defense of her brother was touching.

"What are you going to do?" Fliss was looking at Molly.

What was she going to do? She didn't know.

Molly looked at Brutus, snuggled with Valentine. "So what is happening to Brutus?"

"Someone came to see him the other day. They're coming back to get a second look at him tomorrow, and then there will be a load of checks of course, but if it works out Brutus will have a new home."

Molly remembered how attentive Daniel had been to the dog in the park the day before. An idea formed in her head, and suddenly she knew exactly what she was going to do.

"Can I borrow him for a few hours?"

"Why?" Harriet's tone was a shade cooler and Molly realized that although Harriet might seem gentle, she was more than ready to fight for a cause she cared about. And top of that list was vulnerable animals.

"There's something I want to do. I promise I'll keep him safe."

Harriet relaxed. "I never doubted it. But what are you going to do? I must admit, I'm surprised you're not madder than you are."

"I am mad." Molly stood up and this time her legs felt steady. She was still angry, but she was no longer afraid she might break something. "But there are many different ways of letting out that mad."

"Don't you have a meeting with your publisher?"

"Not until lunchtime. I was going to catch up on some jobs, pick up a gift, but that can all wait. If I move fast, I should still make my appointment later. But I need to take Brutus."

"Okay. But as you're going to be spending one-on-one time with him, there's something else you should probably know." Harriet glanced at Fliss, who rolled her eyes dramatically.

Molly braced herself for more revelations. "What?"

"His name isn't actually Brutus. It's Ruffles."

Nine

"Daniel, there's a woman in reception to see you. She says it's urgent."

Snowed under with the complexities of the case he was handling, Daniel didn't even look up. "She needs to make an appointment."

"It's more complicated than that."

"If it's complicated, then she definitely needs to make an appointment."

"This isn't business. It's, er, personal."

Daniel looked up. He never, ever, allowed his personal life to intrude on his work. It was one of the reasons he'd never hooked up with anyone from the office. "What's her name?"

"She didn't give her name, but she has a dog with her. And this is the weird part—she says it's your dog."

"A dog?" Daniel's internal radar sounded several loud alarm bells. "What sort of dog?"

"A boisterous German shepherd who is creating havoc in reception." Marsha smiled. "When you were asking all those questions the other day, I wondered what was going on. Were you worried it would make you seem more human? Because honestly, that would be a good thing. You should have told me."

"Told you what?"

"That you have a dog."

Tension spread across his shoulders and down his spine. "Are you telling me one of my sisters is in reception?"

"Your sisters? No. I know Fliss and Harry. This woman has dark hair. Very pretty." Marsha looked intrigued. "I assumed you knew her."

He knew her. The description sounded like Molly, and if she was standing in reception with a German shepherd it meant he was in more trouble than he could possibly have imagined.

She'd found out the dog wasn't his.

He pushed away from his desk and stood up just as his cell phone started to ring and Harriet's name popped up.

He ignored the phone. If it was a warning, then she was too late, and right now his priority was handling Molly, not finding out how she'd discovered the truth.

The annoying thing was that he'd been intending to tell her that morning, but she hadn't shown up. He'd assumed that whatever had made her run from him the day before was still bothering her. He'd dropped Brutus back with his sisters and told himself he'd try one more time tomorrow.

Marsha's voice stopped him at the door. "She said to give you a message. Said she hoped she wasn't 'ruffling your feathers' by showing up here. Does that mean anything to you?"

Yes. It meant she not only knew the dog didn't belong to him, she also knew his name wasn't Brutus.

Ruffles.

"How angry is she on a scale of one to ten?"

"Why would she be angry?"

"No reason." *Every reason.* Daniel strode out of his office and took the elevator down to street level to meet his fate.

He didn't have to look far to find it. A crowd of women were huddled together in the middle of the foyer and he could see a brown-and-black tail poking between their legs. It was wagging wildly.

Traitor, Daniel thought, and made a mental note to have a severe word with Brutus later. If the dog had a grain of loyalty he would have sided with Daniel and refused to come into the building. After all those walks. All the sticks he'd thrown. All the belly rubs, and the dog hairs he'd picked off his clothing. He'd never witnessed such a display of canine ingratitude.

Strains of the conversation wafted over to him.

"He's *gorgeous*."

"What an amazing dog, does he really belong to Daniel Knight? I never even knew he owned a dog. He doesn't seem like the type."

"Oh, he's a real dog lover," came a bright, female voice that Daniel recognized immediately as Molly's.

Why didn't she sound angry?

And then he heard her voice again, sweet and a little breathless.

"Didn't you know? He walks his dog every day in Central Park. It's how we met. So romantic."

So that was the way she was going to play it. Clever.

What she had in mind wasn't rage, but revenge.

During one of their conversations he'd told her that he never took his private life to the office, so she'd brought it right here to his door, and from the looks of it she was determined to cause him maximum embarrassment.

Ready to perform damage control, he strode across the marble floor toward the little group. "Molly! This is a surprise."

Molly rose to her feet and for an infinitesimal second her eyes met his. And then she smiled.

It was the first time in his life he'd been afraid of a smile.

"Daniel! Darling." She reached up and kissed his cheek, and his last coherent thought before his senses were caught in the blast was that he wished she meant it. As her lips brushed his jaw he was transported back to the weeping willow, her body pressed against his, his pulse pounding as he felt the erotic slide of her tongue against his.

He wanted to power her back to the reception desk and flatten her to the smooth glass surface, but fortunately for his reputation Brutus intervened. The dog gave a delighted bark and leaped on him, clearly thrilled to see Daniel. Daniel was surprised to discover the feeling was mutual, and not simply because the animal had stopped him from risking arrest for indulging in obscene behavior in a public place.

"Hi, Brutus." He bent to greet the dog, ridiculously pleased that his sisters hadn't yet found a new home for him. The dog licked his hand and wagged his tail so hard he almost lost his balance on the slick polished floor. "This is a surprise."

Molly gave him a playful smile. "But a good surprise, I hope. Don't 'ruffle' his fur, Daniel." The emphasis was faint but impossible to miss. "You know he always likes to look his best."

Daniel straightened, assessing how far she was prepared

to go to humiliate him. "I wasn't expecting the pleasure of a visit."

Her smile told him she knew exactly how much of a "pleasure" this visit was.

"I know we're not supposed to bother you at work, but *Brutus*—" she emphasized his name "—was missing his daddy *so badly.*"

Daniel winced at "daddy." Clearly she was prepared to go all the way. From what he knew about her she was smart and professional. He was pretty sure the word *daddy* wasn't usually part of her vocabulary, especially not in this context.

She dropped into a crouch and held Brutus's face in her hands as she talked in an exaggerated baby voice. "Tell daddy how much you were missing him, you poor baby," she crooned. "You wanted him to snuggle with you and tickle your tummy like he does when he's home, isn't that right?"

The three girls from reception who had left their posts to fondle Brutus were all gaping at him. Clearly the image of him "snuggling" with anything was as alien as thinking of him as "daddy." His reputation was disintegrating in front of his eyes. He didn't care about that. He did care about the major client who was stepping out of a car outside the building. He estimated that he had about two minutes to execute damage control or he'd have a bigger problem than a few dog hairs on his suit.

"Brutus is struggling on the shiny floor, so why don't we take this outside and—"

"We'll be really quick. Brutus brought you a present." She used the same ridiculous voice. A voice he'd never heard her use before.

A voice that told him he was royally screwed.

"Molly—"

"Did you bring your daddy a special present? Shall we give it to him now or make him wait until later?" Her sing-song voice carried across the stark, businesslike interior of his office building and Brutus, whipped into a frenzy of excitement by her tone, whined and wagged his tail so hard he almost sent one of the receptionists flying.

Daniel grabbed Brutus's lead, intending to take him out onto the street where they could continue the conversation in some modicum of privacy, but Brutus was so excited to see him that he leaped up and planted his paws in the middle of Daniel's chest.

Recognizing the ridiculousness of the situation, Daniel laughed. If he ever had decided to get a dog, he would have chosen a dog exactly like Brutus, who had a healthy disregard for people's opinions and society's conventions.

"Oh, he is *so* pleased to see his daddy." Molly sounded delighted and Daniel decided to play her at her own game.

Sometimes, when you were caught in a fast-flowing current, the best thing to do was to stop fighting it.

"And I'm so pleased you dropped by. I left early this morning and didn't want to wake you."

Her eyes widened and color streaked across her cheeks.

Over her shoulder Daniel saw his client close the car door.

One minute until he walked into the building.

He had to find a way to make Molly run, and he only knew one way.

He tugged her against him and she swayed off balance and landed with her palm flat against his chest. She gave a gasp, but before she could protest, he kissed her. He'd intended to keep it brief, but the moment her mouth opened under his he lost track of time. He slid his hand into the silk of her hair, cupping the back of her neck and holding her head steady for his kiss. He explored her mouth, absorbing her, tasting her.

It was only when someone cleared their throat, that he remembered where he was and reluctantly let her go.

They stared at each other, dazed. It was hard to know which of them was most thrown by the kiss.

"I'll see you later." Somehow he managed to speak. "I should be home by eight. Don't cook. I know you have a lot on your mind right now…" *Like a thousand different ways to kill him.* "I've got this." He saw the look of alarm on her face as she realized she was no longer the one in charge.

"There's no need to—"

"I insist. It's my thank-you to you for looking after Brutus while I'm working."

The client walked through the door and Daniel decided it was time to end this encounter. "Rebecca?" He turned to one of the girls who worked on reception. "Ask Marsha to call Rob and get him to bring the car around. He can take Molly and Brutus home."

"Of course, Mr. Knight." She hurried back to the desk and the rest of the women gradually dispersed, no doubt to spread the gossip that unattached, incurably single, man-about-town Daniel Knight was finally involved with a woman. And enjoying sole ownership of a dog.

He suspected office life was about to take a turn for the complicated.

Acknowledging the client with a lift of his hand, Daniel took Brutus's lead and led him out to the street.

Molly turned, a dangerous spark in her eyes. "You borrowed a dog."

"I did."

"Why?"

"I'll tell you that if you tell me why you ran away after that kiss in the park."

She took a step backward, flustered. "That has nothing to do with anything. You used a dog to meet me."

"Yes."

"Were you intending to tell me at some point?"

"Today. But you didn't show up."

"I was busy. I have a meeting with my publisher later, and—"

"And that kiss yesterday freaked you out. Admit it."

Her breathing was rapid. "It was—"

"Yes, it was." He dropped his gaze to her mouth and wondered whether to complicate things by kissing her again right now. He had a client waiting, so probably not the best idea. Next time he kissed Molly he didn't want a time limit.

"You didn't only borrow the dog. You changed his name."

"Yes."

"You're not even going to deny it or make excuses?"

"It's the truth. I'm pleading guilty to all of it. Why did I do it? Because I wanted to meet you. You intrigued the hell out of me, Molly. You still do. And I'm answering all of your questions, but you still haven't answered mine."

She ignored that. "I couldn't work out why he never seemed to know his name. At first I thought he was disobedient and then I wondered if he had hearing issues, but all the time it was because Brutus wasn't his name! That's shocking."

"Brutus!" The dog's head whipped around and Daniel crouched down to make a fuss over him. "He knows his name now."

She scowled at him. "That isn't—"

"Which name do you think suits him best? Ruffles or Brutus?"

She stared at the dog and then at him. "That's not the point."

"It's exactly the point." Daniel straightened. "He's a strong, male dog. He needs a strong, male name."

"That's sexist. And a person's name has no bearing on their identity."

"You really think he's a Ruffles?" He stepped to one side to let the flow of pedestrians pass.

Her mouth opened and closed. "You have to win every argument."

"I'm a lawyer. Arguing is part of my job, just as analyzing behavior is part of yours. But I'm going to save you a job, Molly. You want to know what's going on here? I'll tell you. When I want something badly, I go for it. And I want you. It's that simple." He watched as her breathing turned shallow.

"You don't think it's a touch unscrupulous involving a dog?"

"Brutus was happy enough to join me in Central Park. Happier, I suspect, than he was joining you on a jaunt across New York City when the sole purpose wasn't a run in the park but for him to play a key role in embarrassing me in front of my colleagues." He saw guilt flash across her face.

"I took good care of him."

"You know what I think, Molly?" He leaned closer. "I think you're relieved this happened because now you have an excuse to back away."

"I don't need an excuse. I can simply tell you to back off."

"I mean with yourself. You can tell yourself that you're backing away because I borrowed a dog. But we both know the dog isn't the reason." His phone buzzed and he cursed softly. "I have to go. I have a meeting. But I'll try and get away early. Hopefully I'll be free by eight."

"What? No." She pushed her hair back, flustered. "Daniel, we're *not* meeting up later."

"There are things you need to say and it isn't good for a person to bottle them up. So I'll drop by later and you can say everything that is currently bubbling up inside you and threatening a major explosion. Give me your address."

"You don't need my address. I've said everything I came here to say."

"Somehow I doubt that."

"You made me think you were a dog person!"

Daniel glanced from her to Brutus, who was wagging his tail, a dopey expression on his face. "Turns out I might be a dog person, which is a tad confusing for both of us." He stooped and talked firmly to Brutus, man-to-man. "Look after her on the way home, do you hear me? You're in charge. No running across roads. No drinking from dirty puddles." Brutus nudged his leg and whined with delight. Daniel thought to himself that if half his clients were as relaxed and easy to please as Brutus, his working day would be a lot less stressful.

Molly glared at him. "I suppose you think you're off the hook?"

"No." Daniel straightened. "But we can talk about it tonight. And we can talk about that kiss." He nodded toward the road. "Rob will take you home, or to my sisters' apartment, or wherever it is you want to go."

"The car will be covered in dog hairs."

"Rob is a man who can handle most things. I can't imagine a few dog hairs are going to throw him off his stride. Your address?"

She hesitated and then told him. "If you show up, I might kill you."

Daniel smiled. "I'll see you at eight, Molly. That should give you time to figure out a few million ways to achieve that objective."

Ten

She did not need to figure out how she felt. She knew how she felt. She was mad at him! He'd lied to her. Did he *seriously* think she was going to get involved with him after the stunt he'd pulled? And as for the suggestion that she was using what had happened as an excuse to push him away. It wasn't an excuse, it was the truth.

No woman in her sound mind would get involved with a man who borrowed a dog to meet her.

She simmered as the sleek car purred through the traffic that clogged midtown Manhattan.

When she arrived at the twins' house, Harriet opened the door, looking guilty. "I don't know what to say to you. I feel terrible about this. If you don't want to speak to us ever again, I'll understand. I'll recommend new dog walkers."

"You're the best dog walkers in Manhattan. I don't want anyone different. How's my best boy?" Molly waited for Valentine to come bounding to meet her but instead he stayed where he was, head on his paws, uncharacteristically lethargic. "What's wrong?"

"I was going to ask you about him. He seems a little off-color." Harriet closed the door and then removed Brutus's lead. "Was he fine yesterday?"

"Yes. And he was fine when I took him to the park this morning." She watched as Brutus nudged Valentine. When the other dog wouldn't play, Brutus lay down next to him.

"They're so darling together," Harriet breathed. "Could Valentine have eaten something? He often tries to do that, doesn't he? It's one of the reasons I don't usually walk him with another dog. I have to keep a close eye on him."

"He didn't eat anything. We weren't even there for long." Molly thought back. She'd been lost in thought, preoccupied by Daniel. She hadn't been paying as much attention as usual. Guilt punched her in the stomach, and underneath the guilt was anxiety. It wasn't like Valentine to lack energy. "I suppose he might have eaten something. It's possible."

"I'm sure it's nothing. I'll keep an eye on him and if I'm worried I'll call the vet."

"I'll cancel my meeting." She started to hunt for her phone but Harriet shook her head.

"Don't do that. You're not far away and I'll call if I'm worried. How did it go with Daniel? I hope he apologized."

Molly dropped to her knees next to Valentine, anxious about him. "He's saving that for tonight."

"Tonight?"

"He's coming round to have a conversation."

Harriet's face brightened. "Oh, well that's—"

"It's not anything."

"That's a shame. You're the first woman who might actually be able to handle him. Daniel is used to women falling all over him. It happened the moment he hit puberty. Girls came up to Fliss and I, wanting to know how to attract his attention. He's always had the pick of the bunch. I honestly don't think he has ever heard 'no' from a woman."

"Well, he's heard it now." Except that he didn't appear to be listening.

"You're totally mad at him. I don't blame you at all."

"What upsets me isn't only that he pretended to own a dog that wasn't his, but the convoluted story he made up about his background. Can you believe he actually told me Brutus was a casualty of a bitter divorce case? He told me the man only kept him to punish his wife because he knew how much she loved the dog, and then when he realized he didn't want the dog the wife wouldn't take it back because she thought he deserved it. I believed him. I was upset for Brutus."

"Oh, that part wasn't a lie. Daniel really *did* rescue the dog from that vile divorcing couple up in Harlem. That was the truth. The only bit about that story he conveniently missed out was that he didn't keep the dog—he brought it straight to us."

Wrong-footed, Molly stared at her. "But why would he even have known about the dog?"

As if aware he was the topic of conversation, Brutus stood up and wandered to the sofa to take a closer look at the puppy Harriet was fostering.

Harriet watched him. "Daniel acted for the man in that case, but they parted company in the end because they had a difference of opinion. I don't know why. Daniel can be picky about the cases he takes. He specializes in difficult cases, particularly when they involve child custody."

Molly thought about what he'd told her in the park about

his mother. About how he'd become a divorce lawyer because of what happened.

Damn it, she wasn't going to let him get to her. "He does it for the money, right? Because those are the cases that earn him the biggest paycheck and most publicity?"

"No. He thinks it's really bad for children to grow up in a hostile family environment. He loves fighting for the underdog." Harriet rescued the sleeping puppy before Brutus could nudge him off the sofa. "He's no saint, Molly, but nor is he as bad as you think he is. So how are you going to handle him tonight?"

"I'm not handling him. I can't stop him showing up at my door, but I don't have to let him in." And she wasn't going to think about him defending the underdog, or helping women who couldn't help themselves—

Damn.

"So you're really not interested."

Molly thought about the last few weeks. Of the walks, the talks, the laughs, *the kiss*.

And she thought about the fact that he'd pretended that he was a dog person.

"No," she said firmly. "Not interested."

Worried about Valentine and trying not to think about Daniel, she went to her meeting with her publisher and arrived back to her apartment with an hour to spare before Daniel was due to show up.

Valentine was still listless and off-color, so she settled him in his dog basket where she could see him.

She took a quick shower and pulled on a dress. Then changed her mind and changed into jeans.

That should give Daniel the message that they weren't going out for dinner.

She carefully applied makeup, but only because it gave her more confidence. Not because she wanted him to see her looking her best.

Valentine watched her listlessly.

"Why are you looking so worried?" She stroked mascara onto her lashes. "You're still my favorite man, and always will be. I'm only wearing makeup because it gives me confidence. When he's gone, I'll order in a pizza. And now we're going to do that thing I probably shouldn't do. I'm going to do an internet search on Daniel Knight."

She poured herself a glass of wine, took it to her desk and typed his name into her laptop, wondering if she was going to regret doing this.

What was she going to discover?

Whatever it was, could it really be much worse than pretending to own a dog?

Twenty minutes later, she stood up and topped up her wineglass.

"Well, he's got quite a rep. Brilliant mind, obviously. Tough. Deadly in court, but fair from all accounts. The sort of man you want on your side if you're getting divorced. Which I'm not, of course, and never will be." She glanced at Valentine. He tried to stand up but staggered and then his legs gave way and he collapsed back onto his bed. He was trembling and growling and Molly's heart gave a sickening lurch.

"What's the matter?" She crouched down next to him and stroked his head. Valentine gave a low moan and was sick everywhere. His eyes rolled back in his head and she felt an explosion of panic.

"Valentine! No, no—don't do this to me." Hands shaking, she grabbed her phone, but she'd been so busy thinking about Daniel she'd forgotten to charge it.

Panicking, she tried to think. She'd have to borrow a phone from someone else. Mark and Gabe. Gabe was virtually attached to his phone. It was bound to be charged. She stumbled across her apartment, dragged open the door and walked slap into Daniel. She would have fallen if he hadn't caught her shoulders to steady her.

"Whoa, where's the fire?"

"I need a phone—I have to see if Mark and Gabe have a phone."

"I have a phone." His tone had switched from teasing to serious. "What's the problem?"

"Valentine. He's—" She choked on the words. "He's really sick. I need to call the vet, but my phone isn't charged and—"

"Mine is working." He urged her back into the apartment and by the time she'd closed the door he already had his phone in his hand. "Do you have the number of your vet?"

She was on her knees next to Valentine. "It's in my phone, and my phone is dead—"

"Tell me the name."

She tried to concentrate. To focus. Her mind was blank. "It's the same one Fliss uses. She recommended them."

He dialed. "Fliss? I need the number of your vet." His voice was clipped. There were no traces of his usual light banter. "No—it's Valentine." There was a pause. "Yeah, that's right... Not right now, but if we need you I'll call." He ended the call and dialed another number. While he waited for them to answer, he looked at Molly. "Grab a jacket, and your keys."

She kept her hand on Valentine's head. "I've never seen him like this."

"Molly." His tone was firm, cutting through her panic. "Jacket and keys."

She stood up, following orders on automatic, awful scenarios raining down on her. In the background she could hear Daniel talking to the vet.

By the time he finished the call, she was almost hyperventilating.

"What if he—" She couldn't even say the word. "I don't want to lose him."

"You're not going to lose him. That isn't going to happen." Daniel dropped to his haunches next to Valentine and put his hand on the dog's head. Valentine barely stirred. "They're sending the animal ambulance. They're on their way."

"How do we get him to the ambulance?" She couldn't remember where she'd put her keys. In her purse? On the table? She couldn't think. They had to get Valentine to the vet, fast. But what if they couldn't do anything?

"Keys," Daniel said gently. "They're on the kitchen counter."

She found them and dropped them in her pocket, her fingers shaky and useless. "I can lift him, but I don't think I can carry him down the stairs. He's too heavy for me."

"I can carry him, but I don't want to hurt him so get me a large towel. Something I can wrap around him."

He had taken control and she was glad about that because she wasn't capable of focusing on what needed to be done. The only thing in her mind was what she'd do if she lost Valentine. He was her best friend.

She looked at Daniel properly for the first time since he'd walked into her apartment and realized he must have come straight from the office. "You can't carry my dog. You're wearing a suit—"

"Molly," he said, his voice patient, "grab me a towel. And watch out for the ambulance."

She found a towel and helped Daniel wrap it around Valentine. Then he scooped him up, talking to him the whole time, about how he'd soon be feeling better, about how he'd be back in the park playing with Brutus in no time.

Molly hoped he was right.

She followed him out of the apartment, watching anxiously as Daniel carried Valentine carefully down the stairs.

"Call my sisters and ask them again if there is any possibility he could have eaten something in the park when he was with them. The vet said it would be useful to know. My phone is in my pocket."

"It didn't happen with them, it happened with me." Her stomach gave a sickening lurch. "I took him for a quick walk somewhere different this morning."

"Somewhere different?"

"Not our usual place."

Our usual place. It sounded intimate, as if they'd been meeting in the park for months, not weeks.

She waited for him to ask why she'd taken Valentine to a different place, but he didn't. Probably because he already knew the answer to that one.

She'd been avoiding him.

"And he could he have eaten something then?"

She thought about how distracted she'd been. "Yes," she said miserably. "I don't know that part of the park very well. He could have found something."

"Don't blame yourself. You're the best dog owner I've ever met." Daniel handed Valentine over to the staff from the animal hospital. Then he grabbed Molly's hand and tugged her into the ambulance.

She didn't pull her hand away. She needed the comfort too badly. The other she placed on Valentine's still body, ripped apart by guilt. "I'm sorry. So sorry. I should have paid more attention to what you were eating."

Valentine didn't even open his eyes and she felt tears thicken her throat.

Daniel's hand tightened on hers, and he leaned forward to talk to the driver. "Can you go any faster?" He glanced out of the window. "Don't take a right here, there's construction."

When they finally pulled up outside the animal hospital Valentine still hadn't moved and Molly was gripped by panic.

"He's a really strong, healthy dog. He's never really been sick before—"

"He's going to be fine." Daniel sounded so sure she didn't argue. Instead she grabbed on to his optimism and held it like a lifeline as they walked into the hospital.

The vet appeared immediately. "I'm Steven Philips."

Daniel took over. "We spoke a moment ago. Valentine here is pretty sick."

The vet didn't waste any time. He issued a couple of instructions to the nurse and while she was tending to Valentine he talked to Molly. "Can you give me some history?"

Molly gave him Valentine's medical history, which was brief because he'd never been ill before.

The vet turned his attention back to Valentine. "Try not to worry. I promise you he's in good hands." He washed his hands, snapped on a pair of gloves and focused on Valentine. "So you think he might have eaten something. Any idea what?"

"No. He was listless when I picked him up from the dog walkers, this evening he wouldn't eat and then suddenly he was very sick. He growled at me. He never growls, ever. And he went still. He's so unlike himself."

The vet was examining Valentine, his hands moving carefully. "I suspect you're right about him eating something he shouldn't have. Dogs are pretty indiscriminate eaters."

"I know, which is why I'm so careful. This has never happened before." Feeling horribly guilty, Molly swallowed. "I took him to a different part of the park this morning. I don't normally go there. I wasn't paying as much attention as I should."

"Which part?" The vet carried on examining Valentine as Molly described where she'd been.

"Did you notice daffodils by any chance?" the vet asked.

"I—" She hadn't noticed anything. She'd been thinking about Daniel. "There might have been daffodils. You think that's it?"

"I'm not sure, but if he was well yesterday and only showed symptoms after your walk in the park, I suspect it's some sort of poisoning. I'm going to run some tests."

"What sort of tests?"

"I'd like to take some blood, do an X-ray and an ultrasound, and get a few samples. Given how late it is, and how sick he is, we'll keep him overnight."

Molly's insides lurched. "You want to keep him here?"

"I'm going to start an IV. That way I can give him fluids and electrolytes, and if it becomes necessary to give him drugs, I already have a line in."

Molly felt a rush of alarm at the thought of Valentine with an IV. "You think he's going to get worse?"

The vet hesitated. "Toxic agents often target the kidneys. Flushing them out with fluid helps prevent organ damage.

Often forty-eight hours of fluid replacement is enough to prevent permanent kidney damage from some toxins."

"Kidney damage?" Molly started to shake. The tips of her fingers felt cold. "Then I'll stay."

The vet gave her an apologetic look. "Unfortunately we don't have facilities for owners to stay, but if you leave your number with the reception staff we'll get in touch if there's even the smallest change in his condition."

"If he's that sick, I'm not leaving him. It's not as if I live round the corner, and if something happens—"

"I live around the corner. She'll be staying with me," Daniel said. "My place is a block away. We can get here in five minutes if we need to. You have my number already."

The vet gave the nurse more instructions and Molly lingered. She couldn't bear to leave Valentine. What if something happened to him in the night and she wasn't here? What if he knew she'd left and felt abandoned? What if he—

She sat down on one of the hard plastic chairs. "I'll wait. It's fine. You go, Daniel, and thank you."

"You should both go," the vet urged. "There's nothing you can do here. You need to get some rest. I recommend you take up your friend's offer."

Rest? Was he kidding? Did he really think she was going to be able to rest while Valentine was this sick?

"Molly." Daniel dropped to his haunches in front of her. "I wasn't kidding. I live five minutes from here. It will be no different than being in the waiting room, except it will be a lot more comfortable. If there's any change, Steven will call." He was rock-steady and calm.

Absorbing some of that calm, Molly looked at the vet. "What time do you go off duty?"

"I don't. Tonight is my night shift and I have a new colleague with me so I'm going to be here all night."

That made her feel a little better.

Reluctantly, Molly stood up and gave Valentine's head a last stroke. His eyes were closed and his tail was still. Feeling sick, she stepped back and tried to think about practicalities. "I need to give you insurance details. I don't have anything with me. My card—"

"I've handled it. We can talk about it later." Daniel put his arm around her shoulders and started to guide her to the door when a man appeared.

"Steven, I've put the—" He broke off when he saw Daniel. Molly saw recognition and surprise. And she saw something else.

Caution.

She felt Daniel's arm slip from her shoulders and when she turned her head she saw his jaw lock tight.

She sensed tension, and yet how could there be tension when they were strangers?

"This is Seth Carlyle." Steven introduced them. "He's a critical care specialist who has just joined us."

Molly waited for Daniel to respond, but he was silent, his gaze locked with Seth's.

The silence stretched forever and still the two men stared at each other, like stags weighing up whether to engage in overt aggression.

And she realized they weren't strangers.

They knew each other.

The atmosphere was taut to the point of snapping.

Seth Carlyle was as tall as Daniel, his shoulders as broad. Both men were dark-haired, but where Daniel's eyes were the blue of the ocean on a summer's day, Seth's were almost black.

Molly was bemused.

Maybe Daniel had represented Seth's ex-wife. That was the only explanation she could come up with.

With a brief nod to Steven, Daniel urged her through the door. He strode away so fast she almost had to run to keep pace with him.

"Er—do you want to talk about it?"

"Talk about what?"

"About what just happened in there. Do you know that guy? The other vet? I thought you were going to attack each other."

"We've had dealings."

"Not good ones." It was raining outside and within moments Molly was soaked and shivering. "Did you handle his divorce or something?"

"No. Forget it. It doesn't matter. We need to get you home. You're cold." Emerging from whatever black cloud had enveloped him, Daniel shrugged off his jacket and draped it around her shoulders.

Warmth permeated her skin and the faint, familiar smell of him teased her senses.

It felt ridiculously intimate, wearing his jacket. She probably should have given it back, but instead she pulled it closer.

They were walking toward the park, and every step was taking her farther from Valentine.

She was about to stop and say it was too far, when he turned the corner.

"This is where I live."

"Here?" She blinked. "This is Fifth Avenue."

"That's right. I live on Fifth Avenue."

This time she did stop. "You *live* on Fifth Avenue? Overlooking the park?"

"Yes. And I suggest we get indoors before you die of shock or hypothermia." Without giving her a chance to respond, he stepped into a building, exchanged a few words with the doorman and then there was only the smooth glide of the elevator as it rose.

His shirt was soaked through, the fabric clinging to his skin. She couldn't drag her eyes from the powerful muscles of his shoulders and when she did her gaze met his and the connection was like being stuck by lightning.

"You're soaked, too." Her voice was croaky, but she was just relieved her vocal cords hadn't been fried along with her brain cells. "Sorry."

Daniel yanked off his tie. Raindrops glistened on his hair and his shoulders. "I know it's easier said than done, but try and relax. My sisters have been using that vet practice for years. They're good."

To stop herself from thinking about Valentine, she thought about the guy they'd met. Seth. She wanted to know why Daniel had looked at him with such naked animosity.

She was about to ask him more questions, but the doors opened and he urged her out of the elevator.

His apartment was as spectacular as the address—a duplex with a winding staircase that led to the upper floor and a terrace that wrapped itself around two sides.

Her entire apartment would have fitted comfortably into his living room.

She remembered what she'd read about him. He was considered one of the top divorce attorneys in Manhattan. The lawyer you wanted on your side when things went wrong. And he'd been on her side tonight, despite the fact that she'd taken Brutus to his offices with the sole intention of embarrassing him.

She turned, pathetically grateful. "Thank you."

"For what?"

"For helping me tonight. After what I did to you today, I wouldn't have blamed you for walking away."

"Why would I have walked away? You seemed like you needed help."

She was so anxious about Valentine she could barely summon a smile. "So you really are a Knight? What sort? White or shining armor?"

"I guess that all depends on perspective."

"I think I've lost all perspective."

Dark brows met in a frown. "You need to sit down, but first we should both clean up. Take a shower, then I'll make us something to eat. Whatever questions you have can wait until then." He led the way upstairs. "There's a guest bedroom and bathroom you can use. Help yourself to towels. I'll find something for you to wear and leave it on the bed."

She'd given no thought to the state of her clothes, but now she realized she was almost as much of a mess as he was.

"Valentine ruined your suit. And what he started, the rain finished. I'll pay to have it cleaned. And if it's beyond repair, then I'll—"

"Molly," he interrupted her gently. "Go take a shower."

"Right. Shower. Sounds good." She felt tears sting her eyes and blinked rapidly. Crying on him would be the final insult to his suit. She turned away but Daniel reached out and caught her arm.

"He's going to be fine, Molly."

"You don't know that."

"I do. I have good instincts." He let his hand drop, as if

he'd decided touching her was a bad idea. "You're shivering. Get in the shower. And don't lock the door. If you keel over, I want to be able to drag you out before you drown."

"I'm not going to keel over."

"Maybe not, but don't lock the door." He left the room and she gazed at her surroundings.

If the circumstances had been different she would have been reaching for her phone and sneaking photographs because she was unlikely to see this view again in her lifetime.

She'd never been inside an apartment on Fifth Avenue. The generous expanse of glass that framed the room boasted an incredible view of Central Park. In her apartment, if she stood on the toilet and leaned out of the window, she could see the tops of a few trees, but no way would she ever be able to claim to see the park.

She stripped off her clothes, left them in the room and walked into the shower, letting the hot water wash away the stress of the past couple of hours. She tried not to think about Daniel, a man she barely knew, just a few steps away.

They hadn't even been on a proper date, and yet without him she wasn't sure she would have made it through tonight.

Afraid of missing a phone call from the vet, she didn't linger. Wrapped in an oversize towel, she walked back into the bedroom and saw a pair of jeans and a sweater lying on the bed. The sweater was a soft shade of pink. You didn't need a qualification in psychology to know it belonged to a woman who wasn't afraid to release her girlie side.

She wondered how many women had left clothes in Daniel's apartment.

Her own clothes had vanished, so she had no choice but to wear the ones he'd left her.

The jeans were a tight fit, but the sweater was perfect

and it felt good to be clean, even if she did look like a swirl of fondant icing.

"Are you decent?" The deep tones of his voice came through the door and suddenly she felt self-conscious, which was ridiculous given that she was here because of Valentine. It wasn't romantic, or even personal. In fact her presence in his apartment didn't have anything to do with their relationship at all.

"Yes." She croaked out the word. "Come in."

He strolled into the room and the sudden heat almost suffocated her. Maybe it wasn't romantic, but it felt personal. Suddenly all she could think about was the way his mouth had felt on hers. The searing heat, the urgency, the dizzying chemistry.

"The clothes fit? I would have given you a bathrobe, but it would have swamped you."

The thought of walking around his apartment naked under a robe did nothing to cool the heat pumping around her body.

"The clothes are fine, thank you, although whichever one of your girlfriends left them is a little smaller than me." She tugged slightly at the jeans and saw his gaze travel slowly down her body and linger on her hips.

"They belong to my sister." His voice was huskier. Thicker. Layered with a new intimacy as if he, too, was reacting to the forced familiarity. "I don't entertain a whole lot of overnight guests."

She'd assumed his apartment was as busy as Grand Central Station with women coming and going according to a strict timetable. "Fliss?"

"Harriet." The corner of his mouth flickered. "Fliss wouldn't be seen dead wearing pink. She'd think it was some sort of statement. If you know her, then you probably know that."

"I don't know her well. We exchange a few words when I drop off Valentine, that's all." But now she had a million questions, most of them about Daniel. She'd thought he was a player, but now he was telling her he didn't have overnight guests. "Having a woman in your apartment is unfamiliar?"

"I work long hours, more hours than most relationships can tolerate. When I date—and that is nowhere near as often as rumor would have you believe—I'm often late, or I end up canceling, so most of the time I relax by seeing friends. I sent your clothes to be cleaned, by the way, along with my suit. They'll be back here tomorrow. You must be hungry. Come downstairs and I'll make you something to eat." He walked out of the room and she stared after him, digesting everything he'd said.

Her stomach was knotted with tension, as were her limbs. She wasn't sure she'd be able to force food past her dry throat.

She told herself her lack of appetite was caused by anxiety about Valentine, but in reality she knew the cause was more complicated than that.

She followed him, passing a large book-lined study and a master bedroom decorated in muted shades of green and brown. The place had a feel of understated luxury, but it was lived-in luxury, as if every design feature was there to add comfort for the inhabitant, not to impress.

The stairs were an elegant curve of contemporary glass and the centerpiece of the living room was more glass, the floor-to-ceiling windows framing the dazzling lights of Fifth Avenue and the darkened expanse of Central Park.

Almost as eye-catching was the artwork on his walls.

"Are you interested in art?" He opened a bottle of wine and poured two glasses.

"Yes, but I'm not knowledgeable." Now she wished she was. It would have provided them with a safe, neutral topic of conversation at a moment when she badly needed it. "Are you a collector?"

"It's an interest of mine."

"That's why you chose to live in this area?"

"One of the reasons. Then there's the fact that I like the view, and it's close to my office. I'm not a big fan of commuting."

The mention of his office reminded her that she owed him an apology. "Listen, about today…" She slid onto one of the stools by the granite counter, feeling uncomfortable. "I'm sorry."

"For what?"

"For showing up at your office with Brutus and—"

"And embarrassing me?"

She caught a glimpse of his smile before he turned and reached for his wine. "You didn't seem embarrassed."

"Trust me, it's going to take a while to live that experience down. It's the first time a woman I'm seeing has shown up at my office. And you shouldn't apologize. You were angry, and you had every right to be. Still do."

She was about to say that she wasn't seeing him, and then realized how ridiculous that would sound. She was sitting in his apartment, her hair still wet from the shower she'd taken in his bathroom. And then there was that kiss. The fact that neither of them had mentioned it didn't change the fact that it hovered between them. If anything, not mentioning it increased its significance.

"You carried my sick dog to the vet. Right now you can pretty much do anything and I'd think you were a hero."

"I'm not a hero, Molly." The way he was watching her made her heart beat faster.

"The first time I saw you, I thought I had you sorted. I thought I knew who you were. It was the dog that threw me. You didn't seem like the type to own a dog, and that really nagged at me."

"There's a type?"

"Yes. A dog is a responsibility and you didn't strike me as a man who ties himself down."

"Smart."

"My instincts told me you were all about the light and the superficial."

"I seem to remember I told you that, too."

"Yes, and yet tonight, with my dog sick—what you did— what you're doing—those aren't the actions of a man who is superficial." She broke off and met his gaze.

And then he smiled. "Don't kid yourself. I helped with Valentine because I thought you'd be so grateful you'd get naked with me."

"You want me to sleep with you out of gratitude?"

"As long as you're naked, I don't care about your motivation."

She knew he was teasing her and it made her laugh. "You're outrageous."

"So is that a yes?"

"You'd take advantage of an emotionally vulnerable woman?"

"Definitely." He topped up her wine. "But it won't hurt to get you drunk, too, to make sure I'm covering all bases. Drunk, emotionally vulnerable women are my favorite type."

"I don't believe you for a moment. I think you're a decent, honorable guy."

"Damn. What gave me away?"

"You carried a Dalmatian who was being sick everywhere. And you gave me a place to stay, even though you don't normally allow women to sleep over."

"Just don't leave a toothbrush or I'll expect free therapy." The gentle amusement in his tone made her pulse pound.

To distract herself, she took a sip of wine. Berries and wood smoke exploded on her palate. "This is delicious."

"My neighbor and I share a passion for wine. This was one of his discoveries. We share tips."

"You have neighbors?" She glanced around the spacious apartment. "It feels as if you're in your own private castle."

"There are other private castles close by. Which is useful on the days I need to borrow a cup of sugar."

She laughed. "Or a dog."

"That, too." He topped up his glass. "Is that why you were so angry this morning? Not because I borrowed the dog, but because you misread me?"

"I was thrown." The alcohol slid into her veins and she felt some of the tension in her body ease. "I formed an opinion of you based on your relationship with Brutus. And then it turned out you didn't have a relationship with Brutus, so none of the things I thought about you were true. It was confusing."

He put his glass down. "My relationship with Brutus is real enough."

"You're fond of him. And given that you only borrowed him to make me notice you, that surprises me."

He grinned. "It surprises the hell out of me, too. Brutus

is a great character. Turns out I might be more of a dog person than either of us thought."

Every conversation she had with him seemed to erode another of her defenses. He was charming, that was true, but usually she found charm easy to resist. Charm could be all surface and it could tarnish under certain conditions. But there was so much more to Daniel Knight than charm.

"Are you telling me you're thinking of buying a dog?"

"No. I'm telling you I like Brutus. It's an individual thing." He pushed his phone toward her. "I didn't call the vet. I thought you'd want to do that. While you talk to them, I'll make us something to eat."

"Thanks." She took the phone, almost afraid to use it in case the news was bad.

"Do you want me to do it?"

She was touched as much by the fact that he understood her thought process as she was by his offer.

"No. But thank you." She gripped the phone and dialed, all the time telling herself that if it was bad news they would have called.

It turned out she was right. There was no news. Valentine's condition was the same, and so far none of the tests had shown anything useful.

"No change." She pushed the phone back toward Daniel. "They're still pretty sure he must have eaten something, but without knowing what they can only give him supportive treatment. They said something about trying to maintain normal function of the organs until whatever he ate is flushed out through his body."

"Harriet called twice while you were in the shower. She's worried."

"Harriet is wonderful. When you told me you had sisters, I had no idea it was Fliss and Harry."

"I didn't know you knew them, otherwise I would have insisted on an introduction. Would have been easier than borrowing a dog."

"I still can't believe you did that. Are you always that inventive?"

"No, but you were totally engrossed in your dog and it seemed like the only way to get your attention."

"Was the running in the park for my benefit, too?"

"I've been running in the park for years. It's the best part of the day. After the sun comes up and before the crowds arrive."

She felt the same way. "This morning when I went to your offices I never in a million years dreamed I'd be spending the night in your apartment." In the moment of crisis she hadn't given it much thought. She'd snatched at the chance to stay as close to Valentine as possible. Only now, when the immediate crisis was receding, was she starting to feel the intimacy of their situation. Whatever the reason, it didn't change the fact that she was alone with him, sharing dinner and sleeping under the same roof.

She was acutely aware of him.

She told herself that she was feeling this way because of Valentine. Daniel had been strong, decisive and protective. And it was perfectly fine to lean on someone occasionally. That didn't make her weak or incapable. It made her human. And any woman would feel fluttery under those circumstances.

He studied her for a long, disconcerting moment and then turned and tugged open the fridge. "I wasn't expecting guests, so the level of hospitality isn't going to impress you. I have cheese and cold cuts that will go perfectly with the wine. And don't tell me you're not hungry. You need to eat. If you don't, you'll faint and I've delivered my quota of medical care for one day." He pulled various items from the fridge, removed the wrappings and arranged them on plates. "No bread. Wait there while I make a call."

She took another sip of wine, promising herself that she'd eat a few mouthfuls and then make her excuses and go to bed. She'd close the door between them and everything would be fine.

As she formulated her plan, she heard him say "Do you have any of your delicious bread?" to someone on the phone, and wondered who he could be calling this late. Did he intend to go roaming Manhattan looking for fresh bread? Or was he ordering takeout?

Moments later there was a knock on the door and she heard a female voice. "I brought bread, and you're in luck because I was experimenting with bite-size quiches for an event we're doing next month, so I need tasters. Try it and tell me what you think."

"Isn't Lucas doing that?"

"He already has. His feedback was 'tasty,' but he says if I don't cook a big fat juicy steak sometime in the next twenty-four hours, he's going to put me in a book and kill me."

Recognizing the voice, Molly slid off the stool and walked to the door. "Eva?"

The pretty blonde laughing with Daniel turned her head. "Molly! Well, this is a surprise." She thrust the food she was carrying into Daniel's arms and the next moment Molly was wrapped in a cloud of perfume, warmth and friendship.

"What are you doing here?" She pulled away, thinking

not for the first time that Eva was possibly the friendliest person she'd ever met. "I thought you lived in Brooklyn?"

"I do. I mean, I did. I spend most of my time here now because I'm with Lucas, and I can't drag him away when he's on a deadline. Also his kitchen makes an amazing backdrop for my YouTube videos. What are *you* doing here? Now I think of it, this is the first time I've ever met a woman in Daniel's apartment." She gave Daniel a meaningful look and Molly intervened.

"Valentine is sick, and Daniel helped me, and this place is closer to the vet's so—"

"Valentine is sick?" Eva's expression changed from curious to worried. "How sick?" The horror in her voice made it all the more real and Molly felt the panic she'd suppressed bubble to the surface again.

"Pretty sick."

"But he's going to be fine," Daniel said. "How do you two know each other?"

"Molly is a client of Urban Genie. We were the ones who fixed her up with the Bark Rangers. Do you have everything you need? You're happy with your choice of vet? Can I fill your fridge? Do your laundry? Anything at all that will help you focus on Valentine, just let me know."

Molly was so touched that for a moment she couldn't speak.

Daniel took over. "You can fill my fridge," he drawled. "The contents are pitiful."

"You don't have a meal plan?"

"My plan is to get my guests drunk so that they don't notice the lack of food."

Eva laughed. "I took a call from Marsha today. Do you know about that?"

"Is this about the summer party?"

"That's the one. I knew you were behind it. Thank you."

"Much as I'd love to claim the credit, it was all Marsha's idea. Your reputation is spreading."

"You won't regret it. I promise it will be a party to remember."

"It usually is, although often for the wrong reasons. Certain members of my team tend to let their hair down."

"Nothing we can't handle. Now go and eat." Eva gestured to the food. "The quiches only came out of the oven half an hour ago so they're still warm. Do you have salad? I can get some."

"You should join us," Molly said impulsively. Any moment now the door would close behind Eva and she would be left alone with Daniel. She wasn't sure she could handle the deepening intimacy.

His questioning glance told her he knew exactly why she'd issued the invitation.

"I'd love to, but Lucas is locked in front of his computer and I have some work I need to do. Another time? Call me if you need anything else." Eva vanished and Daniel closed the door and turned to Molly. The look he gave her made her head swim.

"Daniel—"

"Are you afraid of me, or yourself?"

"Excuse me?" She was beginning to wish she hadn't drunk the wine on an empty stomach.

"You invited Eva to join us because you didn't want to be alone with me, but you didn't need to do that." He walked to the kitchen and put the food down on the counter. "When we eventually take this further it will be because you're ready and because you want it as much as I do. And that isn't going to be when you're feeling fragile and vulnerable."

"I'm not vulnerable."

"Valentine is sick and you're staying in the apartment of a man you barely know. That makes you vulnerable."

"Maybe. A little." It was the truth. Why deny it?

"You don't need Eva to protect you from me, Molly." He spoke softly. "When we get together it's going to be because of what we're feeling for each other, and nothing else."

The fact that he made it sound like a foregone conclusion made her heart bump against her chest.

She should probably argue, but the words wouldn't come. Instead she chose a safe topic. "I didn't know you knew Eva."

His eyes held hers for a moment and then he gave a faint smile and accepted the change. "I don't know her that well. Eva, Frankie and Paige run Urban Genie. I happen to be friendly with Paige's brother, so when I found out they were offering event and concierge services, I put them in touch with Fliss and Harriet. Plenty of people in Manhattan need dog walking. I've seen more of Eva since she moved in with Lucas, my neighbor."

She blinked. "Small world."

"It is. But she's gone back to her little world, leaving us in ours. So here's what I suggest. We're going to pretend we've forgotten about that kiss. If I don't look at your mouth, and you don't look at mine, I figure we might manage it. We'll ignore the chemistry and the fact that keeping my hands off you is becoming a challenge, and tonight we'll focus on getting to know each other a little better."

"You're right. We should forget about it totally." Except that trying not to think about the kiss made it the only thing in her head.

"I never said anything about forgetting it totally." His eyes gleamed. "I have every intention of revisiting it once you're not anxious and worried and thinking about Valentine."

"We won't be revisiting it." But she liked the fact that he didn't say "your dog." He made it seem as if he cared.

"I like you, Molly." His honesty was disarming. "I liked you enough to borrow a dog to get to meet you."

"You hadn't spoken to me then, so you couldn't have known you liked me."

"I admit that it might have been your legs I noticed first. And your hair—the way it swings. I want to pull it down and—never mind." His voice was raw. "It doesn't matter what I want to do with it."

"You borrowed a dog because you liked my hair?"

"And the way you ran. As if you were killing the tarmac. Damn it, can we talk about something else?" He paced back to the kitchen, grabbed plates of food and took them to the table in the living room. "Have you ever been to Antarctica?"

"No." She was startled by the question. "Have you?"

"No."

"But you want to? Why mention it?"

"Because I was trying to have cold thoughts. I started off thinking of crushed ice in a margarita but it wasn't enough. Neither was winter in New York. I was trying Antarctica, but I think I might have to give in and settle for a cold shower. No, don't sit next to me—" he gestured with his hand "—sit across from me. I feel safer with a table of food in between us."

Unsettled and more than a little flattered, she sat down.

The sofas were deep and comfortable and had been arranged to make the most of the view. This late, all she could see was darkness and sparkle.

"I always wondered how it would feel to have a view of the park."

"It feels good. When I have time to look at it." He added a few more things to a plate and handed it to her. "Eat. And tell me about Valentine. How did you find him?"

She hesitated and then slid off her shoes and curled her legs under her. "I'd been in New York for a couple of months, and I came across him in the park. Someone had dumped him. I took him to the vet, then to the adoption center and then I realized I didn't want anyone else to have him."

"You'd never owned a dog before?"

Her heart started to beat a little faster. "I had a dog as a child. His name was Toffee. He was a chocolate Lab. I adored him."

"It's always hard to lose a pet."

All she had to do was nod and move on. She didn't have to correct his misunderstanding, but for some reason she wanted to.

"Toffee didn't die—at least, not then. My mother took him."

"Took him?"

"When she left." She leaned forward and cut a thin slice of cheese. She added it to her plate, along with some plump tomatoes and one of Eva's mini quiches. "Turned out that although she could easily live without my father or me, she didn't want to lose Toffee. That was hard."

"I can imagine. You suffered two losses at once. That's tough on anyone. Even tougher when you're a child."

He understood. Not because he'd handled it in his work, but because he'd handled it himself. Maybe that was why she felt compelled to tell him things she'd never told anyone else. "It was especially hard because when she tried to explain why she was leaving, she told me she wanted to be free. But then she took Toffee." She paused. "So what that told me was that she wanted to be free of *me*." The food on her plate lay untouched.

Daniel's lay untouched, too. He was still, his gaze fixed on her face. "Hell, Molly—"

"It's fine. You don't have to work out what to say. There really isn't anything *to* say. I expect you hear stories like that all the time in your working day. You're probably immune."

"I'm not immune." He hesitated. "This is why you don't date?"

"No, of course not! That happened when I was eight years old and I moved on long ago. Am I wary? Of course, but so are a lot of people, yourself included. Dealing with people at the end of their marriage must tarnish your view on life."

He looked as if he was about to say something else and then changed his mind. "Sometimes. But I try and extract the positive from every situation and help people find the best way to resolve their issues. Sometimes that's counseling and conciliation."

The thought made her smile. "You're a guy who talks about his problems?"

"Talking is what I do best. I talk to clients, if necessary I talk in court, in front of a judge."

"I'm sure you're good at that." She decided to confess. "I looked you up."

"On the internet?" He seemed more amused than annoyed. "Now I understand why you were reluctant to stay on your own with me. Which piece did you read? The one where they paint me as being a cross between the Dark Knight and Gladiator, or the one where they call me the Heartbreaker?"

She thought back to what she'd read. About how he was

a master at strategy, finding the weak spot in his opponent. Then she remembered her racing heart rate and her jelly legs and decided that where he was concerned, all of her was weak.

"I know better than to believe everything I read." She thought about what he'd discover if he did an internet search on her. Maybe he already had. If he had, he wouldn't have found anything. There was nothing out there about Molly Parker. And if he'd found out by some means, they'd be having a different conversation. "You have quite a reputation."

"The media like to exaggerate things."

And didn't she know it. "That's why I read everything with a critical eye for the facts."

"And what did your critical eye tell you?"

"That you almost always win your cases, so either you're very, very good or you only take cases to court if you think you can win. Which probably makes you wise as well as good at what you do."

"A contested divorce is never my first choice for anyone. Having said that, I would never recommend that anyone engage the services of a divorce attorney who is afraid to litigate in court. If you do, you have little to no bargaining power. You need someone who is prepared to fight for your best interests, but who also knows when to settle. The ideal outcome is an early resolution."

"You settle? I would have thought you would go after victory every time."

"*'For to win one hundred victories in one hundred battles is not the acme of skill. To subdue the enemy without fighting is the acme of skill.'*"

"Excuse me?"

"Sun Tzu. *The Art of War.*"

"War? That doesn't seem like a healthy way to view a divorce."

"It's about strategy and knowing your enemy. Sun Tzu was a Chinese military general. *The Art of War* is a masterpiece on strategy. You should be interested in it because it's more about taking advantage of the psychological state of your enemy than in applying force."

"So you're telling me you're a disciple of an ancient Chinese military general?"

"I think his ideas have relevance, yes." He finished the food on his plate. "So if you looked me up then you probably already know everything there is to know about me. And I still know next to nothing about you."

Her heart beat a little faster. "What do you want to know?"

"Why did you run from me in the park the other day?"

"You said we weren't going to talk about that."

"No, what I said was that we'll forget about the kiss for now." He added another slice of cheese to his plate. "I'm not asking you about the kiss. I'm asking you why you ran. You're careful. Reserved. Cautious. You don't allow people to get too close. I would have said that has to do with being abandoned at an impressionable age, but if that's not the case then your reaction has to have its roots in something more recent."

"Or maybe I didn't feel the chemistry."

His gaze met hers. "I think it's *because* you felt the chemistry that you ran. It wasn't because you didn't feel, but because you felt too much."

"Hey, I'm the psychologist."

He put his plate down slowly. "Who hurt you, Molly?"

Her mouth dried. "What makes you think someone hurt me?"

"You live alone, your best friend is your dog and you avoid relationships. Those are the actions of someone who has been hurt. Badly hurt. And now you protect yourself. You do whatever it takes to make sure your heart doesn't get broken again. Am I right?"

She could let him think that. She could end the conversation now.

Or she could be honest, and end the relationship.

She stared at her plate for a moment, weighing the options even though she'd known from the start that she couldn't be less than honest.

Acknowledging that, she lifted her head. "You have the first part right. I live alone, Valentine is my best friend and I avoid romantic entanglements. But my heart wasn't broken. You've got it the wrong way round," she said slowly so that there was no misunderstanding. "I wasn't the one who was hurt. I was the one doing the hurting. I'm not the one with the broken heart. I'm the one who does the breaking. Every time."

Daniel stared at her. "What do you mean, 'every time'?"

"My first proper relationship was when I was eighteen. College boyfriend. He fell in love, I didn't. I ended it because I knew I was never going to feel the way he wanted me to and I thought it would only make it worse if we prolonged it. He was so devastated he dropped out. His parents wrote me a letter telling me that I'd ruined his future." She could have elaborated, but she stuck to the basic facts. "After that I picked someone older. I met him in a nightclub when I was with friends. He told me he was only interested in having a good time. I believed him. Maybe he even meant it at the time."

"He fell in love with you, too?"

"He proposed to me after six weeks with the biggest diamond you've seen in your life. He took out a loan to buy it."

Daniel raised an eyebrow. "You seem to have quite an effect on men."

"Adam was great. Really great—" She swallowed. "In theory we had everything going for us. After my experience in college, I only dated men who should have been a perfect match because I didn't want to risk hurting anyone else. Maybe that sounds a little sterile and contrived, but it wasn't. I was simply doing for myself what I'd always done for other people. But still the relationship didn't work out. And believe me, I tried. I tried so hard to fall in love with him. I really *worked* at it. You have no idea."

"You make it sound as if you were trying to pass the bar exam, not fall in love." His tone was mild and she gave a little shrug.

"I accepted that falling in love probably wasn't something that would come naturally to me. Because of my DNA."

"Your DNA?"

"My mother wasn't good at commitment."

"I'm not a scientist, but I'm pretty sure that's not genetic."

"I'm not so sure. Anyway, after Adam, I didn't date for a while."

"I'm not surprised. But somehow I sense this story isn't over." He looked at her expectantly and she sighed.

"You might want more wine."

"How much more?"

"Buy a vineyard."

"Sounds like a great investment strategy." He topped up her glass and his. "Go for it. Who was the next guy?"

"The details don't matter. Let's just say that despite the fact that we were perfect on paper and he was a very special person, I didn't feel a thing. Nothing. I've given up now. I cannot make it happen. Basically I end every relationship I ever begin. And the last one was—ugly."

He glanced at her. "How ugly? Ugly enough to make you leave the country?"

"Yes. And the most upsetting thing about that particular disaster was that I was really careful. I kept looking for signs that he was emotionally involved, but I didn't see any. We had fun, but he never used the L word until the night he proposed. I almost died of shock. And I'm the one who's supposed to understand human behavior." She slumped on the sofa. "They call you the 'Heartbreaker' but I can tell you that people have much less flattering names for me."

"You've surprised me. I assumed you'd fallen in love and had your heart broken."

"I've never been in love. I can't fall in love." And it scared her. It scared her so badly. What was wrong with her? She had no idea. All she knew was that something major was missing. "Other people fall in love multiple times in their lives, and I can't manage it even once no matter how hard I try. You don't want to get involved with me, Daniel. I'm bad news."

"You don't look like bad news." He studied her, and his slow, steady gaze warmed her from the inside out.

"Looks can be deceptive. I don't ever want anyone to fall in love with me again, because I cannot return the feeling." There. She'd delivered a warning, loud and clear.

He didn't move, or shift his gaze from hers. "I'm not going to fall in love with you."

"That's what Adam said before he blew his savings on a ring."

"I'm not the falling-in-love type. Seems you're not either."

"Apparently my heart, and my defenses, are impenetrable. I'm like the Great Wall of China, only without the tourists. You might want to remember that." She stood up, wishing she hadn't had that second glass of wine. "I'll see you in the morning. And thank you again for what you did for Valentine."

Eleven

The vet called first thing and Daniel answered it as he finished buttoning his shirt.

Molly had obviously heard the phone because she appeared in the doorway, her face pale and her gaze anxious. "What is it? Has something happened?"

His brief scan of the shadows under her eyes told him she hadn't had any more sleep than he had.

She looked awful.

"He's better. Making good progress." Knowing that she wouldn't be happy until she'd spoken to the vet herself, Daniel handed the phone over.

He was due in court, but he wasn't leaving until he was sure she was all right.

He reached for a tie, listening as she asked a dozen questions. They were good questions. Thorough. Somehow she managed to keep emotion out of the conversation, although she sank down onto the edge of the bed, as if her legs would no longer hold her.

"Thank you. Thank you." She repeated the words to the vet before finally ending the call. Then she sucked in a few deep breaths before finally lifting her head. "He's better. Making progress. He's going to be okay." She looked exhausted, as if she'd used up all her strength and energy getting through that crisis.

He watched, concerned, as her eyes closed and tears appeared along the seam of her lashes.

"Hey—"

"I'm okay. Ignore me." She pressed her fingers to the bridge of her nose, trying to stem the flow. "I thought— It's a relief, that's all. I was afraid—"

Daniel reached down and tugged her upright, folding her against his chest. He treated it the same way he would if one of his sisters had been upset. "That isn't going to happen. The vet says he will make a good recovery." He felt her go limp against him. Felt her hand lock in his shirt. It took a few seconds for the feelings inside him to shift and change, and to realize that holding Molly was nothing like holding his sisters.

He'd only intended to comfort her, but apparently his body wasn't capable of removing the sexual attraction part.

He stood still, thinking that this was a really, *really* bad moment to get an erection.

He eased away as she stepped back.

"The vet wants to keep him until tomorrow, just to be sure." She sounded flustered. "I'll go back to my apartment."

He didn't bother suggesting that she stay because he knew she wouldn't. And he assumed that, like him, she had work to do. He realized he knew very little about what she actually did. All he knew was that she was a psychologist, but presumably she had places she needed to be, or at least access to her email.

"In that case I'll see you at yours around eight. Don't cook. I'll pick something up on my way over." He saw her expression change as she registered his words.

"Daniel—"

"What? We were supposed to have dinner last night, but circumstances overtook us. So we'll do it tonight instead. I'd take you out, but I think for our first date it might be best if we make it more private. That way you can tell me all the reasons you think what we're going to do is a bad idea, and I can put the opposing point of view."

"What we're going to do?" Her tongue sneaked out and moistened her lips. "Last night I told you—"

"I know what you told me, Molly." He cut her off. "And I can tell you that there is no chance of you breaking my heart. Zero. How do I know that? Because I've been told a million times that I don't have a heart. Not only does that make me safe from your bad-girl tendencies, it also makes me your perfect date."

"I don't date."

"Because you're afraid of hurting someone, but you're not going to hurt me. And now I need to go because a woman who *does* have a heart and whose husband cheated on her and is now trying to make her life hell needs me to be a dragon in court."

"I thought you tried to avoid court."

"*'He will win who knows when to fight and when not to fight.'*"

"More Sun Tzu?"

He flashed her a smile. "There's coffee in the pot downstairs. Close the door behind you when you leave. I need to go and breathe fire."

* * *

Dear Aggie, I've just come out of a bad relationship and I can't imagine ever wanting to get involved with anyone again. How can I learn to trust? Yours, Wounded.

Molly stared at the screen.

Dear Wounded, I don't have a clue.

She had no answer. No advice. No comment.

Her mind was blank. Now that she knew Valentine was going to make a full recovery, all she could think of was Daniel.

Daniel, carrying Valentine to the cab. Daniel, staying by her side at the animal hospital. Daniel, lending her clothes and making her food. Distracting her.

Daniel telling her she'd never hurt him because he didn't have a heart.

Would he really come by after work? No. He'd probably spend the day in court defending some woman emerging from the ruins of a wrecked relationship and decide he didn't want to put himself through that.

She thought about him in court, fighting a battle for a woman who couldn't fight her own.

She stared at the screen again, trying to focus.

She'd arrived back expecting the apartment to be the way she had left it, but it was pristine. She was sure she had Mark and Gabe to thank for that and felt a flash of gratitude.

The first thing she'd done was change into her own jeans and a fresh shirt. Then she'd sat down at her laptop.

There was plenty of work waiting for her, that wasn't the problem. The problem was her attention span.

She needed to stop thinking about Valentine, and most of all she needed to stop thinking about Daniel and what was going to happen later.

She stood up and walked to her bookshelf. Right in front of her was a copy of *Mate for Life*. She pulled it off the shelf and turned it over. She'd written it in a white heat of passion, pouring everything she knew onto the page. Everything she had ever learned about watching people in relationships.

Looking at it now, she couldn't remember how she'd done it.

She felt like an impostor.

What did she know about relationships?

Everything she knew she'd learned from books. From studying. It was all theory. None of it was from experience.

Even though three years had passed, Rupert's voice still rang in her head.

There's something wrong with you.

Was he right? She was starting to think that maybe he was. Even though he'd said those hurtful words because she'd hurt him badly, so badly she'd been careful not to become involved with anyone since, even she could recognize that there was a truth to them. Rupert was a good man and the breakup had been brutal, not just professionally but personally. It had been hard to look at herself in the mirror every morning. She'd hated herself, and what she'd done to him. And part of her believed that if she couldn't love Rupert, who was charming, smart, entertaining and had women falling over themselves to gain his attention, then she wasn't going to be able to fall in love with anyone, was she? She'd decided right there and then that she needed to stop trying and just accept the way she was. Maybe her problems originated in her childhood, maybe they didn't, but nothing changed the facts. No matter how hard she tried, she wasn't capable of falling in love.

She'd given herself a fresh start, but part of that fresh start had included the decision not to put herself in that position ever again.

She could have an active, and interesting, social life without becoming involved with a man.

That resolve had never been challenged. Until now.

She put the book down and made herself coffee. Without Valentine the apartment felt smaller. Empty. As if an important piece was missing.

She was about to settle down to her laptop again when there was a tap on her door.

It was Mark, carrying a huge bunch of flowers. "How's Valentine? Gabe and I were worried sick when we got your text."

"Better. Coming home tomorrow all being well. Come in." Any excuse not to work.

"These are for you. Gabe sends his love." Mark handed her the flowers, a bunch of gerberas.

Staring into their sun-like faces made her smile. "Thank you. It's impossible to feel down when you have gerberas." *And friends.* "Thank you for checking on the apartment last night. I left in a panic and I wasn't even sure I locked it. And you cleaned up. You're a friend in a million."

"You look terrible. Sit down. I'll put these in water." He took the flowers back and walked to the kitchen area. "Have you been working?"

"I thought I'd catch up a little, but I'm having trouble concentrating."

"And that surprises you?"

"I don't usually have trouble focusing."

"You have something major going on in your life. Something else filling your head."

"The vet says he's going to be fine. There's no reason why I shouldn't be focused."

Mark found a vase and filled it with water. "Unless maybe what's filling your head isn't Valentine."

She felt the color in her face give her away. "Meaning?"

"You stayed the night with him."

"Daniel? Yes, but only because his place was nearer. Nothing happened. He didn't even kiss me." But he'd looked at her, and she'd known that if her reasons for being there had been different he would have done more than kiss her. But of course if it hadn't been for Valentine she wouldn't have been there at all, which made her reasoning warped. "I told him I'm bad news. That he should stay away from me."

"And what was his response? He thanked you politely for warning him and agreed to take his interest elsewhere?"

"No." Molly discovered she was desperate to talk to someone. "He said he'd be round with dinner tonight."

"I'm starting to like the guy."

So was she. That was the problem.

"That's the other thing I haven't told you. Did you know Fliss and Harry have a brother?"

"Yes, although I've never met him. Superstar attorney. The sort of guy you'd want on your side if your relationship was falling apart."

"Yeah, well that's him. Daniel. Daniel is their brother."

"Wait a minute, you're telling me that your Daniel is their

Daniel?" Mark dragged his hand through his hair. "Dog-loving fit guy from the park is the twins' brother?"

"Turns out he's not dog-loving. He borrowed the dog to get my attention."

Mark sat down at the table. "I'm starting to understand why you can't concentrate. That's——"

"Dishonest?"

"I was going to say flattering."

"It's flattering to have someone prepared to kidnap and deceive for you? What am I missing?"

"Did he tell you it was his dog?"

"No. But when someone has a dog it's natural to assume it's theirs."

"Not in New York City. In New York City half the people in Central Park are walking dogs belonging to someone else."

"But he borrowed the dog to make him seem like a dog-loving person. What kind of guy does that?" She frowned, thinking back to how he was with Brutus. "In fact he might be a dog-loving person, but I don't think he discovered that until recently."

"From what I know about him, the guy doesn't have to try too hard to get a woman's attention. The fact that he was willing to go to those lengths to attract yours, means something."

"It means he thinks my butt looks good in running pants."

Mark grinned. "Or maybe he's fallen for Valentine. So did he kidnap this dog?"

"No. Fliss and Harriet lent it to him, and I still haven't really had time to process that part."

"He didn't know the dog at all?"

"He did. He was the one who rescued it from a nasty divorce case. They dumped the dog and—" She caught Mark's eye. "Don't look at me like that."

"Like what? I was thinking he's obviously cruel and heartless."

"I need sympathy, not sarcasm. And I didn't say he was heartless, exactly. Just that he pretended to own a dog."

"Did the dog object? Did they ignore each other?"

Molly thought about the way Brutus had almost tugged her hand off to get to Daniel when she'd taken him to the office. "No. They were great together. Will you *stop* looking at me like that."

"Like what?"

"Like I'm crazy for caring that he borrowed a dog. That is not a normal thing to do."

"This is New York City. There is no normal, that's why I love it. Do you know what I think? I think you're looking for reasons to push the guy away."

"You're right. That's exactly what I'm doing, but right now he doesn't seem to be listening. When I told him I always end relationships, he smiled. He said he's my perfect date."

"Maybe he is. I like the guy more and more. Sounds like he knocked down every objection you had."

"That's because he's a lawyer! It's his job. I'm not going to do this, Mark. No matter how sexy he is, how charming and persistent, I'm not going to do this. When I go into a relationship, people get hurt. It's like putting a combine harvester in a field of crops and not expecting them to be chopped down."

Mark eyed her. "Even after a sleepless night you don't look anything like a combine harvester. And he doesn't seem to think there's the slightest chance he'll be hurt."

"That's true, but I don't want to take that chance." She

thought about Rupert. "I've broken someone's heart on a global scale. Not a little crack. Not a dent. A big, massive shattering. In public. Not going to happen again."

The memory made her chest tighten and she felt Mark's hands close over her shoulders.

"I understand that what happened with Rupert freaked you out, but Daniel sounds like a guy who knows himself pretty well. What if he's telling the truth?"

"I'm sure he is, but feelings aren't that easy to control."

"You have no trouble controlling yours. What if he is exactly like you? Think of what an incredible relationship you could have."

Molly stared at him. Right now she couldn't think at all. "I—"

"When did you last have fun, Molly? I don't mean fun on your own, I mean fun with a sexy guy. When did you last have sex without worrying about the emotional side of it, when did you last date without worrying that the guy was going to fall in love and you weren't?"

"It's been a while."

"So think about it. All the fun, none of the fallout." Mark stood up, pulled her against him and kissed her cheek. "Get back to work."

"I can't. Today I'm Molly, and Molly doesn't know anything about relationships."

"Then she should ask Aggie. She knows a hell of a lot."

Molly watched as Mark walked to the door. "He probably won't turn up anyway. He'll think better of it."

Mark turned. "Let's wait and see, shall we? He sounds to me like a man who knows exactly what he wants out of life. Promise me one thing—"

"What?"

"If he shows up, you'll open that door."

* * *

Daniel pressed the buzzer, wondering if she'd let him in.

He'd spent the day untangling messy, painful relationships and the thought of spending his evening with a woman who didn't want emotional attachment was the equivalent of a cold beer on a hot day. Molly was fun, sexy and smart. He liked her. The fact that she wasn't going to fall in love with him was music to his ears. Bring it on.

She opened the door almost immediately. She was wearing jeans, but they were her own jeans this time, and her top was blue, not pink. She looked cute. And fierce. Adorable. Heartbreaker. *Hot.*

Insanely hot.

It wasn't a stretch to understand why guys fell hopelessly in love with her.

"Maybe you should hang a sign on your door," he suggested. "*Beware of the Woman.* That would keep the wimps and losers at bay and ensure you're only bothered by serious bad boys who would rather lose money at poker than waste it on a ring. That's me, by the way." He was rewarded by a slight smile and then she noticed the bottle in his hand.

"Champagne? Are we celebrating something I should know about?"

"Valentine's recovery, judges who see sense and our first date."

"You had a good day in court."

"I had a long, but good day in court. And my reward is tonight." He slid his hand behind her head and kissed her briefly. "You're not falling in love with me, are you? No? Good. Just checking." He took advantage of her stunned silence to walk past her into the apartment. "Where will I find glasses?"

She closed the door, but stayed holding the handle as if she hadn't made up her mind about something. "Shouldn't you be celebrating with your colleagues?"

"I'm celebrating with you. I ordered pizza." He'd intentionally kept it casual. No one could be threatened by a large pepperoni pizza.

"Pizza?"

"When we're in the mood for fine dining I'll take you to a restaurant that will make you wonder if you've ever truly tasted food before, but tonight we're eating pizza." He removed his jacket and slung it over the nearest chair, figuring that the more he made himself at home, the less easy it would be for her to throw him out.

Her apartment was small, but she'd used the space well. A book lay open on the window seat, and the desk in the corner of the room was stacked with papers and notes. The New York sunset sent shafts of golden light shimmering across the hardwood floors. There was a door that he assumed led to her bedroom, and another that presumably was a bathroom. A pair of shoes lay discarded in the corner of the room as if she'd kicked them off while thinking about something else.

She'd stamped her identity on every corner of the place. Everything about her life shrieked that she didn't need anything, or anyone.

He intended to show her there were still some things she needed.

"I like your apartment." The place smelled familiar, and it was only after he'd breathed in the citrus, floral scent that made his head spin that he realized the reason the scent was familiar was because it was hers.

It took him right back to that kiss in the park, when he'd been engulfed by it. *By her.*

"You own a penthouse on Fifth Avenue."

"So? I like what you've done with the place. You've made the most of the light." He popped the cork on the champagne and poured it into the glasses she produced, wondering what it was going to take to get her to relax with him. All he saw in her eyes was mistrust. He noticed the laptop open on the little desk and a pair of glasses next to it. "Bad day?"

"Unproductive."

"Finding it hard to concentrate?"

"Something like that."

Interesting, he thought, and decided to probe a little more. "Thinking about Valentine?"

She paused a beat too long. "Yes."

He felt a flash of satisfaction. He was willing to bet she hadn't only been thinking of Valentine. She'd been thinking about him. He'd got her off balance, which was exactly where he wanted her. She thought she knew him, and he intended to prove to her that she didn't.

"What exactly were you doing? Tell me more about your work. Do you consult?"

"Among other things." She hedged and he wondered if her reluctance to talk about her job stemmed from more than a dedication to client confidentiality.

In his job he'd developed a sense for when people were hiding things, and he was sure Molly was hiding a lot.

"Molly." He kept his voice gentle. "Why don't you just tell me what's on your mind, and then we can do away with the simmering atmosphere where I'm trying to guess what you're thinking? Not only am I a guy, which means I'm not good at mind reading, but I've had a long day."

"I didn't think you'd come tonight. Maybe you weren't listening to me."

"I was listening. I heard every word you said, including the part where you told me I absolutely don't want to get involved with you." He put the champagne down on the table. "I've got it. Loud and clear."

"And yet still you're here. With champagne. And pizza."

"That's right. I wasn't sure how long it would take me to convince you this is the right thing to do, and I thought we might need sustenance as I lay siege to you."

"Sun Tzu didn't believe in sieges."

He was impressed. "You looked him up."

"I was trying to understand you. And I don't. I can only assume that you're here because you don't believe me. You think I'm exaggerating."

"I don't think you're exaggerating. And I'm here because I *do* believe you. I like you, Molly. You're sexy as hell and you're not going to fall in love. For me, that's not a problem. In fact it's a prerequisite for a relationship in my book."

"I once hurt a man so badly he told me I'd ruined his life and he'd never recover." The anguish in her eyes tore at him.

He knew that however badly the guy had been hurt, she'd been hurt, too. For different reasons, maybe, but it didn't take much to see that hurting people didn't come naturally to Molly.

"I've never been in love either, Molly. No time. No inclination. You can relax."

Still she looked unhappy. "I'm bad news, Daniel."

"You're the best news I've had in a long time. Think about it—for the first time ever, neither of us needs to worry about being in a relationship because we're both immune. We've been inoculated by life. Now can we stop talking? The pizza will be here in a minute." There was more he wanted to say, more he wanted to know about her, but he told himself that it could wait. Small steps. He turned to put his glass down and noticed the flowers. "Someone bought you flowers? I have a rival for your lack of affection?"

That made her laugh. "Are you jealous?"

"I think I might be. If you're going to be bad, I want you to be exclusively bad with me."

"Don't you think you're moving ahead a little fast?"

"I carried your sick dog and let you stay in my apartment without laying a finger on you. That qualifies as foreplay."

She opened her mouth to say something but then her phone rang. She checked the number. "It's the vet—"

"Take it." He picked up his glass again and while she answered the call, he strolled to her bookshelves.

He'd once dated a woman who had books on her shelves designed to make a statement about her, and an entirely different set of books on her Kindle. He'd been fascinated that she felt she had to hide what she was really reading.

Molly's selection was eclectic. There were a few biographies, cookbooks, a smattering of literature, crime and romance. Nothing that told him much.

One book caught his eye. *Mate for Life.*

Why did that title sound familiar?

He checked the author and saw the name Aggie, and then remembered Marsha talking about her book being a bestseller. Irritation rose inside him. The woman was everywhere. He couldn't get away from her.

Presumably Molly had consulted it when she was trying to find the perfect guy, but why would a psychologist need help from an advice columnist? What could Aggie possibly teach her that she didn't already know?

It was another indication of how desperate Molly must have felt and he didn't understand it.

Who cared that she couldn't fall in love? There were plenty of people who *had* fallen in love who would think she was lucky.

Molly ended the call. "I'm picking up Valentine tomorrow morning."

"That's good." Daniel decided not to embarrass her by mentioning the book. "Is that the door? Sounds like our pizza."

He paid and carried the box to the table.

"It smells good." She pulled out a chair and sat down. "This is why I don't often eat pizza. I find it hard to stop at just one slice."

"So you're a bad girl with self-control issues and a big appetite. The news gets better all the time. This is turning out to be the best first date I've ever had."

"I bet you were the kind of kid who played with knives and climbed trees."

"And fire." He flipped open the box. "Don't forget fire. Mostly caused by my sister who is a terrible cook. I loved doing anything that might risk injury."

"Seems to me that you haven't changed much."

"Is that another subtle warning? You're not going to injure me. So anytime you want to give in to the chemistry, lose control, rip my clothes off and use my body for your own gratification, go right ahead." Pleased to see her smile, he chose a slice of pizza. "So I have a question. And it's personal."

She stopped smiling. "How personal? You want to know if I like olives on my pizza?"

"No. I want to know when you last had sex."

"What?" She gave a shocked laugh. "Did you seriously just ask me that?"

"I seriously did. And the answer is…?"

She reached for a slice of pizza, avoiding his gaze. "Let's just say it's been a while."

"How long is a while?"

"I think I can probably remember how it's done, but it's possible my memory has faded with time." Her cheeks were pink but her eyes were bright with challenge. "Are you scared?"

"I'm carbo-loading as we speak." He took another large slice of pizza. "So why so long? Because the last guy made you feel guilty, you stopped having sex?"

"He didn't 'make' me feel guilty. I produced that emotion by myself."

"Spoken like a psychologist."

"Which I am."

"Which you are, but not falling in love with someone isn't a crime, Molly. People fall in and out of love all the time. I see it every day in my work. It's not something you can control. We all want things in life we can't have. Happens all the time. Jobs we don't get, houses we don't live in, health issues we sure as hell don't want—people we love who don't love us back. Not feeling the way someone wants you to feel doesn't make you a bad person." There was more to it. He could tell from looking at her face. And he knew she wasn't ready to talk about it. "And now you can tell me your other innermost secrets. Like whether you like olives on your pizza."

"I love olives. Did you want a plate or something? You're wearing a suit and you don't strike me as a pizza-out-of-the-box kind of guy."

"I'm wearing a suit because I've been in court, and you're judging again—" He pushed the box toward her.

"My judgments are usually correct. I didn't think you were a dog kind of guy to begin with, and it turned out I was right." She took a slice and bit into it with a moan of pleasure. "This is good."

Daniel stared at the movement of her throat. He never thought watching someone eat pizza could be sexy. "Just because I don't own a dog doesn't mean I'm not a dog kind of guy, but I'm flattered to know you were paying me that much attention."

"It's what I do. Study people." She chewed slowly, savoring every mouthful.

"Admit it, you studied me longer than the average person."

She stopped chewing. "Your ego is bigger than this pizza."

"I feed it well. And I know you were studying me, because I was studying you, too." Daniel glanced at the bookshelves. "You read a lot?"

"Yes. You?"

"Yes. Mostly crime and thrillers."

"Written by your neighbor Lucas Blade. He does get into the mind of his characters. His books are as much about the person as the actual murder."

"He has a psychology background. Next time he and Eva take pity on me and invite me over for a meal, I'll take you with me. He's an interesting guy." He waited for her to protest, but she didn't.

"So what else do you read?"

"Apart from fiction?" He took another slice of pizza. "I read biographies, some history, art catalogs."

"Art catalogs?"

"Catalogs of exhibitions I'm too busy to enjoy in person. There are too many of those. I need to carve out more time."

"You work long hours."

"But I enjoy what I do." He stretched out his legs. "I wouldn't do something I didn't enjoy. How about you? Do you love what you do?"

"Yes." She stood up and cleared up the pizza box. "That was delicious, thank you. Coffee?" She strolled to the kitchen area and he watched as she ground beans and made it fresh.

She poured it into two cups and then turned. He smoothed her hair away from her face and she planted her hand in the middle of his chest.

"You said you weren't going to kiss me."

"That was last night. Tonight all bets are off."

"Sun Tzu?"

"No. Me." And he lowered his mouth to hers. Her body melted into the heat of his, her softness curving around his hardness. He tasted her on his lips, felt her scent tease his senses.

By the time he pulled away he was ready to have sex on a kitchen countertop, something he'd never done in his life before.

She staggered slightly, her hand locked in the front of his shirt. "That was—"

"Yes, it was. Which is why I've decided to leave." He dropped another lingering kiss on her mouth and unpeeled her fingers from his shirt before easing away from her. It was the hardest thing he'd ever done.

"You're leaving?" Her voice sounded husky. "I thought you were carbo-loading."

"I was." He caught her face in his hands and trapped her gaze with his. "But you're still not ready to do this. You're a little wary, a little suspicious and afraid you're going to hurt me. And you're afraid you're going to hurt yourself again, by being forced to reexamine the possible reasons you can't fall in love. But I'm going to make that part easy for you. No woman in her right mind would fall in love with me so don't even waste energy asking yourself that question."

She looked a little dazed, a little vulnerable. "You really are leaving?"

"Yes, because when we have sex, there are going to be no doubts. No holding back."

"So what was the kiss for?" The note of wistful disappointment in her voice almost made him change his mind.

Almost.

He smiled. "It was a taste of things to come."

Twelve

Molly picked up Valentine the following morning and was relieved to see him back to his normal self. He greeted her as if they'd been parted for a century and she wrapped her arms around him, feeling his whole body moving as he wagged his tail.

"Thank you," she muttered to the vet, her face in his fur. "Thank you for everything you did." Her heart was so full she could hardly speak.

If something had happened to Valentine. If she had lost him—

"You're welcome. He's a beautiful dog." Steven gave Valentine a pat and then returned to his surgery.

There was no sign of Seth.

Realizing that Daniel still hadn't told her how he knew him, Molly clipped on Valentine's lead. "From now on I'm not taking my eyes off you for a single second. Anything you're planning on eating, I need to see it first."

She'd had a text from Daniel, inviting her to his apartment for dinner. The fact that he'd also invited Valentine sealed it for her.

"You're invited to dinner. What do you think?" It was a perfect New York day. The rain had given way to perfect blue skies. Sunlight glinted off glass towers and the streets were clogged with traffic and people. "Do you think we should go?"

Valentine wagged his tail enthusiastically.

"Before you make your decision, you should probably know that Brutus won't be there. He doesn't actually live with Daniel. And you'd have to behave. He has a very expensive apartment. Chew anything and you're out."

Valentine gave a single bark.

"Right, then. I'll take that as a yes." She stroked his head. "If we're going out tonight, we'd better go home and get some work done."

* * *

A few blocks away in his office, Daniel had started his day early.

He had the place to himself, which suited him perfectly because having been in court for the previous two days he had a mountain of work.

He glanced out of the window and imagined Molly and Valentine enjoying the park. Maybe he should ask his sisters if they needed him to walk Brutus occasionally. Not that he was particularly attached to the dog, but they were busy. Overstretched. It would be a way of helping.

According to Fliss, two families had come to see the dog. The first had said that he was a lot bigger than they'd thought and decided they didn't want a German shepherd, which Daniel found unfathomable given that they knew the dog's breed before they'd visited. The second had been worried Brutus would be a risk to their two very boisterous children.

Daniel was outraged that anyone would imply Brutus was aggressive. He'd never met a better-natured animal.

Not that he was an expert on dogs, but he'd indulged in some pretty rough play with Brutus when no one was looking and both had emerged without a bruise or a scratch. And he had the funniest face Daniel had ever seen. He'd never thought a dog could look guilty until he'd met Brutus.

If the family hadn't immediately fallen for him, then in his opinion Brutus had had a narrow escape.

The sun rose, people started arriving at the office and by eight o'clock the phones started ringing and Marsha appeared with coffee. "Have you been here all night?"

"Feels that way." The aroma of coffee wove itself into his brain. He reached for it, allowing himself to savor the smell before taking a mouthful. The caffeine delivered a much-needed electric shock to his system. "You're a lifesaver."

"That bad?"

"People keep trying to sell me malpractice insurance. I hope they don't know something I don't. You're hovering. Something wrong?"

"Elisa Sutton is on her way up and this time she has the children with her. She turned up at reception, very upset."

"If she's upset, we should refer her to a therapist. My expertise ends at legal advice. And I'm more expensive than a therapist."

"She trusts you. She knows you're not one of those lawyers who would take advantage and let a client run up a huge bill because they're always on the phone moaning."

"My job is to come up with a winning divorce strategy. That's it."

"Judging from how upset she is, that might be what she's about to ask you to do."

Hearing bawling coming from outside his office, Daniel stood up. "Do we know what has happened?"

"No, but I'm willing to bet Henry hasn't delivered on his promises."

"Now, isn't that a surprise." Daniel walked out of his office into Marsha's. Elisa was jiggling the toddler and Kristy was crying so hard she was almost choking.

Daniel made a rapid assessment and decided to start with the older child.

"Hey, Kristy." He dropped into a crouch in front of the little girl. "What's wrong?"

Kristy sucked in a juddering breath. "Lost—R-Rosie."

"We bought a new doll from the toy shop on Broadway and she dropped it somewhere." Elisa shifted the howling baby onto the other shoulder as she explained. She looked exhausted. "My fault. I was rushing. She probably dropped it on the sidewalk. I don't know. We'll look again when we leave here."

Seeing Kristy's face crumple again, Daniel intervened swiftly. "What does Rosie look like?"

"B-black hair," Kristy hiccuped. "R-red skirt. Why?"

"Because if we're looking for a missing person, we need a name and description. That's how it works." Remembering the time Harriet had lost her favorite doll only to discover their father had tossed it in the trash, Daniel stood up, reached for the phone and hit the button for reception. "This is Daniel Knight. Contact security and tell them we have a missing person. Black hair. Red dress. Name of Rosie. She's a doll… Yes, that's right, you heard me correctly. Have them send someone to take a look outside the building… Yes, it's a priority." He put the phone down and turned back in time to see Marsha hide a smile. "Kristy, I have my best team dealing with it. We're sending out a search party."

Kristy stopped sobbing and stared at him, wide-eyed with wonder.

Elisa's eyes filled. "That's kind of you. I'm sorry to show up like this without calling you, but—"

"Let's take this into my office." Realizing that if he didn't deal with this quickly there would be more crying, he held out his hand to Kristy. "I have something to show you." Daniel led her toward a cupboard at the far end of Marsha's office. "Marsha keeps a secret box in here. But she only shows it to very special people."

Kristy studied the cupboard. "What's in the secret box?"

"I don't know. I'm not special enough, so she won't show me. You'll have to ask Marsha."

Marsha picked up the cue. "Shall we take a look together?"

While Kristy opened the door and peered inside, Daniel turned to Marsha and spoke in a low voice. "If they don't find the doll, call the store and have them send another one over."

She nodded, and Daniel reflected that one of the many reasons he loved working with Marsha was that nothing threw her. Leaving the problem in her capable hands, he walked into his office and left the door slightly ajar. "Kristy will be fine with Marsha."

"You're brilliant." Elisa blew her nose. "There are days when I wish I was married to you. You're better with my kids than Henry."

Daniel kept his expression neutral. "If you need to talk to a therapist, Elisa, then Marsha can—"

"It's not that. I know you're not here to listen to my problems, but sometimes it's not so easy to detach the emotional stuff from the practical stuff. I don't know what to do, Mr. Knight. He yelled at Kristy this morning. That's why I bought her the doll. I can't believe I'm turning into that person who thinks buying stuff compensates for bad parenting." Her eyes filled again and she took a deep breath. "I know it's a lot to ask, but could you hold Oliver while I go to the bathroom? I've been trying to stay calm because when I'm tense it makes his asthma worse—"

Daniel took the wriggling toddler and held him firmly. The child grabbed a handful of his hair and stared at him, intrigued.

Elisa's tears spilled over. "You see? He'd rather be with you, a stranger, than with me. He knows I'm tense. I'm a terrible mother."

"You're a great mother." Daniel spoke gently. "Sit down." He handed her the box of tissues and she took a handful and plopped down as if she was too tired to do anything else.

"Sorry. Henry keeps telling me I should pull myself together."

Daniel refrained from voicing his opinion on Henry. "You have two young children. Even without marital tension, that's enough to put pressure on you."

Elisa blew her nose hard. "I'm trying to do what's best for them, but I don't even know what that is anymore. One minute I think they'd be better off growing up in a two-parent family, but then Henry snaps at Kristy and Oliver's asthma is getting worse daily, as are his tantrums. Henry takes it personally, and he accuses me of poisoning the kids against him." Taking a deep breath, she stood up. "Right. I'm pulling myself together right now. Back in a moment." She left the room and Marsha popped her head around the door, her eyebrows lifting as she saw Daniel pointing out various New York landmarks to a fascinated Oliver.

"Do you want me to take him? At least turn him the other way. He might freak when he sees the crowds in Times Square."

"Good point." Daniel shifted so that the toddler could see the Empire State Building. His eyes widened with wonder and he stretched out a chubby finger to the glass. Daniel smiled. "He's pretty cute."

Marsha leaned against the door. "Keep your voice down. If all those people who call you the Dark Knight and the Rottweiler could see you now, you'd be in trouble."

"Then it's a good thing they can't. And just so we're clear, if this little guy deposits body fluids of any kind on my suit we'll be charging double."

She folded her arms and tilted her head to one side. "You know, Daniel, the tough-guy act doesn't quite work when you're cuddling a toddler. I had no idea you were so good with children."

"I had two little sisters. Plenty of practice."

When Elisa came back she'd brushed her hair and applied more lipstick. She took the little boy back and Daniel settled himself on the edge of his desk.

"What happened?"

"Two days." Elisa settled Oliver on her lap. "That was how long he lasted. He moved back in and then I caught him calling her two days later. Can you believe that? When he said we should get back together, I thought he meant it. I thought he was committed to doing this for the children, but it was all lies. Apparently I'm the one supposed to make sacrifices for the children, but not him. I can't live like this

but he tells me it will be bad for the kids if we split up."
Elisa's eyes filled again. "Aggie said—"

"What do *you* think? Not Henry and not Aggie," Daniel
kept his tone neutral, but he was starting to think that if he
heard that name again he'd break something.

"Honestly? I think it sounds like a life sentence. Not because I don't love him, but because I do. Can you imagine how it would feel to spend your life with someone who
doesn't feel the same way about you as you do about them?"

Daniel was careful to listen and remain neutral.

Molly might think that not falling in love was a problem,
but from where he was sitting falling in love with the wrong
person didn't look so great either.

Elisa sniffed. "I don't want to be with someone who
doesn't love me. But he told me if I leave, he'll stop me
from seeing the kids."

Daniel felt a pressure in his chest.

In his head he heard another voice, another time. Another
woman sobbing.

*If I leave, he'll take the three of you. He told me he'd make
sure I never see you again. It's hard, but I have to stay. I
won't lose my babies.*

"Mr. Knight?" Elisa's voice cut through the memories,
tentative. Unsure. "That's why I'm here. I know you told
me only to come to you for the legal stuff, but now I'm really scared that if I go through with the divorce he will stop
me from seeing my kids. He said if I want to keep the kids,
I have to stay."

Daniel hauled himself back into the present.

He hadn't been able to help his mother, but he could help
his client, just as he'd helped countless others. "He's not
going to stop you from seeing the kids, Elisa. New York cus-

tody laws protect the best interests of the child. And judges take a dim view of parents who use their child as a weapon or a bargaining chip."

"Are you sure? He's so convincing—you probably don't believe me…"

"I believe you." Daniel had witnessed something similar firsthand. Witnessed his father's threats and seen his mother cowed and intimidated, too afraid to fight back.

"Elisa, look at me—do you trust me?"

She looked and nodded, her eyes swimming with tears.

"Good." He handed her another tissue. "Have you been keeping that written record we discussed? Doctor's appointments for Oliver? Parent-teacher conferences for Kristy? You remember everything we talked about?"

She nodded again.

"So this is what we're going to do." He talked to her for an hour, devised a strategy and then left his office to find Kristy and Marsha playing with a doll.

Kristy beamed at him. "The search party *found* her."

"That's great." Daniel looked at that smile and wondered how much of her childhood this girl would take with her into adulthood. Would she be wary of relationships? Would she take the risk or decide to stay single?

Maybe she'd become a divorce lawyer.

Whatever the future held for her and Oliver, he was going to make damn sure this family didn't go through the same hell his had.

* * *

Molly had chosen her outfit carefully. She didn't want to seem overdressed, but still the occasion warranted more than a pair of jeans. After a few false starts, she had settled for a stretchy dress in a rich shade of blue that made her feel sexy. She took advantage of the ride in Daniel's elevator to change into heels and replenish her lip gloss. And as for what was under the dress—she gave a small smile—that was for her to know and him to discover.

Valentine wagged his tail approvingly.

"You're going to have to look the other way," she murmured. "You're definitely too young to witness what's going to happen tonight."

And she'd made up her mind that it would happen. She'd subdued the part of her that thought this was a bad idea. It had been a long time since she'd even been tempted to do something like this, which made it both nerve-racking and exhilarating.

As he opened the door, her heart kicked up a notch.

His gaze held hers for a moment and then moved lower, lingering on her mouth before sliding down her body to her heels. He didn't touch her, and yet it felt as if he had. Her skin tingled and her tummy did a gymnastic flip.

The moment was threaded through with a delicious tension, the atmosphere electric. She had a sense that he was going to reach for her right there and then in the hallway, but Valentine decided he wasn't getting enough attention and pawed his legs by way of a hint. Daniel transferred his attention from Molly to her dog. It could have been a moment of respite but her body and brain refused to take it. Instead she found herself looking down on his wide shoulders, at the powerful jut of his thigh and the gentleness of his hands and imagining what lay ahead. His kiss had been all things. Gentle and decisive, demanding and intimate. It was impossible not to imagine the next step.

He rose, held her gaze again for a protracted moment and then gestured inside his apartment without speaking.

She was well acquainted with body language and nonverbal cues, but she was sure that never before had so much been said by two people who hadn't even opened their mouths.

She followed him into the kitchen, her eyes fixed on his shoulders, her heels tapping on his floor. She wondered whether she should remove her shoes, but when she paused and reached down he turned and caught her arm.

"Don't." Just that one word, and a look that offered up a thousand more.

She could feel his tension. It was in his shoulders, the set of his mouth and the way he clattered around the kitchen.

He'd changed into jeans and a shirt, but his hair was still damp around the edges, suggesting he hadn't long left the shower.

"I hope you eat steak. It's one of the few things I can cook." His words added a touch of normality, and a brake on her imagination that was sweeping her away on a dizzying ride.

"I love steak." She put her bag down. She didn't tell him she felt so nervous she wasn't sure she could eat. She hadn't been involved with anyone in such a long time and it was impossible not to think about how it had ended the last time. She pushed that thought away. If she thought Daniel was anything like Rupert, she wouldn't be here. "How was your day?"

She could do this. She could conduct a normal conversation, or at least behave as if every thought in her head wasn't jumping forward to the point where they were both naked.

"Let's just say it became a whole lot better when you showed up at my door." He opened the fridge. "You?"

"I-it was fine." Maybe she couldn't do this. She was starting to doubt her ability to speak normally, or focus on anything except the way she was feeling.

She was standing right behind him and she could see the way his shirt pulled across his shoulders and biceps as he braced his arm on the side of the fridge.

She felt the punch of cold air and wondered if there was some way she could fit her whole self inside.

"Wine or beer?" He spoke without turning his head and she closed her eyes.

"Beer." Her mouth was dry. Her heart was pounding. "No, wait. Wine. I—I'll have wine."

His hand closed around a bottle and he turned.

His eyes gleamed, steel and slate, and then with no warning he cupped her head with his free hand and brought her mouth to his. She fell against him, dizzy, and he stepped backward. There was the sound of rattling, glass against glass. Something smashed. All she felt was the searing punch of heat, the stab of desire. Nothing existed but the moment. Everything else was forgotten. His day, her day, the past, the future, all of it vanished as their world centered on the moment.

His kiss was deep and explicit and her response was instant and equal. She kissed him back, sliding her arms around his neck and lifting herself on her toes. She felt his arms come around her and pull her in, felt the hard strength of his body locked against hers as he hauled her close.

Without lifting his head, he pushed her back a few steps and kicked the fridge closed with his foot. His mouth was skilled, demanding, and she melted under the scorching heat of his kiss, the rush of sensation overpowering her. They tore at each other's clothes in an intimate collusion, ripping fabric and popping buttons until he was naked and she was standing only in her high heels. They'd planned nothing, and yet it felt planned, as if they already knew the moves, as if this was something they'd experienced a thousand times before. It was unfamiliar and yet familiar, and as he explored her with lips and hands he spoke only three words. *I want you.* And those words were said with such raw savagery that for a moment she felt her own power and reveled in it. And then she felt the warmth and strength of his hand on her back and the urgency of his mouth on her skin, and realized that he held an equal amount of power. She'd never felt this way before, the sexual energy, the desperation, the *need*. There was no question of making it to the bedroom. No question of pausing. She felt dizzy, unbalanced, and closed her hands over his shoulders, feeling the hard swell of muscle under her fingers.

She felt his hand lock in her hair, felt his mouth scald her skin and lock over the tip of her breast. The flick of his tongue made her cry out and he teased and tormented, using his hand and mouth to explore what turned her on until she was a seething mass of desperation. She could no longer think, only feel. As she closed her hand around the solid thickness of him, she heard him groan and felt him harden in her hand. Then he was powering her back to the sofa, although she had no recollection of moving from the kitchen to the living room. For a moment she was weightless, and she realized dimly that he'd lifted her, lowered her, and then she felt the solid weight of him, trapping her, caging her. Excitement streaked through her and she wrapped her thighs around him, arching in an agony of anticipation. She wanted him now, right now, but just when she needed him to speed up, he slowed down. She couldn't make sense of it, couldn't think. Her senses were swamped. She pressed her mouth to his shoulder, tried to speak, but then she felt him move down her body and felt the heat of his breath and the slick stroke of his tongue against sensitive flesh.

He savored, tortured, delayed, unmerciful in his determination to drive her to the highest peak of pleasure until she was sobbing and writhing under him. When he slid his fingers deep she came in a series of intense spasms that racked her whole body.

He eased himself up her body and gathered her against the warmth of his chest. She felt shell-shocked. In her pleasure-filled stupor she realized she'd never given herself so fully before this moment. She'd always held part of herself back. But this felt different. And it felt different because for the first time ever she wasn't worrying about where this might lead or what came next. Nothing came next. There was just this moment. Now.

Liberated by that knowledge, she rolled him onto his back and lay across him, looking down into his eyes, relieved to see nothing there that worried her.

His eyes were hooded, his mouth curved into a satisfied smile. "Sorry. Did you say wine or beer? I might have been a little distracted."

"I don't remember. I was a little distracted, too." She lowered her head and traced the roughness of his jaw with her lips.

"I was going to cook you steak."

"Don't say that word in front of Valentine." She glanced at the dog, but he was dozing on the opposite side of the living room. "He's made himself at home. I think he approves of you."

"That's good to know." He groaned as she slid her hand

slowly over the taut, flat planes of his abdomen and lingered. "We should go upstairs while I can still walk."

"Do we have to?"

"We'll be more comfortable."

She wouldn't have cared where she was, as long as he was there with her. "If you want comfort, I should remove my shoes."

"Keep them on." He cupped the back of her head in his hand and drew her mouth down to his, his message clear. This was a pause, not a halt.

She had no idea how they made it to his bedroom, but they did and he kicked the door shut and tumbled her down on the bed, ravishing her mouth, his hands skimming over her in intimate exploration until she was trembling and dizzy. She felt it all, every touch, every breath, every sensuous flick of his tongue, and finally, when she could stand it no more, she rolled on top of him. His eyes seemed darker, and he lifted his hands and framed her face in a possessive gesture, drawing her down for his kiss. It was as if he couldn't not touch her, and she understood because she felt the same urgent need. Her hair fell forward, sliding over his hands, enclosing them both in a place where the outside world couldn't intrude. For a while they stayed like that, kissing hungrily, holding nothing back, and then he speared the soft silken strands with his fingers and drew it back from her face before rolling her onto her back with intent and purpose.

Desire engulfed her, heated and sharp. She was dimly aware of him reaching for something from the nightstand and then she was aware of nothing but her body and his body, and the way he made her feel. She wrapped her legs around him and he entered her in a single silken thrust that drew a sob from her throat. She dug her nails hard into his shoulders, felt the hard bunching of muscle as he held himself back and forced himself to slow the pace. But she needed the pace. She needed it as much as he did. She moved her hips, arching into him, and then there was nothing but the pleasure, the slick, skilled rhythm that matched the hunger in both of them. She needed all of it, *all of him*. She held nothing back. Neither did he. It bordered on wild. Uninhibited, intimate and unrestrained, they didn't slow down or pause until release thundered down on both of them. They came together, the intensity of it blinding, and afterward they lay in breathless silence, limbs and bodies still intimately entwined. She felt the pressure of his hand, strong and protective as he held her, and of the slide of his hair-roughened thigh against the smooth silk of hers.

Keeping her entwined with him, he rolled onto his back. "How long did you say it had been since you had sex?"

"I might have been a little desperate." She kept her head on his chest, waiting for her heart rate to steady. What they'd shared had been unlike anything she'd ever experienced before. Because their relationship was simple, she thought. Yes, that had to be the reason. She wasn't worrying about what might happen next because nothing was going to happen next. Except maybe more sex. "You have an impressive amount of stamina. I hope I haven't exhausted you."

"Not a problem. I'm sure I'll recover in a month or so, although I might need extra nutrients." The light humor kept the moment from tipping into anything more serious. "Maybe I should cook dinner now."

"You might have to do it on your own. I'm not sure I can move."

"I'm not sure I can either. That was a perfect end to a hell of a day."

"You had a hell of a day?" Concerned, she raised herself on her elbow so that she could look at him. "Tell me."

"I can't even remember now. I think you might have fused my brain." His eyes were closed and she stroked her hand over his chest, tracing the line of hair that led lower.

"Do you want a beer? Wine?"

He opened his eyes. "It might not be cold. Did we close the fridge door?"

"I have no idea. But I do remember something breaking."

"I think that might have been my self-control, but just in case it wasn't we'd better not walk around in bare feet." He sat up, delivered a lingering kiss to her mouth and sprang from the bed. "Don't move. I'll grab us drinks."

"Or we could take the drinks onto your terrace."

He hauled on jeans without bothering to button them. "You want to have sex in public and risk falling off my balcony?"

"I was thinking more of having wine and conversation."

"Conversation. I can probably do that. As long as you stay on one side of the terrace and I stay on the other." He threw her a shirt. "Put that on."

"I have a dress somewhere."

"Your dress is what got us to this point. If you put it back on I'll be taking it off you again in under four seconds. Your only chance of wine and conversation is if you wear a shapeless shirt. And even then there are no guarantees. I suggest you button it up to the neck."

She felt giddy, happy and ridiculously flattered, but she did as he suggested, pulling on one of his shirts. It fell to midthigh and flopped past her fingers so she rolled back the sleeves.

Because she had nothing else to wear on her feet and

she'd definitely heard the sound of breaking glass, she slid her feet back into her high heels.

As she walked downstairs she could hear him cursing.

"You're right. We did break something. Don't come in here. I'll clear up and bring the wine onto the terrace. That's if I can find a bottle we didn't break."

Molly checked on Valentine and then wandered outside, feeling the air cool her skin.

The roof terrace wrapped itself around two sides of the apartment. Up here they were insulated from the bustle and the street noise, the craziness of New York City. Far beneath her she imagined people strolling along Fifth Avenue, pausing to gaze in shop windows, jostling the crowds. Friends, lovers, strangers, all crammed together in the small area that was Manhattan. She heard the shriek of a siren, the muted blare of car horns. No one bothered to look up as they hurried about their business. Coming home from work, going out to dinner, walking on air, walking off a temper. Everyone had a different reason for being there. It fascinated her to think of all those separate lives. People passing each other, but never meeting, oblivious to the highs and lows of each other's lives.

She stood for a moment, content, and then turned as she heard him behind her. "I've lived in this city for three years and there is still a point in almost every day when it takes my breath away. The view from your apartment is incredible."

"It was the roof terrace that sold me on the apartment. That and the fact that the craziness is far beneath you." He was holding a bottle of wine and two glasses. "Sometimes, after a bad day, I sit out here."

"And today was one of those days?"

"It started out that way." He poured the wine and handed her a glass. "But it ended well."

"Do you want to talk about it?"

"Definitely not." He leaned his forearms on the balcony railing and stared over the park. "I'm the guy who has full control over his emotions. I don't need to talk about anything."

She stared at his profile, waiting, and eventually he turned his head to look at her again.

"What?" He sighed. "Okay, I'm lying. Generally I am that guy who has full control over his emotions. When I'm working, I'm the lawyer. I'm there to do the best for my client. Nothing else comes into it. I pride myself on my professional objectivity. I'm as neutral as Switzerland."

"But?"

He breathed deeply and ran his hand over his face. "Undone by a little girl and her doll." He muttered the words so she wasn't sure she'd heard him correctly.

"Excuse me?"

"Lately it's been harder for me. My personal experience is coloring my professional life. It's creeping in, so that mostly I don't notice. Then I'll react differently than usual. A little more extreme. A little less detached."

"And that's usually when you're dealing with cases involving children?"

"I've spent my career dealing with cases involving children. I don't know why this is happening now."

She was silent for a moment. "Sometimes something happens in the present that makes us think about the past. For example, if you were dealing with a case that mirrored your own childhood experience, that might make it harder than usual to stay detached. Because whether you like it or not, you're bringing your personal experience, and feelings, to the situation."

"Yeah, that makes sense." His voice was husky. "I'm particularly sensitive to cases where child custody is used as a threat."

"You mean when one party threatens to deny the other access in order to manipulate the marital situation?"

"Yes. And I worry about the damage that witnessing conflict does to a child."

Molly took a sip of her wine, marveling at how comfortable she felt with him. "Conflict in a relationship isn't necessarily bad. What's more important is the way the conflict is played out and resolved. When kids witness their parents fighting, but then resolving the fight, it reassures them. That's not disturbing in the way that other marital conflicts might be."

He frowned. "Such as?"

"For example where one parent just gives in. That isn't resolution, that's avoidance."

"Wait—" he lifted his hand "—you're saying screaming rows can be good?"

"Obviously it's better if there isn't *screaming*, because screaming doesn't exactly create a calm and positive environment for children and it can be scary, but if the argument is heated and leads to a clear resolution that the child can see, then yes, it would be widely recognized that it might not be so damaging. If one parents screams at another and the response is that the other parent walks out and doesn't come home for three days, and then there is no discussion, or resolution, that's likely to be more harmful."

"Because they don't see it resolved." He listened attentively. "They get all the tension, but never see it fixed."

"That's right. If one parent continually capitulates and the atmosphere is fraught with unspoken resentment, that's more harmful than an explosion that clears the air and ends in a resolution. A child doesn't understand what's happening. There's uncertainty, fear, insecurity."

"So it's all about resolution." He put his wineglass down. "I never thought of it that way."

"Seeing parents argue is a lesson for life. We experience conflict all the time. Not just with partners, but with friends and in the workplace. Learning how to handle conflict is a life skill, and it's a life skill that's ideally learned in the home, in a safe forgiving environment. Good parents will show their children how to resolve conflict in a positive, healthy way where both sides feel heard. That way the child goes out into the world and they resolve conflict the same way. It's self-perpetuating."

"So what's your view when a couple aren't good at resolving conflict in a healthy way? You're saying their child grows up unable to solve conflict?"

"It's not quite as simple and linear as that, but yes, that's always a possible outcome. Maybe they're afraid of expressing an opposite point of view in case the other person becomes upset. If they've seen a parent never argue back, but bottle up resentment, that may be the only way they know to deal with conflict. They walk away instead of dealing with it in a calm, mature fashion."

"Or maybe they go the opposite way and they're the aggressor."

Was he thinking about his father? "That, too. But sometimes what they don't learn from parents they can learn from other people around them. Siblings. Schoolmates. So it isn't necessarily cause and effect."

He let out a long breath. "You know a hell of a lot."

"It's my job. I'm sure you know a hell of a lot about yours."

"So do you deal with this sort of stuff on a daily basis?"

"To a degree. I'm not as deeply involved as you are. I skim the surface. I've written blogs on handling conflict within a marriage." She almost mentioned her new book, and then realized that would steer the conversation to a place she wasn't ready to go. Not yet. It was too soon. The relationship was too new and that was a part of her life she wasn't ready to share. "It's an important issue. You can't spend the rest of your life with someone who doesn't listen to you, who tramples over your views and your hopes."

"That was what happened to my mother. My father was a control freak with anger management problems. It took very little to set him off. If my mother disagreed with him, he'd explode. If she tried to voice a view he didn't share, the outcome was the same. If she wore something he didn't like, smiled in a way that annoyed him—" He broke off, staring at the glass in his hand. "What you said just now—I hadn't thought of it that way. That conflict in the home can be good for a child. I think I'm naturally wary about advocating to keep children in what I see as a destructive family environment."

"Don't misunderstand me. I'm sure there are plenty of times when a child would be better off if the parents divorced. But simply witnessing conflict isn't necessarily one of them." She watched him. "I gather your parents weren't good at conflict resolution."

"Does throwing plates at the wall count?"

She felt a stab of sympathy. "I suppose it's one way to go about it. That must have been pretty scary to witness."

"It was. My father had a terrible temper. My mother was

terrified of him. Everything she did, the way she lived her life, was designed to soothe him and keep him calm. 'Don't annoy your father' were the words we heard most growing up. My mother was the woman you described—the one who walks away and closes the door. I used to hear her crying through the bedroom door."

She put her hand on his arm, feeling the hard muscle through the soft fabric of his shirt.

"I don't know how you coped."

"I was too occupied protecting the twins to think much about myself. It was never physical, but verbal can do as much damage. Fliss fought back, which wasn't great either. But Harriet—" He frowned and shook his head. "He only had to raise his voice for her to be paralyzed by fear. She had a severe stammer as a child. It drove him insane. The more he yelled, the more she stammered. There was an incident at school…" He hesitated. "She had to recite a poem. Fliss and I had helped her practice. Over and over again. Not a single stammer. She was so excited and proud. Then she got up onstage and saw our father in the back row. He never showed up to school events. I swear he only did it that night because he knew how important it was to her to recite that poem perfectly."

Molly felt a rush of cold horror, only too able to imagine what had happened. "She saw him and couldn't get a word out."

"Yes, and that single cruel act undid all the hard work that Harriet had put in. Fliss was so angry she flew at him with a skillet."

Molly was appalled. "How old were you?"

"I don't know. Sixteen? The twins would have been around eleven. Occasionally life was fairly normal. We used to spend every summer with our grandmother in the Hamptons while my father was working in the city. She owns a house right on the ocean. It's spectacular. She's been offered a small fortune for the land by developers but she won't sell. So there's my grandmother in her modest beach house, surrounded by mansions. Apart from the few occasions he visited, those were our happiest times. Mom told me later that she used to dream of us living like that, just the four of us, by the beach."

"So you became a lawyer so you could make that happen for other people. What happened to your father?"

"He had his first heart attack five years ago. The second one a year after that. It mellowed him a little, but only because he's afraid. He's spent his life driving people away, alienating them, and now he's discovered that he's alone."

"You see him?"

"He won't see me because he blames me for the fact that Mom eventually divorced him. Which suits me fine." He leaned on the railing, watching as darkness spread across Central Park. "He won't see Fliss either."

"And Harriet?"

"Harriet sees him occasionally, but it stresses her. In a way she suffered more than any of us. Even now, if she's upset, her stammer sometimes reappears. It's one of the reasons she works with animals and not people."

"And your mother?"

His expression softened. "After the divorce she finally rebuilt her life. It was a bit like a child learning to walk. Small steps. A thrill of achievement and the realization that taking steps leads to places. It was wonderful to watch. She trained as a nurse and then last year she decided she wanted to see the world. She's currently in South America with three friends she met at a support group she attended."

"That's a nice story."

"Yes. She finally has the life she's always wanted." He took a deep breath and drained his glass. "And I've just told you a ton of stuff I've never told anyone in my life before. That must be what happens when you hang around long enough to have a conversation after sex."

She smiled. "Maybe. Or maybe it's what happens when you trust someone." If anything the conversation had deepened the intimacy, rather than lessened it.

Daniel turned to look at her, a strange expression in his eyes. "Maybe it is." He brushed his hand over her cheek, his fingers lingering on her jaw. "You look good in my shirt. How can you look good in my shirt?"

His touch made her pulse quicken. "It's the light," she said. "It's very forgiving."

"I just realized I still haven't cooked you that steak."

"I'm not hungry."

"Tomorrow. We'll try this whole thing again." He lowered his head. "I'll buy you dinner. We'll go out. That way I can't rip your clothes off. And we'll talk about you, not me."

"I'm busy tomorrow."

"You're prioritizing a spin class over sex?"

"It's not a spin class."

"Cooking class? Salsa? I don't even know what day it is—"

"It's a work thing." A work thing that right now, with his eyes on hers, she was tempted to cancel, but she knew she couldn't. It was too important.

"What time does it end? Come here afterward." As his hand slid under the hem of the shirt, she felt herself weaken.

"I'm free the night after."

"Good." The words were muffled as he trailed his mouth down her neck. "That will give me time to clear up the rest of the glass."

Thirteen

"The father didn't exercise his parenting time on any weekend in the first three months of this year, and his behavior isn't consistent with—" Daniel paused as Marsha walked into the room and then returned to his phone call. "Yeah, that's right. That's what I'm saying… He missed two parent-teacher conferences so I don't think so, but let's talk later." He put the phone down. "You're wearing your serious face, but I can tell you nothing is going to stress me today."

He'd had the best night of his life. And it hadn't just been the sex, although he'd been thinking about that for most of the morning. It was more than that. The way she'd listened. The way they'd talked. He would have expected to feel a little uncomfortable about all the things he'd told her, but for some reason he didn't. He could have talked to Molly all night. He could have had sex with her all night, too. In fact he had, for most of it. The only thing they hadn't done was eaten, but he was going to fix that. He was going to take her to dinner somewhere special tomorrow. Somewhere romantic.

He sat back and smiled at Marsha expectantly. "Well? How do you intend to burst my happy bubble today? As long as you're not about to tell me you're leaving me, everything is good."

Marsha's expression told him that everything was far from good. "What did you do last night?"

It was unlike her not to get straight to the point, but Daniel played along. "I had a date with Molly. You?"

"Dinner with my girls." She put coffee on his desk. "Molly is the girl you met downstairs? With the gorgeous dog?"

"Yes, she's the one. You'd like her. She's smart, funny and a great listener." *And phenomenal in bed*, he thought, not to mention sexy. One minute she was an athlete with her cute ponytail swinging across her back as she ran, the next she was rocking a dress and sky-high heels. Remembering made his whole body heat. He had a feeling there had been lace underwear, too, but he'd been in too much of a hurry to get her naked to pay attention. Next time, he was going to pay attention. It was more than a little annoying that "next time" wasn't going to be tonight. He, who had previously not had the time or the inclination to date on consecutive nights, was feeling mildly irritated that she already had plans.

He forced himself to focus on work. "What was it you wanted to talk to me about?"

"You wanted Max to find out the identity of 'Aggie.'"

"Judging from your expression, I'm not going to like what I hear."

"I think she does good work. I don't approve of your mission to unmask her and take her to task."

"Aren't you being a little dramatic?"

She gave him a long look. "Once you find out who she is, you're going to wish you'd never asked."

"So she is a person? I was starting to think Aggie might be a call center with a hundred people dishing out random advice based on something written by a computer. I'm glad to hear there is at least someone I can connect with and she's human."

"She's definitely human."

"Great." He held out his hand for the file and Marsha hesitated.

"Sometimes it doesn't pay to ask too many questions. We might find out things we would rather have not known."

"Another topic on which we disagree. I prefer to ask as many questions as possible. Then I can make an informed decision." He kept his hand outstretched and she handed the file over reluctantly.

"Aggie is the pen name of Dr. Kathleen Parker." She said the name slowly, with emphasis, waiting for a reaction from him.

He glanced from her to the file, wondering what he was missing. "Doctor? Doctor of what? Deception? Bullshit?"

"Dr. Parker, Dr. Kathleen *Molly* Parker, is a behavioral psychologist."

Daniel looked up. The blood pounded in his ears. "Did you say Molly?"

"That's right."

"My Molly?"

"I don't think she's going to be yours for much longer when she finds out you did a background check on her. Or maybe you already told her."

"I didn't do a background check on her. I did a background check on Aggie, although technically it was Max who did it."

"Turns out Molly and Aggie are one and the same person. Aggie is her pseudonym."

"It has to be a mistake." Daniel stood up and paced to the window, his brain racing. No, it couldn't be possible. She would have mentioned it. After everything they'd shared, she would have mentioned it. Wouldn't she?

He thought about the times she'd changed the subject when he'd asked about her work. The times he'd probed for a little more information and got nothing back.

She'd told him she was a psychologist but she had never given him specifics.

He kept his back to the room. "Tell me."

"It's in the file. Or I could call Max and he could—"

"I want you to tell me." Although part of him didn't want to hear it. For the first time in his life he was enjoying a relationship with a woman, and now it turned out she wasn't who she said she was.

He could respect her desire to protect patient confidentiality, but he knew that wasn't what was going on here. The issue was that she didn't trust him. He'd trusted her with personal information about himself, about his past, that he'd never shared with anyone before but she hadn't been willing to return the gesture.

He didn't turn, just listened as Marsha read from the report.

"She has a postgraduate degree from Oxford. Her blog, *Ask a Girl*, currently has 8 million hits a week—" She broke off as Daniel uttered an expletive. "Yes, she's popular. Her first book, *Mate for Life*, sold over half a million copies in the first two weeks of sale, and her second book—"

"Wait—" He dragged his hand through his hair. That was

why she had a copy of the book in her apartment. She hadn't bought it for advice. She'd written the damn thing.

Slowly, his image of her changed shape.

Do you deal with relationships in your work?

Yes.

He turned to find Marsha was watching him as she might watch an escaped tiger, unsure whether to say more.

Daniel clenched his jaw. "Go on."

"She's just signed another book deal with Phoenix Publishing, but the details haven't been announced yet."

"Phoenix? They're the people who wanted me to write a book on surviving divorce?"

"That's right. Do you want to know the rest?"

"No." He'd already heard more than enough. What he needed now was a conversation with "Aggie." Or Molly. Or whoever the hell she really was.

How could they be one and the same person? One of them he wanted to have sex with, and the other he wanted to strangle with his bare hands.

He'd thought Aggie was an ignorant charlatan, and in fact she was a smart, professional woman.

The coffee Marsha had brought in earlier sat untouched and forgotten on his desk.

Why wouldn't she mention that she worked as an advice columnist? Why so secretive? It didn't make sense. He was confused, and underneath the confusion was outrage. She'd accused him of deception, but her deception was greater than his. All he'd done was borrow a dog. She was concealing an entire identity.

Marsha was still watching him. "Are you angry for professional reasons or personal reasons?"

He thought of Molly naked, laughing down at him. Then

he remembered the way she'd listened to him that night on the balcony.

She had a way of encouraging people to talk, without doing any talking herself.

"Professional." He spoke through his teeth. "It's professional. Wasn't I invited to a party at Phoenix Publishing?"

"Cocktails at the Met tonight. You told me to make your excuses."

"Un-excuse me. I'm going."

"To discuss the project they had in mind? Because if you're going to make an embarrassing scene, I don't want to be part of that. I like Aggie. Her book is brilliant, and—"

"Her name is Molly. Call Phoenix. Invited or not, I'm going. And tell Max to delete this particular project from his memory. I don't want it mentioned again."

Marsha looked upset. "I hate to see you hurt."

"Hurt?" He barely recognized his own voice. "I'm not hurt."

"But I thought you and she—"

"What? I don't do relationships, you know that. Molly and I had fun, but we're not emotionally attached."

"Are you sure? Because I wondered if possibly, perhaps—" Marsha licked her lips and he scowled at her.

"What?"

"These last few weeks, you seem different. I thought, I wondered, if maybe you're starting to care about her."

Daniel stopped dead, genuinely astonished. "What are you suggesting?"

"Nothing," Marsha said hastily. "It's just that you seem very upset, that's all."

"You're right, I'm upset. And I'm upset because I don't like being lied to." It was obvious, wasn't it? He couldn't understand why she'd think it could be anything more. And of course he cared about Molly, but not in any deep or meaningful way. He'd meant what he said about not falling in love with her. He had no concerns about that. Their relationship was perfect.

Except that apparently it wasn't perfect enough for her to trust him.

* * *

The roof terrace of the Metropolitan Museum of Art offered a perfect view of Central Park and the skyscrapers of midtown Manhattan. Tower blocks rose behind treetops, as if the city was determined to remind the awestruck spectator exactly who was the star of the show.

And who could forget?

Smiling, Molly took a glass of champagne. She probably didn't need the drink. She already felt as if she'd downed an entire bottle of champagne without pausing for breath. She'd sailed through the day on a cloud of happiness, dizzy with excitement. Part of her wished she had made her excuses this evening so that she could have seen Daniel instead. If she'd done that, they'd be in bed now.

She surreptitiously drew her phone out of her purse, but there was no message. Maybe he was still deciding where to take her to dinner tomorrow. She probably should have told him that she'd be happy to eat a bowl of corn chips in his bed.

Lost in a dream, she moved to the edge of the terrace, taking the weight off her feet one at a time. Why did shoes that felt comfortable when you put them on turn into torture devices after a few hours of wearing them? It was one of life's mysteries.

She gazed down at the park. She ran there every day, but she never saw it from this angle. Through the canopy of trees she could see paths winding their way lazily through wooded glades, framed by buildings beyond.

She rose on her toes, trying to pick out the spot where she'd first met Daniel. She couldn't stop thinking about him. For her, sex had always been part of a relationship. That in itself had been enough to hold her back. Only now was she realizing that she'd rationed her responses. She'd never had sex that was so uninhibited, so *real*. It had been crazy, electrifying and so exhilarating that she wasn't sure how she was going to get through a whole twenty-four hours until she saw him again.

She stood staring at the view, listening to the clink of glass and the hum of voices behind her when she heard someone say her name.

She turned and saw Brett Adams, the CEO of Phoenix Publishing, approaching. With him were a man and a woman.

"Aggie!" He leaned in and kissed her briefly on both cheeks, New York style. "Glad you could make it. We're excited about the next book. We have big plans."

"I'm excited, too." She was relieved and grateful that he used her pseudonym. She'd been assured by Brett that her identity would be protected at this small, exclusive party. There were no photographers, no journalists to write up her story.

"I want you to meet my brother, Chase, and his wife, Matilda. Matilda is one of our rising stars. She writes romance fiction and she's a big fan of yours. She's been nagging me for an introduction."

The woman was pretty, with tumbling brown hair and friendly eyes. "I just *loved Mate for Life*. I used it for inspiration when I was writing my last book. You have a way of putting things that makes so much sense. I wish I'd had your book when I was single." Matilda reached out to shake her hand, spilling some of her champagne in the process. "Oh. I'm so sorry—"

"Let me take that." Chase carefully removed the glass from her hand, the speed of his movements suggesting it wasn't the first time he'd rescued his wife from disaster.

Matilda shot him a grateful look, which he acknowledged with warmth and amusement that was touching to watch.

Molly decided these two were in no need of any relationship advice from her.

"I'm glad you enjoyed it. Have you written many books for Phoenix?"

"I'm on my third, so I'm still very new."

"She's being modest," Brett said. "Her first book hit the *New York Times* bestseller list. Rare for a debut author. The heroine was engaging and relatable and seemed to strike a chord with many women. You'd enjoy it, Aggie. I'll have my assistant send you a copy."

"I'd love that! Are you working on a book at the moment?"

"Yes, and I need to get it written before the summer." She placed a hand over her abdomen and beamed up at Chase. "Because in August we're going to be busy."

Molly smiled. "Congratulations."

"We're very excited."

They talked for a few more minutes and then someone approached Brett and Matilda and Molly stepped away, giving them space, only to slam straight into a solid wall of male muscle.

"Hello, Molly."

She would have recognized that deep, male voice anywhere. She felt a thrill of pure adrenaline and turned. "Daniel? What are you doing here?"

She was so, so happy to see him. For the first time in her life she wanted to behave like Valentine and wag her tail and jump all over him.

"I was about to ask you the same question." His tone was cool. Cooler than she would have expected given that twenty-four hours earlier they'd been intimately entwined.

It puzzled her. Maybe there hadn't been emotional involvement but there had been friendship. A connection that had added an extra dimension for both of them.

But that connection was no longer in evidence and she sensed something different about him.

Was it because they were in public? No. It was something more than that. There was a glint in his eye that she didn't recognize. A hardness she hadn't observed before. Oh, she knew he was tough, but he concealed it under layers of charm and charisma that made you forget his reputation.

It was like playing with a tame lion, she thought, and forgetting that at the end of the day he was a wild animal.

She was looking at Daniel the lawyer, not Daniel the lover.

Her excitement dimmed, only to be replaced by panic as she realized something that hadn't immediately occurred to her.

She wasn't here as Molly.

He was going to want to know what she was doing here.

"Daniel!" Brett stepped forward and shook his hand firmly. "Good to see you. I hope this means you're considering our proposal. And I see you've already met Aggie. I think you'll have a lot to talk about. Aggie is a psychologist, and she writes the most insightful books on relationships.

She was Phoenix's biggest seller last year and we're hoping for similar success with her next book."

Molly closed her eyes briefly. By introducing her by her pseudonym Brett assumed he was helping protect her identity, instead of which he'd inadvertently revealed it.

She felt hideously embarrassed and aware that she'd laid herself open to accusations of hypocrisy. She'd been outraged when she'd discovered that Brutus didn't belong to Daniel, but how much worse was this? What would he do? She felt a little sick. He'd told her things, personal things, and now he was probably feeling vulnerable. A man who felt vulnerable often fought to defend himself. Some might seek revenge, and what better way to take revenge than to blow her identity wide-open?

She waited for Daniel to challenge her, but he didn't. Instead he listened attentively to Brett, who seemed oblivious to the tension in the atmosphere.

"Daniel is one of Manhattan's top divorce attorneys. I'm trying to persuade him to write a book on how to make the divorce process as civilized as possible. Maybe we should commission the two of you to write something together."

Daniel gave a noncommittal smile.

Molly felt a flutter of nerves. Was he going to say something right here and now, or would he at least wait until they were in private? She almost wished he'd get it over with because the suspense was killing her.

She downed her champagne in four large gulps, only vaguely aware that Brett had wandered off to talk to another group of people who were waiting for his attention.

Daniel lifted two more glasses of champagne from a nearby tray and balanced them on the low wall. "Help yourself. You look as if you need it, Molly. Or should I call you Aggie? I'm confused."

He didn't look confused. She wasn't sure how to interpret his expression. The setting sun made sure she couldn't get a good look at his face.

"Daniel—"

"And you have a popular blog and an impressive following on social media. Now that's something you didn't mention while we were getting hot and sweaty together." He leaned in, his breath warming her cheek. "I've never had sex with two women at the same time before. I'm interested—did I go to bed with Aggie or with Molly? Do you have any advice for me on that?"

The couple standing close to them sent them curious glances.

Mortified, Molly finished her second glass of champagne and moved away a few steps. "Plenty of writers use a pseudonym. Look around this party and I doubt you'll find many people who write under their own names."

"And I doubt you'd find many people who fail to mention it to their friends. Especially friends they've been naked with. If 'Aggie' is simply a pseudonym, why didn't you tell me?"

She felt the anger pulsing from him.

"Probably for the same reason you didn't tell me Brutus wasn't yours."

"That's different! That's—" He swore under his breath and raked his fingers through his hair. The light of his eyes had darkened to pewter. "I didn't know you then." Something in his tone made her breathing jam in her throat.

She wanted to say that he didn't know her now, but that

would be lying. He did know her. Not every detail of her past, but more than anyone else ever had.

"I keep a separation between my work identity and my real self. I prefer it that way."

"So you trust me enough to get naked with me, but not enough to tell me that?"

She could hear the hurt in his voice. Pride. That had to be it. She'd damaged his pride. He'd told her things, but she hadn't done the same. "You told me what you wanted to tell me, nothing more."

"This has nothing to do with what I told you, and everything to do with what you didn't tell me."

Whatever his reasons for being hurt, there was no denying that he *was* hurt and she was the cause of it. And she hated that. Hurting him was the last thing she'd ever wanted to do. "You seem to have a big problem with the fact that I'm Aggie and I don't get it because you've never even heard of me before tonight."

"I've heard of you." His laugh was devoid of humor and she stared at him, wishing she hadn't drunk champagne on an empty stomach. She needed her wits about her, and right now her wits felt...well, blurry.

"Are you saying you read my blog? I don't believe you."

"I don't, but my clients do."

Someone touched his arm and he turned, impatience masked by a quick smile.

He shook hands, listened as if he was interested in what was being said, responded to their effusive thanks with a few polite comments. Then he turned back to her, his body language making it clear that the next person who disturbed them would find themselves dropped over the edge of the terrace into the park below.

Despite the champagne, her mouth felt dry. "Your clients? Which clients? What are you talking about?"

"One of my clients was getting a divorce, until you talked her husband out of it. You said that because they had children, they had a duty to persevere with their marriage."

Her head throbbed. She lifted her hand and pressed her fingers to her forehead, trying to remember. How was she expected to remember a few words among the thousands she wrote? "I would never give advice on a specific situation. I make general observations, that's all."

"Well, your 'general observations' have caused a great deal of emotional anxiety and turbulence in a family that already had far too much of it."

"I will not apologize for suggesting that a marriage might be worth another try before abandoning it. If there are children involved, there's nothing wrong with trying again."

"You know nothing about their situation."

That was true, and she also knew this conversation wasn't about his clients. On the surface, maybe, but underneath it was about something else. It was about them. About the fact that she hadn't trusted him.

She lowered her hand and chose her words carefully.

"I know a lot about it, both professionally and personally. People write to me outlining their situation, and I give them my thoughts. That's all. Have you even read the advice I gave? Maybe you should, before flinging accusations. Good night, Daniel."

Hand shaking, she put her empty glass of champagne back on a passing tray and turned to leave.

He caught her arm. "Wait," he said, his voice urgent. "Something doesn't feel right about this. Why didn't you tell me the truth? And don't talk to me about 'professional distance.' You're afraid of something. You're hiding something. Does this have to do with why you left London? Something to do with the last guy?"

Her heart was pounding. She didn't answer and his hand tightened on her arm.

"Tell me."

Why not? He was going to find out anyway. Nothing she did, or said, now was going to change that. "If you type Dr. Kathleen Parker into a search engine, you'll find the answers you're looking for."

"Kathleen Parker? Any other names I should know?"

She pulled away, trying to work out why she felt so sick. She'd hurt men before. Men she'd been more deeply involved with. What she and Daniel shared was nothing more than superficial fun, so why did she feel so bad?

"Kathleen Molly Parker is my full name. These days I use Molly. Once you've looked me up, you'll understand why." And that would be it. No more secrets. He'd watch that awful, humiliating video on YouTube. He'd see for himself what she was like. Telling him about it was one thing, but witnessing it was another.

There's something wrong with you.

Turning away, she hurried across the terrace to the stairs, her shoes biting into her feet.

She made it into the elevator and heard his voice.

"Molly! Molly, wait."

There was no way she was waiting.

She hit the button hard, decisively, and the doors closed just as he reached her.

She shut her eyes with relief, knowing that once he'd looked her up, he wouldn't be following her.

Whatever they'd had, whatever they'd shared, it was over.

She had no idea why she felt so bad about that.

Fourteen

Molly hammered on the door of Mark and Gabe's apartment.

Mark answered the door, his distracted look turning to a smile when he saw her. "Molly! I wasn't expecting you this early. Valentine is glued to a reality dog show on TV. You can't pull him away now."

"I'm in trouble." Her pulse was racing and her palms were clammy.

"Trouble?" Mark scanned her face and his smile faded. "What kind of trouble?"

"He knows." She pushed her hair out of her eyes and realized her hand was shaking. "I wasn't expecting to see him until tomorrow, but he showed up at the Met and Brett introduced me as Aggie. Not his fault. He thought he was helping. And he was angry."

"Brett was angry?"

"Daniel. And—I've upset him. I always upset people. I warned him, but he didn't listen. He should have listened.

But he didn't and now I've managed to screw up my whole life in one evening. And I was so *happy*. But that's how it goes, isn't it? One minute you're minding your own business, living your life, building a good career, and the next moment there's a hashtag and everyone has an opinion, and suddenly you're that woman who gives advice on relationships even though you have no *actual* experience of relationships, and truly I never really got that part because you don't have to travel the world to teach geography, but most of all I didn't want to hurt him." And what was he going to think? Maybe she would have told him about the whole Rupert thing eventually, but not right now, not like this. She would have waited until they knew each other better. Until there was less likelihood of him judging her.

"Whoa, wait a minute, back up. Who have you hurt? Daniel? Why was he at the Met? You look fabulous, by the way. Love the dress. That blue and those crisscross straps—gorgeous."

She didn't care about the dress. She didn't care about anything except what Daniel was doing right now. *What he was going to think of her.*

Valentine came bounding to the door, barking in ecstasy.

She bent to hug him, soothed by his presence. She stroked his smooth coat and breathed in his familiar doggy smell, overwhelmed by love. "I should have stayed in with you tonight. You're my best boy. I don't know why Daniel was at the Met." She straightened, her head still spinning, the panic eating away at her stomach. "They want him to write a book, or something. What are the chances? And last night was so great, Mark. For the first time in my life I had wild, crazy sex and it was amazing because I wasn't worrying about love or any of that stuff. It's the first time I've ever broken anything during sex. I thought it was all great, but it isn't—"

"Wait. You broke something?" Mark stepped back, scanning her for signs of injury and she gave a wobbly smile.

"Not me. We knocked over wine. Or beer. I don't even know. We were kissing and the fridge was open—"

"You'd better come in before you tell me any more or you'll shock Mrs. Winchester." Mark hauled her inside the apartment, closed the door and led her into the living room.

"I wasn't planning on giving you details."

"If you had sex in a fridge, I want the details. We'll open some of Gabe's champagne."

"I didn't say I had sex in a fridge! And I don't need any more champagne. I've already drunk more than enough. Where is Gabe?" Distracted, she glanced around and noticed some of Mark's drawings scattered over the table. "You're working?"

"Gabe has dinner with a client, so I'm catching up."

"I'm disturbing you—"

"There's nothing I'd like more than to hear about your sex life."

"It's not the sex I want to talk about, it's the other stuff! I don't want him to know all that." She groaned and covered her eyes with her hands. "His phone will probably self-destruct. I should never have gone to that publishing thing, and I never should have gone to bed with him. He said there was no way he'd get hurt because neither of us has feelings, but I've hurt him and now I feel so, *so* bad."

"But if neither of you have feelings, how can you have hurt him?"

"Pride, I guess."

"Pride." Mark gave her a long look. "You think this is about pride?"

"What else?"

Mark opened his mouth and closed it again. "I don't know. Never mind."

"I shouldn't have slept with him. No matter what I do, it always goes wrong. He'll look me up and discover what everyone else already knows. That when it comes to relationships, I'm lacking."

Mark sighed. "Sit down."

"Do you think he's going to blow my cover? Tell people who Aggie is? I don't want to trend on Twitter twice in a lifetime."

"You don't have a Twitter account."

"I'm on Twitter as Aggie. Not as Molly."

"It's a wonder you don't have an identity crisis. Why does it matter? Why does it matter if you use a pseudonym? That's your choice. And does it really matter that he knows?"

"I can't afford for this to explode again. There are only so many times I can emigrate. And I love New York! I don't want to have to move to Brazil."

"Brazil?"

"It was a random choice."

"I'm confused. Are you worried about the fact that Daniel might blow your cover or the fact that your relationship might be over?"

"We don't have a relationship. But whatever it was we had, I liked it."

"Maybe it isn't in the past tense. Maybe it isn't over."

"Of course it's over. Once they find out, people treat me like someone with a highly infectious disease. And I understand it. Who needs that in their life?"

Mark nudged her toward the sofa. "Take off those killer heels and relax. You are not moving to Brazil. Who would I cook for? We'll figure this out."

His kindness cut the last threads of her self-control. "If this blows up, if it's everywhere, you need to pretend you don't know me. Just because you have the misfortune of being a neighbor, doesn't mean they'll find out you're a friend. You can look blank if they ask you things. Just maybe don't mention that this is the first time in three years you've known a man to be in my apartment."

"If anyone asks me," Mark said, "I will tell them to mind their own damn business, and I'll tell them that because I'm your friend. When a friend is in trouble you keep them close, you don't throw them overboard. I know your friends let you down badly in the past, but that isn't going to happen this time. I wouldn't do that. Nor would Gabe."

"Don't—" she slid off her shoes "—don't make me emotional. I'm already a wreck."

Mark pushed her onto the sofa. "We're in this friendship for the long haul. I'm going to be godfather to your kids."

She didn't know whether to laugh or cry. "If I'm pregnant on top of everything else, I'm really going to freak out." She watched as Mark opened the fridge and pulled out the champagne. "I don't know what we're celebrating, unless it's my ability to complicate even an uncomplicated relationship."

"There's no such thing as an uncomplicated relationship. And you went to bed with a guy." Mark eased the cork out of the bottle and caught the eruption of bubbles in a glass. "That's something to celebrate." He handed her champagne.

She took a sip, feeling the light tang and the tingle of bubbles. "This might be the champagne talking, but you and Gabe are the best friends anyone could have."

"You've only had two sips of champagne, so I'm going to accept that for the compliment it is."

"Two sips on top of the two glasses I drank at the Met."

"Keep drinking. I want you to tell me if he's good in bed."

Despite everything, that made her smile.

"Insanely good."

"You haven't had sex in three years and that's all the detail you're giving? You're cruel and heartless."

"I've been telling you that for a long time. All this is probably for the best. It was bound to end at some point, so it might as well be now."

"Molly—"

"What? I have serious abandonment issues, I know that. I'm a professional and I'm well able to diagnose my own condition. But it turns out knowing what's going on doesn't mean I can fix it."

"I don't see how you could have hurt him. From what you've told me, the man's defenses are more impenetrable than yours, and he went into this with his eyes open."

"He told me some things. I told him some things, too, but maybe not as much as he told me." She bit her lip. "I probably made him feel vulnerable and now he's defensive." Yes, that was probably it. The more she thought about it, the more it made sense.

"I'm amazed the two of you managed to kiss without first agreeing on terms."

Oh, they'd managed it. They'd done more than manage it. They'd knocked it out of the park.

Remembering sent a slow, sinuous heat sliding into her pelvis. She finished her champagne. "I didn't expect it to be so good."

"So you kissed someone because you thought they would

give you a really bad experience? Honey, I love you, but I will never understand you." Mark topped up her glass again and she groaned and shook her head.

"Don't give me any more."

"Your apartment is one floor down. I'll throw you over my shoulder and carry you if necessary. And if you've been labeled a Bad Girl you might as well live up to your reputation."

"I feel horrible. How can I feel horrible when I warned him? I shouldn't feel guilty but I do."

"And you're sure it's guilt you're feeling?"

"What else could it be?"

Mark hesitated. "Nothing. Look, maybe it's a good thing that he knows your secret."

"It isn't. That part is scary."

"I understand about being scared." Mark picked up his pencil and reached for a piece of paper. "I spent my teens being scared. And with reason. People can be vicious, as we both know. But hiding has a downside, too. It means you live a small life. A life much smaller than you deserve."

"People think I deserve a lot of things I didn't get. Most of them bad."

"The judgment of people you don't know and don't care about shouldn't have an impact on your life. You should never be afraid to be you. Flaws, faults, weaknesses—that's what makes us human."

"You make it sound so easy."

"It's not easy. But hiding isn't easy either."

"Where do you get all this courage from?"

"It comes from having friends who feel like the best type of family." Mark put his pencil down. "Once you have a group of people who know who you are and love you for it, you realize that what other people think doesn't matter."

"That's one of the reasons I love Valentine. He doesn't judge me. And then there's my dad, of course—"

"And Gabe and I." Mark gave a crooked smile. "And I'm pretty sure Mrs. Winchester would go to bat for you, too, if she had to. If Daniel Knight is difficult, or upsets you, we'll take him between us."

She thought of Daniel's powerful shoulders and razor-sharp intellect. "He wouldn't be easy to take." She stood up and instantly felt dizzy. "Shouldn't have had that last glass. Too much champagne."

"No such thing. Here—a gift for you." He handed her the paper and on it was a sketch of Valentine. He'd captured the dog perfectly. She touched the dog's heart-shaped nose with the tip of her finger, her heart swelling with love.

"This is brilliant. I love it so much. Thank you." She stood on tiptoe and kissed Mark's cheek, feeling decidedly unsteady. "I'm going home, that's if I can get downstairs without falling over." She picked up her shoes and walked to the table, examining his sketches. "These are gorgeous. Is this a new idea?"

"I'm playing with a few themes. Too early to know if it will work."

"Is he a hare or a rabbit?"

"He's an Arctic Hare. I'm working on a story about camouflage. Hiding from predators." He gave a humorless smile. "You know all about that."

"So do you." With her free hand she picked up each of the drawings, following the story. "The snow melts and suddenly he's visible."

"That's right."

"Please tell me he doesn't get eaten. In my emotionally vulnerable state, I might not be able to stand it."

"He makes friends and they shelter him until it snows again and he's safe."

"A family of friends. I like that." She put the drawings down. "You're so talented. I'm going to frame my picture of Valentine. One day when you're even more famous than you are now, someone will offer me a fortune for it and I will tell them it isn't for sale. I should go. Thanks for listening and for getting me drunk enough not to care about my problems."

"If he gets in touch, let me know."

"He won't. This is a man who doesn't want complication. I'm a bigger complication than most people can handle." She called Valentine and the dog came bounding toward her, tail wagging.

It didn't matter what was happening in her life, there was nothing that having a dog didn't make at least a tiny bit better.

"Thank goodness dogs can't read. You love me unconditionally, don't you? You're part of my family." She stooped to hug him and Valentine licked her and wagged his tail so hard he almost took her eye out. "You don't care that I can't fall in love."

Mark grabbed the dog. "Not being in love isn't a crime." He opened the door and guided her through it. "Want me to walk you home?"

Hearing the word *home*, Valentine bounded out of the apartment and then paused at the top of the stairs, waiting for her.

She looked at his adorable face and smiled. "No, I can

stumble down one flight of stairs. And if I fall, Valentine will rescue me. But thank you for offering."

Giving Mark a quick hug, she followed the dog.

What was Daniel doing right now? Looking her up, probably. Forming judgments.

She walked carefully, shoes dangling from her fingers, her feet silent on the stairs.

Valentine kept glancing at her, tail wagging, checking she was all right.

"You're my best boy," she said. "My favorite man."

As she followed the turn in the stairs, Valentine started barking happily and she saw Daniel leaning against the wall next to her door.

For a moment she thought she must be hallucinating, but Valentine's reaction suggested that what she was seeing was real.

She'd been so sure she would never see him again. She felt a rush of happiness and her heart kicked against her ribs, and then she remembered that he was angry and that he was probably only here because he wanted to finish the conversation she'd walked away from.

His bow tie dangled around his neck and his eyes glittered. In his hand was his phone. "Well," he said. "You're a woman with one hell of a reputation."

Fifteen

Daniel watched as Molly walked toward him. Her feet were bare, her hair hung loose over her shoulders, and her shoes swung from her fingers. The slinky blue dress exposed just enough skin to make a man forget what he was thinking.

As she drew closer he saw that her eyes were bright and that she wasn't entirely steady on her feet.

He eased away from the wall. "Where have you been? I was worried."

"Why would you be worried? I'm not your responsibility." Her words were slightly slurred, her eyes challenging.

"How much have you drunk?"

"Nowhere near enough, but I'm working on it so don't even think about spoiling it for me."

"You're drunk because I upset you?"

"No, I'm drunk because I left the party before the food was served and because I've just drunk half a bottle of champagne. I really, really like champagne."

"We need to talk."

"Not a good time." She waggled her finger at him. "If I can't walk in a straight line, I can't have a serious conversation. I'll mean things I don't say. No—" She frowned. "That's not right. I'll say things I don't mean. Yes, that's it."

"I want to have the conversation now."

"You're here to take advantage when I'm weak and vulnerable?"

"I'm here because I owe you an apology." He slid his phone into his pocket, thinking that he'd never found a situation so uncomfortable. "I acted like a jerk, and when I act like a jerk I make a point of apologizing fast."

"Jerk. That's not a very lawyerly word. The defendant is a jerk, Your Honor."

"Plaintiff."

"Sorry?"

"Never mind. I'm not here as a lawyer."

She delved into her purse for her key, removing lipstick and tissues. "You were angry."

"I'm not angry now." His anger had lasted as long as it had taken him to type her name into the internet. What he'd found had shocked and sickened him. And it had explained a lot about her. About the reasons she held herself at a distance and her reluctance to embark on relationships. The difficulty she had trusting people. "Where were you? Who did you drink champagne with?"

"Mark. He was taking care of Valentine for me." She glanced up from her purse and focused her gaze on him. "Why are you here? Did you already tell me that?"

"No. Do you want me to help you find your keys?"

"I can find my own keys, thank you. See?" She pulled them out of her purse and jangled them in front of him. "Keys. How long have you been here?"

"An hour? I tried to follow you but I kept getting waylaid by people wanting free advice on divorce."

"Be grateful you're not a doctor. People might have removed their clothes and shown you their rashes." She fumbled with the keys and dropped them.

"Mark is your neighbor? The cook?"

"He's an artist. He illustrates children's books. Cooking is a hobby."

"Does Mark know your true identity? Does he think you're Molly?"

"I am Molly. But if you're asking if he knows I work under the pen name of Aggie, the answer is yes. He knows. He's a friend."

"And I'm not?"

"You're just some guy I met in the park." She bent to retrieve her keys at the same time he did.

Her mouth was so close to his he could feel the warmth of her breath, but he knew if he kissed her now she'd probably blacken his eye. And he wouldn't have blamed her.

"I'm more than that, Molly."

He kept thinking about the things she'd told him. He imagined her, eight years old, watching as her mother left her, taking the dog she loved. He thought about everything she'd achieved, and how vulnerable she was under the tough, smart exterior. He thought about her naked and uninhibited in his bed and how scared she must have been when she realized that he knew her secret.

Her gaze dropped to his mouth and lingered there for a moment as if she was making a decision. Then she shook her head. "No."

"No?"

"I am not kissing you." She stood up, her keys in her hand. "Not going to happen."

He refrained from pointing out that it had already happened. Several times. "Any particular reason why?"

"Because this relationship has already gone far enough. I hurt you tonight. I saw your face. I have a record of hurting men. You should have seen what I did to Rupert." She poked the key at the door, missing the lock.

He felt a rush of different emotions. Exasperation, sympathy and tenderness because she obviously thought she was a danger to men. "From what I can see, he was the one who hurt you. He tried to destroy you. Your professional reputation. Your personal life. All of it."

She stilled. "That's what happens when you make someone really mad."

"No. That's what happens when someone is an asshole. An adult can be angry without throwing a fit."

"I did warn you it was ugly. And it wasn't his fault. It was the media. The public."

Did she really believe that? He looked at her face and decided this wasn't the time to put her right. "Give me your keys." He held out his hand but she shook her head.

"I can open my own front door, thank you. It's best if you leave. And if you're really a decent person you will forget about what you learned tonight and you'll forget about me."

"You're not an easy woman to forget, Molly."

"Rupert would agree with you. He told a journalist that he would never get over me, but that he hoped that one day he would learn to live alongside the pain of losing me."

"Rupert needs to man up. Do my sisters know you're Aggie?"

"No. Gabe and Mark are the only two people who know

apart from my publisher. And now you know. So I'm doomed." The way she said it tugged at something inside him.

"Why are you doomed?"

"Because I don't know you, and it's not a nice feeling being exposed to someone you don't know."

"You spent an entire night naked in my bed." And he couldn't get a single moment of that night out of his mind.

"That's an entirely different type of exposure. Physical exposure is nowhere near as scary as emotional exposure." She swayed slightly. "You can see my naked body any day but I'd rather keep my naked feelings covered up, thank you very much. They don't look as good as they're supposed to." She jabbed at the door again. "My key doesn't fit. It's the wrong key. Or maybe it's the wrong door..." She swayed again and he gently removed the key from her fingers and opened the door.

Valentine squeezed past them and bounded into the apartment, sniffing the floor and wagging his tail.

"Thank you." Molly followed him in, dropped her purse and shoes and collapsed facedown on the sofa. "You should leave now."

"I'm not leaving."

"If you're hoping for more juicy gossip, I'm not talking." Her voice was muffled and Daniel shook his head and made straight for the kitchen.

"You need strong coffee."

"I don't want coffee. I want more champagne. It was delicious. It made all my problems seem lighter. Fizzier. Floatier. Is that a word? If it isn't, it should be." She rolled onto her side and closed her eyes. Valentine trotted up to her and nudged her hip.

When she didn't move, the dog sent Daniel a worried look.

"Yeah, I'm dealing with it. I've got this, buddy." Daniel made coffee and took it across to her. Valentine sprawled like a sentinel next to the sofa and Daniel moved Molly's legs and sat down. "Drink this."

"I never drink coffee after two o'clock. It keeps me awake."

"I want you awake. I want you to talk to me."

"Too tired." Her eyes remained closed. "I've told you. No more gory details. It's like feeding the piranhas. Whatever you throw at them it's never quite enough. They're not happy until they've stripped off all your flesh."

From what he'd read, it was a good analogy.

"I'm not a piranha. I'm a friend. I want facts."

Her eyes opened. "I thought you'd already looked me up?"

"We both know that what gets reported isn't necessarily the facts."

"It's all true. I'm Molly the Man-eater. The Black Widow without the hairy legs. Most men would rather swim with a great white shark than date me. But you were warned. I warned you, and you ignored the warning so now I'm probably going to bite you in half or sting you with my scorpion tail—or something." She rolled onto her back, one arm flopping over the edge of the sofa.

Valentine was on his feet instantly, licking her hand, trying to persuade her to sit up.

Daniel thought to himself that if humans were as devoted as dogs, life would be a lot smoother and calmer. "I ignored the warning because I didn't care about any of that." He reached out and stroked Valentine's head, reassuring him. "You can sit down, boy. She's going to be okay."

Valentine didn't budge. He nudged at Molly's chest, encouraging her to sit up, but she didn't.

"It's okay, Daniel," she said, and flung her forearm over her eyes, "you can take your heart, and your humor, and your superior bedroom skills and put them somewhere safe."

"I'm not going anywhere. Sit up and drink this coffee."

"I can't sit up. The world is moving. If I sit up, I'll fall off the edge." She gave a moan and Valentine whined, too, looking at Daniel as if to say it was time someone did something.

"Sit up. You're scaring your dog." Daniel pushed aside a stack of books and put the coffee on the table. Then he stood up and scooped Molly into his arms. She flopped like a rag doll.

Valentine stood up, his tail wagging with approval. Molly didn't share the sentiment.

"What are you doing? Where are we going? Can you stop moving? I'm getting motion sickness."

"I'm going to sober you up."

"I don't want to be sobered up. I like myself just the way I am. Fizzy. I was anxious about what you might do, and now I'm not so anxious. I'm anesthetized."

Hating the fact that he'd made her anxious, he walked to the bathroom and lowered her carefully to the floor.

"Stand there and don't move."

"I can't promise. My legs aren't doing what I want them to. Why are we in my bathroom? Is this another excuse to get me naked?"

"I don't need an excuse for that." He slid the crisscross straps off her shoulders and let the dress slither to the floor.

Holding her upright with one hand, trying to ignore her body, he leaned into her shower and turned it to cold.

"You are *not* putting me in a cold shower. If you put me

in there Valentine will bite you. There is no way you're going to—agh!" She gasped as he deposited her under the freezing stream of water. "You're a torturer. Valentine, help, help! Seize!"

The dog came charging into the bathroom, his feet slithering on the tiles in his haste to reach her. He hesitated for a fraction of a second, and then hurled himself into the shower to be with Molly. Knocked off balance, she slipped and landed on Daniel, who swore fluently.

Struggling with a wet woman and a wet dog, he shifted position to give himself more traction. Molly started to giggle helplessly and he tightened his grip on her arms to stop her falling, soaking himself in the process.

"Valentine," he said through his teeth, "can you get out of the shower? You're not helping."

The dog wagged his tail, sending droplets of water flying everywhere.

Daniel swiped his hand over his face to clear his vision.

"I've never had a shower with a man and a dog before." Molly grabbed the front of his shirt to support herself. "It's a whole new experience."

"I've lost count of the number of suits I've ruined since I met you. Right now I wish he didn't love water so much."

"Valentine hates water, but he really loves me. That's why he's in here. Isn't he the most adorable perfect dog?"

"I'm not sure what I think of him. All I know is that he is costing me a hell of a lot in dry-cleaning bills." He held her there, and then grabbed a towel from the rack. His shirt stuck to his skin and he was pleased he'd at least thought to remove his shoes.

He draped the towel around her, managed to reach around

her to turn the shower off and ran his hand over his face to clear his vision.

"Coffee. Then you're going to talk to me."

Her head flopped onto his chest. "There's nothing to say you haven't already read."

He rubbed her hair with the towel and grabbed a robe from the back of the door. "There are things that don't make sense."

"It all makes perfect sense. I tried to fall in love again and it didn't happen. No love. No feelings." She swayed as Daniel tied the robe at her middle.

"I get that part. What I don't get is how ending a relationship meant you were labeled as a man-eater." He stripped off his soaked shirt and saw her gaze drift to his chest. "Don't look at me like that."

"Why not? I am a man-eater. And you're seriously hot."

"And you're seriously drunk."

"Not really. I can walk in a straight line. Maybe you should take the rest of your clothes off. Then I can lick you all over."

He decided it was less taxing on his willpower to keep as many clothes on as possible. All the same he struggled to keep his focus. "And I don't understand how you could have been fired from your job. An affair gone wrong is not cause for dismissal. You should have sued them."

"Viewing figures plummeted and it was my fault. They did the only thing they could do."

She stumbled back to the sofa and curled up. Without makeup and with her hair hanging in damp tendrils, she looked small and vulnerable. "You want the whole sorry tale? Why does it matter?"

"It matters to me."

"We have no emotional commitment, remember?"

His eyes darkened. "Just because we're not in love, doesn't mean I don't care."

"What are you going to do with the information?"

He was about to make a sharp comment and then he saw the vulnerability in her eyes and realized she was genuinely scared.

The thought of her being scared ripped something inside him. "I would never expose your secrets."

"If you hadn't shown up at that party, you would never have known."

Should he tell her the truth? Should he tell her that he'd known before the party? No. There was nothing to be gained by telling her. The only thing that mattered was that he knew. The rest was just mechanics.

And his view of "Aggie" had undergone a huge transformation in the past few hours. He'd had no idea that his Molly was the woman behind the popular advice column. That changed everything. For a start, Molly knew what she was talking about.

He handed her the mug of coffee. "Drink and tell me everything. From the beginning."

She curled her hands around the mug. "My postgraduate research was in an aspect of human behavior and relationships and because of that I was asked to act as a consultant for a new reality TV show called *The Right One*. There had been dating shows before, but the producers wanted to increase the credibility and interest by adding in sections of the show where a psychologist talked about a different aspect of finding a partner. I was Dr. Kathy. Don't ask me why, but the moment it aired my section became the most popular segment of the show."

"That doesn't surprise me."

"They had two presenters, but the show was really all about Rupert. He trained as a doctor, but he left soon after qualifying. He presented a medical show first before he was poached to front *The Right One*. He was great in front of the camera. Good-looking, charismatic, funny—and he played up the doctor side even though he'd never laid hands on a patient once he'd qualified. He had a massive female fan following." She took a sip of coffee and eyed him over the rim of the mug. "They called him Dr. Sexy."

Daniel wanted to punch him. "I get it. The guy had an adoring audience."

She lowered the cup. "People tuned in to watch the show partly because of Rupert. There was a female co-presenter, Tabitha, but she didn't get anywhere near as much attention. I was supposed to represent the serious side. I interviewed the participants and then recorded a piece to camera. I was never live. It was a very comfortable role for me. Then one day Tabitha was sick half an hour before they were about to go on air and they asked me to step in."

"And you were a natural."

She shook her head. "Far from it. I was out of my comfort zone and it was Rupert who saved the day, and the audience loved it because they saw it as another example of what a great person he was. He was a big star, but he took time to make sure I was comfortable. Tabitha was off for a month. By the end of the month viewing figures had tripled. Tabitha decided she didn't want to come back—she was tired of always being in Rupert's shadow. I replaced her. We had an on-screen chemistry, and soon the public was tuning in to watch our relationship develop. The producers milked it.

They suggested Rupert ask me to dinner on air, so he did. The story made some of the tabloid newspapers."

"Did you go?"

"Yes. I liked him. He was good company, and he wasn't called Dr. Sexy for nothing. The entire viewing public was in love with him."

"But you weren't."

"No, but I didn't think it mattered. We were having fun, that's all."

It was like watching a car crash in slow motion. "He thought differently?"

She put the mug down on the table, her hand shaking. "We'd finished recording the show and were backstage one night when he told me he loved me. He asked me to marry him. Right there and then he went down on one knee and produced a ring. I thought it was a joke. I was worried he was going to electrocute himself because there were wires everywhere. I told him to get up. That was when I realized he was deadly serious. He told me he'd never felt this way about anyone before. He was crazy about me and wanted to spend the rest of his life with me. Everyone loved him. He assumed I loved him, too. How could I not? And I couldn't answer that, obviously. I don't know why I can't fall in love." Her voice rose slightly. "All I know is that I can't. And maybe it's because of my mum. It would make sense that I'm worried about being rejected, but deep down I think it's something more. That it's not what I've witnessed or experienced, it's part—" she swallowed hard, struggling to speak "—it's part of who I am. There's something missing in me." She covered her face with her hands. "I've never actually said that aloud to anyone before. It must be the champagne."

He hoped it was because she trusted him, but he didn't say

anything. Instead he drew her hands away from her face. "I presume he didn't take it well?"

"No." There was a long pause, as if she was deciding whether she'd already said too much. "And it turned out the production team had somehow found out what he was planning and filmed it live. I had no way of knowing, but what I thought was a private moment between us was in fact beamed live into millions of homes. It was seen by an entire population of women who thought Rupert was the catch of the century. Dr. Sexy being jilted. Did you watch it? It's right there on YouTube. It had thirty-five million views last time I looked, but that was a few years ago." Her voice shook so badly he decided this wasn't the moment to tell her there had been a few million more since then. Watching that video had been one of the most uncomfortable experiences of his life.

"You looked different." He'd barely recognized her. "Your hair was shorter. But you were still beautiful."

"Not beautiful enough according to Rupert's legions of fans. No one short of Helen of Troy would have pleased them. I was supposed to count myself lucky that someone as gorgeous as him wanted me, and yet I'd turned him down in a horribly public way. Afterward the press tried to get a comment from Rupert but all he would say was that he was too upset to talk about it."

"Did he know what they were going to do?"

"No! And I felt terrible for him and totally mad with the production team. They'd said before that they wanted to film a proposal live on air, but I'd always stopped them. I'd told them it was a private moment and not something that should be shared, and I'd also pointed out that the outcome was never sure. So they decided to film mine. It backfired on them, too."

He could imagine her horror when she'd discovered that it had all been streamed live, her insecurities about herself witnessed by millions. "You made a choice, Molly. I don't see why that led to the witch hunt."

There was another long pause.

"Rupert went home, humiliated. He didn't emerge from his house for a week. There were rumors that he'd harmed himself—" Her voice broke a little. "It was truly awful. Everyone's attention and anger turned on me. The media dug up details of my old relationships. Collectively they decided I was a heartless bitch who needed punishing. And perhaps they were right. I'd hurt another good, decent man. I never should have agreed to date him."

"Molly—"

"Rupert stayed in hiding, fueling the rumors. One tabloid newspaper took my picture and captioned it *The face of guilt.* I stopped switching on my laptop. To try and protect my dad, I moved in with a friend, but after a day they surrounded her house, too, and she told me I had to move."

Daniel ground his teeth. "Not a great friend, then."

"She did what she could. Finally Rupert appeared looking gaunt and told people he was fine."

"Which gained him even more sympathy." Daniel was starting to seriously dislike Rupert. "Did he call to see how you were holding up with all this going on? Did he tell the press to leave you alone?"

"He was too hurt to think about anyone but himself."

Or too selfish. "What about the show? You carried on presenting?"

"Yes. I recorded the show on my own while he was off sick, but people were outraged that I was carrying on with my life when his was ruined. I was followed to the supermarket, to the gym. People I'd thought were my friends waded in and fed the media with stories. A couple of my old boyfriends joined in."

"None of your friends stood by you?"

"To be fair, the attention was hideous and then it escalated. The public started a campaign—Dump Dr. Kathy. There were literally millions of people who didn't know me and had never met me, hounding me and the TV company, saying that I shouldn't be allowed to do the job. That I shouldn't be described as an expert on relationships when I'd never had one myself. They were judge, jury and executioner." She spoke faster and faster, her distress almost painful to watch. Valentine clearly thought so, too, because he shot to his feet and trotted to her side, nudging her with his nose, checking she was all right. She stroked his head, calming down a little. "And I didn't particularly love being in the spotlight but I did love the show. They picked people who genuinely struggled to find a partner. These weren't self-obsessed narcissists who wanted to make a name for themselves on TV, they were real people with real problems. My skills genuinely helped them and I felt as if what we did was truly positive, so to have all that taken away—they made me look like a fraud." She hesitated. "I suppose it tapped into all those fears I'd buried, about not being enough. They made me feel as if I was lacking. But the worst thing was seeing Rupert looking so awful. It reminded me of the way my dad had looked in those first awful weeks and months after my mum left. I couldn't bear to think I'd broken Rupert's heart the same way my mum broke my dad's."

"So you resigned from your job?"

"No, they fired me and I was left with nothing but a bucketful of guilt, low self-esteem and a permanently damaged reputation." She breathed. "And I had all these feelings. Feelings I'd buried. Feelings I didn't want. About how it had felt when my mum left. About how I wasn't capable of falling in love."

"You should have sued them." He kept his anger under control. "So they fired you, and then what? Did you look for another job?"

"Who was going to hire me? I was a pariah. Fortunately the show had paid well. I had savings. Enough to support myself for a while. So I moved here, kept a low profile. I stopped using the name Kathy and called myself Molly, my middle name. I was so afraid the press would track me down, or someone on social media would find me and broadcast my whereabouts. I closed all my online accounts. Fortunately, the media lost interest. I guess once they'd destroyed me, ripped away my reputation and my job, and driven me from my home, they were satisfied. No one seemed to care where I'd gone."

"You knew people in New York?"

"I didn't know anybody. And that was a good thing. I moved into a tiny walk-up in Brooklyn, paid cash and cried myself to sleep for a month. I didn't leave the apartment except to buy groceries. And then one day I decided I'd punished myself enough. I started the blog just for me, as a way to get my confidence back. To begin with I posted the questions myself and answered them. Then real ones gradually started to trickle in. If I'm honest I never expected it to grow the way it did. And the attention it gained got me more attention. My blog was featured by a couple of big news sites. People started asking questions. I refused interviews. I never put a photograph up. There was nothing that could associate my name with Aggie. I wasn't interested in any sort of publicity. When I was approached by Phoenix Publishing, I made it clear I didn't want my photo or real identity used."

"So you kept your name out of it."

"Yes. Fortunately writers use pseudonyms all the time. I don't have my photo on the book jacket and I don't do book signings or personal appearances, so there's no way my face will be recognized. I've covered my tracks and been careful. I've rebuilt my life. And then I met you. I should have known I couldn't hide forever. Whenever you're hiding something you don't want people to know, you can be sure it's going to come out." She rolled onto her side and buried her face in the cushions. "You should probably go."

"Go? Go where?"

"I don't know." Her voice was muffled. "Anywhere. I'm sure you don't want to be here."

"This is exactly where I want to be."

"I screwed up so badly."

He couldn't work out if she was crying or not, so he eased her away from the cushions and pulled her into his arms. "You didn't screw up. None of that was your fault. And I'm impressed that you not only survived, but thrived. That's an experience plenty of people wouldn't have recovered from."

"I ran away."

"No. You removed yourself from the line of fire. That's sensible, not cowardly. Clever tactics. When your enemy attacks, you make yourself small."

"Sun Tzu?"

He smiled into her hair. "I'll make a disciple of you yet."

"Earlier tonight, you were angry. You said I'd given bad advice to one of your clients. What did you mean?"

"I was wrong. After we talked this evening, I went back

over some of your older blogs and I found his letter and your answer."

Her brow wrinkled. "How? It's anonymous."

"I know this person. I recognize the way he writes. The way he thinks. And you were right, your advice was general, not specific."

"But he took it to be specific?"

"He took it in a way that suited him and used it to manipulate his wife into staying with him."

"Oh no." She looked worried. "I know you can't talk about your clients, but just tell me—did you fix it?"

"*She* fixed it. She called him on his very bad behavior. She kept documentation. There won't be a problem."

"Good. Did you say you came here to apologize? I'm guessing you're not a man who often apologizes."

"I always apologize when I'm wrong."

"You didn't apologize for borrowing Brutus."

"That wasn't wrong. If I hadn't done that I wouldn't have met you."

"Bet you're wishing you hadn't done it."

"That's not what I'm wishing." He stood up and held out his hand.

She stared at it. "Where are we going?"

"I'm taking you to bed so that I can be sure of you getting there without falling over and banging your head."

"After everything you've just learned about me, you want to go to bed with me?"

"I'm not going with you, but that has nothing to do with what I learned and everything to do with the fact that you've had too much to drink. You need to sleep off that champagne or you'll feel terrible tomorrow." He took her hand and pulled her to her feet.

"Sadly I'm not so drunk that I'm not going to remember all this. I already know I'll feel terrible tomorrow, and you don't need to make excuses. I totally understand why you wouldn't want to hang around after everything I told you tonight."

Was that really what she thought? "Molly—"

"It's fine. Totally fine. No explanations necessary, but just tell me one thing—" She looked up at him anxiously. "Are you going to post my real identity on social media?"

"You really think I'd do that?"

She stared at him for a long moment and then shook her head. "No, I don't. And I suppose one other person knowing isn't the end of the world. My secret is still safe."

It was more than one other person, but since both Max and his sources were bound by confidentiality there was no point in worrying her by telling her that.

"Your secret is safe."

Sixteen

Molly woke to hammering inside her head, and then Valentine barked and she realized the hammering wasn't coming from her head, but from the door.

With a groan of denial she slid out of bed, clutched the wall to balance herself and fumbled her way to the door. The whole of the night before came back to her in a flash. The party. Daniel's anger. Drinking champagne with Mark and then everything that had happened afterward. Spilling her guts to Daniel.

Oh *God*, had she really done that? Told him everything? Yes, she really had. She'd been like a waterfall in full flood. No wonder he'd left in the early hours.

She gave a moan of regret.

She was never, *ever* drinking again.

Valentine was barking frantically and she put her hand on his head.

"Please, *please* don't bark." She opened the door and a dog that looked exactly like Brutus barged his way into her apartment. He greeted Valentine like a long-lost brother, proving that he was in fact Brutus. The two dogs growled and rolled on the floor and Molly stared at them, wondering if she was still suffering from the effects of too much champagne.

"Brutus?" She rubbed her eyes but the dog still looked the same. And there, standing in her doorway, was Daniel. She felt a thrill of relief and delight. After what had happened the night before she'd thought he wouldn't want to come within a million miles of her. "I thought a family had taken him."

"They didn't like his temperament." There was an edge to Daniel's voice. "Turns out he isn't easy to rehome so he's still with Fliss and Harriet."

"So you're walking him?"

"Yes, but don't read anything into it. I'm just helping my sisters."

"Because you're not a dog person." She watched as Brutus charged back to Daniel, checking he wasn't leaving. She felt like doing the same thing. She watched as he gently scratched the back of Brutus's neck, reassuring him. "I don't think you used Brutus to get close to me. I think you're using me to get closer to Brutus. Do you know that some people call you the Rottweiler?"

"You've been reading my press again."

"Seemed only fair as you read mine. Is that coffee?"

"It is." Daniel thrust a cup into her hand and followed Brutus into the apartment.

"I was planning on going back to bed."

"Forget it. We're going for a run. It'll wake you up."

"Run? Do you know how hard it was to walk from the bed to the door? I couldn't run if you threatened my naked body with a cactus." She glanced at the sofa and saw a pillow. "What's that doing there?"

"I slept there. You need a bigger sofa."

"You slept on my sofa?" She looked at his running gear and the coffee in his hand. "But—"

"I went home an hour ago. Took a shower, changed, bought coffee and then picked up Brutus."

He hadn't left her? He'd been here almost the whole time she'd been asleep?

"Why would you sleep on my sofa? And why didn't I know?"

"I put you to bed and you passed out. Valentine was so worried about you he didn't want me to leave. Every time I walked to the door he blocked it and dragged me back. Generally I'm good at arguing, but I have no idea how to argue with a dog, so in the end it seemed easier to stay. But that was before I knew how uncomfortable your sofa is."

"It's comfortable." The knowledge that he'd stayed the night made her feel strange. Vulnerable, yes, because she had no secrets left from him, but also a little touched that he'd cared enough to sleep on her sofa.

"Maybe it's comfortable for people under six foot two." He seemed supremely energetic for someone who had been up for most of the night.

"About last night—I apologize."

"For what?"

"For all of it. For drowning you in the floodwaters of my very messy past. It was the champagne." She told herself it was definitely that, and not the fact that Daniel Knight was an exceptionally good listener. "Let's go to the park. I can't promise to run, but I can crawl behind you and moan."

In the end she managed a gentle jog and being in the park

made her feel better. The air was fresh and cool, and seeing Valentine back with his friend made her smile.

"I don't understand why that family didn't snap Brutus up."

"I don't understand either." He threw the ball for Brutus, who charged after it, grabbing it with a tumble and a roll.

It was all so normal, *he* was so normal, that she gradually stopped feeling self-conscious.

"So are you going to write a book for Phoenix?"

"I don't know. They first approached me two years ago. They wanted a book on divorce written by a lawyer. They wanted it to be the equivalent of a free consultation, giving you just enough information to understand the process. At the time I was too busy."

"But now?"

"I'm considering it. I have another meeting with Brett in a few weeks. How about you? You're working on something new?"

"*Mate for Life* sold really well, but it's mostly about choosing a partner, evaluating what makes you happy in a relationship, identifying what you won't compromise on so you don't make a mistake. My next book tackles how to maintain a relationship. How to keep it going when life gets tough." Still sensitive, she sent him a glance. "That's your cue to laugh."

"Why would I laugh?"

"Perhaps because I've never maintained a relationship of my own? I don't exactly speak from personal experience."

"But you do speak from professional experience, which is what people want. Anything else is just someone's opinion."

His comment lifted her mood.

After her life had exploded one of the hardest things to

cope with was the feeling that she was a fraud. An impostor. Someone who shouldn't be advising people on relationships.

"Tell me something." Daniel pulled her toward him and took her face in his hands. "Do you believe in the advice you give?"

"Of course, but—"

"There is no but. As professionals, we give the advice we believe to be correct. If someone chooses not to take it, that doesn't make us wrong. It's crazy to say you shouldn't be offering advice on relationships, and the fact that your book sold so many copies suggests that there were plenty of people who respect what you have to say and value your professional opinion."

"But people buying that book wouldn't know that I haven't ever had a long-term relationship."

"I've never been married and I spend my days advising people on divorce. I have no personal experience of either of those things. Brutus!" He called, and the dog hesitated and then came charging back to him, skidding to a halt at Daniel's feet.

Molly stared at him, openmouthed. "Well—wow."

"We've been working on it."

She heard the pride in his voice and watched the way he made a fuss over Brutus before throwing the ball again. "He's going to miss you."

Daniel frowned, as if that possibility hadn't occurred to him. "I should get to work. Will you be all right?"

"Of course. Why wouldn't I be?"

"I opened wounds." He lifted his hand and brushed a strand of hair away from her face. "Made you talk about things."

"I think I managed that part by myself."

"Do you regret it?"

"Telling you? No." She hesitated. "I suppose if I'm honest I feel a little exposed."

"Exposed?" He gave a slow smile, leaned forward and said something into her ear.

She felt heat pour into her cheeks. "Did you seriously just say that?"

"Yeah, I seriously did. I'll see you at eight, Dr. Parker. Bring your whole bad self over to my place so I can expose parts of you I've never exposed before."

* * *

Daniel hammered on the door of his sisters' apartment. He should have felt tired, but instead he felt energized. The stress he'd felt, the anger, the hurt—it had all vanished when Molly had opened up to him. She'd told him everything. Trusted him with everything. And she was a person who didn't trust easily. There were no more secrets between them.

He was seeing her later that night. Dinner, he thought. And then bed. No more deep conversations.

Maybe he'd text her and tell her to wear the same dress she'd worn the other night. And the lacy underwear he'd been in too much of a hurry to remove.

Harriet opened the door with three tiny kittens under her arm.

Brutus strained toward her and Daniel looked down at him sternly.

"Sit."

Brutus sat and gave Daniel a dopey look.

Harriet's jaw dropped. "You trained him?"

"Molly made some suggestions. She knows a lot about dogs." And she knew a lot about other things, too, like how to make the perfect cup of coffee, how to salsa dance and how to use her mouth to drive him wild. Knowing that thinking about that would compromise his ability to walk, he wiped the image from his mind and strolled into the apartment.

Brutus was quivering with expectation and Daniel snapped his fingers.

Brutus charged into the apartment, almost flattening Harriet.

Steadying herself, she closed the door. "I made coffee. Help yourself while I settle these little ones."

"You're fostering kittens?"

"Just for a couple of days." She put them down and tucked a blanket around them. "I'm so glad Valentine is better. And it's going well with Molly? Has she forgiven you for borrowing Brutus and not telling her?"

Yes, because it turned out there were plenty of things she hadn't told him, which made them equal in his book. "She seems to have come to terms with it."

"Good." Always generous, Harriet smiled. "I like her a lot. I was worried she'd be mad with us."

"I'm the one responsible, not you. Where's Fliss?"

"In her bedroom. She's about to leave to see a new client."

"I need to talk to her." And it wasn't a conversation he was looking forward to. He'd pondered on it, run some checks and come to the conclusion he had no choice but to talk to Fliss himself. Better that she heard the news from him than from someone else.

"I'll give her a shout. I suppose Molly was ready to forgive you anything after what you did for Valentine."

"He was sick and she was scared." He'd witnessed a lot of anguish in his career and handled it with a detached empathy, but Molly's agony had been almost painful to watch. "That's why she stayed at my place. Because it was closer."

Fliss emerged from her bedroom in her socks. "Molly stayed at your place? Overnight? The *whole* night?"

"It was a matter of convenience. She slept in the spare room. Fliss, I need to talk to you about something." He wondered how best to break the news to her. Straight-out? Should he prepare her first? Drop some hints?

The last thing he wanted to do was hurt his sister, but what choice did he have? If she found out that he'd known and hadn't told her, she'd never forgive him.

"You had a woman stay the night? Damn right you need to talk to us." Fliss picked up her running shoes and grinned at him. "You are in *deep* trouble. We're here to save you. That's what we do, isn't it Harry?"

Daniel felt a prickly discomfort in his skin. "I am not in trouble."

"Has a woman ever slept over at your place before?"

"No, but—"

"And—let's be honest here because we're all grown-ups—when you've seen women in the past, it's always been just for sex."

"I don't know what you're talking about. I have invited plenty of women out for dinner."

"Fueling them up as a precursor to sex."

"Could you two stop talking about sex?" Exasperated, Harriet checked on the basket of kittens. "It's a good job they're asleep. I don't want them corrupted."

"All I'm saying is that this whole scenario is different." Fliss grabbed her backpack and a light sweater. "He had a woman sleep over. That means something."

"Molly was worried about her dog."

"Yeah." Fliss tugged on the sweater, her gaze sharp and questioning. "And it's normal to offer overnight accommodation to women who are worried about their pets. Hey, maybe we could offer that as an extension of the Bark Rangers. Fur B and B."

"I think you're reading too much into this."

"And *I* think you really like this woman."

"Which is great," Harriet said quickly. "*Really* great. I never thought I'd see you so interested in a woman."

"We're just having fun. It's not serious."

Harriet looked at him expectantly. "You wanted to talk to us about something?"

"Not you. Fliss." He paused, wishing he didn't have to do this. His sister seemed so happy. So strong. She was running her own business. She was confident. Sure of herself. And what he was about to tell her was probably going to set her back ten years to a time none of them wanted to remember. "Sit down, honey."

Fliss froze, her weight on her toes like a deer about to run. "I'm not sure which part of that sentence freaks me out the most. The fact that you're calling me 'honey,' or the fact that you want me to sit down. That's what cops say in movies before they break bad news. If something bad has happened just tell me straight-out."

"Seth Carlyle has joined the Animal Hospital." He watched the color drain from his sister's cheeks and heard Harry's murmur of alarm and horror.

"My Seth?" Fliss sat, so hard and fast that it was like a stone dropping from the sky. "Is that a bad joke? No. I know it can't be. You're annoying but you're never cruel, and making that up would be—" Her breathing was shallow and she pressed her hand to her chest. "I don't feel so good. Can't breathe—"

Harriet sat down next to her twin and wrapped her arms

around her. "Breathe slowly. In through your nose, out through your mouth. That's it." She looked at Daniel. "Are you sure? How do you know?"

"I saw him the night I was there with Molly and Valentine. Steven, the vet, introduced us. Obviously he didn't know Seth and I had a prior connection and I didn't say anything."

Fliss gave a wan smile. "Then you're more restrained than you used to be. I suppose I should be grateful you didn't punch him."

"I already did that."

"I know. I remember." She sucked in a shuddering breath. "Did he say anything?"

"About you? No. But it wasn't exactly the time or place."

She lifted her gaze to his. "How did he seem?" The anguish in her eyes made him feel helpless, and he hated feeling helpless.

He dropped to his haunches in front of Fliss and took her hands in his. It said a lot about her state of mind that she didn't immediately pull them away and slap him. "He looked okay to me. It's you I'm worried about. What can I do? Tell me what I can do."

"Nothing. It's—" She breathed deeply. "This is my problem."

"We share problems." Harriet was glued to her side. "Always have. Always will. I can do all the vet visits if you like, then you'll never bump into him."

"If he's working here on the Upper East Side, then I'm bound to bump into him. And anyway, it would be cowardly of me to avoid him. Why would he be here? Is it a coincidence? Yes, of course it's a coincidence. We haven't seen each other for ten years—" Her eyes filled and Harry hugged her, exchanging a helpless glance with Daniel.

"Don't give me sympathy. The whole thing was my stupid fault, all of it." Fliss saw her brother's eyes darken and glared at him. "Don't start."

He let go of her hands and stood up. "I haven't said a word."

"I can handle this. A decade is a long time. Water under the bridge, right? We're both adults. I'll get my head around this. I just need some time. And a boyfriend."

Harriet looked bemused. "A boyfriend?"

"Of course. If he realizes I'm single he might think I never sorted my life out, and I absolutely wouldn't want him to ever think that." She caught Harriet's eye. "Because it wouldn't be true. I've moved on."

"Of course you have," Harriet said stoutly. "You haven't talked about him for a couple of years. I don't suppose you've even given him a thought."

"Not a thought," Fliss echoed.

Daniel said nothing, but he hoped she could up her acting game before she met Seth.

"Did he mention me? Did he ask how I was?"

"We didn't have a conversation. We acknowledged each other and didn't cause each other physical harm. That was the extent of our joyous reunion."

"So as far as he knows I could be married or anything." Fliss stood up and paced across the apartment. "I definitely need to date someone. Fast. Who do we know who might help?"

"Don't look at me." Daniel raised his hands in a gesture of surrender. "I don't know anyone who would date you unless they were medicated first."

"Thanks." But some of Fliss's spirit had returned and when she glanced at him he was relieved to see the usual spark in her eyes. "I'm late. I have to go. But thanks for the heads-up. I appreciate it." She scooped up her keys and flew out of the door, leaving Harriet and Daniel alone.

"Shit," Harriet muttered and Daniel lifted an eyebrow.

"That's the first time I've ever heard you swear."

"Seth coming back into Fliss's life is a reason to swear. She was broken, Daniel."

"Yeah, but it was a long time ago. She was vulnerable, and now she's not."

"I'm not so sure." Harriet looked unhappy. "Where Seth is concerned I think a part of her will always be broken. I've often wondered—"

"What?"

"Nothing." Harriet avoided his gaze and he frowned.

"What? Is there something you're not telling me?"

"No. I'm worried, that's all."

"Me, too, but she'll be fine. She always is." Daniel finished his coffee. "I'm late. Call me if you need anything, but otherwise we can finish this conversation tomorrow when I pick up Brutus."

Harriet was distracted. "You can't have him tomorrow. The people who want to adopt him are coming to take him."

Daniel was surprised by how much that news bothered him. "I thought they didn't like his temperament."

"These are different people. They're specifically looking for a German shepherd. I think they'll be the perfect family for him."

Daniel felt as if he'd been kicked in the gut. He told himself it was seeing his sister upset that was responsible for the hollow feeling.

Harriet peered at him. "You look upset, but it's not as if you need a dog to walk anymore. Now Molly knows the truth you can just walk because you enjoy walking. Or jog. Or whatever it is you do."

"Two families have rejected Brutus already. I want him to have a good home, that's all."

"The people in the adoption center know what they're doing."

"Are you sure? Because it's not as if what they've done so far has been particularly impressive. They should talk to Molly. She's good at knowing what people and personalities would work together."

"Her expertise is humans."

"Brutus is smarter than many of the humans I know."

Harriet's gaze softened. "You really like him. You're attached."

"He's a dog, and I'm never attached." Feeling like a traitor, he gave Brutus a final back rub and walked to the door. "Make sure they know he has a problem coming back when he is called. They need to be careful where they let him off the lead. And don't let them call him Ruffles."

Seventeen

Dear Aggie, I'm married but I'm attracted to another woman. I love my wife, but life with her is predictable. Should I stay or should I go? Yours, Bored.

"He's going to need a divorce attorney." Daniel leaned over her shoulder. "Do you want to give him my number?"

Laughing, Molly shoved him away. She was working at Daniel's desk. Valentine lay sprawled by the window, asleep. "As surprising as you might find this, I don't generally start by recommending divorce."

"Why not? If he goes through with the torrid affair he's obviously considering, that will be the eventual outcome. Might as well save himself, and his wife, years of anguish and file for divorce now. Cut out the middle man. Or the middle woman, in this case." He bent to kiss the back of her neck and Molly felt heat consume her.

She closed her laptop. "I'll answer this later."

"No." His lips moved to her shoulder. "You have to answer

it now. We're having dinner with Eva and Lucas, remember? We're due there in an hour. Carry on and work. Ignore me."

Ignore him? How?

Molly opened the laptop again and tried to focus, but it was impossible with Daniel's mouth on her skin. His touch felt so insanely good she closed her eyes, forgetting the computer screen in front of her. Right now she didn't care what Bored did with his life. The only thing on her mind was what Daniel was doing to her.

She hadn't ever felt like this before. Not with Rupert. Not with anyone. For the first time in her life she wasn't hiding anything and it was surprisingly liberating. Daniel knew about her mother. He knew about Rupert. He knew all of it. It was the simplest, easiest relationship she'd ever had and as a result she felt relaxed and uninhibited.

She turned and stood up, winding her arms around his neck. She felt his fingers tug at her ponytail until her hair came loose and tumbled over her shoulders. He gave an appreciative groan and speared it with his fingers.

"What about Bored? You owe him an answer."

"I think he needs to ponder on his problem a little longer. It's not good to rush these big decisions." She grabbed the hem of his shirt, jerking it upward, and he ripped at her top, his movements frantic. Everything about it was unsteady and uneven, from his breathing to the urgency of his hands as he stripped her to her underwear. It turned her on to see him so out of control because she felt the same way herself.

"I don't want to go out." His tone was rough and raw, his mouth fused to the smooth flesh he'd just exposed. "I want to stay in and feast on you instead. I'll cancel."

"No! We have to go. I love Eva and I want to meet Lucas." She slid her fingers into his hair and then his mouth collided with hers and talking plummeted right to the bottom of her list of priorities.

She glided her hands over his shoulders and he lifted her onto the desk as if she weighed nothing. She felt a delicious shiver of shock and wrapped her thighs around him. And still they kissed, as if it was something it wasn't possible to stop doing.

She felt the powerful thrust of him against her and instinctively moved her hips to be closer.

His hands stroked down her thighs and then she felt the skilled, gentle slide of his fingers as he explored her intimately.

She wanted him desperately, frantically, and she reached down, fumbling with his zip and the fabric of his jeans. He covered her hand with his, forced her to pause while he reached for a condom and then slid into her with a smooth possessive thrust that sent electric excitement shooting through her. For a moment she stayed still, allowing her body time to accommodate the thickened thrust of him, and then he moved and there was only the perfect driving rhythm, the bite of his fingers on her thighs and the heat of his mouth on hers. They kissed all the way through it, through the frantic, sweaty coupling, through the shuddering excitement, through the explosive orgasm that gripped both of them.

It was so intense, so shocking, that afterward Molly didn't move. She stayed with her head on his chest, feeling the strength of his arms holding her, locked together in the most intimate way possible.

"Dear Aggie," he murmured, scooping her hair back from her face, "there's this woman, and I'm so crazy about her that if she walks past me I want to grab her and strip her naked. What can I do? Yours, No Self-control."

She eased away and looked up at him, still trying to process what had just happened. They were both out of breath and his shoulders were slick with sweat. "Dear No Self-control," she said, her voice husky, "sexual attraction that intense can be exciting, but no relationship can flourish if one party is arrested for performing a sex act in a public place. I suggest you make sure the woman in question only ever walks past you when you're in private. And I'm sure that intense chemistry will soon wear off."

"You think so? For the sake of my sanity and physical comfort, I'm banking on it." He eased away from her. "Just in case it doesn't, you'll need to sit on the other side of the table tonight."

"Good plan." She slid off the desk and grabbed her clothes from the floor.

She just hoped being on the other side of the table would be enough.

* * *

"So your next book is out in July?" Daniel reached for some of Eva's delicious homemade walnut bread. "When do I get my advance copy?"

"They came in yesterday." Lucas poured the wine. "I can get you one if you're interested."

Eva shuddered. "Take my advice and refuse. The cover alone is enough to make me want to sleep with the lights on."

Molly smiled. "You don't read Lucas's books?"

"I don't let her," Lucas drawled. "The only time she did, she woke me up with screaming nightmares." He glanced at Daniel. "Remember that time she answered the door to you with a knife in her hand?"

"I assumed it was your special brand of hospitality."

"It was the night he made me watch Hitchcock." Eva was laughing so hard she could hardly speak. Turning to Lucas, she said, "I blame you totally. If you choose to scare me, you have to live with the consequences."

Lucas shook his head. "I have to lock the door to my office when I'm not in there because she's been known to change a sentence here and there."

"It doesn't hurt to make the characters kinder."

"But that's one of the things that's so *great* about his characters." Molly leaned forward, her food temporarily forgotten in her enthusiasm. "They're complex. That guy in your last book was incredibly kind to his neighbor. He was a fascinating mix of sociopath and psychopath with a sprinkling of narcissistic personality."

Daniel watched her, trying to delete the image of her naked on his desk. He couldn't remember an occasion where he'd been so desperate for a woman he'd wanted to have sex with her on a desk. And it wasn't as if that had solved the problem. He wondered how soon it would be reasonable to leave and go back to his apartment.

Lucas looked amused. "You psychoanalyze my characters?"

"Impossible not to, although the way you mix up different traits makes it pretty hard to come up with a specific diagnosis or profile."

"She probably picks the perfect partner for them," Daniel teased, but he was intrigued that Molly enjoyed Lucas Blade's books as much as he did. He watched her face as she talked to Lucas. She was animated, intelligent and had plenty to contribute.

Her level of knowledge always impressed him and Lucas

was clearly impressed, too, as they exchanged thoughts on personality types.

"The thing that makes your books so scary is the characters. It's not what they do, it's the fact that the crime is committed by someone we could all know. The friendly local cop, or the nurse on the ward. Your books challenge our intrinsic belief that we're safe."

"And you think that's a good thing?" Eva put her fork down. "I do not want to think that I know anyone who might be capable of committing murder. We'd better change the subject or I'll be waking up screaming again."

"I'll lend you Valentine," Molly said. "He's a terrific guard dog. I never feel unsafe when he's with me."

Hearing his name, Valentine lifted his head and his ears pricked up.

"Yes, we're talking about you," Eva said. "He's beautiful and you're lucky. I'd love to have a dog." She glanced hopefully at Lucas who raised an eyebrow.

"Are you looking at me with those big blue eyes for a reason?"

"There's no point in having big blue eyes if I can't use them to elicit an emotional response from you. You're the one who has sent my fear levels soaring into the stratosphere. I never used to be suspicious of people until I met you. I trusted everyone. Now I'm wary."

"Being wary can be a good thing," Molly said, and Daniel sensed she was thinking of her own experience. She hadn't just been let down by strangers. She'd been let down by people she'd called friends. It was hardly surprising she was wary.

Lucas topped up the wineglasses and looked at Eva. "You only want a dog because we rescued that abandoned dog from the park at Christmas. It wouldn't work. We can't handle a puppy, Ev. You're out for most of the day and I'm shut away in my study working."

"I don't want a puppy, I want a rescue dog who needs a loving home. I want to make a difference to a dog's life, the way Molly did with Valentine."

"He's the one who made a difference to my life," Molly said. "When I first moved to New York, I knew no one."

Daniel thought about Brutus and wondered how he was getting on in his new home. He hoped the dog had ended up with people as loving as Molly. He made a mental note to ask Harriet next time he saw her. "Walking a dog is great exercise."

"Don't give her yet more reasons to persuade me. And anyway," Lucas said, frowning, "you don't have a dog."

"I've been walking one of my sisters' rescues. To help out." He met Molly's gaze and saw a dimple appear at the corner of her mouth.

"That's how we met," she said, and he wondered if she was going to tell them that he'd borrowed the dog, but she didn't.

Instead she held his gaze, her eyes alight, teasing him.

He loved her smile. It started at her mouth, with the slow curve of her lips and the flicker of the tiny dimple, and finished at her eyes. He could tell she was enjoying their secret.

"You met walking the dogs?" Eva stood up. "That's romantic." She started clearing the plates, but Daniel took them from her.

"I'll do it. Sit down."

"You're the guest!"

Lucas pushed her gently into her chair. "You cooked. We've got this."

"If you insist." Eva turned back to Molly. "You must have been lonely moving here from London and knowing no one. Do you often go home? I've only been to London once. It was a school trip, and I remember it rained the whole time."

"I think of this as home now."

"But you left everything behind. That's brave. What made you do it?"

Seeing how uncomfortable Molly was, Daniel intervened. "She had a job offer." He stacked the plates on the kitchen island. "And who wouldn't want to move to New York? It's the best city in the world."

"True. New York actually *is* the best city in the world, although to be honest I found the place a little scary when I first arrived. I guess it's a little easier moving from one big city to another, though. I was raised on a small island off the coast of Maine, so Manhattan was a bit of a culture shock for me. Fortunately I came with friends." Eva chatted away, filling Molly in on her life story and the background to her going into business with her friends. "At the time we thought losing our jobs was the worst thing that could have happened, but it turned out to be the best."

The conversation moved on to more general topics and by the time they returned to Daniel's apartment, Molly was yawning.

"That dessert was incredible. And you have lovely friends." She slid off her shoes and wrapped her arms around him. "I've forgotten what it's like to hang out with good people. You really *know* them, and they know you. Lucas and Eva would be there for you if something bad happened. And you'd be there for them."

He didn't deny it. "You have people who would be there for you, too."

"Maybe. No, not maybe." She frowned. "Gabe and Mark. They're like brothers to me. They'd be there." Her expression cleared. "That's a good feeling."

"Not just Gabe and Mark."

Her gaze lifted to his and something flickered in her eyes. "You don't owe me anything, Daniel. This is just fun. Sex. You like my ponytail, my butt and my legs."

"I love your ponytail, your butt and your legs. And yes, it's sex, but it's also friendship. I like you, Molly. I like you a lot. It doesn't matter how hot you are, I never would have gone to bed with you if I didn't like you. You're a friend." He stroked her cheek with the backs of his fingers. "Don't you think we're friends?"

"Yes, but—" she looked shaken "—this will end at some point."

"And when it does we'll stop having sex but we'll still be friends. And the day you need me, I'll be there. That's what friendship is." He could tell by the look in her eyes that she didn't believe him and it hurt him to think that her experience had stripped away her belief in people. It also shocked him just how much he wanted her to trust him. "Molly—" He broke off as his phone rang.

He checked the number and stepped back. "I need to take this. It's Fliss."

"Of course."

They walked into the apartment, and he spoke to his sister. "Everything okay?"

"No." There was a shake in Fliss's voice. "Are you on your own? Can I come up?"

"I'm not on my own—" his gaze met Molly's "—but you

can come up. Where are you? Do you want me to come and get you?"

"No need. I'm right outside your building."

Eighteen

Molly made hot chocolate in the kitchen, trying not to listen to the conversation between Fliss and Daniel in the living room. They sat with their heads close together, dark against blond, the bond between them unmistakable.

His sister needed him, and Daniel hadn't given a thought to turning her away. She respected that. She not only respected it, she envied it. How would it feel to call someone in your time of need and know they'd be there for you?

She didn't know, because she hadn't had that when she'd needed it most. The one person who she could have turned to, her father, had been the person she'd been determined to protect. She would no more have burdened him with her problems than she would cut off a limb. He'd been hurt enough in life without her adding to it. She'd shouldered her problems alone, first when her mother had left and later when her life had fallen apart.

Whatever issues Daniel might have had growing up, it

was clear that he had a close relationship with his sisters. They were there for each other.

Was life easier when you had a sibling?

She thought about all the people she knew who were estranged from family and decided that the bond of family was no more reliable than any other.

And anyway, she didn't have siblings so there was no point in thinking about it.

This wasn't about her, it was about Fliss. And Fliss clearly had a problem. A big enough problem to drive her to her brother's door late at night.

Judging from the apologetic glances she'd sent Molly, it was obvious she hadn't been expecting him to have company. No doubt she was wishing Molly wasn't here. She'd heard his response to the question of whether he was on his own. The fact that Fliss had made that call from outside his apartment building told Molly how badly she'd wanted to see him. And she didn't want to put the brakes on the conversation.

She walked over to them and set the hot chocolate down in front of Fliss. "I'll call you tomorrow, Daniel."

"Why? Where are you going?"

"You two have things to discuss." She smiled at Fliss. "I thought you could do with privacy."

"Don't leave because of me." Fliss sat slumped next to him. "I'm the one who should be leaving. I didn't mean to intrude. Daniel doesn't usually have overnight guests. I haven't got used to the idea, so I didn't think." She stood up. "I'll leave. I'll call you tomorrow, Dan."

His hand shot out and he tugged her back down. "You're not leaving and you're not intruding." His voice was rough.

"If you want to talk privately, I'm sure Molly can catch up on some work. I distracted her earlier."

"No." Fliss seemed to pull herself together. She shifted her gaze from her brother to Molly. "You're a psychologist, aren't you? Maybe you can find a way to fix my brain." It was the pronounced shake in her voice that convinced Molly to stay.

"Does it need fixing?" She sat down opposite, so that she could see both of them.

"I need to cure myself of these thoughts I'm having."

"What thoughts?"

Fliss chewed the corner of her fingernail. "Have you ever absolutely not wanted to feel anything, and then felt it really badly?"

Daniel handed her the hot chocolate. "Drink this instead of eating your nails. I'm assuming what you're feeling has to do with Seth?"

"Seth?" Molly couldn't work out why the name was familiar. And then she remembered. "That was the guy we met the other night?"

Fliss snatched in a breath. "You met him?"

"In the reception area at the vet clinic. It was obvious Daniel knew him. You had a relationship with him?"

"You could say that." Fliss gave a choked laugh. "We were married."

Molly hid her surprise. Not that she knew her well, but she never would have guessed Fliss had been married. Did that explain Daniel's animosity toward the man? "I didn't know that. I didn't know you'd ever been married."

"Not many people do. I was eighteen. It wasn't my finest hour and it's not something I generally bring up in conversation. I've moved on. I thought I was doing pretty well…"

Her eyes filled and she turned to Daniel. "Do *not* tell Harry I'm upset. Promise me?"

"Sure, but—"

"No buts. I told her I'm fine. I want her to think that. That's why I'm crying here on you, and not there with her."

"She's your twin. You don't think she'd want to know?"

"She probably already does know, but that doesn't mean I have to confirm it." Fliss wiped her cheek on her sleeve. "I'm here because you know a lot about difficult relationships, and seeing as my relationship with Seth was difficult I need to know what to do. What I'd *really* love to do is not see him, but it seems that isn't going to be an option. So the next best thing is to be in charge of the meeting. I don't want to bump into him when I'm not prepared. But I don't want him to know I'm prepared. I need to make it look casual. Like I'm totally fine."

Daniel let out a long breath. "He saw me, Fliss. He's going to know I've told you he's here."

"I know, which means I can't pretend it's a surprise." Fliss put the hot chocolate down untouched and looked at Daniel in despair. "I don't know what to say to him. My palms are sweaty, my heart is racing, I'm a mess. And I hate it. Men don't make me feel this way. Not ever."

One man clearly does, Molly thought, but she kept that thought to herself.

"You and he are history," Daniel said. "Is it such a big deal?"

Fliss was silent. "It's a big deal," she muttered. "There's stuff—"

Daniel frowned. "Stuff?"

She shook her head. "Never mind."

"What stuff, Fliss?"

"Nothing, so you can drop the stern lawyer tone. But I need to know how to behave. What should I do and say? I don't want to get this wrong."

"Molly?" Daniel looked at her. "You're the psychologist."

Molly was wondering what Fliss was hiding from her brother.

Fliss poked at her chocolate with the tip of her spoon. "Molly doesn't know Seth."

"But she knows people. And she knows a lot about relationships."

Molly snapped her attention back to the present. If there were things Fliss chose not to tell her brother, that was none of her business.

"I think how you handle your first meeting depends on what impression you want to create. What you want the outcome to be." It was hard to make any useful comment without knowing the details, but she sensed Fliss didn't want to talk details.

"I want him to know I've moved on." Fliss stared blankly ahead. "That what happened is history. Something that happened as part of my rebellious phase."

"You had a rebellious phase?"

"Things weren't great at home." She caught Daniel's eye. "She doesn't know?"

"She knows some of it."

"You told her?" Fliss looked surprised. "Okay, well, I just want to get this first meeting out of the way, that's all. Ever since you told me he's here I haven't been able to sleep or eat. I feel sick."

"If it's upsetting you that much, then maybe you should engineer the meeting," Molly said. "That way you'll be in control. You pick the time and the place. I'm guessing that will be the clinic. And you should do it sooner rather than later. The longer you leave it, the more stressed you'll be. How often do you take animals there?"

"Some months we seem to live there, and then we go weeks without taking any animals to the vet." Fliss wrapped her arms around herself. "Harriet is supposed to be taking Noodle for his vaccinations next week. I could take him instead. What if I start shaking, though? I might drop the cat."

"Do some breathing exercises before you go in. Practice what you want to say in front of the mirror. And smile. That helps you relax."

"Right. Practice. And smile. I can do that." Fliss bared her teeth. "How am I doing?"

Daniel opened his mouth and then caught Molly's eye and obviously thought better about whatever he was going to say. "I'm sure it will look more genuine with practice. Do you want me to come with you?"

"No. That would look as if I still had feelings. Or worse, as if I was scared."

And she wasn't scared, Molly thought, she was terrified.

She didn't know what had happened, but it was obvious Fliss still had very strong feelings for her ex. Feelings she didn't want him to know about.

"Work out what you'd like him to know," she said, "and write yourself a script. Keep it neutral. Tell him he's looking well. Ask him what he's been doing. Then tell him what you've been doing. Focus on your business, and how it's growing. Tell him how busy you are. Then talk about Harriet."

"Business. Growing. Harriet. Okay, this is good. I can do all that." Fliss stood up so quickly Valentine jumped to his feet in alarm. "I'm okay now, thanks for listening. I'm going to write a script. I'm going to hijack Noodle's appointment so that I can control this." She bent and kissed Daniel. "All things considered, you're not the worst brother in the world." She smiled awkwardly at Molly. "Thanks. Your advice is brilliant. And I'm so glad you're finally reforming Daniel of his wicked ways."

Molly tried to speak but Fliss was already halfway out of the apartment.

She jumped as the door slammed.

Daniel sighed. "Thank you." His voice was gruff. "It's not part of your brief to handle my family problems, but I'm not going to pretend I'm sorry you did. You were great. Really great."

His praise warmed her. "This is why you were upset when you saw Seth? Because you knew his being in New York would upset Fliss?"

He nodded. "We used to hang out together every summer at my grandmother's beach house in the Hamptons. We were great friends and then suddenly he had this thing with Fliss—" He shook his head. "It's history. But thanks again for helping with my family drama."

She sensed there was a lot left unsaid. "If you want to talk about it—"

"I don't." He turned to her and pulled her into his arms. "Instead, I think you should take me to bed and cure me of my wicked ways."

They fell into an easy routine. Sometimes they stayed at Daniel's apartment, and sometimes at hers. As the evenings grew warmer they strolled along the tree-lined blocks of the Upper East Side. They discovered wine shops, bakeries bursting with sugary temptation, and little boutiques tucked away off the beaten track. They ate steak tacos and sipped frozen margaritas in a romantic restaurant in Lenox Hill and strolled along the East River Promenade. He took her to a performance of *Tosca* at the Lincoln Center, and showed her his favorite parts of the Met and the Guggenheim. Together they explored the northern end of Central Park, an area often overlooked by tourists.

They were both busy, but he sent her texts during the day, and she texted him back. She worked with her phone next to her laptop so that she didn't miss a message from him.

When they stayed in they took it in turns to cook, and sometimes they ate with friends.

The dinner they'd enjoyed with Eva and Lucas had been the first of many evenings they spent with the couple. The four of them got on well together, and one day when Eva called her, not to speak to Daniel but to ask her advice on something, she realized that his friends were becoming her friends. She'd slotted into his circle. Trusted who he trusted. Her group of friends was smaller of course, but she'd introduced him to Gabe and Mark, and even Mrs. Winchester had declared him very handsome when she'd met him on the stairs.

She still went to her spin class, but she dropped salsa because she enjoyed getting up close and personal with Daniel more than she enjoyed doing it with a stranger.

As spring tipped over into summer, the borders grew lush with color, the air was thickened with scent and the evenings grew longer. When Daniel worked late, they walked in darkness, breathing in the scents and sounds of New York.

They talked about everything, from politics to people. They discussed books, wine, art, dogs.

"It's so much more than incredible sex," she told Gabe one night over dinner when Daniel was working late. "I look forward to seeing him. When I'm not with him, I think about him. I find myself sending him emails when something funny happens and I really need to share it. And he listens. I've never met a man who listens the way he does. Sometimes I think he knows what I want before I do. I've never had a relationship like this before. It's so uncomplicated. I don't even know what that's called. There's no name for it."

Gabe raised his eyebrows. "I think it's called l—"

"Life," Mark said quickly. "It's life. Sometimes relationships just work. Why do we have to label it?"

Gabe opened his mouth and closed it again. "Sure. Life. And you're right. We don't have to label it. If it works, it works. It can take any shape or form that works for you."

"Do you know the best part? That he knows who I am. He knows it all. With him, I'm not hiding."

"That's great." Mark stood up and grabbed dessert. "So this party he's taking you to—"

"It's a summer party that his law firm has every year. Fancy. What should I wear? I'm thinking a short dress. Maybe black?"

"Not black. Wear color. Red looks great with your hair."

They debated the options for a while and she decided she probably needed something new. "How's the champagne ad campaign going, Gabe?"

"Fizzing away. The client loves what we've proposed." Gabe stood up and started clearing the table. "Which is a relief, because I'm enjoying the spoils. This is one account I don't ever intend to lose."

Mark grinned. "It's champagne for breakfast, lunch and dinner."

Molly helped clear the rest of the plates. "Don't even talk

to me about champagne. I'm never drinking again after that night at the Met."

Mark made coffee while she and Gabe finished clearing. Then she called Valentine and said good-night to them both.

Gabe closed the door behind her and looked at Mark. "What's going to happen when she realizes what she's feeling is love?"

"I don't know. But I have a feeling it's not going to be pretty."

"Maybe you should see if you can switch classes from Italian cooking to Serious Comfort Food."

Nineteen

It was the first time Daniel had ever taken a date to the annual summer party, so their arrival immediately attracted attention.

"Is my skirt too short?" Molly paused, aware that everyone had turned to look at them. "Do I have spinach stuck in my teeth? Why is everyone staring?"

"They're staring because this is the first time I've brought a date to this event. It was bound to attract some curiosity and interest. And then there's that red dress." It fell to midthigh from tiny shoestring straps. It was perfectly decent, so maybe it was simply that he knew what lay underneath that made him find the dress sexy.

She gave him a wicked smile. The same smile she'd given him when she'd joined him in the shower earlier that evening. Her smile was the reason they'd arrived late.

"Want me to tell them that our relationship is physical and that's all?"

He thought about the hours they spent talking, arguing,

exchanging views. The number of times they'd laughed until neither of them could speak, and eaten from each other's plates in restaurants. "Sure." He managed to keep his voice normal. "Tell them it's just incredible sex."

It's what he would have said himself a month ago. But now?

He knew what he felt went far deeper than that.

He'd never fallen in love before. But he was sure, he *knew*, that he was in love now. With Molly. That discovery hadn't come to him in an instant. It had been a gradual realization and at first he'd rejected it. Love? No way. He'd searched for other words to describe the way he felt about her. Friendship? Definitely. Sexual attraction? That went without saying. But neither of those labels explained the depth or breadth of his feelings. The truth had hit him when he'd heard a married colleague describe him in tones of deep envy as a free agent. Daniel had realized he didn't want to be free. Not if free meant being without Molly. To him that sounded like being given the choice between a life in a barren desert or a life in a lush rain forest.

His state of mind bothered him less than he would have expected.

What bothered him was *her* state of mind. Molly was a woman who never wanted a man to fall in love with her. It was her worst-case scenario. Which gave him a problem for which, right now, he had no solution.

She'd made him promise that he wouldn't fall in love. He couldn't change the way he was feeling, but he could keep those feelings to himself.

"I need to circulate." For him, this event was all about work. He and the other partners were expected to mingle, say a few motivational words and then tactfully leave before the rest of the staff drank too much and danced on the tables. "Let me introduce you to a few people." Resolving to keep the evening as short as possible, he did the rounds, introducing Molly to various members of the team.

The weather was perfect for an outdoor summer party and the event struck exactly the right balance between sophisticated and casual. The terrace was illuminated by discreet lighting and outdoor furniture was arranged in a way that encouraged people to come together in small groups and enjoy the food and the company. Candles flickered in Mason jars and bunches of flowers added a sweet, heady aroma to the night air.

The band was good and knew what to play to draw people to the dance floor. There was a hum of conversation, a ripple of laughter and interspersed between the sounds of revelry were the sounds of New York. Sounds that were part of the rich tapestry of the city. The blare of cab horns, the wail of sirens, helicopters, garbage trucks, barking dogs.

Across the terrace he saw Eva talking to someone serving food. She caught his eye, gave him a little wave and turned her attention back to work.

"Now that you've spoken to what felt like a hundred people, are we allowed to dance?" Molly finished her drink and slid her arm into his.

"I have a reputation to maintain."

"You'll be safe with me, I promise. I won't let you make a fool of yourself in public."

"You've never seen me dance."

"People are staring at us anyway. We might as well give them something worth looking at."

"I thought you said you wouldn't let me make a fool of myself?" But he took her hand and walked her to the dance floor before pulling her into his arms. Her hair brushed against his chin and he breathed in the scent of it and was instantly transported back a few hours to their steamy encounter in the shower.

The moment her body brushed against his, he knew it was a mistake. Their connection was too intense, too alive and real to ever be concealed from those watching curiously.

He couldn't remember the last time he'd danced, but what they were doing now didn't feel like dancing. It felt like an extension of what they did in the bedroom. And the hallway. And his office. And any other place where there was a door separating them from the outside world.

He heard her breathing change and felt her hand rest on the front of his chest.

Then she lifted her head and looked at him with those green eyes that made him think of fields and forests. What did she see when she looked into his eyes? Did she see the change in his feelings? He hoped not, because he had yet to come up with a strategy.

He wasn't the first man to fall in love with her, but he intended to be the last.

"Let's go." He forced himself to step back to a safe distance and pulled her to the edge of the dance floor, only to find the way blocked by Max.

Tension rippled through him. If there was one person he wouldn't have wanted to introduce to Molly, it was Max.

"Daniel! And with the best-looking woman in the room, as usual." He winked at Molly and gave what he probably thought was a charming smile. "I'm Max. I'm here to lighten the tone of the place. You must be Molly. And before you ask how I know that, I should tell you that you are the first woman Daniel has ever brought to this event so you're already famous. Congratulations."

Daniel saw a tiny frown appear between Molly's brows, as if she didn't quite know what to make of Max.

"We're on our way out," he said bluntly, but Max had drunk just enough to ensure that his reactions were blunted.

"You can't leave yet. What do you do for a living, Molly? Your face looks familiar. Have we met?"

Daniel ran his hand over the back of his neck. "Max—"

"I'm a psychologist."

"Whoa!" Max's reaction was exaggerated drama. "Is this the point where you tell me what you think of me? Because I'm not sure I want to know."

Daniel was more than ready to tell his colleague what he thought of him but he bit his tongue.

Molly tipped her head to one side. "I think you're drunk. But it's a party, so why not."

Max was clearly enchanted. "I like her. I like her a lot." He slapped Daniel on the shoulder. "So you now have your own personal psychologist, whereas the rest of us still have to write to Aggie."

The amusement in Molly's eyes faded. "You've written to Aggie?"

"Of course. We all think she's brilliant. Except Daniel, of course. He thinks he knows better. In fact her advice has driven him so mad he made us track her down and find out her real identity. Can't give you details, of course. All confidential," he said, and winked at Molly, "but between you and me I can tell you she isn't fifty people working in a call center. She's a real person. And I'm guessing she's a babe."

"We need to go," Daniel said smoothly. "And you need

to lay off the champagne, Max, or you'll be the subject of a lawsuit, not the solution."

"Wait! You tracked her down? You did a background check?" Molly turned her head to look at Daniel and now her eyes weren't field or forest, they were fire and fury.

He felt her anger like a punch to the gut, but he also felt something else that worried him far more. He felt her panic and her anxiety. He could almost see her mind racing forward, trying to work out what this meant.

Max was oblivious to the destruction he'd wrought. "Don't be shocked," he said. "It's the reason Daniel never loses a case. He's a detail man. He doesn't just look at the surface, he X-rays everything underneath it until there's nothing he doesn't know. It's the reason he's so fearsome in court. Nothing gets past him. He and 'Aggie' would actually make a great couple. Can you imagine that? The guy who knows everything about relationships dating the woman who knows everything. Now *that's* something I'd like to see."

"I doubt you're ever going to see that." Molly's voice was so cold it was like being dipped naked in an ice bucket, and then she turned and left the party without looking back.

Max stared after her, bemused. "Did I say the wrong thing?"

"You said a thousand wrong things." Daniel followed Molly and caught her at the elevator. "Wait. *Wait!* Please." He caught the doors before they could close. As he strode into the elevator he expected her to back away but instead she stepped forward and jabbed him in the chest with her finger.

"You had me investigated?"

"Molly—"

"*You had me investigated*, and you didn't think that was worth mentioning?"

"Hear me out." He was the one with his back against the wall. As the doors closed, Daniel loosened his tie and undid his top button.

Her eyes sparked. "Nervous?"

There was no sign of tears. Instead there were shards of anger. He decided he could be the object of her anger more easily than he could be the cause of her tears.

"Neither. Just hot."

"Don't flatter yourself." The doors opened and she stalked away from him, her balance impressive given the height and spindle-thin delicacy of her heels.

He could have let her go, but he knew that would be a mistake.

"I did not investigate you. I investigated Aggie, who was, if you remember, giving what I considered to be unhelpful advice to my clients. I had no idea it was you."

"And you didn't think to mention it? It slipped your mind? I don't think so. You're not a man who has lapses in memory. So how long have you known? Wait a minute—" She narrowed her eyes as she calculated. "That night of the Phoenix Publishing party—you didn't seem surprised when Brett introduced us. You already knew."

"Yes."

"You had sex with me, knowing who I was?"

"No. I found out the day of the party." Although if he'd known before, it wouldn't have stopped him. Nothing would have stopped what happened that night. From the moment she'd walked through his door wearing that stretchy blue dress, the outcome had been inevitable.

"That was why you came to the party?"

"Yes. I wanted to talk to you."

"You were so angry." She lifted her hand to her throat,

trying to slow her breathing. "But you didn't tell me you'd had me investigated."

"How I found out wasn't at the top of my mind."

"So you were angry with me because I'd been hiding something from you, even though the method by which you discovered that information was something you chose to conceal from me. Do you see the irony of that?" There was no warmth in her tone. It was as if she'd hauled all her emotions back behind a wall. Gone was the girl who had exposed her emotions when Valentine had been ill. Gone was the girl who had laughed with him and confided in him. This was the Molly who protected herself. "You could have told me you knew."

"After Brett introduced us, there didn't seem any point."

"You mean you wanted to stay safely on the moral high ground where you wouldn't get your feet wet."

"If I didn't already know I would have found out at that party."

"No, you wouldn't, because you wouldn't have gone. You weren't planning on going anywhere that night. You asked me out. If you'd already been busy, you would have said so. You accused me of hiding myself from you, but you were hiding plenty yourself."

"Put yourself in my position. Aggie's name kept coming up. Her—*your*—advice contradicted mine. You don't use your qualifications, or even a photo. I was suspicious. I wanted to protect my clients. That was professional. When I found out you were Aggie, I was angry that you hadn't shared the information. That was personal."

"I understand the conflict, but at the very least you should have told me what you'd done!"

He hailed a cab. This wasn't a conversation to have on the

street. "Let's go back to my place and we can talk there." Within the security and familiarity of his apartment, hopefully she'd relax and listen.

"I'm not going back to your place, Daniel."

"Fine, we'll go to yours."

"No. I—" She rubbed her fingers across her forehead. "I'm not going anywhere with you. You're the first man I've ever trusted, do you know that? I told you everything. And now I discover that—" She broke off, her breathing unsteady. "I don't understand why you didn't tell me."

"Because I was afraid." The confession was dragged from him. "Because there is no good way to tell a woman you really like that you accidentally had her investigated." It was more than like, a lot more, but timing was everything when breaking unexpected and possibly unwanted news, and this wasn't the time.

She stood, poised on the sidewalk, oblivious to the flow of people around them.

This was Manhattan, and life carried on. Through love, marriage, divorce, sickness, friendship, loss, the city kept moving. It didn't sleep, nor did it rest.

"I can't think." She sounded dazed. "I need time to think."

"Come home with me and think about it there." He reached out to her but she lifted her hands to ward him off.

"No. You think you know everything about women," she said, her breathing shallow and uneven, "but let me tell you, Daniel, you don't know anything at all."

He wasn't about to disagree. "Will you call me when you're ready to talk?"

"I don't know."

The thought that she might not call him was like being kicked in the ribs.

"Molly—"

She turned away, looking so vulnerable the pain in his chest intensified.

He wanted to stop her, but before he could find the words that might persuade her not to climb into the cab, she was gone.

He told himself that he'd figure it out. She was mad right now, but she was also reasonable. When she calmed down, she'd see his point of view. At least, he hoped she would.

At least now she knew everything.

Things couldn't get worse.

That hope lasted until he woke up the following morning, checked his messages and discovered things had just got a whole lot worse.

Valentine's gaze followed her as she clattered her way around the small, sun-filled kitchen.

"All right, maybe it wasn't *that* different." She glared at him. "Stop looking at me like that. You're making me feel guilty."

Valentine yawned and thumped his tail.

"You want me to feel guilty? What sort of a friend are you?" A good friend. The best. Except that lately, Daniel had been a good friend, too.

She made her coffee strong, breathed in the aroma and took several restorative sips before taking it to the window seat. It was the place she did most of her thinking. "I love talking to you, but talking to him felt good, too." She leaned against the cushions, curled her legs under her, and stared down into the street.

"I should probably call him."

It wasn't as if he was the only one who had been stingy with the truth. She had, too, hadn't she? In fact, if she'd told him the truth from the beginning, none of this would have happened.

His behavior had been no worse, or better, than her own Valentine watched her, his mellowing paws, clearly deciding that this was one of those days when it was best to keep a low profile.

"I'm upset," she told him, her bad mood lessening as he thumped his tail on the floor. "He should at least have told me, don't you think?"

Valentine watched her in silence and she sighed.

"He was doing the best for his clients, I know." And it was hard to criticize a man for that. "I mean, I know I kept secrets from him, but that was different."

Twenty

Molly didn't sleep much, and the wakeful moments were punctuated by the knowledge that Daniel had investigated her and hadn't told her.

Of all the arrogant, outrageous, lying, arrogant—had she already said arrogant? Well, hell, he deserved to be called twice.

Abandoning hope of sleep, she stomped to the kitchen. She should definitely call him.

With a sigh, she reached for her phone.

"Here's the thing," she told Valentine. "It's okay to make mistakes, just as long as you're not afraid to admit when you were wrong. I was wrong. In his position, I probably would have done the same thing. Give me five minutes to drink this and recover and then I'll call him and take you for a walk in the park. Maybe he'll even meet us there."

Valentine's ears pricked up at the promise of a walk, but before she'd had a chance to finish her coffee there was a hammering on the door.

"Molly?"

Valentine sprang to his feet and shot across the room, barking with delight as he recognized Daniel's voice.

Molly, who was having much the same reaction, walked to the door, her coffee in one hand and her phone in the other.

He'd come to her. That was good, wasn't it?

She unlocked the door and opened it.

Daniel stood there. He was still wearing the shirt he'd had on the night before, although he'd replaced tailored trousers with jeans. His face was ashen, the blue of his eyes intensified by the pallor of his skin. At the sight of him the last of her anger evaporated and all that was left was concern.

"What's wrong? What's happened?" Had he lost a client? Was he ill? "You look awful."

"You didn't answer my text." He pushed his way into her apartment without waiting for an invitation and she closed the door.

"I was just going to call you, but you beat me to it. What did your text say? My phone was switched off." She switched it on, wondering what the message was. Something affectionate? Another apology? Or was he waiting for an apology from her? She had a feeling she owed him one.

"Sit down." His mouth was tight. His expression grim.

Her stomach gave a little lurch. "Look, I admit I may have overreacted a little last night. I've had time to think about it and—"

"I'm not here because of last night."

"Oh. I assumed…" She swallowed. "So why are you here?" She'd never seen him like this before. She'd only ever seen him calm and in control. "What's wrong? Has something happened to you?"

"It's not about me, it's about you."

"Me? I don't understand." And then her phone came to life and she saw his text.

Don't look at the internet.

He removed the phone from her hand. "You have to believe that I had no idea this would happen. Not that I'm making excuses." He inhaled deeply. "There is no easy way to say this and I take full responsibility—"

"For what?"

"They've made the link between Aggie and Dr. Kathy. They know who you are."

Her limbs turned to liquid. "Max? The background check you did—"

"It wasn't Max."

"Then how—"

"Last night someone took a photo of us together."

She cast her mind back but remembered nothing specific. "I don't understand how that would expose me. And I don't remember anyone taking a photo of me."

"You weren't the target of the photo, I was." He ran his hand over his jaw. "That was the first time I've ever taken a woman to that event. I'm the eternal bachelor. Someone took a photo of me and posted it. It was retweeted a lot, and somewhere in that round of retweets someone recognized you. Someone who was at the Phoenix Publishing party that night, and knew you as 'Aggie.' That's the power of social media."

She knew all about the power of social media. The good side and the bad.

"How bad is it?" Her mouth was so dry it was hard to speak. "They've made the connection and named me?"

"Yes. They've talked about your TV role as Dr. Kathy. About how you were targeted by the online community. How you lost your job." He hesitated. "And that you moved to the US and started *Ask a Girl*."

She closed her eyes as the enormity of it descended, along with the implications. "So they know all of it."

"Yes, and I understand that this is the one thing you dreaded. It shouldn't have happened and I'm the reason it did." His tone was raw. "I'm truly sorry."

She shook her head, numb, and reached for her laptop.

He caught her arm. "Don't."

"I want to. I have to know what I'm dealing with."

The story wasn't hard to find.

The identity of the woman behind the popular relationship blog Ask a Girl, *has been revealed as Dr. Kathleen Molly Parker. Writing under the pseudonym of 'Aggie,' Dr. Parker has spent the last three years advising people on how to manage their relationships, despite the fact that she has never managed to sustain one herself. Fired from the hit British TV show...*

Molly carried on reading, even though she already knew the content. Only one part was new, and that related to Daniel.

She read it aloud. *"'An ex-girlfriend of Daniel Knight's commented that "she won't break his heart because he doesn't have one." Mr. Knight was unavailable for comment.'"*

Scrolling down, she saw the picture someone had taken of her and Daniel at the summer party. They'd caught the moment when they were dancing, eyes locked.

No wonder we didn't notice people taking photographs,

she thought. He'd been the only thing in her field of vision and she'd been the only thing in his.

She won't break his heart because he doesn't have one.

She stared at the words and then looked away, confused. Why was she focusing on that one sentence when it was the rest of it that was important?

There was an ache behind her ribs.

Shock, she thought. That had to be it. What else could it be?

And of course she would be shocked. Her life was unraveling.

Still, it was that one phrase that went round and round in her head.

She won't break his heart because he doesn't have one.

Well, that was good to know, wasn't it? She didn't want to break anyone's heart ever again.

"Actually I was available for comment," Daniel drawled, "but seeing as my only comment would have been unprintable there didn't seem much point in answering the phone."

"Your phone has been ringing?" It was happening again. Only this time Daniel was in the line of fire. She flipped her laptop closed, unwilling to read any more. "I'm sorry you've been dragged into this mess. You'd better leave."

"Why would I leave?"

"Because sooner or later someone is going to show up here asking questions. Probably taking photos. You should get out before it gets tough." That was what people did, wasn't it? Her mother. Her friends—

Her friends.

"You think I care about that?"

"You'll care, Daniel. When they've dragged your reputation through the mud, interviewed all of your ex-girlfriends and plastered the sordid details of your life all over the internet, you'll care. All my friends should stay away." What if they bothered Gabe and Mark? What if their friendship wasn't as strong as she believed it to be?

"It's because I'm your friend I have no intention of staying away. We'll formulate a plan together."

"A plan?"

"Of course. I'm a lawyer. A master of strategy. It's my job. But first I need coffee. I didn't get much sleep last night."

"Daniel—"

There was a knock on the door and Daniel's expression darkened.

"Don't answer that," Molly warned, but he strode to the door and checked the identity of the visitor.

"It's Fliss and Harriet." He opened the door and then locked it behind them.

Harriet was carrying three kittens in a basket and she set them down next to Molly. "Sorry to bring them, but I couldn't leave them on their own."

"You shouldn't have come at all." Molly stared at the twins. "I don't understand what you're doing here."

"When we see our brother's name on Twitter it's generally something we want to follow up on," Fliss said, turning to Daniel. "Not to mention the fact that some pea-brained journalist stopped me in the street this morning and asked me whether the reason you'd chosen to become a divorce lawyer was because your childhood was so unstable."

It was like adding a few drops of poison to a water source, Molly thought. Pretty soon everyone was infected.

She expected Daniel to be annoyed, but to her surprise he grinned.

"And your reply was?"

"I asked him if he became a journalist because he was nosy and led a boring life." Fliss thumped her bag down on the sofa and looked around approvingly. "Nice place."

"Thank you." Molly felt awkward. "I'm sorry."

"Why are you sorry? It's the journalist who should be sorry for asking questions that were none of his damn business. And he *was* sorry, I'm happy to tell you. I was walking a rescue dog who has a very snarly temper. I didn't actually allow sharp teeth to snap tight on sensitive flesh but it was a close enough thing to ensure he won't be back in a hurry. And I might have mentioned in passing that the dog's favorite food is testicles." She sat down next to Harriet on the sofa, looking unreasonably happy about the outcome.

Molly pulled a curious Valentine away from the kittens and joined the twins on the sofa. "I've already told Daniel he should leave. Perhaps he'll listen to you."

"He never listens to us. And why would he leave? He's big and bad enough to look after himself and if the press steps over a line legally he will go after them like the wrath of…of…someone wrathful. We're here for you." Fliss patted Molly's leg awkwardly.

"For *me*? Why?"

"Because that's what friends do when life implodes. Not that I know a lot about your past, but it looks to me as if your life is definitely imploding."

"But—you don't even know me that well."

"Not true. We've been walking Valentine when you're busy for the past two years. You're kind, sensible and you love your dog. Also, I know my brother is crazy about you, and given that he's never been crazy about a woman before, I figure you're someone worth knowing." She caught her brother's eye. "What? Why are you looking at me like that?

Did I say something I shouldn't have? I mean, she has to know you're crazy about her, right? And she's crazy about you, or you wouldn't be spending all this time together. And then there's the fact that you helped me when I had a meltdown. So I owe you for that, too."

Molly felt her head spin.

Crazy about her? Fliss had that totally wrong, but this wasn't the time or the place to put her right. She'd obviously misinterpreted all the time Molly and Daniel had been spending together. Read more into it than was there. They were spending a lot of time together, that was true, but not because they were crazy about each other. Because they had fun and enjoyed each other's company, that was all. What was wrong with that?

Harriet, who was in the process of tucking a blanket around the kittens, glanced at her twin. "You had a meltdown? Was it about Seth? Why don't I know about this?"

"Because I didn't want you to have a meltdown, too. You and me together would have escalated global warming. I went to Daniel because he never melts down. And Molly was very helpful. I don't care what those idiots say, you know what you're talking about."

"Have you spoken to Seth yet?"

"No. Still planning that part. I'm building up to it." Fliss stood up. "Given that we're now besties, can I make myself coffee in your kitchen? I'm so desperate, I'll chomp on the beans if you have any."

There was another knock on the door and Valentine went racing across the apartment, startling the kittens.

"This place is busier than Times Square." Daniel opened the door again and this time it was Gabe and Mark who stood there.

He let them in and Gabe walked straight to Molly and folded her into a giant hug.

"Are you doing all right?"

"I'm not sure. What are you doing here? Shouldn't you be at work?"

"I'm the golden boy since we won the champagne account. I can work at home if I need to."

"You probably should have gone into the office while you could. After today, you won't be able to leave your apartment." She thought about what it had been like for her friends the last time. "There's still time to move. They'll want to interview you."

"The front door is locked. And if it's any consolation I heard Mrs. Winchester having a go at someone." Gabe strolled to the window and glanced down into the street. "Don't worry, sweetheart. We will form a protective circle around you."

Molly felt her throat thicken and her eyes sting.

She reached behind her to the box of tissues she kept on the shelf, tugged one out and blew her nose.

What was wrong with her?

Maybe she was getting the flu.

"Here. Hold him." Harriet placed the smallest kitten in her lap. "Nothing like a fluffy kitten to lift the mood."

Valentine, who seemed confused to be sharing his space with so many people, sat close to her, nudging the kitten gently with his nose.

Molly looked around her crowded apartment, feeling a little dazed. Gabe and Daniel were discussing how best to handle the situation. Mark and Fliss were clattering around the kitchen, finding mugs and making coffee. Harriet was trying to settle the other two kittens in the basket. "I can't believe you're all here."

"We're your urban family." Cheerful, Fliss poured coffee into mugs. "That means we can argue, be generally annoying, hang around when you really wish we'd leave, drink your coffee, eat your food—do you need me to go on?"

The thickening in her throat grew worse. Not flu. Emotion. "I don't know what to say."

"Save your words for handling what's happening. You should blog about it." It was Daniel who spoke. "There isn't a man or woman out there who hasn't struggled with relationships at one point in their lives. Post something. That way you tell it from your point of view. Control it. The only comment you make on this situation is on *Ask a Girl*. That way, people who want to know more will go directly to your blog."

"Increase traffic." Gabe nodded. "I agree. Write something heartfelt and honest. Want me to help? I write advertising copy for a living."

"We'll all help you write it." Fliss handed out mugs of coffee. "For the record, I think it's so cool that you're Aggie."

"You do?" Molly felt overwhelmed. She'd never solved a problem by committee before.

"Yes. From now on anytime we have a problem with our relationships, we can call you." Fliss tapped her mug against Molly's. "It's *very* cool."

"It feels weird everyone suddenly knowing something I've been hiding for years."

"We're experts on that." Gabe winked at Mark. "We can advise. And we can watch your back."

"Someone needs to, because Daniel's mostly watching

her front," Fliss said cheerfully and earned herself a warning look from her brother.

They stayed all day, and by the time everyone left the apartment, it was dark.

Between them they'd written and posted the blog, eaten six large pizzas, consumed two bottles of champagne and talked. They talked about the good and the bad, the embarrassing and the scary. They shared secrets and feelings. Twice Harriet had quietly slipped out of the apartment and taken Valentine to the park for a quick run. Fliss had insisted on tagging along as her bodyguard, and had returned the second time with a large box from Magnolia Bakery.

"Everyone knows a sugar rush is the perfect cure for tension," was all she'd said when Mark had made a comment about the threat to their arteries.

Eventually, in the small hours of the morning, the only person left was Daniel.

Molly tidied the cushions, stacked the empty pizza boxes in the kitchen and cleared what felt like a hundred dirty mugs. She should have felt stressed, but instead she felt warmed, as if she'd been wrapped in layers of soft blankets. That was what friends did. They acted as an insulator. A layer between a person and the cold, hard world.

She realized that Daniel was watching her. He stood, legs braced and arms folded, the stance pulling the fabric of his shirt tight across his muscle-packed shoulders. His jaw was dark with stubble and his eyes were tired. He'd been here all day and still showed no signs of leaving. She sensed there was something he wanted to say to her and was waiting for the right moment.

There were things she needed to say to him, too, but right now she didn't have the energy for another emotional conversation. "You should go. You've already done more than enough and I'm grateful. You don't need to feel guilty."

"You think I'm here because I feel guilty?"

What other reason could there be? "You must be exhausted."

"I'm not leaving. If I'm tired I'll sleep on your sofa."

"You hate my sofa."

"True. There's always the bed."

He was talking as if nothing had changed. As if their entire relationship hadn't been shaken up in the past twenty-four hours. If she let him back into her bed, what would that mean? "I don't think that's a great idea. Not that the sex isn't good—"

She saw the sudden flare of heat in his eyes and knew it was mirrored in hers. She'd been trying not to think about that side of things, but of course now she'd said it aloud she could think of nothing else.

A muscle flickered in his jaw. "Sex isn't why I'm here either."

She was missing something.

Obviously she was missing something.

She searched for the answer in his face, but found nothing. Long lashes shielded his gaze. His mouth was a firm, disciplined line, revealing nothing.

"Friendship?" Yes, that had to be it. "You're here because you want to prove your friendship and today you've more than done that. I'm grateful."

"I don't want your gratitude. And I'm not here as your friend."

And yet he'd been by her side all day. Everyone had chipped in, but no one had been in any doubt about who was in charge. Daniel was the one who had stayed cool when four people were talking at once. Daniel had picked the good ideas from the bad.

Today she'd had a firsthand glimpse at the skills and qualities that made him such a fine lawyer.

Maybe he wasn't here as her friend, but he *was* here, standing between her and another disaster, and that made her lucky.

"If it's not friendship, then I don't know what it is, but I'm grateful for it."

"I don't want your gratitude." He hesitated and then shook his head. "You've had a hell of a day. We should talk about this another time."

"Talk about what?" She felt a rush of unease. "If something else is wrong, then I want to talk about it now. Are you upset that they dug into your past?"

"I don't care what they say about me, but I care what they say about you. Gabe, Mark, Fliss and Harry—they were here as your friends. I'm here because—" He paused, ran his hand across his unshaven jaw and muttered something under his breath.

She couldn't make out the words.

Something about it being the wrong time? About him picking the worst possible moment? The worst possible moment for what?

She felt a rush of alarm.

"Daniel? Finish your sentence. You're here because...?"

"I'm here because I care about you." He let his hand drop and his gaze met hers. "I love you."

It took a moment for the words to sink into her brain and even when they did her reaction was muted. *Shock.* "You don't mean that."

She won't break his heart because he doesn't have one.

"I mean it. I love you."

She stared at him and then turned and paced to the window, her arms wrapped around her waist. "You feel that way because the sex is good."

"The sex is good. But that isn't the reason I feel this way."

She turned to face him, pure panic rising up inside her. "I can't believe you're saying this, Daniel. Not now. I can't handle it along with everything else."

"I'm telling you how I feel, that's all. You don't need to handle anything."

"But you don't—you can't—" She couldn't get the words out. "You promised me. You told me you'd never been in love."

"I never have been in love. But I'm in love now. With you."

This couldn't be happening.

She pressed her fingers to the base of her throat, trying to calm her breathing. "You need to leave. Right now."

"Molly—"

"I'm serious. It's for the best. You need to meet someone else. Get over me. Go and have rebound sex." She was stammering, falling over her words in her panic.

"You want me to go and have sex with another woman?"

It was as if he'd driven a knife under her ribs. She had a fleeting image of him with someone else, smiling for someone else, tilting his head when he listened, eating pizza, walking in the park, laughing, talking— "Just go." She grabbed his jacket from the sofa and thrust it at him. "Go."

He didn't budge. Instead he stood, rock-solid and calm. "You have no reason to panic."

"You think you're in love with me. That's the best reason I know to panic! That's more terrifying than anything that has happened here today. You know why? Because no matter what you say, the next thing will be you expecting me to fall in love with you. And I can't. I'd try, I'd try really hard, and when nothing happens I'd feel crap about myself and—"

"Hush." He covered her lips with his fingers to silence her. "Stop talking and open your laptop, Molly." He let his hand drop.

"What? Why? I've seen all I need to see."

"There's something else you need to see, and if you still want me to leave after you've seen it, then I'll leave."

"But—"

"It has to do with Rupert."

The name made her freeze. "Rupert?" What did any of this have to do with Rupert?

"Give me five minutes. That's all I'm asking. Five minutes."

Right now she wasn't sure she was going to make it through five seconds.

"I don't understand what you want me to look at. I don't understand what this has to do with what just happened."

"What happened was that I told you I love you, and you freaked out. I know you're scared of love—"

"I'm scared of hurting people. And now I've hurt you, or if I haven't already I will soon! And you're the *last* person in the world I'd ever want to hurt—"

His response was to walk to her laptop and tap a few keys. "Read this. Humor me. You owe me that much." He pulled out the chair behind her desk and nudged her into it, then sat on the desk beside her. "You thought you'd damaged his heart. Broken it. Has it ever occurred to you that it was his ego you damaged rather than his heart?"

Why was he raking all this up now? They'd already talked about it. She'd told him everything.

"Losing me almost killed him."

"Those were his words, yes? I want you to forget what he said, and look at the facts. This was a guy who loved the limelight and attention. He was king of the show until you came along. It was you who sent the ratings rocketing."

"The public liked our relationship."

"They liked you. And your relationship was part of that. And he knew it, which is why he pursued you."

"You're suggesting he was with me because it increased the ratings? That he was raising his own profile?"

"The evidence would suggest so." He paused, obviously choosing his words carefully. "You thought he didn't know the proposal was being filmed but he knew, Molly."

"No. He never would have agreed to it. He never would have taken that risk."

"He was wearing a microphone."

"No!" Her instinctive denial died on her lips as she saw the look on his face. "You— What makes you think that?"

"I have a friend in the business. He checked the sound quality. Rupert was definitely wearing a lapel microphone. If you look closely, you can see the wire."

A wire? She would have noticed. Wouldn't she? On the other hand, she'd been panicking too much to notice anything. Maybe he'd been counting on that.

"But why would he propose if he wasn't in love with me? I might have said yes."

"He knew you wouldn't say yes. He knew you didn't love him."

"You're saying he proposed, *knowing* I'd turn him down? But that would have meant he was setting himself up for public humiliation. What guy would ever do that? What did he possibly hope to gain?"

"He gained public sympathy, a massive boost in his popularity and he got you removed from the show, although I suspect that was an added bonus rather than part of the original plan."

It was too much to take in. Too far apart from everything she'd believed for so long.

"I broke his heart. Just as I broke the hearts of all the guys I dated before him, even though I tried really hard not to."

"I can't comment on the guys before, but I can comment on Rupert. Take a look at this." He tilted the laptop screen toward her. "Take a look at what the man whose life you supposedly ruined is doing now."

She stared at the screen. "I— He's married? To Laura Lyle. She was a researcher on the program when I was there. How long have they been married?"

"Almost three years."

"Three—" Even in her confusion she could still do basic math. "So he must have started dating her almost immediately after we broke up."

"I don't know, but I don't think he was brokenhearted for long. And now that's enough." He closed the laptop. "You didn't damage his heart, honey. You damaged his ego. He couldn't handle the fact that you were more popular. He staged the whole thing as a publicity stunt to boost his career."

She'd carried it for so long, the belief that she'd hurt someone badly.

Knowing that it wasn't the case should have given her instant relief, shouldn't it?

"I'm angry."

"Good. Anger is better than guilt."

She was silent for a long minute. Then she stood up and turned to look at him.

"I'm glad you showed me this, but none of this changes the fact that I don't want you to fall in love with me. I care about you, Daniel. I don't want you to be hurt."

"I know you care about me. That's why I'm sharing the way I feel about you."

"I care about you as a friend. A lover. I don't want anything to change."

Everything had already changed.

He knew it. She knew it.

It was the reason she was panicking.

"This isn't about Rupert." He stood up, too, refusing to allow her to back away. "It isn't about any of the other men you dated. It isn't even about your mother. It's about you."

"Me?"

"Yes. You've always been made to feel you're not enough. Your mother made you feel that way, and so did Rupert. Two people who supposedly loved you forced you to question yourself, personally and professionally. And it has left you worried you'll never be enough for someone. But you're enough for me, Molly." He framed her face with his hands, forcing her to look at him. "You're enough for me. Everything you are, the person you are—" he lowered his forehead to hers, holding her gaze "—you're *more* than enough. You're everything."

She couldn't breathe. She couldn't speak.

Her chest was full. Terror, excitement, exhilaration, despair.

She needed to think, but there was no chance to think with his eyes on hers and his hands in her hair.

"I love you." He said it again, softly this time. "And I think you love me."

The words roused her from her trance.

"No." She pulled away from him, stepping backward so fast she nearly stepped on Valentine's paw. "Yes, we've had fun, but part of the reason for that fun was that neither of us was in love. For the first time in my life I wasn't even *trying* to fall in love. There was no pressure. No expectation. It's the most relaxed I've ever been, the most myself I've been. I've told you everything about me, shared all of me." She felt a flash of panic as she met his steady gaze and realized how that probably sounded. All right, so she'd been relaxed and herself, but that didn't make it *love*, did it? So why was he still looking at her, as if he was waiting for her to have a lightbulb moment? "I don't mean *all* of me, obviously. My heart is still exactly how it was before I met you. I don't know what I'm saying because you're looking at me in that way and—"

"What way? How am I looking at you?"

He was looking at her with kindness, amusement, patience and a million other things she didn't expect to see in the face of a man she'd rejected.

"You know how! As if you're waiting for me to say something I'm never going to be able to say! I'm so, *so* sorry to hurt you but I'm definitely not in love. Not in love. No. Never. It isn't something that happens to me and believe me, I should know because I've tried—" She broke off as he covered her lips with his fingers and nodded.

"All right. I get it." He let his hand drop, but she could still feel the pressure of his fingertips against her mouth.

All right? That was all he was going to say? No argument or recriminations? No emotional blackmail? Perhaps he didn't believe her. "You need evidence?" She scrabbled around for something that might convince him. "I don't look at you with starry eyes and talk to you in a baby voice."

The corners of his mouth twitched. "Good. I'm not big on baby voices."

"My appetite is fine. At no point has being with you ever put me off my food."

"That's good, too." There was a tenderness in his voice that almost crushed her.

"I don't even dream about you." That wasn't quite true, but it had been just a couple of times so those didn't count.

He was silent for a moment and then he slowly reached for his jacket.

"I thought you weren't leaving." Her heart kicked against her ribs. "Where are you going?"

"I've changed my mind. I probably should leave." He sounded tired.

"But—you— I just told you I don't love you."

"I heard you." His voice was level. "You've told me how you felt, so we're good."

Good? He didn't seem good. She'd hurt him. She'd really hurt him. And knowing that made her feel physically sick.

"So—am I ever going to see you again?"

"Of course. We're friends. Friends don't stop being friends just because they don't agree on everything." He stooped to stroke Valentine and then strode to the door. "It's been a long night. Get some sleep, Molly."

Sleep?

She watched as he closed the door behind him. How was she supposed to sleep? There was a weight crushing her chest and she felt as if someone was squeezing her lungs. She couldn't breathe. Couldn't focus.

She rubbed her chest with her palm, trying to ease the ache. The last person in the world she wanted to hurt was Daniel, so of course she was going to feel bad about that.

That's what the pain was. Guilt. Nothing else. What else could it be?

Twenty-One

"She broke it off. The first time I have ever said 'I love you' to a woman, and she virtually threw me out of her apartment." Daniel paced to the window of his sisters' apartment. Was this how it felt? All those people who had trailed through his office, devastated at the end of their relationship—had they felt as bad as this? If he'd known, he might have been more sympathetic. On the other hand he was paid for legal advice, not sympathy. He felt as if something vital inside him had been torn. Internal injuries, not visible from the outside. "Now what?"

He never should have said those words to her. At least not right then, when her brain had been occupied trying to process everything else that was going on.

He'd picked the worst possible time.

On the other hand their relationship had been one long sequence of secrets and misunderstandings. He'd thought it was time to put the truth out there and see how it went down.

It hadn't gone down well.

Harriet spoke first. "Was that a rhetorical question or are you actually asking us for advice?"

"I'm asking. I need help." He turned and looked at both of them. His sisters. His family. "I'll take anything you've got."

Visibly awkward, Fliss rubbed her toes on the wooden floor. "When it comes to relationship advice, I don't have much. Harry?"

"Not personal experience, but I've read a lot." She rescued one of the kittens who was about to dive from the sofa. "Quite a bit of what I've read was written by Molly."

"That could be a good thing, and in any case, I'm desperate."

Fliss exchanged glances with her sister and shrugged. "Not that I'm an expert, but I would say your timing sucked."

"I know my timing sucked!"

"Hey, you asked for advice! You said you'd take anything we've got, and that's what I've got."

"I'm sorry." His head crowded with emotions that were unfamiliar and uncomfortable. If this was love, he wasn't sure he liked it. He felt helpless, and he'd never felt helpless in his life before.

Fliss sighed. "Molly was having a *really* bad day. She was all freaked out that people would be talking about her again, and if you've looked online you'll know that wasn't a picnic last time, and then suddenly in the middle of all that emotional crap you tell her you love her. She was already set to panic stations and you sent her into meltdown. It's like everything going wrong at once. And she's a kind person. She probably hated hurting you."

"You're saying that if I'd waited, she might have given me a different answer?"

"I don't know! Maybe."

"I need to talk to her again."

"Not yet," Harriet intervened. "You need to give her space, Daniel."

"Yes. Give her space. Good plan. Maybe you should spend a month in Texas. Then you can't be tempted to drop around and see her." Fliss stood up and started clearing the living room. She stacked magazines that were already neat and straightened a plant that didn't need straightening. "This is tough for you to handle. The first time you fall in love with a woman, and she doesn't love you back. That's got to hurt."

"She loves me." He ignored the internal voice that suggested he might have got that part wrong.

"What? I thought you said—"

"She loves me. That isn't the problem." At least, he hoped it wasn't. He hoped he was right about that part.

"Well, if she loves you, why did she throw you out of the apartment?" Fliss slammed a stack of books down on the table. "I don't want to dent your confidence or your ego, Daniel, but why would she tell you she doesn't love you if she didn't mean it?"

"Because she doesn't know. She doesn't recognize it. She's convinced herself she can't fall in love, that something is missing inside her. And she's so scared of not being able to feel the way she thinks she's supposed to feel, she doesn't want to recognize it. *That's* my problem. How do I make her see she's in love with me?"

Fliss shook her head. "Solving that problem is way beyond my pay grade." She picked up a plant and Harriet shot off the sofa and took it from her hands.

"Don't take your stress out on my plants. They've taken enough punishment lately." She placed it carefully back on the windowsill, positioning it so that it had exactly the right

amount of light. Then she turned back to her brother. "If
you're right, and she is in love with you, then that's good,
isn't it?"

"No. It isn't good. Falling in love is the thing she is most
scared of. For some people it's heights, for others it's the
dark—"

"For me it's ex-husbands who show up in my town," Fliss
said darkly but for once Daniel couldn't focus on anyone's
problem but his own.

"Maybe it would be easier to handle if she didn't love me.
I could have accepted that."

"Are you sure? Because accepting things isn't really in
your nature. Generally you try and change things you don't
like."

"That's true, but I wouldn't have tried to change this. I
would have respected her decision."

Harriet frowned. "You still have to respect her decision,
Daniel."

"I know, but it's the wrong decision, made for the wrong
reasons. That's what makes it all so difficult to handle."

And he wasn't handling it. Right now, he wasn't handling
it at all. He didn't need to see the way his sisters were looking at him to know that.

"I never thought I'd fall in love. I never thought I'd feel
this way, but now I do and not being able to act on those
feelings is—" he ran his hand over his jaw "—hard."

"I still think you need to give her space," Harriet said.

"I agree. Stay away from her," Fliss said. "Maybe she'll
miss you or something. Maybe she'll call. Not that she has
any chance of reaching you, because you're always on the
phone."

Daniel surreptitiously checked his phone but it was depressingly silent. It was the first time in his life he'd been desperate for a woman to call.

"How long should I wait to call her? Five hours? Five days? A week?" He wasn't sure he could make it through a week. And it wasn't just his own emotions that were torturing him, it was hers. Was she really panicking? The thought that he'd upset her was as hard to deal with as his own issues.

What was she doing now? Was she on her own in the apartment? Had she gone to talk to Mark and Gabe? Was she walking Valentine?

"Sit down, Daniel." Harriet spoke calmly. "Let's work this through and come up with a plan."

"Plan? Isn't that a bit ambitious?" Fliss looked at her sister. "Let's be honest, the only person around here who knows anything at all about relationships is Molly. Which kind of makes the whole thing awkward. Maybe we should call her and ask her to come over and help fix this." She pressed her fingers to the bridge of her nose and then let her hand drop, triumphant. "Okay, I've got it. You write to her."

Daniel looked at her blankly. "What?"

"She's used to analyzing emotional problems that are written down. Everyone else writes to her. You should do the same."

"I have never had to ask for advice on my love life before."

"Yeah, well, you've never been in love before." Fliss shrugged. "If it bothers you, use a fake name or something. You could be 'Clueless.' I mean that's pretty accurate in the circumstances. Or you could be—"

"I get the picture." Daniel paced again, and one of Harriet's kittens that had wandered away from the sofa sprinted to safety. "I don't know what else to say to her."

"You always know what to say. People pay tons of money

precisely because you know what to say and how to get them the best outcome."

"This isn't a court of law."

"But you're fighting for the best outcome. The difference is that this time it's for yourself."

"I'm finding it a little hard to stay objective."

"Yeah, I'm getting that," Fliss said, eyeing him, "and so is our rug. If you wear it out, you're going to have to buy us a new one."

"Enough!" Harriet vanished to the kitchen and emerged with cookies and cans of soda. "If we're going to make a plan, we need sustenance."

Fliss took a cookie and bit into it savagely.

Harriet glanced at her twin. "I don't understand why you're so angry. This isn't even your problem."

"I'm not angry." Fliss let out her breath in a little huff. "All right, maybe I'm a little angry."

Daniel stopped pacing. "Why?"

Fliss glared at him. "Because you're my brother and I don't like seeing you hurt! And don't say it's not our problem because it is our problem. We're a family."

Harriet's eyes misted. "Fliss—"

"What? Don't read anything into it. I still think you're annoying," she addressed Daniel, "but that doesn't mean I don't want things to work out for you."

The phone rang and Harriet answered it, her expression turning from serene to anxious. "He did?" She paused, listening. "Where did you last see him?… Yes, you're right, that *is* close to the road… You tried looking?… I'll come now." She ended the call and reached for her keys. "I have to go out. I'll be back soon."

"Where are you going? Who was it?"

"It was the family who have Brutus." Harriet glanced nervously at Daniel, clearly reluctant to give more bad news. "They let him off the lead in the park and he didn't come back. They don't know where he is."

* * *

Molly rapped on Gabe and Mark's door.

When Mark opened the door, she walked into the apartment without waiting to be invited. "It's over."

"What's over?" Mark looked alarmed. "Everything looked fine last time I looked. You were swamped with supportive comments on your site. People are impressed at how you picked yourself up again when your life crashed. They're saying you're an inspiration. An—"

"Not my career. My relationship. I ended it."

Mark closed the door. "In that case we need to talk. Where's Valentine?"

"I left him in the apartment. He was getting upset seeing me upset. And I stepped on his paw. Twice. And talking would be great, but do not give me champagne. Bad things happen when I drink champagne." She saw Mark's drawings scattered across the table. "Did Gabe go to work today?"

"Yes. Emergency client meeting."

"And I kept you both up most of the night. I'm sorry."

"Don't be. That's what friends are for."

"Don't make me cry. I've had no sleep, so it's not going to take much."

"I'm not going to make you cry." He pushed her gently onto the sofa. "We didn't leave you until three in the morning. I assumed Daniel would stay."

"He would have stayed. But I told him to go."

"Why?"

"Because that's what I do when someone tells me they love me. And as usual I feel completely horrible about it."

"He told you he loved you? He said those words? You didn't misunderstand him?"

"Unfortunately, no."

"Why unfortunately? You told me this was the best relationship you've ever had."

"It is. It was. But that was because he said he wasn't capable of falling in love. For the first time in my life I felt completely free and safe. We had so much fun."

Mark leaned against the table. "So it was good, but you've ended it."

"What choice did I have? He told me he loved me. It's not going to be safe and fun anymore. It's going to get deeper and more complicated. I never wanted that! He's never fallen in love before. Why did he have to pick me as the exception to that rule? It's so unfair." She saw the corner of Mark's mouth twitch. "Are you laughing?"

"Molly, you have to appreciate the irony. I don't know the guy that well, but I'm guessing there are plenty of women who would have done anything to hear him say those words."

"Which makes me feel a thousand times worse because it's wasted on me."

With a sigh, Mark sat down next to her and put his arm around her. "You're not abnormal. If you don't love him, that's okay. Daniel is going to understand. He's not Rupert."

She leaned her head on his shoulder. "I know he's not Rupert. For a start, I told him far more than I ever told Rupert." She'd told him far more than she'd ever told anyone. And telling him, sharing, had brought a new level of closeness to their relationship. When someone knew something about you that no one else did it was like giving them a key to a locked door. They had access. They knew what was inside. She'd let him in, and now she had to find a way to get the key back from him. "You know the stupidest thing? He had this crazy idea that I was in love with him, too! Have you ever heard anything more ridiculous?"

Mark took his time answering. "Is that ridiculous?"

"Of course it's ridiculous. I've never fallen in love and you have *no idea* how hard I've tried. I'm not in love with him, Mark."

"I heard you. You're not in love with him."

She shifted so that she could look at him. "You sound as if you're humoring me."

"I'm not humoring you."

"You're humoring me, and I don't get it. I mean it's true we had a good time, and yes I told him a lot of things. Things I haven't told anyone before. But that's because he's easy to talk to. Not because I'm in love."

"Right."

"And it's also true he has qualities I admire greatly. For example, I liked the fact that he was strong. I don't mean physically, although his shoulders are like something from a superhero movie, I mean emotionally. When Valentine was sick and I was falling apart, he was so calm. Steady."

"He was calm and steady last night, too."

"Exactly. Calm and steady. And he didn't care that Valentine was sick on his favorite suit. And I like the fact that he knows all the best restaurants in Manhattan but he's equally happy to eat pizza out of the box."

"Can't beat pizza out of the box."

"Then there's the fact that I have hormones and he's sexy!" She shrugged, dismissing it. "But that's sex, right? Not love."

"Totally sex. Nothing else."

"And of course it would never have worked, because he's not a dog person."

"True. He's not a dog person." Mark carefully removed a piece of fluff from his jeans. "Although he was good with Valentine."

"Yes, but he's generally good in a crisis. I guess that's to do with his training. He's used to handling things."

"And he walked Brutus—"

"He did that to meet me."

"But after he met you he still walked Brutus."

"The dog is friends with Valentine. That's all it was."

"Sure. Of course, I'm sure you're right." Mark paused. "So that's it then?"

"That's it." Her mouth was dry. "All my life I've felt as if I wasn't enough. I grew up knowing that, that whatever I was, it wasn't enough to stop my mother leaving. Then my professional life fell apart because I wasn't enough there either. I live with this fear that people will judge me and find me lacking. Everything I have here—my work, my friendships—it all still feels fragile."

"And Daniel didn't understand that?"

"Oh no, he understood perfectly. In fact he said—" she snatched a breath "—he said I was enough for him."

Mark stared at her. "Wow." His voice cracked. "Well… that's—"

"Unrealistic?"

"I was going to say it's the most romantic thing I've ever heard."

"You think so?"

"He's telling you he loves you, Molly. You. The real you. He doesn't want anyone different, and he doesn't want *you* to be different. You're the relationship expert, not me, but

isn't that the goal? Isn't that what we all want? To meet someone who will love us as we truly are? No pseudonyms, no
online personas, no hiding and no fakery. Just honesty." He
swallowed. "If you were Aggie, advising someone on this
situation, what would you say?"

She tried to find objectivity in the swirl of emotions.
"I'd say they were lucky to have met someone who felt that
way. I'd say that finding someone who truly knows you, and
loves you for who you are, is a rare gift in today's world.
I'd advise them to think hard before turning down something so special." She stared at him, heart pounding. "But
I've thought hard. I've thought really hard. And I feel guilty
that I can't return his feelings, but I can't. And I told him to
go, and he's gone."

"Well, then, you have nothing to worry about." Mark
patted her leg and stood up. "You've got the outcome you
wanted. You should be happy."

Happy? She'd never felt more miserable in her life. "I've
hurt him."

"He'll get over it. Daniel Knight is a catch, Molly. His
heart will mend, he'll meet someone else, get married, have
a million babies and be fine." His words punched the air
from her lungs.

"You think he'll have a million babies?"

"Not literally. It was a figure of speech. I'm telling you
he'll be okay. He'll find someone else. And in the meantime, your reputation is intact and you will go on to do
great things with your career. So in the end, everyone lives
happily-ever-after."

This was happily-ever-after? It felt as if someone had
gouged out her insides with a sharp object.

But Mark was right, wasn't he? Daniel would get over her.

He'd meet someone else, and they'd get married and have lots of babies and they'd never get divorced because Daniel wouldn't marry someone unless he was sure—

"I don't feel too good." She pressed her fingers to her forehead, her breathing rapid. "Light-headed. Weird."

"Lack of sleep. Lack of food. I'll get you something." He headed for the kitchen and brought her a glass of water.

"I feel dizzy. I think I might faint."

"Damn it, Molly." Mark put his hand behind her neck and pushed her head down. "You're the same color as mozzarella. And you're hyperventilating. I'm no good at first aid. Do *not* faint. Do I call Gabe or 911?"

"Neither." She closed her eyes and slowed her breathing and finally her head stopped spinning. "You're right. This is just because I haven't eaten. That's all it is."

"Except that we all ate pizza at two in the morning. So it can't be that." He put the water down next to her.

"Lack of sleep, then."

"Possibly, except that it came on when I told you Daniel would get over you and meet someone else."

"Relief, then. Eventually I can stop feeling guilty."

Mark sat down next to her. "Are you sure that's what it is?"

No. No, she wasn't sure. "Maybe I'm getting sick. There are always bugs going around, aren't there?"

Mark hesitated. "Or maybe you feel this way because you've finally worked out that he's right. You love him."

"He can't be right. Think of all the times I tried to make that happen and it didn't."

"Maybe this time it has happened because you weren't trying. Instead of focusing on your feelings, you were focusing on him. On having fun."

There was a buzzing in her ears.

She still felt dizzy.

She kept thinking of Daniel laughing with someone else. Sharing everything with someone else. The thought didn't bring her relief. It made her feel sick. It made her feel—

"I'm in love." She shot to her feet, her heart racing. "You're right, I'm in love. All these years I've thought there was something wrong with me, that there was something missing, and it turns out that the only thing missing was the right man. Daniel." She broke off as Mark grabbed a handful of tissues and shoved them at her. "What are those for?"

"You're crying."

Was she? Yes, she was crying. Her cheeks were wet. How could she be crying when she was happy?

"I love him, Mark."

"I'm getting that." Mark handed her more tissues. "It's great. It's all good."

"It's better than good." And then she remembered the look on his face as he'd left her apartment. "I have to tell him. I have to tell him." She grabbed her purse and fumbled for her phone. "I've been stupid, so stupid. I have to tell him that he was right and I was wrong."

She called him, but the call went to voice mail.

"He isn't answering. Why isn't he answering? What if he's alone and miserable somewhere? I'll call the office." She paced, thinking. "No, that would embarrass him. I'll call Fliss." She did that, but Fliss's phone went to voice mail, too.

Was she comforting her brother?

Anxiety shot through her. What had she done?

"I've messed it up. The first relationship in my life that has truly mattered to me, and I've messed it up. I told him to leave. He said all those amazing things to me and I threw them back as if they didn't mean anything. As if they weren't important. I told him I didn't love him. That he was wrong." Molly grabbed her bag and shot toward the door, knocking over the glass of water.

"Where are you going?"

"I don't know. To try and find him. I'll go to his apartment. Then I'll go to his sisters' apartment. Someone has to know where he is." She walked to the door, knocking into the table on the way and sending a few of Mark's drawings flying.

"Don't worry, I've got this." Mark rescued them and guided her the rest of the way so that she could reach the door without injury.

Twenty-Two

There was no answer from his apartment, nor from Fliss and Harriet's.

Frantic, Molly kept calling, wondering why none of them were answering their phones.

She'd keep trying. That was all she could do.

In the meantime she'd do what she always did when she needed to clear her head. She'd go for a walk in the park.

Valentine kept checking on her, glancing over his shoulder and wagging his tail, sensing her anxious mood.

"I've made a terrible mess of things," Molly told him. "And I don't know how to fix it, but I have to find a way. Even if I'm too late, I have to at least tell him that he was right. I can fall in love! I'm not like my mother! He's shown me that and even if it doesn't work out—" She swallowed. It was ironic that finally she'd fallen in love and she'd realized too late.

Was it too late?

There was only one way to find out and that was to talk

to him, and that wasn't proving easy. What if he was screening her calls?

Maybe she should email. No. Too impersonal. Make an appointment at his office? No. Too stalker-like. She'd call one more time. And then she'd stop embarrassing herself because she didn't want to turn into one of those women who dialed the same number until the guy had thirty-five missed calls.

"Last time." She stooped to hug Valentine. "If he doesn't pick up this time then I'll back off." Straightening, she pulled her phone out of her pocket.

She called his number, her palms so sweaty the phone almost slid from her hand.

This time it rang instead of going to voice mail and suddenly she felt light-headed again.

What if he didn't answer? What if he'd decided that she wasn't worth the trouble?

Somewhere in the distance she heard a phone ringing, but she ignored it until she heard someone calling her name.

Daniel.

Daniel was calling her name.

He was here?

She turned, confused, and saw him sitting on the bench. Their bench. Holding his phone. For a moment she thought she was hallucinating. Lack of sleep. Something.

But Valentine bounded over to him happily and she realized she wasn't conjuring him up from the depths of her imagination.

He really was here.

She hadn't prepared exactly what she was going to say and now that she was with him in person everything vanished from her head.

As she moved closer she saw he looked even rougher

than he had earlier. Whatever he'd done after he left her, it clearly hadn't involved going home and getting rest. Or going to the office.

He looked shaken. No, worse than that. Devastated?

It horrified her. She felt as if her heart was being crushed. "Daniel?"

"Did Fliss call you?" He slid his phone back into his pocket, his voice scratchy and raw. "It was good of you to come. I appreciate it. The more people who are here, the better."

He wasn't making sense. He wanted to talk to her in front of an audience? She was hoping for something a little more private.

"I haven't spoken to Fliss. Maybe we should go back to my apartment. Or your apartment."

"No." His gaze shifted from her to the park. "He doesn't know his way there. He's probably lost, but I thought it was worth coming here in case he remembered this bench. The others are searching the other side of the park. And the road."

"The road? Searching for what?"

He dragged his gaze from the trees to her face. "Brutus. What else? I'm grateful to you for coming to help with the search, especially since I know what I said upset you."

Search?

Slowly his words sank in. "You're looking for Brutus? He's missing?"

"You didn't know? The people who were thinking of adopting him let him off the lead. He didn't come back." He sounded exhausted. "This was last night, but they only called Harriet this morning. We've been searching for hours. There's no sign of him."

"I didn't know. No one called me."

"I guess they thought you had enough going on. But if no one called you why are you here?"

"I've been calling you and calling you. When you didn't answer I called Fliss and Harriet. I've been to your apartment and theirs—"

"We were all searching for Brutus. You couldn't get through on the phone because we were all talking to each other." He frowned. "Why were you calling?"

Now that the moment had come, she felt shaky. "It doesn't matter—it can wait."

"No. It can't wait. If it was enough to make you turn up at my apartment, then I want to know what it was."

"We should be looking for Brutus—"

"We've searched the park and there's been no sign of him. No one has reported an unattended dog. All we can do is wait and keep looking. I keep hoping he might show up here, at our bench." He leaned forward, resting his forearms on his thighs. "You had a tough night. I'm sorry I made it worse. I was wrong to say what I said."

"You weren't wrong, but I was."

He sat up and turned to face her. "You were?"

This wasn't how she'd planned on telling him, but she'd given up trying to find the right way or even the best way. "I was wrong about all of it. I was wrong to send you away. I was wrong about not wanting you to love me. And it turns out I was wrong about not being able to fall in love." Her mouth was dry, and she wished she'd taken the time to bring her usual bottle of water. "The reason I know that is because I'm in love with you. The first time in my life I wasn't actually trying to fall in love, I fell in love. And because I wasn't trying to make it happen I didn't even know it was happening. I didn't recognize it, but you did. I love you."

She couldn't believe that words she'd never said before could be so easy to say. "I love you. And I was trying to work out how to tell you. I didn't know whether to call and do it on the phone, or write to you, or—"

He didn't give her a chance to say all the other things she wanted to say. His mouth came down on hers, his kiss demanding and layered with more than a touch of desperation. He yanked her against him and her last coherent thought was one of gratitude that he hadn't changed his mind. That he still felt everything he'd felt earlier that morning.

She didn't know whether to laugh with joy or cry with relief. She gave up trying to speak and let herself go, hurtling into the kiss. She slid her fingers into the silk of his hair, stroked her palm over his rough jaw, whispered breathless words of love against his seeking mouth. And now she'd said the words once, she couldn't stop saying them.

"Love you, love you, love you—"

And he said the same words back to her, his hands in her hair, his mouth urgent on hers. She felt the heat in his kiss, and other things, too. Sweetness, sincerity, security. And still he kissed her, words punctuated by greedy kisses until speaking stopped being a priority.

It felt as if they kissed forever, and when he finally lifted his head, he still didn't release her. Instead he wrapped his arms around her and rested his chin in her hair.

"I was sure you loved me, but then I kept thinking I must have been wrong."

"You weren't wrong. And I'm so happy about that. You have no idea how happy. I was scared there was something missing in me." She lifted her hand and touched his face.

"I never want you to be scared. Or sad." He broke off and

flashed her an apologetic smile. "I'm the guy who always knows what to say, but right now I don't know what to say."

"You already said the most important words."

"That I love you?"

"Yes. And you said that I'm enough. You have no idea what hearing you say that meant to me." She rested her hand on his chest, feeling the beat of his heart under her fingers and knowing that she'd never, ever, do anything to hurt that heart. She stayed like that for a moment, breathing in the scent of him, the scent of the park, the scent of the city. "I've written about love all my life, but I've never felt it. Until now."

"How does it feel?"

"Like a legal high." Before she could elaborate, there was a commotion behind her and she saw Daniel's face break into a smile. She turned her head and there, racing toward them was Valentine, and right behind him was another dog. Heavier, clumsier, but wonderfully familiar.

"Brutus!" She was filled with joy and relief. "Valentine found him. He's safe."

Valentine shot up to her and Brutus lurched to a halt next to Daniel, who for a moment said nothing.

Molly was beginning to think he didn't recognize the dog when he dropped into a crouch and pulled Brutus toward him.

Brutus whined and licked him, put his paws on Daniel's shoulders until he had to brace himself to keep his balance.

Still he didn't speak, and it was only when she looked closely that Molly realized that the reason he didn't speak was because he couldn't.

Witnessing the emotion in his face made her heart contract.

She put her hand on his shoulder. "He's safe."

"I imagined him being hit by a car. I thought—"

"He's here and he's fine. We should call the twins. We'll get him checked. We'll take him to see Steven. He shouldn't go back to those people."

"He's not going back to them." Daniel rose unsteadily to his feet. "He's going to live with me."

"You?"

"Brutus is a difficult character to handle and I can't risk having to interrupt my working day every time he goes missing."

Deciding that this might not be a good moment to smile, Molly simply nodded. "Good point."

"So it's easier if I keep him myself."

"That is a sound and logical decision. And a generous one," she added, "given that you're not a dog person."

"But you *are* a dog person. And you'll be living with me, so he'll have someone who knows about dogs." His hand was on Brutus's head, but his eyes were on her. And what she saw in his eyes made her breathless. How could she ever have thought she could live without him? She didn't want to, not even for a moment.

"I will?"

"We could live at your place if you prefer, but there's more room at mine. And two dogs are going to take up a lot of space. Especially as they're not exactly small dogs."

"I'm not clear about this. You're suggesting I move in with you?"

"It wasn't a suggestion. It was a command, with an alternate close."

"An alternate close?"

"Your place or my place."

"That's it? That's my choice?"

"Yes, although it shouldn't be that hard a choice. After a day with Brutus in your apartment, you'd have to remodel. He lacks spatial awareness."

"In that case, I don't think there's a decision to be made." She felt light inside. Light, and so happy she wanted to dance. Warmth flowed through her.

Daniel took her face in his hands, everything he felt visible in his eyes. "I wrote to you. I sent Aggie a letter this morning. I was waiting for her answer."

She wrapped her arms around his neck, her heart forever lost. "I haven't been online since you left, but I can tell you what her answer would be."

"I haven't told you the question." He murmured the words into her hair and she smiled, holding him tightly.

"Whatever the question was, her answer would be yes. Yes to all of it. Yes, to love. Yes, to living together. Yes, to anything. I'm desperately in love with you. That's the only thing that matters."

He brought his mouth down on hers again. "I can't stop kissing you," he murmured against her lips, "and there are about a thousand people in the park. Think what I'm doing for your reputation."

"You're probably enhancing it, although people will warn you that I'm going to break your heart."

"I never believe what people tell me. I prefer to check out the evidence for myself."

"Good." She looked into those wicked blue eyes and wondered how she'd lived without him all this time.

"So we're a family. You, me and two unruly dogs."

"Seems that way."

He smoothed her hair back from her face. "And one day,

a long way in the future, I'm going to ask you to marry me, so you'd better write to Aggie and ask for her advice on how you should answer."

"I think I know what she's going to say."

Sensing her happiness, Valentine barked his approval. Brutus joined in, and through the crazy barking she heard cheering and pulled away to see Fliss and Harriet beaming at them.

"Of course when you marry me, you'll get two sisters," Daniel drawled. "If that's a problem, we could always move to another city."

She laughed and wrapped her arms round his neck. "I'm never moving again. I love your sisters, I love you and I love this place. New York actually is the best city in the world."

"You could be right about that."

And he lowered his head and kissed her again.

* * * * *

Thank You

There are still days when I wake up and can't believe writing is actually my job, but writing the story is only the beginning of the publication process and I'm grateful to my publisher, HQN in the US and HQ in the UK, for their continuing support for my writing. A particularly big shout-out to the sales team in both the US and the UK who work so hard to make sure readers can find my books on the shelves. With so many books published daily they have a difficult job and it's lucky for me they're all so good at what they do.

Social media makes it possible to connect with so many readers, and I'm grateful to the wonderful group of people on Facebook who were so generous with their help when I asked for inspiration for dog names, and a special thank-you to Angela Vines Crockett who gave me the idea of making the dog's name "manly."

Thanks to my wonderful agent Susan Ginsburg and the

team at Writers House, and also to my editor Flo Nicoll, who is brilliant in every way.

Without the support of my wonderful family I doubt I'd write a single word, so I'm eternally grateful to them, but my biggest thank-you goes to you, the reader, for choosing to buy my books. I'm so lucky to have a place on your bookshelf or e-reader.

Love, *Sarah*
xxx

Loved this book?

Visit Sarah Morgan's fantastic website at **www.sarahmorgan.com** for information about Sarah, her latest books, news, interviews, offers, competitions, reading group extras and much more...

...and connect with her online, at:

 @SarahMorgan_

f facebook.com/AuthorSarahMorgan

g goodreads.com/SarahMorgan_

instagram.com/sarahmorganwrites

Pinterest pinterest.com/SarahMorgan_

HQ
One Place. Many Stories

The home of bold, innovative
and empowering publishing.

Follow us online

 @HQStories

 @HQStories

 HQStories

 HQ Stories

 HQMusic2016

Fall in love with New York City...
and fall in love with Sarah Morgan

Let Sarah Morgan whisk you away to the Big Apple in
the all new *From Manhattan with Love* series!

Follow best friends Paige, Frankie and Eva as they
navigate the streets of Manhattan and find their own
perfect New York fairy tales along the way.

One Place. Many Stories